THE SCENT OF EUCALYPTUS

BY THE SAME AUTHOR

The Middle Platonists (1977/1996)
Salt and Olives: Morality and Custom in Ancient Greece (2004)
The Heirs of Plato: A Study of the Old Academy (2005)
The Roots of Platonism (2018)

As editor

The Greek Sophists (Penguin Classics, 2003)
The Enneads by Plotinus (Penguin Classics, 1991)

THE SCENT OF EUCALYPTUS

John Dillon

451
Editions

The Scent of Eucalyptus

2nd Edition Published by
451 Editions, Dublin, 2019
www.451Editions.com

ISBN: 978-1-9999075-6-3

First Edition, 2006 by
The University Press of the South

John Dillon worked as an English teacher in Ethiopia in the early
nineteen-sixties, a sojourn which inspired this book. *The Scent of
Eucalyptus* is, however, a work of fiction. Names, places and incidents
are either the product of the author's imagination or are used
fictitiously. Any resemblance to actual persons living or dead, events,
institutions or locations, is entirely coincidental.

Cover design by Clarisse Faber

FOREWORD

"You won't find a new country, won't find another shore ... " Cavafy's classic lines, quoted in the book's opening pages, provide an epigraph for this *Bildungsroman* concerning a young Irishman's migration to Ethiopia to teach English following his graduation from Oxford in the mid-sixties. Narrator/hero Luke La Touche has two contacts in Addis Ababa: "Cousin James" a British-colonial service veteran whose ostensible role is to help Emperor Haile Selassie modernise the judiciary, and Yohannis, formerly a fellow-student from Oriel College and the eldest son of the richest man in the city.

The stage seems set for an Evelyn Waugh style novel with an Irish accent, and indeed, a series of characters offer themselves to Luke as guides to the mores of expatriate society. The author draws these characters – English, Irish, Ethiopian, Greek – simply and efficiently, ensuring that by the end of the book, the reader feels they have experienced something of Ethiopia's multi-faceted society. For Luke, his adventure unfolds with one introduction and one social event succeeding another as he strives to find his way in this Brave New African World. Except that it's not that new. The dominant figures remind him of the dominant figures of Oriel and indeed to some extent the dominant figures of the protestant Wicklow of his upbringing. The difference is the scene of their business of manipulation, not the business itself.

Luke dutifully tries to make sense of each individual he meets. He tries to be fair to everyone, like a Wicklow Candide. He tries to understand how they operate together as a society and how they relate to their host country. Luke's confidence increases as he comes to feel, that step by step, he understands what is going on. He is surrounded by friends, after all, who are guiding him. If one were to express his situation in the terms of a lyric his jazz combo might have performed, it would be Louis Armstrong's "It's a Wonderful World".

Plato affirms that the Republic must be based on friendship, and author John Dillon is a celebrated Platonist. The narrator of *The Scent Of Eucalyptus* looks at things in a way that Plato might have recognised. Luke La Touche discovers that his Ethiopia is based on false friendships and it that it seems to disintegrate as quickly as it had taken shape. The darkness behind the country's political machine, which Luke glimpsed on his first day in the country, comes to threaten his very own freedom. Those whom he holds most dear turn out either to have fooled him for much of his life, or contrive to cynically betray him. The entire narrative may be read as a pitch to the last word in the book: nothingness. If Luke's relationships were based upon illusions, is Ethiopia an illusion too? If they are illusory, where is the reality for Luke to inhabit?

On its face, the book is a simply conceived and lucidly executed novel about growing up which might afford little to distinguish it from others in the genre. Yet it is transformed by the hard philosophical gaze which informs the story; one which asks questions about the nature of truth, falsity, friendship and society in a way that engages the reader without putting them off through overblown philosophical language. An outstanding work.

Ronan Sheehan
Dublin, August 2019

THE CITY

*You said: "I'll go to another country, go to another shore, find
another city better than this one.
Whatever I try to do is fated to turn out wrong
and my heart lies buried like something dead.
How long can I let my mind moulder in this place?
Wherever I turn, wherever I look,
I see the black ruins of my life, here,
where I've spent so many years, wasted them, destroyed them
totally."
You won't find a new country, won't find another shore.
This city will always pursue you.
You'll walk the same streets, grow old in the same
neighbourhoods, turn grey in these same houses.
You'll always end up in this city. Don't hope for things
elsewhere: there's no ship for you, there's no road.
Now that you've wasted your life here, in this small corner,
you've destroyed it everywhere in the world.*

C. Cavafy

(trans. E. Keeley & P. Sherrard)

7

CHAPTER ONE

Addis Ababa from the air: I smiled slowly as it came into view. After hundreds of miles of apparent emptiness, slashing gorges and improbable lunar mountains, there appeared over the crest of the last ridge of hills a tree-like bristling, expanding soon into a mass of dark green on a scale not previously observed on the journey. This flowed down an amphitheatre of mountain towards the plain below, with occasional bare patches and flashes of white, to where the apparent emptiness took up again, and stretched on to the horizon as before. It was mid September and the Big Rains were just ending, and the land was green, making the contrast between the eucalyptus groves of Addis and the bare land surrounding them not as violent as it would otherwise be, though still notable.

Of the city itself, no obvious pattern was visible, an impression only confirmed on closer acquaintance. As the plane came in to land at Haile Selassie I International Airport to the south of the city, I took in a snapshot view of a wild jumble of native huts, shanties, old French colonial-style buildings, along with the occasional modern skyscraper; the whole scene liberally laced with eucalyptus trees.

I stepped out of the plane door, blinking in the bright African light, down the steps, and onto the tarmac. My foot touched the soil of Africa – or rather nothing so romantic – the grubby, oil-flecked cement of Africa. Weighed down with various precious parcels, my antennae out, with each sense at maximum alert for a new sensation. The airport building itself was unremarkable, obviously a fairly recent construction, yet already small pieces were missing from the neon sign above the entrance doors. The first things that struck the senses, however, were not visual. Rather, they were the sounds and smells; the sound of orders shouted in a strange language; and an indefinite but pervasive odour, a compound of dust and burning eucalyptus leaves, seasoned with stale piss.

The early evening sun was already casting long shadows on the runway, both from the terminal building itself, and from a clump of eucalyptus trees rising above the building to the left. The sun was hot, but not any longer with the cloying heat of Athens airport, which I had left five or six hours before. Here there was a certain crispness and clarity in the air which raised the spirits, and gave a much-needed new charge of life.

It was a short walk to the Arrivals lounge. Once in the door, I caught a glimpse of myself in a mirror just inside. A sorry sight. The long journey had left me dishevelled and baggy about the eyes – not at all in the sort of shape in which I wanted to confront a rather important person in my life, at the start of this most reckless of adventures.

I put down my bags and parcels, made an effort to quell my hair into some sort of order, closed the top button of my shirt, unbuttoned somewhere over the Sudan, and straightened my tie. Even so, a pretty shop-worn vision looked back at me. A casual observer, I reflected, would see only a slightly stout, dark-haired figure, neither tall nor short, neither handsome nor conspicuously ugly – regular features, one might say, but with a somewhat tentative look, anticipating rejection. What the hell was I doing here, I suddenly thought to myself, with a dart of terror. How on earth am I going to explain the impulse that drove me to this? But no; no going back now. I shook off these thoughts, straightened myself up, and walked firmly through the swing doors marked EXIT, matched by an incomprehensible inscription in Amharic, to collect my baggage.

My cousin James, as I had hoped, was waiting just outside the Arrivals lounge to meet me, accompanied by a leathery, dark figure who turned out to be his personal servant, Wolde-Gabriel. It was a few years since I had last seen my cousin – it was relatively difficult for him to get back to Ireland from Ethiopia – and I noticed immediately some changes to the familiar profile. The spectacles were still perched forward quizzically on the nose, but the imposing shock of hair rising from the forehead was now, in late middle age, peppered with grey, and somewhat receding; the jowls beneath somewhat more florid and ample. But it was still a thoroughly familiar figure that loomed before me, beaming in welcome, very much like an animated Toby jug. In these thoroughly alien surroundings, amid the swirl of figures of every hue, in every sort of Western and native costume, he constituted a most welcome oasis of familiarity.

My cousin had filled out considerably since I had first made his acquaintance, when he used to come over for short escapes from the privations of wartime Britain to the large rambling house in County Wicklow where I grew up with my mother and grandmother. We had lived there ever since Mother and I'd had to flee Malaya in 1940 in face of the oncoming Japanese, leaving my father behind us.

We had all been in Malaya together, though I was too young to remember that. James Mallory – who, by the time he met me at the Addis arrival gate was, in fact, Sir James Mallory, KCMG, in recognition of his many services to His Majesty in the colonial justice system – was my mother's second cousin, from the London branch of the family, and my godfather. Having retired some years previously from the Colonial Service, he had accepted an invitation from Haile Selassie (whom he had got to know when the Emperor was in exile in Britain before the War) to serve as his legal adviser and help him modernise the judiciary, which was one of the Emperor's ambitions.

James had actually introduced my father to my mother, it seemed, not long after my father had moved up to Penang from the Dutch East Indies, where he had been working as an oil engineer. He had remained a good friend to my mother and myself ever since, especially after my father's death in a Japanese prison camp.

James had never married himself, and I always felt that he had something of a soft spot for my mother. Indeed, I was uncomfortably aware that he had actually been instrumental, over the years, in both the planning and financing of my education, all the way through Oxford, from which I had just come down. It was with a certain apprehension, therefore, that I faced him now, since this adventure of mine must have seemed to him seriously irresponsible.

However, I got a warm welcome, without any shadow of reproach, at least for the moment. He clasped my hand in both of his, as had always been his habit.

"Well, dear boy, you made it. Welcome to Ethiopia! How was your flight?"

Both groggy from the journey and rather overwhelmed by the situation facing me, I stammered a positive reply.

"Good, good. Splendid. And now let me look at you. Grown a bit since I last saw you, I think. Put on a bit of weight, possibly?"

I nodded guiltily, conceding that this might indeed be so. Conditions at home in Wicklow tended to be conducive to this.

Cousin James chuckled. "Ah well, it's a problem I can sympathise with. I'm afraid we may after all have something of the same metabolism. But enough of that. Now we need to get you out of here. Let us go and find your bags."

And with that he swept me off, first to the baggage reclaim, where fortunately my rather battered suitcase had been gathered up by Wolde-Gabriel, to whom James solemnly introduced me. Then, he strode with authority through Customs – shaking hands and exchanging a few words with various relevant officials, who then bowed us through. Wolde-Gabriel packed my bags and parcels into the trunk of the waiting Mercedes, held the door open first for me in the back, then for James in the passenger seat, and settled himself behind the wheel. The car purred away effortlessly. I nestled back, luxuriating in the cool leather against my shoulder blades.

From the airport, we drove along a magnificent sweep of highway into the splendid modern expanse of Adowa Square, and I wondered why all this modernity and signs of rational organisation had not been more apparent from the air. Only later did I discover how much this fine approach to the city resembled a film set, behind which lay the chaotic jumble that was the real Addis. However, for the moment we continued on our fine avenue, a little tattier now, but still impressive, up the hill towards the older part of the town, to another, rather asymmetrical, older square which I later came to know and love as the 'Piazza'.

James, who had been enquiring about my journey and the health of my mother, as well as showing me interesting landmarks along the way, was at this point, struck by an idea.

"Now let me see. What road shall we take home? I could make a detour, but on the whole I think I ought to blood you. Wolde, straight up the hill, I think".

"*Eshe, getoich,*" said Wolde impassively, and he turned the car at the corner of the Piazza and left up the hill.

I didn't quite know what to expect, but I was not left long in suspense. Immediately behind the Piazza there was a large open space

– one could not dignify it with the title of park, though it largely served that purpose – and in the middle of this open space there stood a gibbet, and on this gibbet there hung a corpse.

Now, a corpse hanging on a gibbet is not a sight that one often sees nowadays, and I must say that, at the impressionable age of twenty-two, it gave me something of a shock. Cousin James told Wolde to stop the car, and turned round to me in the back.

"Well now, dear boy, I expect you're wondering who that gentleman is, and why he is hanging there."

I nodded dumbly, gazing at the scene. A number of people were gathered round the hanging corpse at a little distance from it, some gossiping, others just looking on.

"Well, if you'll possess yourself in patience till we get back to the house, Wolde-Gabriel will make us a gin and tonic, and I'll tell you the story of that corpse. Drive on, Wolde!"

"How long will he hang there?" I asked, rather faintly.

"Normally till nightfall. Then his relatives can come and cut him down. Until then, he's part of the public domain."

We drove on, and the spectacle faded from sight.

A little later, on his spacious verandah, while we waited for Wolde-Gabriel to prepare dinner, James told me the whole story. Some months before my arrival, there had been an abortive coup. During the absence of His Majesty on a state visit to Brazil, the Palace Guard and some disaffected regiments had seized power in the capital, imprisoned the government, and induced Haile Selassie's eldest son Asfa Wossen to assume the throne. All this might just have worked, had the Little Man been an ordinary tinpot dictator. He would have seen the game was up, and retired gracefully to Cannes, or the coast of Portugal, to live on his Swiss bank account. But if one is offspring of Solomon and the Queen of Sheba, Lion of Judah and King of Kings, one does not give up so easily. The Emperor directed his pilot to fly straight home, and when news came to Addis that the Emperor's plane had landed at Asmara in the north of the country, the coup collapsed.

In any case they were in trouble, since tribal levies, armed to the teeth with ancient muskets, spears and clubs, were by this time converging on the capital from all sides to do battle in defence of the Emperor. Haile Selassie returned in triumph, the ringleaders were tried and executed, and to his errant son the Little Man is said to have declared, "I will forgive you, and forget you."

James took on board a generous draught of gin and tonic, and came to the point.

"This fellow you saw hanging there was a lieutenant in the Imperial Bodyguard. He had been part of a detachment set to guard members of the cabinet, who were being detained in a room in the palace above them. At one stage in the proceedings, the guards on duty, either on orders from somebody, or out of pure exuberance, began firing through the ceiling at random, and as a result a number of ministers were killed – a fate that at least some of them richly deserved, but that is beside the point. The lieutenant was tried for his part in this, and sentenced to life imprisonment. He decided to appeal the sentence. The judges in due course agreed to hear his appeal, listened to what he had to say, and on mature reconsideration, condemned him to death. So there the poor bugger hangs. The ceremony was carried out this morning at dawn."

"My God," I said. "But how can the Emperor claim to run a civilised country, if he still practises public executions?"

James smiled. "Before you go much further in expressing your shock and outrage, dear boy, I should perhaps reveal something. When I came out here, one of the problems the Little Man raised with me was the following. Some years before, as part of his general desire to modernise society, he had abolished public executions. The problem was, however, that, in many cases, when rebels and other malefactors were executed, the public refused to believe that this had happened, because the evidence was not available, and thus the point of the execution was considerably lessened. I advised him, therefore, if he proposed to continue executing people (which he did), that he should reintroduce public executions. In this country, if you're not prepared to hang someone publicly, people simply conclude that you're afraid to do so for some reason, and that the condemned man has just been spirited away somewhere, from where he very well might return some day. So there we are! That was one of my first legal reforms."

I gazed out through the eucalyptus at the tangled city stretching away below, and sipped my gin and tonic. James' story had the effect of bringing home to me the essential relativity of all values, and I found that strangely soothing, in the context of my present enterprise. On the face of it, this was relatively prosaic and rational. I was going to take up a position teaching English, and a little Latin, at The English School, Addis Ababa – a position secured for me, at my request, by Cousin James himself. But this rational purpose concealed a much darker and more chaotic state of mind.

Strange smells and sounds caressed my senses. The sun began to go down, in that sudden way the sun goes down in the tropics. Wolde Gabriel came in to refresh the drinks, and then melted away again in the direction of the kitchen, from which exotic scents were also arising. A pleasant tingle of anticipation ran up and down my spine. I still did not know what I wanted out of life. I did not even know what would face me tomorrow. But I had wanted something different, and it looked as though I had got it.

Cousin James in turn was in a reflective mood. He seemed pleased to see me, but as my godfather he was plainly also rather disturbed at my state of mind.

"Well now," he said, "what are we going to do with you? This is a very large step to take at your time of life, to head out to the ends of the earth like this. What got into you? Your letter from Oxford back in May sounded distinctly frantic. Is normal civilised existence really that bad?" He looked at me archly over his horn-rimmed spectacles.

I wriggled uneasily in my chair, and sipped my drink.

"I don't know," I said. "Maybe I was just working too hard or something. Things were getting pretty frantic, coming up to Greats. I just found that this feeling was building up in me, all last year, that I had to get away. I felt stifled, somehow, by the idea that, after jumping through all these hoops, I had to go out and get some sort of respectable job – settle down, and so on ... " I spoke rather desperately, aware that I was not making much sense.

"But there was really no reason to worry about that, dear boy. You're intelligent and studious. You could have thought about doing some postgraduate work, for instance. What *did* you get in the end, in fact?"

"Oh, a Second, I'm afraid. It was quite a *good* Second, as they say, but still... My tutors were disappointed. They were expecting a First. But that was very much the problem. I just wasn't motivated any more by the end of it."

"Well, a Second is perfectly respectable, if it comes to that. You could go on to do graduate work with a Second, I should say, if you wished."

"Yes, I suppose I could. But I really felt I needed to get away and *think* for a while. And have some different experiences. I'm sure I'll have got all this out of my system after a year or so," I added. James *was* my godfather, after all, and a particularly good one at that, and I owed it to him, I felt, to sound reasonably purposeful.

James contemplated me, rubbing the side of his nose.

"No doubt you will, my dear fellow, no doubt you will. But meanwhile, we must see that you are properly provided for. I have arranged to bring you round to the school tomorrow morning and introduce you, since they are, after all, starting term on Monday, leaving you not much more than the weekend to settle in – and tomorrow will be already Thursday. Fortunately you have a bungalow and furniture all ready for you, by courtesy of your unfortunate predecessor, whose fate I told you of in my letter, I think."

I nodded.

"An excellent fellow in his way, Davies, but a warning to you as to what *not* to become. "You see, *he* came out to the colonies straight from College, as I recall – though I rather think with a less promising degree than you; in fact I'm not sure that he wasn't sent down – and started teaching in Rhodesia, and afterwards in Kenya for a while. Then, when things began to go bad down there, he gravitated up here. But after a certain number of years it comes about that you find you *can't* go home, even if you want to, because you've become used to the life out here, and everyone at home has forgotten about you, and you have no real qualifications anyway. So you're stuck. And then you're here, or somewhere like this, till you die. That's what happened to poor Davies, and that is what I do *not* want to happen to you, my dear fellow. So I would suggest two years at the outside for this adventure, and then we must take serious thought for your future."

"That sounds fair enough," I nodded, "so long as I don't have to think about that now. For the moment, I just want to immerse myself in Ethiopia, if that's all right."

Cousin James signified his approval.

"And so you shall. That's a good attitude to have. I commend it.

I have seen so many wretched fellows coming out here on secondment from their governments, or with international firms, who make no effort at all to get to know and appreciate their surroundings, but simply moan incessantly about how inefficient everything is, and how obstructive the officialdom is, and how far away they are from London or New York, and all that they're missing. Then they go back where they came from in no way the wiser. And these are people who in many cases are meant to be *helping* the country!

You should try to learn the language," he continued, "and something about the history and the people. I can lend you some books, and I can put you in touch with an old friend of mine who can give you Amharic lessons, if you like. He's the Anglican chaplain to the British community here, and a delightful eccentric – Padre Matthews. Been out here for years. It's a fascinating place, as you will discover, and an ancient and noble civilisation – *despite* practising public execution!"

Wolde-Gabriel now appeared at the french windows, and announced that dinner was served. Wolde was a solid little man, with a kindly weather-beaten face, radiating loyalty and quiet efficiency. His snow-white *shamma,* draped over his shoulders above what appeared to be the almost universal national uniform of khaki jacket and trousers, set off his features to advantage.

We rose, leaving our glasses on the wicker table in front of us, and followed him, through the drawing room, into the dining room. I had been stealing glances, since my arrival, at the many treasures of James' house. It was a spacious old bungalow of colonial type with a wide verandah all round, three large rooms downstairs, drawing room, dining room and study, with the kitchen and Wolde's domain behind. Upstairs there were two spacious bedrooms with sloping eaves and dormer windows, each with its own bathroom. I was lodged in one of the latter.

This was all delightful, but what really fascinated me was the array of works of art, furniture and books that James had assembled over the years. Stuff from South-East Asia and Polynesia jostled with artefacts from East Africa and Ethiopia itself, together with a certain amount of Mallory family heirlooms (including the silver at dinner) in bewildering but tasteful profusion. The house contrived to be full of treasures without appearing cluttered.

Dinner was uncompromisingly Ethiopian, although James said he had ordered Wolde to go easy on the red pepper. Again, though, he was, as he said, concerned to blood me.

"If you're going to live here," he said, "you must come to terms with the food. At first it seems quite uneatable, but then, I assure you, it becomes almost addictive. I wouldn't eat *wat* myself more than once a week at the most, or I'd have no stomach left, but you're young. And another thing. Not only do you have to come to terms with it; you have to learn *how* to eat it, since you must forget about knives and forks. You have to re-learn how to eat with your fingers. Like this!"

I looked first at what Wolde had placed in front of me, and then at my godfather, who was grinning wickedly. I found myself faced with what looked like a thick soup or stew, reddish in colour, and graced at intervals with strips of chicken and small hard-boiled eggs. Beside this, to the right, there was what appeared to be a large, dirty napkin. This was the unleavened bread, *injera*, with which one approached the stew, which was called *wat*. James reached out his hands to this, tore a strip off it, and dipped it in the *wat*, and popped what he gathered into his mouth.

"Remember, " he said, "to use your *right* hand. You may use your left for wiping your bottom, but not for anything more exalted. You as a left-hander, as I recall, must be especially careful to avoid what would be a grave social solecism, to put it no stronger."

Watching him, I tore off a piece from the *injera* with my right hand, and dipped it in, fastening on a piece of chicken. I inserted it cautiously into my mouth. The red pepper hit me with devastating force, seeming to lift off the roof of the mouth. Cousin James emitted a satisfied chuckle. He was enjoying the initiation of his godson.

I looked at him balefully through tear-filled eyes.

"How on earth is anyone expected to eat this?" I gasped. "It must do extraordinary things to your stomach."

"No, no," he assured me. "Very good for you. Clears out the nasal passages. Sharpens the mind. Not unlike the Classics, in fact." And he chuckled again.

Eyes streaming, I persevered, and gradually became somewhat acclimatised. For dessert, though, I was very glad to get to the fruit and curiously aromatic homemade ice-cream.

As we ate, James continued to expatiate on the ancient and rich culture of the country. He explained to me the complex political and social structure which the Emperor had set up, securing an essential alliance with the *Galla*, the dominant tribe in the southern part of the country (the Amhara really came from the North, around Gondar), by himself marrying a princess of that tribe. The Empress Menen must have been a fine-looking woman in her time, but she had in her latter years become woefully stout, and, being both diabetic and imperiously addicted to sweetmeats, had recently died, to the accompaniment of a full month of national mourning; but she had served her purpose, it seemed, and the country was ruled by an alliance of *Amharas* and *Gallas*, dominating the many lesser tribes.

James obviously had a great regard for the Emperor himself, but he was concerned to warn me that, though I as a foreigner would be perfectly free to mind my own business and have a good time, this was *not* a democracy or a free society, and I should always remember that. The Little Man liked the ideas of progress and constitutionality in theory – he had established a parliament, after all, and decreed that elections should be held for it, and he had set up a network of secondary schools, where all subjects were taught through English (for the most part by Indians, admittedly, with rather fractured results), and a university in the capital, called after himself – but he did not like to be contradicted. He ruled with a rod of iron, and all the apparatus of a police state.

"I'm not sure that I blame him for that, I must confess," he added, "because I don't think that this country can be run in any other way – for the foreseeable future, anyhow. But he's creating a class of well-educated young bureaucrats, many of whom he has sent for education abroad – to Britain, America, Germany and even Russia – and he is certainly building up trouble for himself. He has also trained up a highly sophisticated officer corps, taking many of the top graduates of his secondary schools into the army, and that is going to come back to haunt him before very long, I shouldn't wonder. We have already had one attempted military coup, as I've related to you, and of which you've seen one result, and I'm afraid it's only a matter of time before we have another one."

"Gosh," I said apprehensively. "I hope they can hold on just a little while. I don't want to have to run for my life after just arriving."

James smiled. "I wouldn't worry too much. They are most unlikely to target foreigners. They need the continued investment. The only thing is not to get caught in the crossfire."

Stimulated, no doubt, by having a neophyte like myself to discourse to, he turned next to the Emperor's foreign policy.

"On the international front, the Little Man is engaged in a very delicate balancing act between East and West. He pleases neither side entirely, but he shrewdly manages to keep his independence of each bloc. For instance, he recently persuaded the Americans to build him an oil refinery down on the coast, at Assab, and then he proposed to refine Russian oil in it! There was a devil of a row, but he got his way. And then he got the Russians last year to build him a fine new hospital here in the capital – and arranged to staff it with Canadian Jesuits. The Russians tried to argue that the Jesuits wouldn't understand how to handle the technology, so he told them to teach them! And he gets away with it! So far, anyhow. He really most favours countries like Sweden and Yugoslavia, and even Israel, because they're more or less non-aligned. You'll find a lot of enterprises here being run by nations like that – a lot of Indians, too – and you'll find a lot of their offspring at this school of yours. I think I remember Graham – that's your headmaster – telling me that there were over twenty nationalities represented at the school, at last count."

All this was fascinating, but it was becoming too much for me, in my exhausted state. James could see my eyes drooping, and wisely judged that this was enough for one day. He led me back out to the verandah for a nightcap of Ethiopian brandy, before dismissing me to bed.

"Not bad stuff, actually," he said, commenting on the brandy, if you take it on its own terms. Made by an enterprising Italian – Melotti – also makes beer, gin and whiskey. The beer isn't bad, but I wouldn't touch the other two."

I sipped it cautiously, but found it quite pleasant, not unlike the Greek Metaxa, which I'd had a chance to sample on a visit to Greece the previous year.

Then – from just the other side of the compound fence – an uncanny whooping noise broke in above the chatter of the cicadas. I jumped.

"What on earth was that?"

"Oh, just a hyena. You'll get used to them. They come down the ravines at night, and poke around all through the city for what they can find. They're fairly timid creatures, though. No need to worry about them. They're also very useful garbage collectors."

A moment later there was an answering whoop, a little further away. "One has to keep the compound gate shut, though, of course, or they would get at the hens as well as the garbage."

"You keep hens?"

"Oh, Wolde keeps a few out the back, beside his vegetable garden. I like the beasts. Always enjoyed your mother's hens. She still keeps them, I hope?"

"Of course. You can't imagine Mother without hens, can you?"

"No, it would be unfamiliar, certainly. You must drop her a line, by the way, without delay. Just assure her you've arrived safely. And give her my love."

"Yes, indeed. I'll do it tomorrow morning, if we have some time."

"We'll make time for that, you may depend on it. In any case, there's no rush. We're not expected over at the school until eleven or so."

As we downed our brandies, Wolde-Gabriel appeared from inside, and shuffled respectfully in the shadows, waiting to be excused. James turned, and waved a hand.

"All right, Wolde, we can look after ourselves now. You can go, thanks."

"*Eshe, getoich.* Good night. Good night, Mr Luke. And welcome to Ethiopia!"

"Good night, Wolde," I replied. "And thank you for everything."

He bowed, and glided away.

"A very good fellow, Wolde," commented Cousin James. "Been with me nearly ten years now, ever since I first arrived. Absolutely honest, and the soul of discretion. I got him from the Stanfords. He worked out on the farm, and then in the school for a while. He's a *Guragi*, from a village just north of here. I think they've found you a boy of more or less the same background. I'll explain the ropes to you in that regard tomorrow."

Here another new and troubling challenge loomed, to be the master of a personal servant. Of course, we'd had servants around the place in Wicklow, but that was not quite the same thing. Anyhow, it would be enough to worry about that the following day. By that point, it was all that I could do to drag myself upstairs in the wake of my godfather, undress, and flop into oblivion in a capacious and comfortable bed, lulled by the myriad sounds of the African night.

CHAPTER TWO

I awoke in the morning to the courteous voice of Wolde-Gabriel in my ear.

"Mr Luke, Sir James ask if you like get up, have breakfast now?"

I struggled into consciousness, propping myself up on an elbow. Wolde drew the curtains, in anticipation of my assent. The sun beamed in the window, lighting up the otherwise rather dark wood of the bedroom. It was a pleasant, cosy room, but with its sloping eaves, wood beams, and walls lined with books and trophies from Cousin James's journeys about the world, it needed a good shot of tropical sunlight to brighten it.

"Oh, thanks, Wolde," I said. "Looks like a nice day."

He looked round at me, a slightly puzzled look on his kindly face. He plainly was not used to commenting on the weather, in the way that our servants back in Wicklow, or even my scout in Oxford, would automatically have done.

"Yes," he said thoughtfully, "now is very nice weather, good time of year. We are coming to Meskal in one week, end of rains, new year. All the country is green." He waved a hand at the eucalyptus-covered heights of Entotto, visible through the window.

"Oh?" I said, intrigued. "You have New Year now?"

"Yes!" A smile lit up his face. "New Year one week, big feast, everybody happy!"

And he glided respectfully out. I resolved to ask James more, over breakfast, but for the moment the task was to get out of bed, take a much needed bath and shave. I heaved myself upright, and lurched over to the window. My bedroom faced north, up towards the hills surrounding the city, rather than down upon the city itself, which had been the view from the verandah. Beyond the compound fence, within which there was a neat vegetable garden, and a little enclosure for Wolde's hens, I could see a profusion of circular native huts, in a forest of eucalyptus. Between the huts wisps of smoke were rising. I opened the window, and immediately there wafted in, on the crisp morning air, the intoxicating scent of burning eucalyptus leaves mixed with red pepper. I had caught a whiff of this yesterday, but this morning it impressed itself on me very strongly.

I remained a while transfixed at the window. From somewhere in the jumble of huts there came the slow, irregular beat of a pounding stick, perhaps grinding corn for the daily bread. Outside a hut, a dog turned around twice, sniffed, settled down again. In the space between two huts, a small black hen stopped in the red dust, scratched her eye, ruffled her feathers, uttered a sharp complaint. The sun was already beating down on the leaves of the eucalyptus and false banana trees. A thin song eddied up from one of the huts, perhaps from the woman pounding the corn. Looking out from my vantage point, I had the curious, disquieting sensation of intruding on this scene of everyday existence, so exotic to me, but utterly banal and ordinary to those who lived it.

I turned my gaze back within the compound, and stood watching Wolde's hens for a brief while, as they scratched around in their pen. Unremarkable, somewhat scrawny fowl, I found their actions vaguely comforting, providing an element of continuity between this strange new world and the one I had left. It was probably some of their rather puny eggs that had found their way into the *wat* the previous night.

I turned away from the window, and made my way to the guest bathroom next door, where I found that Wolde had thoughtfully run a bath, in anticipation of my desires. I luxuriated in it for as long as I dared, shaved and dressed briskly, and presented myself downstairs in the dining room for breakfast, taking with me a present that my mother had sent out. It was a consignment of homemade fudge of which Cousin James was particularly fond, and it seemed to have survived the journey in pretty good shape.

Cousin James was already in place at the breakfast table, immersed in the airmail edition of *The Times*.

"Ah, there you are, dear boy. Take a pew there, and help yourself. There's coffee, bread and honey or marmalade, and Wolde will bring you some eggs in a moment. Did you sleep well?"

He folded the paper, and surveyed me.

"Yes, thanks," I said, taking a seat. "I slept very well. I feel more or less recovered, actually."

"Excellent! I should warn you, though, it will be wise to take things pretty easy at first. You must remember that we are up at well over seven thousand feet here. A lot of people come to Addis and forget that, and find themselves unexpectedly in a very sorry state. Altitude sickness is no joke!"

"Gosh," I said. "I hadn't thought of that. I did notice, though, how crisp and clear the air seemed."

"Yes, that's one side of it. It can also be a bit enervating, though, till you're used to it. Just bear it in mind for the first few days. And now let us discuss what I've planned for you today." And he looked at me over his spectacles.

First, though, he clapped his hands, and called into the kitchen. "Wolde, Mr Luke is down. You can put on his eggs now."

"Eshe, getoich," came the reply from the kitchen.

"Well now, plainly the first thing to do is to take a drive over to The English School, and introduce you to your new home. Before we do that, though, it might be as well to fill you in a little on the history of the place, as there some aspects that it is particularly important to understand."

I poured myself some coffee, and looked expectant.

"That coffee, by the way, comes, as does the honey, from Nyala Farm, the Stanfords' country place. I like it, but it takes some getting used to."

I took a cautious sip, and saw what he meant. It was strong, smoky and aromatic, but strangely attractive. Brigadier and Mrs Stanford, I knew from James' letters, were the founders of the School, and I was impatient to know more about them. From the hints he had given, they sounded a fascinating and delightful pair.

"I like it, I think. But I can see what you mean. It's powerful stuff."

"Yes indeed, and most distinctive. Their bees plainly live interesting lives – as, indeed, has the Brig himself." James pushed his chair back from the table, took off his glasses, and fell to polishing them with a corner of the tablecloth.

"The Brig – he was only a Colonel then – came out here first before the First World War, as military attaché to the British embassy. Like many another, he fell in love with the country, and after the war, he declined to be moved, resigned from the service, and decided to settle down here. He got into the import-export business. What exactly he imported or exported I couldn't tell you, but he made a living – running things down to East Africa as well as to Europe – until the Italians came.

His wife Louise fortunately shared his enthusiasm – a great old girl, by the way. If she likes you, as I hope she will, your life will be greatly enriched, not least by weekends at Nyala! All their three children were born out here, and have largely grown up here – two boys and a girl.

"When the Italians took over in '36, Andy Stanford took his family back to England, and got some sort of desk job – I think he was actually made treasurer of Guildford Cathedral at one point, of all things – but he wasn't happy. Africa becomes very difficult to leave, I warn you, if you stay here for any length of time. When the War started, he tried to enlist, but he was too old for any normal service, so they kept him on ice."

Cousin James paused, took a sip of coffee, and continued.

"Then, in late 1940, came the opportunity to dislodge the Italians, and bring the Emperor back. That's how I first met him. You may recall that I was assigned to liaise with the Little Man when he was in exile in Bath? Now that interesting lunatic Orde Wingate was given overall command of the operation, but, because he knew the country so well, Andy was promoted to Brigadier, and assigned the job of leading an advance party, including the Emperor himself, back in from the Sudan.

"That was a dangerous, daring operation, but it worked. The Italians were in fact in considerable disarray by this time, and in May 1941 Andy and Wingate led the Little Man triumphantly back into Addis. This was much more of an achievement than one might think, because there were powerful British interests in the invading force who wanted to sideline the emperor, and take over the country as a British colony. That would have been appallingly short-sighted as well as dishonourable, of course, and Andy and Wingate did well to stand out against it."

At this point Wolde Gabriel appeared with a pair of attractively presented fried eggs, swimming in oil, and I started in on them, mopping them up with chunks of excellent home-made bread, while I continued to listen to James' narration.

"In the aftermath of that," he continued, "the Brig was very much persona grata, naturally, but he didn't want to go back into business. He had a good war pension by then, so he just wanted to retire and do a bit of farming. The Emperor, though, had another idea. In the confusion following on the liberation, he needed someone to educate his children, and the children of his chief associates. Various of the great *Rases* and *Dejazmaches* had children or grandchildren of the right ages, and nowhere suitable for them to go. The emperor had been brought up in a French tradition himself, but after his experiences in exile, he had decided that English was the coming language. He he very much liked Andy – and Louise, when she came out to join her husband.

He summoned Louise to his presence, and asked her if she would be prepared to start a school for the children of his nobility. Louise had been a teacher for a while in her youth, and while she had never done anything like this before, she didn't like to refuse an imperial request. And so The English School, Addis Ababa came into being. It's still known unofficially, by the way, to taxi drivers and others, as the 'Stanford School', *ya-Stanford tamari bêt,* in case you're ever trying to get back there from the Piazza or elsewhere.

"The Emperor gave them a piece of land on the east of the city, not far from the Imperial Palace. The main bungalow is rather fine, and that is now the headmaster's house. Most of the other buildings they had to put up themselves, but your little bungalow is old – and it's not at all bad. I'm sure you'll be very comfortable there. Your predecessor certainly was."

"The school is now, as you will see, quite a flourishing establishment, recognised by the British Council, and catering to a wide cross-section of the expatriate community, and to resident foreigners, such as Greeks and Armenians, as well as, still, to many prominent Ethiopians – despite the fact that the Emperor has by now established quite a network of good secondary schools."

The narrative intrigued me, almost leading me to forget my breakfast. I finished my rapidly cooling eggs, set the plate to one side, and turned to try the honey, with some more fresh bread. James refilled my coffee cup, and then his own, and continued.

"Louise based herself in town, but at the same time the Emperor presented the Brig with a fine stretch of land about twenty-five miles north of the city, where he built a bungalow and set up "Nyala Farm". He has a couple of hundred acres out there on the upland, including a native village, which supplies him with servants, and then a whole valley two thousand feet below – God knows how many more acres – in one of the gorges that run eventually into the Blue Nile.

"It's a fascinating place; it has two different climates. One is nearly seven thousand feet up, like a good English summer. There, he grows all sorts of temperate crops and vegetables. Then down in the valley it's tropical, and he grows coffee and bananas, and so on, and you'll find colobus monkeys and baboons and waterbuck and leopards. Very tricky mule ride down, though. I've done it a couple of times in my day, but not any more!

"So that's the Stanford background, anyhow. Now, more to the point, a bit about your headmaster. Graham Wiggins is a good enough chap, and he runs the school very well."

I nodded.

"Good," said James, continuing. "He was one of the first group of recruits to answer an advertisement that the Stanfords placed in the English papers soon after the end of the war, with a view to setting up a proper school in the autumn of 1945. Previous to that, Louise had simply tutored the young Ethiopian nobles in her drawing-room! Then came two married couples (one of whom, the Lonsdales, is still here), and your predecessor, who was a good teacher, I believe, but a rather older man – so Wiggins was the only presentable young bachelor in the group. He quickly caught the eye of the Stanfords' daughter Isabel, who was then in her early twenties, and was helping out in the school.

"This relationship flourished, I'm glad to say, and within a year or so Wiggins had, in effect, married the boss's daughter. This suited Louise very well, as she had never really wanted to spend her later years as a headmistress, so after another year or so, she handed over the reins to Wiggins, and retired to Nyala Farm.

"Wiggins is a good manager, as I say, and the school has been doing very well, despite all the other schools that now exist. You see, the advantage The English School has is that it is truly cosmopolitan, and English-speaking, while at the state schools, though the language of instruction is officially English, most of the teaching is done by non-mother tongue teachers and the pupils are all Ethiopian, so that not much English of any quality is spoken. The aristocracy, therefore, still like to send their offspring to the Stanford School. You'll find a number of interesting persons there.

They may not be particularly diligent, but I think you'll find them well-behaved and entertaining. The Emperor's grandchildren are there – Asfa Wossen's children – and those some of his chief Rases, and of a number of his ministers. In fact, the son of my particular colleague, the Minister of Justice, will probably be doing Latin with you. I believe his father is rather keen on starting him on it. He was very pleased to hear you were coming."

"Gosh," I said. "I'll have a Latin class, will I? That was raised as a possibility."

"Yes, that's part of the plan, I believe. I think it counts as an extra, but it is offered. They used to get old Padre Matthews up to do it – that's the delightful old boy I told you about last night – but having you there will be more convenient."

This talk of young aristocrats jogged my memory. In my second year in Oxford, when I was still in College rooms, I came back in October to find that the room opposite to mine on the staircase was occupied by a black man. I suppose I was no more tolerant or broad-minded than any other British public schoolboy of the 1950s (except that being Irish had sensitised me, at least, to that aspect of British upper-class intolerance). And I was mindful of one of my Cousin James' earlier injunctions, when I went up first: "Remember, my dear boy, always be nice to black men, if you come across any at Oxford, because they are probably very interesting people if they have got that far, and they will probably go home afterwards and become someone very important – if they don't get themselves shot in the meantime."

So when I met this fellow going into his rooms one afternoon soon after the beginning of term, I greeted him, introduced myself, and asked him if he would like to come over for tea. He was plainly surprised, and at first rather hesitant, but then accepted gladly, and over tea and crumpets toasted at the gas fire I learned who he was, and what he was doing. His name was Yohannis Tessema. He was from Ethiopia, he told me, had spent some years at Harrow, which he had not enjoyed, and was now trying Oxford for a year, to see how he liked that. He was officially reading Politics, Philosophy, and Economics, but he was taking his duties pretty lightly, so far as I could see. Money seemed to be no object, and his father seemed to want him to sample the best in British education, but the whole experience was not agreeing with him very well. I got the impression that I was more or less the first person who had been spontaneously polite to him since he had arrived in the country. A few days later, he asked me back, for some properly brewed Ethiopian coffee, as he emphasised.

Well brewed it certainly was. I had never tasted such coffee. He ground it himself, and then boiled it up in a brass pot on a primus stove, talking to me over his shoulder as he did so. It was an education in the making of coffee. Of course, as Yohannis explained, with a delightful arrogance that I came later to recognise as characteristic of the upper echelons of his nation, it was not surprising that it was excellent coffee, as the Ethiopians had actually invented coffee.

In the event, we became pretty good friends over that year, in a funny sort of way. He was fairly reticent about who exactly his father was, but he seemed, from various incidental references, to be well acquainted with members of the Ethiopian royal family, and he owned a red Maserati sports car, in which we took periodic trips into the Oxfordshire countryside, so I assumed he was pretty comfortably off and well connected. I remember Yohannis once remarking that on his way back from Addis Ababa after the holidays, he had stopped off in Paris, and while there had attended the funeral of Sidney Bechet. "I passed myself off as the son of the Duke of Harar." He laughed to himself. "Actually, my father is rather more important than the Duke of Harar, but there's nothing like a title to impress the natives."

So I thought I would ask James about Yohannis, while he was in my mind. "By the way, talking of young members of the aristocracy, I was up at Oriel with a chap from this part of the world. I wonder if you know of him. His name was Yohannis Tessema. He certainly seemed pretty prosperous, but I don't know what his background was, really."

Cousin James raised his eyebrows, and looked at me over his spectacles, which he had returned to his nose.

"Yohannis Tessema, eh? I should say I do know of him. You have certainly been moving in interesting circles!"

"I was just following one of the bits of advice you gave me when I went up first actually, "Always be nice to black men!" He happened to live across the staircase from me in my second year."

"Well, well. To answer your question, your friend Yohannis is the eldest son of one Tessema Gesesse, who is probably the richest man in Addis Ababa. At any rate, he owns most of it. Ras Tessema is a younger brother of the Empress Menen, so he is very well connected, as you can gather.

But young Yohannis is a bit of problem. I'm not sure that I would advocate having too much to do with him. Since he came back, he has been combining a very dissolute lifestyle with rather radical politics, and being generally outspoken and scandalous. His Majesty is not pleased with him at all. He hasn't cared to intervene yet, out of deference to the family, but I don't know how long that will last. The Little Man will put up with a certain amount of immorality among his extended family – if anything, it renders them more ineffectual, and he doesn't mind that – but he dislikes anything that smacks of political activism. He has Yohannis pretty closely watched, I understand, though the young fool seems unaware of that, or at least unperturbed by it. I shouldn't be surprised, though, if your friend wasn't packed off somewhere remote before very long – perhaps to a minor embassy post – where he would be out of mischief. Meanwhile, though, my advice would be to avoid him."

"Oh darn. I had been hoping to look him up. We got on very well. But I see your point."

"Yes, I'm sorry, but I do think I'm right. My original piece of advice is in general a sound one, but it doesn't always work, I fear. Sometimes a man will go back home and get into every sort of trouble. But now," said he said, pushing back his chair and rising from the table, "I would propose that you sit down in the study and write a note to your mother, and then in a little while we can go over and visit Wiggins and Isabel. I will find you some notepaper."

He led me into his sanctum and settled me down at his desk. Only now did I get round to presenting him with the fudge, which he received with great delight. I remembered how much he used to enjoy it when he visited us in Wicklow. My mother always had a supply ready for him.

Faced with a blank sheet of paper, I was suddenly at a loss. The events of the last twenty-four hours, transporting me as they had from one mode of existence to another, seemed somehow to defy description. And yet my mother was certainly entitled to a letter. I decided to compromise, dashing off a preliminary bulletin, along with a promise of something more substantial very soon. After all, I still hardly knew where I was, or what I was doing.

Then I sat back, sucking the end of my pen, visualising for a moment the arrival of this letter at Bellevue Lodge. Seamus, the postman, would probably come round to the kitchen door with such a sensational document, a letter with a very furrin stamp on it, and one which he would know was eagerly awaited. Bills in brown envelopes he would tactfully leave in the letterbox at the front door, but for such a welcome item as this he could reasonably hope for a cup of tea, and even some of my mother's homemade biscuits, or a piece of cake.

To deal with the letter properly, Mother would have to make herself a cup of coffee, get out her cigarettes and her glasses, and settle down at the kitchen table. She was not a demonstrative woman, but I knew she would be worrying. After all, I had turned my back on any of the sensible job prospects that might seem to open up – if not in Ireland, then at least in England – after a reasonably respectable Oxford degree, and had headed out virtually into the unknown – to do what? To drop out, really.

But Mother was a stoic. She had argued with me rationally, pointing out the folly of the adventure, and asking what in the long term I proposed to do with my life (a question to which I had no clear answer), but she did not indulge in any tearful appeals, or lamentations as to what was to become of her if I was eaten by savages, and when it became clear that I had made up my mind she left it at that, and turned to practical plans.

I could see, though, that the whole thing was gnawing away at her though the summer. It made me feel very bad, though without deflecting me from what I felt I had to do. I had accumulated over the last few years a nest of demons that had to be exorcised.

No, I could not have settled down to any normal occupation without making some effort to sort myself out. Whether Ethiopia was the place to do that remained to be seen. At least, I reflected, I would be earning quite good money while doing this – around £1200 a year had been mentioned, along with free accommodation – so that I should even be able to send something back to support the tottering economy of Bellevue, and this made me feel somewhat better.

My mother was used to living from hand to mouth, and she was quite good at it. Ever since returning early in the war to her mother-in-law's crumbling establishment, she had managed to make ends meet by means of a sort of barter economy – a system of arrangements with the local shops and farmers according to which very little money actually changed hands, and goods and services were exchanged in extremely complicated but effective ways. Mother would provide cabbages or new potatoes or eggs or cream or raspberries or cooking apples to Mr Byrne's Stores in the village, and would use the credit to get other things we might need. The Long Field would be lent to Gerry Walsh for his bullocks, and in return some ploughing or weed cutting or repairing of sheds would get done when needed. Someone else would be given the use of another field one year to plant a crop of potatoes or turnips or cabbages, and for a season we would have all we wanted and more of that particular commodity. In this way two minuscule pensions, Granny's and Mother's, were made to go quite a long way.

Growing up in a household such as that, and surviving boarding schools from the age of seven to that of nearly eighteen, should theoretically leave one able to face almost anything that life can throw at one, but I found myself, at the age of twenty-two, still in a curiously helpless state. Life was austere, certainly, both at home and at school, but most decisions were out of my hands. Mother had developed a deep-seated conviction, presumably as a result of looking after my father in Malaya, that men were unable to care for themselves on any practical level, and in my case this became a self-fulfilling prophecy. Life in Oxford was admittedly a rudimentary step in the direction of self-sufficiency, but between the efficiency of scouts and the solicitude of landladies I did not find myself challenged too radically. How would I manage running my own household, even with a servant?

But there was really no time for daydreaming. Envelope in hand, I went out to find Cousin James. He had returned to the dining room and his perusal of *The Times*. I waved the letter.

"All done?" he said. "Good man. You sent her my love, I hope?"

I nodded.

"Splendid. Well, I can find you a stamp, and we will mail it in the Piazza, on our way over." He looked into the kitchen.

"Wolde, we will go now. I will drive myself. Back for lunch."

"*Eshe, getoich,*" came back from the kitchen, where Wolde was washing up the breakfast things.

"I think I'll hold onto you for today," James said, "since we don't know what's waiting for you in this bungalow that Wiggins has assigned to you. My understanding is that it's pretty well furnished, but we'll see. We can check it over, and I may be able to fill a few gaps. If it's habitable, you can move in this evening, and try it out ... I thought, by the way, that on Saturday we might take a picnic down to the Awash River, if you'd like. Show you a bit of the countryside. "

"That sounds lovely," I said. However, I was also conscious of an unwillingness to leave the haven of luxury that was James's bungalow.

"Yes, I think it should be. I've asked an old friend of mine, Willy Buhagiar, to join us, and the Hardimans, from the Embassy – a very pleasant pair. Willy is acting as Chief Justice here at the moment, until he can train his successor. He's Maltese himself, but educated in Cambridge, and then at the Inns of Court. Very good man. Right then, let's be off."

As James manoeuvred the Mercedes cautiously out of the compound, other things occurred to him.

"We need to think of a few practical matters. You are going to need some money, for one thing. I can take you past the bank on the way back, and you can open an account. I know the manager – a pleasant Armenian fellow, Boghossian by name. Has his children in the school, I think – so I can introduce you. I can lend you a few hundred dollars till your first paycheck. I'm sure Wiggins would be glad to, but blood is thicker than water."

"Well, that would be just great," I said. "I wasn't able to get any Ethiopian dollars in London. I just have sterling."

"Well, we can settle that this afternoon, I think, after Mr Boghossian's siesta. We'd better not delay now, as Wiggins is expecting us."

As we drove, Cousin James filled me in on some aspects of doing business in this country. When dealing with officialdom, it was necessary to take one's time, and observe the proprieties, such as accepting cups of coffee and discussing the state of the world before getting down to business. It was also extremely helpful to have personal introductions, he emphasised, as there was little or no sense of impartial public service. An official had really to have a personal reason for obliging you.

"Which reminds me," added James, looking across at me, "you will need to go in without delay about your residence and work permit, to the Ministry of the Interior. We might even call in there this afternoon as well, if there seems to be time. Fortunately, I know the Director-General quite well. I was in a position to get him out of a spot of bother a little while ago. So I can introduce you there too."

"Gosh," I said, a little dismayed, "that's all a bit discouraging, if you don't happen to know anyone."

"Ah yes," said James, with a quiet smile, "but you do know someone. You know me. And I know various people, who in turn know various other people. So don't forget to ask."

I laughed. "When you come to think about it," I said, "it's not that unlike Ireland. At home, after all, it does make a great difference if you know someone, or even if you're prepared to chat to them. And once again, it's not really a question of bribery and corruption. It's just the personal nature of society. The amount of parking tickets that Mother has talked herself out of, around the centre of Dublin, just by chatting up young guards! She's very good, also, with agricultural inspectors – and bank managers."

"Yes," said James, smiling. "Your mother has always been good at that sort of thing. Well, now you'll have a chance to practise the same skills. We'll start on Ato Kebede Degachew in the Ministry, possibly tomorrow afternoon. Tomorrow, I'm afraid, I am tied up with the Minister of Justice for most of the morning."

We drove back down the hill, retracing our route of the previous evening, towards the Piazza. Just before we reached it, as we passed the open ground above it, I cast a sidelong glance at yesterday's scene. The gibbet still stood, but the corpse was gone. I made no comment.

The Piazza was full of varied life. James pointed out notable landmarks, such as the Italian-style State Bank, the Ras Makonnen Bar, a very popular expatriate meeting place, and Giannopoulos' Bookshop, where the foreign newspapers came in, and which stocked an interesting, if eclectic, range of novels and non-fiction. I was to become thoroughly familiar with both these latter venues before very long.

"The official title of the Piazza," he explained, "which nobody uses, of course, is Haile Selassie Star Square – 'Star' because it is the meeting place of five roads. We came up the southern one from the airport yesterday evening, Churchill Street, but we're going to go out now to the east, along Haile Selassie Avenue. It's not such a fine modern boulevard as Churchill, but it is far more interesting and characteristic of Addis. However, first you must post your letter."

We pulled up outside the Post Office, a pleasant old French Colonial-style building. When I had dealt with the letter, evading the attentions of one or two shoe-shine boys who had already gathered round me, vying for the privilege of shining my shoes, we headed off to the left, along the long, ramshackle street which James had introduced as Haile Selassie Avenue.

Hardly had we left the Piazza when I began to see what he meant by declaring the avenue interesting and characteristic. It wound its way deviously up one of the main gorges which slash the city, until it found a place to cross, near the head of it, by means of a small bridge, after which it made its way laboriously down again, though edging eastwards all the time. It was lined by the most extraordinary assortment of dwellings I had ever set eyes on in a single street, representing a fair cross-section of the various layers of development that made up Addis Ababa.

There were gracious old French Colonial-style buildings dating from the twenties and thirties, jostling with rather grim Italian Fascist erections from the occupation years, and the occasional post-war modern office or apartment block; there were also little Arab or Indian shops, jerry-built and precarious, with all their wares on display, and the proprietor, as often as not, seated out in front, fingering his worry-beads; but in between and behind all these flourished the usual chaos of native *tukuls,* stretching down, along little paths, deep into the ravine. I peered out of the car window, avidly taking in the scene, which went by all too fast.

"This is quite an historic avenue," said James, responding to my interest. "One of the earliest to be developed in the Emperor Menelik's day. It's chaotic, of course, but rather charming in its way. There's an interesting old hotel there," he pointed out to his right, at an elegant old building with a deep verandah, and various curlicues and buttresses, "The Itegue Menen – used to be the Hôtel de France. A little dilapidated nowadays, but still delightful. It's been superseded by the grand modern hotels, like the Ras, down on the way to the airport, but it still has great character. Worth dropping in on for a drink, at least."

I nodded, and took note, but then my attention was attracted by a curious row of little shacks with neon lights above their doors, set side by side a little back from the roadway. Most of the lights were straight, but some were in the form of a cross. Most of the shacks were shut, but in front of one a young woman was washing clothes. I had seen some similar ones on James' road, just before we got to the Piazza, and they looked somehow intriguing.

"What are those shacks with the red lights above them?" I asked. "Are they some sort of medical service?"

Cousin James chuckled broadly.

"Ah! You've been deceived by the red cross, like many an innocent visitor to this city before you. Well, medical service is hardly the right word for them, though they constitute a service of a sort, certainly. Not to beat about the bush, those are brothels. The commonly used term for them is *tej-bêt,* meaning simply 'house where you can drink *tej*', which is a form of mead that I personally find quite vile, but which you should at least try. You can, I believe, always get a beer or a *tej* in a *tej-bêt* if you ask for one, but that is not the main service provided. All I would say to you on that matter, as your godfather, is that, if you are tempted to visit one of these places, do provide yourself with some suitable rubber goods. These are easily obtainable, as you will quickly discover, from any street trader or shoeshine boy, but I would strongly recommend them, as most of these ladies are riddled with diseases."

I looked at the rows of little shacks with new interest.

"Thanks for the warning. There seem to be an awful lot of them, I must say. How do they all survive?"

"I imagine", said James, "that there are proportionately at least as many brothels in Addis Ababa as there are pubs in Dublin, and that is a reasonable index of the priorities of the respective cultures. As to how they all find enough business, I'm not sure that I can answer that. But it is a curious aspect of this culture that it seems quite acceptable for young girls to come up from the country to earn their dowry by selling their favours for a while. When they have amassed enough savings, they go home in triumph, get married and settle down to raise a family. It gives the whole trade a pleasantly amateur aspect. You get comparatively few hardened old whores, and no system of pimps, or of the exploitation that goes with that. The girls seem largely to manage their own affairs."

We meanwhile had come to the end of the Avenue, and out into a large modern square.

"This is Arat Kilo", James said. "Thus named because it's *four* kilometers – *arat* being the Amharic for 'four'– from the Piazza, which is regarded as the centre of town". He pointed at an impressive complex of modern buildings facing us, behind large gates, which he identified as Haile Selassie I University.

"It was actually the Little Man's palace, the New Ghibbi," James explained, with a wave of his hand, "but he very nobly handed it over to form the campus of a university, and retired into the Old Ghibbi, which was Menelik's palace, down the road there." And he pointed down a broad avenue to our right, where the wall of a large compound could be seen.

We turned up to our left, along a suburban avenue, flanked by pleasant western-style villas, interspersed with little Arab shops and a few *tukuls* (no further red lights were visible), and came soon to another roundabout and square just up from which a large compound came into view, with a neat sign outside proclaiming:

The English School, Addis Ababa
Est. 1946.

"Well," said James, "here we are: Siddist Kilo ('six kilometers'). A little out of town, but quite an easy taxi ride, as you'll discover."

To my surprise, a warm feeling of familiarity welled up in me as I surveyed the scene from the car. Perhaps it was some infantile memory of a similar establishment in Malaya, but the place seemed strangely welcoming. Facing us, at the top of a gentle slope, was the impressive dormer bungalow that James had mentioned as the headmaster's residence. Two collie dogs rose from its verandah, and came down the steps to greet us, barking and wagging their tails. The approach of the Mercedes stirred up a quantity of red dust, which hung in the air behind us. Back to our right, nearer the gate, was a cluster of buildings which looked like classrooms, and dotted about to the left and right of the main bungalow were a number of smaller ones, doubtless residences of staff members. One of them, I reflected, was going to be mine for the next few years.

We pulled up in front of the main bungalow. I climbed out, and stood looking around. The dogs bustled around me, barking, wagging, sniffing. James climbed out more slowly. The front door opened, and a large, untidy, friendly-looking woman emerged, calling to the dogs, who retreated obediently. Her piercing blue eyes surveyed me. I shook the welcoming hand, and said how pleased I was to be here.

"Did you have a good journey? No hitches? James looked after you this end, of course."

"Yes, very well indeed," I said, smiling.

"Yes, I'm sure he did. You're a lucky fellow. It's no harm at all to have someone to meet you who knows the ropes, I can tell you. They'll try anything on if they think they can get away with it. They're not bad, really, as a nation, but you have to know how to handle them."

Isabel Wiggins certainly looked as if she could handle anything. She struck me as one of those indomitable ladies who constituted the true sinews of the empire, before whose gaze dishonest or unruly natives simply quailed. She led the way indoors.

The décor was delightful. The hall was full of Ethiopian hangings and trophies of various sorts, but also family items such as coats, hockey sticks and roller skates, making for a pleasantly chaotic and homely atmosphere. An elderly servant appeared in the hall, and she gave orders to him in a stream of Amharic. He bowed respectfully, *Eshe, Mem,* and bustled off on his errands.

As he did so, a door at the back of the hall opened, and a small, sandy-haired man with a well-trimmed moustache and thin face, lean and muscular, marched out to greet us, hand outstretched.

"Ah Graham," said Cousin James, "there you are! I thought I would just bring over young Luke here, and introduce him to you. I very much hope he will prove satisfactory."

"Sir James!" Graham Wiggins beamed, and shook him vigorously by the hand. "You're most welcome indeed. We are most honoured. And I have no doubt that any cousin of yours will be a credit to you."

"You're very welcome, young man," he said, extending his hand again. "I'll call you Luke, if I may. We're pretty informal here, as you'll find out."

"Oh please do, sir," I said.

Mr Wiggins did not, I noted, disdain being addressed as 'sir'. Indeed, he seemed rather pleased. He waved an arm, to usher us into a large room on the left. This proved to be a pleasant, low-ceilinged room, looking out on the compound, with comfortable cane chairs and a sofa, covered with a rug and cushions of native design, arranged around a large open fireplace. We settled ourselves on these, Isabel Wiggins inviting me to sit with her on the sofa.

"Well now, we'll have some coffee, and then I can show you the ropes," said Wiggins. "We can have a look at your quarters. I think you'll find them agreeable. Poor old Davies had nice things, and he kept the bungalow always spick and span. We picked out a few things of value to send to a niece of his back home – only relative he seemed to have – but all the furniture and fittings are yours to make use of."

"That sounds marvellous," I said. "It makes things so much easier."

"Yes," said James, "I was thinking about sheets and towels and so on, but do I gather we have those?"

"Oh yes," said Isabel, "I think you'll find everything you need. Unless the designs don't appeal to you!" And she laughed.

I laughed in return. "Oh, I'm not inclined to be particular. I'm sure they'll be fine."

"Well then," said James, "I wonder if he shouldn't move in this evening, just to try it out. I was going to take him on a picnic to the Awash on Saturday, and I can hold onto him for that night, but he could spend tomorrow learning the ropes here, couldn't he? I'm going to be fairly tied up tomorrow in the Ministry, in any case."

"Fine," said Wiggins, "splendid idea. We have a boy lined up for him, in fact. Young fellow called Tekla-Mariam. I borrowed him from the Nyala household, so he knows his job. English a bit elementary, but he can get along. Good excuse for you to pick up some Amharic, Luke," he added, turning to me. "We'll call over, and instruct young Tekla-Mariam to stand by. Ah, here's the coffee!"

And for the second time that day strong, aromatic Nyala coffee was served, along with some excellent homemade biscuits.

After this interlude, during which I offered compliments on both the coffee and the biscuits, to the great pleasure of Isabel Wiggins, we set off on a tour of the compound. The large building opposite the main bungalow, near the gate and the road, was indeed, as I had supposed, the main assembly hall, containing also most of the classrooms and a library. Then there was another row of classrooms to the side of it, a long low building with a verandah and a series of doors opening off it, where I was told I would be chiefly teaching, as that was where the senior classes met. We looked into one of the rooms, and it seemed bright and cheerful.

"This, this all looks very pleasant," I smiled.

"Yes," said Wiggins, "I'm sure you'll like it. There's a good spirit around, if I may say so myself, and they're a fine, enthusiastic group of kids. Usual teenage problems and exuberance, of course, and some of them are a bit lonely, if they've just arrived, but basically they all want to learn, and that's the main thing, isn't it?"

I nodded agreement. "It's a very cosmopolitan place, I believe? Cousin James was saying that he thought you had over twenty nationalities represented."

"Yes indeed. We have no less than twenty-two nationalities represented in this year's enrolment. You see, besides quite a selection from the top families of Ethiopia, we have a good number of the children of the various resident alien groups, Armenians, Greeks, Indians, Arabs and Italians – yes, there are still quite a few Italians around, in spite of everything! That gets you six nationalities so far. And then there are expatriates from all over the world except for the French and the Germans, who have their own schools. And you'll find children from both sides of the Iron Curtain in your class – quite a few Yugoslavs, in particular.

I insist, though, that while they're here they are all equal, and they all have to accept the British way of doing things – which I think is very good for them, don't you?" He laughed, and patted me on the arm. "You're Irish, of course, I realise, but I understand you've had a fair dose of British education yourself."

"Yes," I said, "I've certainly had enough to know what you mean, I think. And I'm sure it is good for them." I was concerned to be diplomatic.

"Oh yes. Yes indeed," said Wiggins confidently. "Actually, I think we do have one Irish pupil this year – a girl in her late teens. I imagine she'll be in your class for English. We'll have to check on her standard of preparation, but I'd expect her to be in Sixth Form, which will be you. Her father is here with the UN, seconded from your civil service, I think."

"Ah," I nodded, though I wasn't sure how warmly I welcomed the news. They would hardly be my sort of Irish, after all, and I doubted that they would welcome me as a compatriot. We would see.

We walked on round the compound, the Headmaster and I ahead, James behind, in conversation with Isabel. We came to a number of pleasant bungalows occupied by staff, my future colleagues. Some had not yet returned from various travels, but the Geography master, Alan Lonsdale, and his wife Ruth, were at home, and gave me a friendly welcome. When they found out I was moving in that evening, they urged me to call over for a drink, before going to dinner in the 'big house'.

"That'll be a drink before a drink, of course," said Wiggins, "because we're not going to be done out of our drinks, are we, dear? But no matter. Young Luke is not going to be driving anywhere tonight. It'll be a good chance to see how well you can stand up to colonial drinking habits, what?"

"Oh, I'll be very cautious," I said. "I have to take account of the altitude as well, of course, I believe."

"Ah yes," he laughed, "the altitude. That gets blamed for a multitude of sins out here." We passed on, with a promise from me to drop in around six.

Finally we reached the whitewashed mud-brick bungalow, with a wooden verandah, set back to the right of the main house, which was to be my home. There was a little garden in front of it, with a profusion of flowers and bushes, surrounded by a low picket fence, and a well-laid stone path ran up to the front door. Bougainvillea flourished on the pillars of the verandah. Some loving attention had plainly been given to all this, and I took to it immediately.

"Mr Davies liked gardening, did he?" I said.

"Oh yes," said Isabel. "John was really devoted to his plants. Fortunately, though, you won't have to take a great interest in them if you don't want to. We have an excellent gardening boy, who used to work closely with him. Indeed John taught him quite a lot. Now he can practise it. All you need to do is pay him a few dollars."

"Fine," I said. "I'll be glad to do that."

As we approached the door, it opened, and a young Ethiopian emerged, smiling, to welcome us. Wiggins addressed him first in Amharic – fluent enough, but much more of the 'kitchen' variety, I judged, than that of Isabel – and then in English, introducing me.

"Tekla-Mariam, this is Mr Luke, whom you are to look after. We want you to make him very comfortable."

"*Eshe, getoich,*" said Tekla-Mariam, bowing. I shook him by the hand, and addressed him, a little nervously.

"Hello, Tekla-Mariam. I'm very glad to meet you. You'll have to try and teach me some Amharic." To my relief, he did at least seem to understand English.

"Yes, *getoich,* " he said, "I will be happy to. You must also excuse me my English. I learn just right now."

"That's fine," I said. "I'll be glad to help you with that. I'm sure we'll get along very well."

Wiggins now gave orders to Tekla-Mariam to collect my luggage from the car and he bustled off to do that.

We went in, and Isabel showed me round my new quarters. Cousin James stepped in also, and cast a quizzical eye around the facilities. It was small and cosy and neat. Just a large front room, serving as a living room, dining room and study, with, behind it, a bedroom and bathroom. To the side was the kitchen, Tekla-Mariam's preserve. The furnishings were comfortable, a sofa, two armchairs, dinner table and four chairs, capacious bed, good-sized bath, fridge, radio. Good bachelor quarters.

We made our way back out into the open air, where the midday sun was beginning to make itself felt. The smell of dust and, from beyond the compound fence, burning eucalyptus leaves hung on the air, as midday meals were prepared in the native huts.

"Well," said James, "we had best be getting on. Many thanks for your hospitality, Isabel and Graham. You and Luke can get down to business in more detail tomorrow, I expect. I'll deliver him back here this afternoon about four-thirty or so, in time for his drink with the Lonsdales. First, though, I want to introduce him to my friend Mr Boghossian at the bank."

"Ah yes," said Wiggins. "By the way, Luke, your first pay-packet won't come until the end of the month, I'm afraid, but we can make you an advance before that if you need it."

I thanked him, but said I had brought a hundred pounds with me, and all agreed that this would certainly see me through comfortably. Even that was a loan from my mother, which I would have to repay as soon as possible, but it was good to hear that it sounded ample to live on for the rest of the month. My salary, Wiggins confirmed, was to be £1200 a year, with a free bungalow, and that seemed princely to one just out of college, who had never hitherto made any serious attempt to earn his living.

Tekla-Mariam's salary, it also emerged, was to be twenty-five Ethiopian dollars a month – about five pounds sterling – and a new suit of clothes – plain khaki fatigues – twice a year. Pretty minimal, but Isabel assured me that he would live like a lord on that.

As we drove back, James commended me on my performance, and judged that everything had gone very well.

"I certainly felt very welcome," I said. "I must say the whole set-up seems very attractive."

"Well," said James, "don't jump to any conclusions, good or bad, for the moment. Just takes things cautiously. Keep your mouth shut and your eyes and ears open. You've got to get the feel of things. I think you will in fact have a very good time, but it is best to be circumspect to start with. Expatriate society here, as you will discover, has a rather hothouse atmosphere. As Graham Wiggins remarked, the altitude can do funny things to people. But I think it's just the fact of being rather thrown together in a very strange environment, with, in many cases – especially in that of the wives – not quite enough to do. At any rate, you need to find out who is talking to whom, and indeed who is sleeping with whom, and who is regarded as notoriously eccentric, before you plunge in."

"Fair enough," I said. "I'll just try to be quietly pleasant to everybody."

"Yes, that is more or less my policy and it seems to work. Of course, I am a bit old by now to get up to very much mischief, but one still needs to be on one's guard."

We reached James's to be greeted by attractive smells from the kitchen, and indeed Wolde-Gabriel had prepared an excellent, if rather copious lunch, in a European mode this time. James questioned me closely about the state of affairs back in Wicklow, and how well Mother was surviving, and then told me something of his work with the Ministry of Justice. The Minister himself, Abebe Retha, he was high in praise of, and promised to introduce me to before long. He was a nobleman of royal blood himself, a descendant of the Emperor John, who had reigned in the previous century. He was also highly educated, extremely efficient, and incorruptible, and he was prepared to answer the Emperor back when he thought he was wrong. According to James, all this made for a rather uncomfortable relationship with the Little Man, whose claim to descent from the royal line of Solomon and the Queen of Sheba was tangential at best, but he found he could not dispense with Lij Abebe, for the moment at least. As lunch was ending, the sky clouded over, and a sudden breeze whipped the eucalyptus trees.

"Now," said James, "I'm afraid we are not quite through with the rains yet, so you are going to experience a little touch of monsoon. It will only last for an hour or so at this stage of the year, and it should be over by next week, in time for Meskal, if it is behaving properly. I would propose that you follow my example and try to take a little nap till about three o'clock, and then we will go down and visit Mr Boghossian. I have made an appointment for half past three."

So I found myself a little while later lying on the bed in the guest bedroom, listening to the soothing roar of rain beating on the roof, and reflecting on my various adventures. And so doing, I dozed off.

CHAPTER THREE

This time it was Cousin James himself who woke me, with a prod at my shoulder.

"Well, well. Managed to snooze a bit, did you? It's a great benefit if you can do that. Many northern Europeans can't, and it makes them irritable in the tropics. I'll leave you to get up. We'll need to go down the hill quite shortly, though, if we're to catch Mr Boghossian."

I rose and dabbed some water on my face in the bathroom. The rain had stopped, the clouds were clearing away, and a smell of damp freshness floated in through the window. In the back yard, the hens were scratching about as before, and a scrawny black cat had settled down to sleep on an old piece of sacking near the fence.

As we drove down the hill, James filled me in briefly on Mr Boghossian. The story was an intriguing one. Boghossian's father, it seemed, was one of the Armenian orphans that the Emperor Menelik rescued and brought out to Addis at the time of the Turkish persecutions. Most of those orphans had done very well for themselves, since the Emperor, sharp old boy that he was, recognised their potential for generating commerce and industry, and set them up in business, but few had done as well as Mr Boghossian.

He had started in textiles, and in general import and export, but gradually, through developing a reputation for honesty and reliability, he developed a private banking system, which many of the native aristocracy and other merchants made use of. He survived the Italian occupation without compromising himself – indeed, he managed to give some significant help to patriot elements without the knowledge of the Italians. After the war, when the Little Man wanted to reconstitute the Bank of Ethiopia, he asked Mr Boghossian to take it over, merging his operation with it.

This was a bit of a sacrifice for Boghossian, but it was also worth his while to accept, from the point of view of security, there being a certain amount of prejudice against the Armenians among the native population, precisely because of their success. And it gave him an ideal vantage point for practising what he was very good at, which was doing favours for all and sundry. The actual governor of the bank, James said, was an Ethiopian grandee – a rather silly old Ras, whom the Little Man wished to conciliate – but there was no real question that the bank was run by Boghossian.

"So the thing is," concluded James, "in introducing you to Mr Boghossian, I am not just introducing you to your local bank manager, but to a man who, if he likes you (and he will be predisposed to like you, being a relation of mine), can be very useful to you if you are ever in difficulties. He is also, I may say, a most attractive character, extremely cultured, speaks five or six languages, loves music, and is an excellent conversationalist. I value him at dinner parties. His wife Mimi is also delightful, and much devoted to amateur theatricals; but you may have to keep her at arm's length, especially if you confess to a liking for acting, as she will certainly endeavour to rope you in."

We reached the bank, and drove round the back of it into a private carpark, supervised by a guard. We then presented ourselves at the front desk, and were ushered up to Mr Boghossian's spacious office, which commanded a fine view over the lower part of the city.

Mr Boghossian rose briskly from behind his desk to greet us. He was a large (though not by any means fat), balding, olive-skinned man, with a friendly though shrewd expression, and a number of flashing gold teeth.

"Sir James, Sir James, this is a great pleasure, as always! And this is your young cousin! I am most pleased to meet you – Mr La Touche, is it not? Do have a seat. I am at your service."

He clapped his hands for a waiting boy, and called for coffee.

"Well, well, it is very fortunate that I could be here today to meet you. Tomorrow I must go to Asmara, and then I will be in Eritrea for almost a week. But as it is, I can have the pleasure of setting things up for you."He then turned to me, and asked about my journey, how I liked the country, what I would be teaching, where I had studied and what.

As I contrived suitable answers, I found myself increasingly attracted to this enormously urbane figure. He had informed himself

45

about me, and he seemed genuinely interested in my situation. Having discovered that I enjoyed drama and had even done a little acting at Oxford, he declared that I must certainly meet his wife, and that he would see to that before long. In fact, Mr Boghossian appeared to be what he was, a consummate politician.

The coffee came in, accompanied by some particularly delicious *loukoumi*, and still the talk proceeded in elaborate circles. Mr Boghossian turned his attention back to Cousin James, and they discussed various items of local gossip that were obscure to me.

At last our host rose, and declared that he would escort us to a man who would open my account for me. We went downstairs, and into a room at the back of the ground floor of the bank, where an efficient young Ethiopian accepted my £100 and performed the formalities without delay. Mr Boghossian, having given the necessary orders, excused himself most gracefully, with a promise to get in touch very soon.

I now had a comfortable wad of Ethiopian dollars in my wallet. As far as I could see, finances were not going to be a problem, if I lived moderately. James assured me afterwards, as we drove away, that this simple process could have taken weeks without the proper introduction, with many hours of tedious waiting in anterooms; but that had not been his main reason for introducing me to Mr Boghossian.

"Partly," he said, "I just wanted to show how business should be done in this society, and partly I wanted to introduce you to a very interesting and useful man to know. Boghossian has, over the years, built up an elaborate network of contacts, among people for whom he has done favours of one sort or another, so that he is both personally unassailable and extremely influential if he wants to help somebody else. I naturally hope you won't have much need of him – you can always come to me, in any case – but he is a good man to know, certainly."

"Yes, thanks very much," I said. "I'm sure he is. I liked him a lot, I must say."

"Well, I think he liked you, which is good, and more to the point. You will probably hear from him again before too long, and then Mimi may get you into her clutches."

I laughed.

"Oh, I don't think I'll mind that too much. I've always liked amateur theatricals."

Cousin James chuckled to himself, but made no further comment. He delivered me to The English School compound at around a quarter to five, leaving me a reasonable time to settle in to my new quarters before going across to the Lonsdales for drinks.

"I'll leave you, then, for the moment," he said. "I am conscious that we did not get to visit Ato Kebede in the Interior Ministry, but I didn't really think we would. This residence and work permit business is important, though, and can be a tedious process. What I will try and do is to set up an appointment with him tomorrow afternoon, and you can go down yourself in a taxi and practise your new-found skills of diplomacy on him. I don't think I'll be able to join you, as I say, but that won't really matter. Just remember to bring your passport, and a chit from the school to say you work there. I'll phone Graham to confirm that during the morning, and he can pass on the message. And I will call back for you, or else send Wolde, before dinner tomorrow, let us say about six-thirty. You might as well start from my place, since we will be leaving quite early for the picnic, before it gets too hot. And then you can come back and spend Saturday night, if you like. I'm having a few people in to dinner that you might like to meet. I'll get you back here on Sunday afternoon. We usually take a walk on Entotto in the morning, after church, and you might like to join that."

"Great!" I said, rather overwhelmed at this timetable. "That would be lovely. And thanks again for everything."

Cousin James saluted gravely, the Mercedes rolled away, and I was on my own, for the first time since I had arrived in this odd corner of the world.

I wandered slowly up the path into my bungalow, half afraid to confront my new life, and my new servant. But all these things had to be faced up to, and I steeled myself to adopt a benign but authoritative air. Tekla-Mariam, as it happened, was not in residence, but he had been at work. My suitcase and bag had been unpacked, and clothes hung up and stored away in drawers in the bedroom, while my wash things were laid out neatly in the bathroom. Plainly, my manservant was no slouch, even if he was just in off the farm.

I had intended to spend the hour or so in doing my unpacking, so I now found myself slightly at a loss. I pottered around for a while, examining the furniture and fittings in the front room; then into the kitchen, to check the contents of the fridge (which seemed pretty well stocked with essentials); then out the back door from the kitchen. Here I found a little kitchen garden, now somewhat overgrown, stretching away to the periphery fence, over which the tops of *tukuls* could be seen, amid a forest of eucalyptus. In the riot of vegetation in the garden, I could discern some tomatoes, green beans, and peppers of various sorts, all intertwined rather chaotically.

Back in the house, I began to check the books that Davies had left behind. He had interesting, civilised tastes – a few detective stories, by Agatha Christie and others, and a thriller or two, but no real junk. I saw Waugh, Huxley, Anthony Powell, Virginia Woolf, Lawrence Durrell, Faulkner, Camus, Sartre, Thomas Mann. Some I had read; more I hadn't. There was a lot of good reading to look forward to. There were also some interesting works on Ethiopia, and Africa in general, particularly East Africa. Last but not least, I found a little record player, which seemed to be in working order, and a small collection of classical records. This was a very welcome discovery, as I had brought out a number of my own favourite records, just on the off-chance – mainly modern jazz, but some folk and pop as well.

I settled down in one of the two armchairs with a book by a man called Ullendorf, entitled *The Ethiopians*, and began to read. This was a recent book, having appeared just two years previously, and it looked like a very good means of orienting myself. I was still immersed in it three-quarters of an hour later, when Tekla-Mariam appeared from the kitchen. He greeted me respectfully, and asked me if I would like tea.

"No thanks, Tekla-Mariam. I am just going to visit Mr and Mrs Lonsdale, and then I will have dinner with Mr and Mrs Wiggins, so I won't need anything till breakfast, thanks."

"Okay, *getoich*, so I go then, perhaps? I hope everything all right."

"Yes, indeed. Thank you for tidying everything away so nicely."
He bowed acknowledgement, smiling. Then an inspiration came to me.

"Oh, Tekla-Mariam," I said. "I think I will give you your wages for the month now, if you like. You'll probably need some money to settle in."

This went down very well. He must not have been expecting anything till the end of the month. He opened his eyes wide and grinned.

"Oh thank you very much, *getoich*. That is very good. I stay now with my brother, but he have no money, and he is much far away, and it is difficult. Now I find myself a house, perhaps, quite near to here."

So I peeled off a number of notes, to the amount of $25, and he went away highly pleased. I was impressed at what such a sum of money could do, in the native economy.

I waited until about five past six, and then strolled across the compound to visit the Lonsdales. The sun was still hot, but not unpleasant at this time of the evening, and shone golden through the eucalyptus. The air was clear after the rain, and I felt pleasantly invigorated. The altitude, perhaps, would not disagree with me.

I knocked on the Lonsdale's front door, which was slightly ajar, and heard Alan Lonsdale's voice calling to me cheerily to come on in. Then he appeared himself, beer glass in hand, from a room on the left, which turned out to be their living-room. The Lonsdale bungalow was somewhat larger and more elaborate than mine, with a little hall, and rooms leading off it to either side, and even stairs leading to a room or two upstairs.

He saw me looking around, and waved his glass at the scene.

"Not a bad little place," he said. "Does us, anyhow. We just have the one kid, young Judy – going to be ten next month – she lives upstairs. Wouldn't want to have many more, though, from the space point of view!"

I followed him into the living-room.

"It looks very pleasant, I must say, but I see what you mean. Mine suits me well enough, but I certainly couldn't put a family into it."

"Oh, you'll like it there. Nice cosy little place. Real Ethiopian craftsmanship – look around it, you'll see there isn't a straight line in the whole place."

And he laughed loudly. It occurred to me that this had not, perhaps, been his first drink of the evening.

"Ruth's just collecting Judy from a friend's, I'm afraid. She'll be back soon, but we'll have to forage for ourselves for the moment. Now, what can I get you? They make reasonably good beer out here – an outfit called Melotti – Italians. But I've got whisky and gin as well."

On request, he made me a gin and tonic, which turned out to be a distinctly generous one, and sank into one of the cane armchairs in the living-room, inviting me to do likewise.

"Well," he said, broaching a question I would have to face many times in the coming weeks. "How are you finding it all, eh? Pretty damn strange, I suppose."

Alan Lonsdale spoke with a distinct Midlands accent of a type which in the class-ridden world of 1960s Britain was clearly identifiable as 'grammar school'. I was suddenly slightly uncomfortable about my conspicuously public school intonations.

"Oh Lord," I replied, "it's all been a bit dream-like so far. I'll need a bit of time before I can give you an intelligent answer to that. At the moment I'm having a very good time, but I don't think reality has quite struck home yet."

Again he laughed, rather louder than seemed called for.

"Well, it is a strange enough place, God knows. I can tell you that. But at the same time, you'll find it has its fair share of everyday drudgery, like any other place, really. You've still got to get out of bed, wash your teeth, eat your breakfast, take a shit, buy the groceries, pay the bills. And then of course face your class, and correct the little buggers' exercises at the end of the day. Same old routine, anywhere in the world." He glanced at me narrowly, over his glass.

"What brought you out here anyhow, if I may ask? Search for adventure? Escape from the past? No, you're not really old enough to have a past, are you? An unhappy love affair, perhaps? How about that?" And again he laughed rather loudly.

I hesitated as to how far to unburden myself.

"Oh," I said lightly, "search for adventure, really. Coming up to my final exams last spring, the prospect of an ordinary job behind a desk just didn't look too attractive, and, on an impulse, really, I wrote out to my cousin here, to see if he could find me a teaching job for a while."

Lonsdale raised his eyebrows.

"Ah! So Sir James Mallory is your cousin, eh? That's a good start! He's a useful man to have on your side, by all accounts. Knows his way around the power structure here. Has the ear of the Emperor, too, I believe. That's one thing about this place – if you want anything done, it's as well to know someone. Saves a lot of frustration. I reckon we'll all be coming to you when we get into a spot."

I laughed. "He's certainly been full of good advice, I must say, and he does seem to know people. I haven't had to test him very far yet, though."

I decided then to turn the conversation around, rather than answer any more questions myself. "But if I may ask you a question in turn, how did you come to be out here, and how do you like it? Have you been here long?"

50

Alan Lonsdale smiled slowly and took a deep draught of his beer.

"Well," he said, "it's a long story, but basically it's what you'll hear from most people out here from the UK if you ask them. Ruth and I were both teaching at a big secondary modern in Birmingham, just got a little house, had a kid – doing all right, really. But the dullness and the drudgery were just getting us down. I mean, there was still rationing when we left. Your money didn't seem to go anywhere. Life was drab. We used to ask ourselves did we really want to go on like this for the rest of our lives. Then one evening I saw this ad in the TES – The English School, Addis Ababa, needed someone to teach Geography and a bit of English. It just caught us at a weak moment, and we went for it.

We went down to London, I had an interview with old Graham, who was over scouting around, we got on fine, and he offered me the job, with the option of a job for Ruth as well, in a kindergarten he was starting. So here we are, six years later, and I don't regret it for a moment. The only problem I would say we have is how the hell we could ever face going back, in case this place blew up – which you have to reckon it might do some day."

"Yes," I said, "I suppose one does have to worry about that. But the Emperor looks pretty solid at the moment, doesn't he?"

"Oh yes, I reckon he's good for a few years at least. But who knows? He's only just survived a coup, after all. And he's not young. Of course, the end of him doesn't necessarily mean the end of civilisation, but most people I talk to do feel that he's the only man that can really run this place."

"But meanwhile," I said, "you enjoy it."

"Oh yes, it's a great life, really. There's servants to look after your house and kids, endless round of parties, very interesting lot of people – not just British, loads of different nationalities. And fine countryside out there to explore. We go camping about once a month, I should say. Must bring you along some time, if you'd like. Very fascinating country, especially if you're interested in geography, like me."

At this point there was the sound of a car drawing up at the side of the house. Then car doors slamming, and a child's voice, telling some exciting piece of news. A slightly hunted look, I thought, passed over Lonsdale's face, but he spoke cheerfully.

"Oh, here they are now! Sounds like Judy had a good time."

And indeed Judy came bounding in, full of news, and with a trophy to show her father, followed at a short interval by her mother. Lonsdale gave his daughter a hug, and introduced her.

"Say hello to Mr La Touche, sweetheart. He's just arrived to teach in the school, instead of poor Mr Davies."

Judy looked at me with a frank and open stare.

"Hello," she said, politely, "I'm very pleased to meet you. Are you going to live in Mr Davies' house, then?"

"Hello, Judy," I said. "Yes, I just moved in this afternoon."

"I hope Mr Davies won't come back and haunt you."

I laughed."Yes, I hope so too."

But Ruth Lonsdale, who had just come in, was most embarrassed by this sally, and Judy was packed off upstairs to do her homework.

"Sorry about that," she said. "What an awful thing to say!"

"Oh no," I said, "Quite a nice thought, really. I think he'd probably be a friendly sort of ghost, if he found his way back. I've been looking around his establishment, and it seems like the home of a pretty contented man."

"Now that's perceptive of you," she said. "Isn't it, Alan? John Davies was a contented man, I should say. He was a bachelor, of course, so he might have had his lonely moments, but he had lots of friends. He was a very good cook, and he liked entertaining. We'll all miss him." She looked at my glass. "Good, Alan fixed you a drink? Let me freshen it up."

I tried to protest, but not very effectively.

"Just a small one, then, thanks. The first one was quite strong, actually, and I've got some more drinking to do, after all."

"Ah well," she said, smiling, "you're in the colonies now, so to speak. You'll have to get used to hard drinking."

I found Ruth Lonsdale agreeable. She had seemed slightly reserved at first, but I now discerned a dry, ironic humour. She was, I also noted, quite pretty, in a slightly faded way – small, slight, brown hair and eyes, a scattering of freckles on pale skin.

"That's all very well," I said, "but when one is facing one's future headmaster for the first time, one would prefer to be reasonably sober."

"Oh, I wouldn't worry too much about old Graham," she laughed. "He'll probably be pretty sloshed himself before the end of the evening."

She brought me back a second drink not much smaller than the first.

"I'm sure your cousin's giving you a good time, and filling you in on things." Ruth seemed to know more than her husband about my connections, I noted. Perhaps she gossiped with Isabel Wiggins.

"Oh yes, he's being magnificent. I'm going back to him tomorrow evening, after settling in here, and he's going to take me off for a picnic on Saturday to somewhere called Awash, and then I think there's a dinner on Saturday evening. I hope I'm in a fit state to start teaching on Monday."

"Oh, I wouldn't worry too much about that," said Lonsdale. "There'll be a fair bit of chaos for the first few days in any case. You'll like the Awash, by the way. That's the big river south of here. Lots of wildlife – hippos and baboons, mainly, and the occasional leopard, if you're lucky – and hot springs. We often go down there to camp, don't we, darling?"

"Yes, you'll like that," said Ruth. "Watch out for the baboons, though. They throw things, if you go too near them. And there's a little stream there you mustn't step into by mistake. It's boiling hot!"

Conversation turned back to the topic of expatriate social life. There were a good many young or youngish married couples out from the UK, it seemed, either teaching in the various secondary schools of the capital or in the university, or as representatives of various large companies, and there was a round of cocktail parties and dinner parties which I might expect to be asked to.

"But bachelors have most of the fun," teased Ruth. "There's only one bachelor on the staff, besides you, Simon Blakeney – he teaches the senior science classes – and he's dying to get together with you, I know. He's away at the moment, camping up country for a few days with the Barneses, but they'll all be back tomorrow, so you'll meet them then. Simon's great fun, but he's a bit wild, I have to warn you. He gets into scrapes when he has a bit of drink inside him, and the police here don't like that sort of thing. We've had to bail him out a few times, haven't we, dear?"

Alan Lonsdale laughed loudly. "Yes, by gum, we could tell you some tales about our Simon. Maybe you'll be a sobering influence on him, eh? You'll like the Barneses, too, in the bungalow next to yours. They're a bit like us, really – came out two years ago, fed up with the teaching scene back home. Got two little kids. John teaches History, and some English to the juniors, Amy does French. Very good colleagues to have, aren't they, dear?"

Ruth nodded agreement.

"How are the students?" I asked. "They must be an interesting bunch, coming from so many nationalities."

It seemed to me that a slight constraint entered the conversation here. There was a pause before Alan Lonsdale answered.

"Oh, they're an interesting lot, no doubt about that. And easy to teach, I must say. No real discipline problems, at any rate, though some of them find the going a bit tough because of language difficulties. We have quite a lot of Ethiopian aristocrats, as Graham may have told you, and they're mostly lazy as sin, though very civilised about it, it must be said. Graham keeps them all up to the mark, though, as you'll see. All have to start the day with a prayer and a hymn at assembly, never mind if they're Arabs or Hindus or Commies. Good for them, I expect. It's The English School, after all. If they don't like it, they can go somewhere else."

The Lonsdales' conversation was sufficiently intriguing to make me lose track of time. When it occurred to me suddenly to glance at my watch, with a shock I saw that it was already half past seven.

"Gosh," I said, "I'd better go across to dinner, I suppose, while I can still walk. You were both most generous with those gin and tonics, I must say." I rose, a little unsteady. "Well, this was a very pleasant introduction to my new life. I look forward to returning your hospitality very soon."

We parted at the door with all sorts of good wishes, and I headed across, a little apprehensively, to the main bungalow. I mounted the steps onto the verandah, and knocked, rousing the dogs. There was a scampering sound, and sounds of a struggle, and the door was opened by two small persons, who stood looking at me with eager faces. Then Isabel appeared, beaming, and quelling the dogs.

"Come in, come in, Luke, you're very welcome. Don't pay any attention to them, they're perfectly friendly. All guff."

"It's fine, I said. "I'm used to dogs." And I bent down to scratch their backs, which they greatly appreciated, curling around under my hands, though I had to be careful to divide my attention equally between them.

"And these are our offspring, Sarah and Edward. Sarah's five and Edward is three.

"Three *and a half*," said Edward."

"No, you're not," said Sarah.

"Yes, I *am*."

"Say hello to Mr La Touche," said Isabel. "I'm sure you'll be seeing a lot more of him."

The little eager faces said hello, demurely, and were then herded away by their Ethiopian nanny, a fine-looking woman in a white *shamma*.

"Go on in, Luke," said Isabel. "You'll find Graham in the sitting room, and he'll fix you a drink. I just have to supervise this pair to bed, or we'll have no peace."

I found Graham Wiggins waiting beside the drinks cabinet.

"So," he said, 'what'll it be?"

"Well," I said, "if it's all right with you, I'll just start with tonic water or fruit juice or something. I seem to have had quite a bit at the Lonsdales. I was on the gin and tonic."

"Oh come, come", he laughed, "That's giving up at the first fence! I'll make you a light G&T, how about that? That's a compromise."

I assented, weakly, and this was presented to me. It turned out to be approximately normal UK strength, but it was admittedly weaker than the previous ones. I resolved to sip it slowly.

"So," said Graham. "You've had a little visit with the Lonsdales?"

"Yes," I said. "They were very hospitable."

"Oh, Alan's a good man. One of our best. Gets on very well with the students."

"Yes, he was telling me a bit about them. It sounds as if he does a lot with them, camping trips and so on."

"Yes, that's true." Graham paused a moment, and then continued. "However, while Isabel's dealing with the children, I should perhaps fill you in on something, in case you put your foot in it later. Alan actually had a spot of bother last year with one of the senior students – rather smashing Italian girl called Maria Farinacci. Father owns a big clothing business in town. You'll see it advertised on various hoardings around the place. She developed quite a crush on him – he's a good-looking fellow, of course, Alan. He rather foolishly responded, and the upshot was that they seem to have had a brief affair. It all blew up last spring, when her father got to hear of it.

Ruth's been splendid about the whole thing, I must say. It was just a piece of foolishness, after all, no one got pregnant, and I think the fair Maria was just practising on poor old Alan. She was no virgin, I'm pretty sure of that, though her doting father seemed to believe so. At any rate, we managed to hush it up, because he didn't want a scandal any more than we did, and spoil his daughter's marriage chances! So she finished up the year with a reasonable number of O Levels, and is now off our hands."

My slightly open-mouthed reaction to these revelations seemed to bring home to Graham that all this might appear somewhat indiscreet. He stroked his moustache, and added, slightly defensively.

"Sorry for springing a story like that on you in the first minute, so to speak, but I think it's better that you know these things, rather than be saying the wrong thing in company and not knowing why. There's a warning in the story too, even for bachelors like yourself. You'll come across some pretty attractive girls, both among our students and around the foreign community at large, and many of them – from other cultures, especially, but even British too – just don't have the inhibitions we might expect at home. Now, of course, your private life is your own, as long you keep it that way, but we really don't want scandals attaching to the school, so if you decide to be indiscreet, I'd appreciate it if you did it off the premises."

I nodded firmly. "Oh, I can quite understand that, sir. I have no present plans to cause mayhem, certainly."

"Oh no, I'm sure you don't," he laughed. "But then you don't know what's out there waiting for you, do you? I do notice that chaps go a little wild out here, for some reason or other. It may be the altitude. I don't know. Anyhow, I don't want to spoil your fun. I hope you'll have lots of it. But I just wanted to put a word in your ear, at an early stage."

"Oh yes," I said. "I quite understand. I'll certainly bear it in mind."

Then we heard footsteps descending the stairs and Isabel came in, looking apologetic.

"Oh Luke, I hope you don't mind. I'm afraid you're rather popular. I have a special request that you read a story. They like to capture guests like that, if they can. Please say if you'd rather not. It needn't be long, of course."

"No, no," I said. "I'll be glad to."

"You're awfully good."

So I was led upstairs to the brightly decorated nursery, where two little persons looked out of two little beds at me, overawed by what they had achieved. I sat with them for ten minutes or so, and read a story about Noddy to two small English children in this strange land. Then I said good night to them, they snuggled down in their beds, I turned out the light, pulled over the door, and went softly downstairs. Again I had the strange sensation, as I'd had that morning, looking out at the hens – the shock of the familiar, in the midst of an exotic environment.

"That was very kind," Isabel greeted me on my return. "Thank you. I hope they weren't troublesome."

"Not at all," I said. "They were very good. I read them a Noddy story, on request. They were born out here, presumably? Have they ever been back to England?"

"Yes, both born here. We took them back once, when Sarah was two and Edward was just a bit, to visit Graham's parents, but they would hardly remember it. We're hoping to go again next year, when they'll really be able to appreciate it. It's expensive, though, as you can imagine – even with a bit of help from the British Council."

"Yes, it must be." I said. "Of course, you were born out here yourself, I suppose?"

"Yes, indeed. I didn't see the UK till I was twelve, and then we were stuck there till almost the end of the war, though Daddy, of course, came back here before that, bringing home His Majesty."

"I've heard about that. It must have been a great adventure."

"Yes, it was, though we only heard about it too, of course. By the time we got here, things were quite settled, really."

Graham refilled his drink, having checked that I was still nursing mine.

"Yes," he said, "it's all just history to me. But it's exciting to hear the Brig tell about it, if you can get him going. He has to be in the right mood, though. Doesn't he, dear?"

"Yes," said Isabel, "but I'm sure he'll talk to Luke. He likes an intelligent and appreciative audience. Just ask him a leading question – show you know a bit about it – and he'll be off."

"I'll look forward to that very much," I said. "Cousin James has been describing the beauties of Nyala to me."

"Yes, it's a marvellous spot," said Graham. "An oasis of peace. And stunning scenery of course. Just the place to relax after a hard week."

At this point the cook appeared to announce dinner, so we went in procession into the room at the back of the house which served as both dining room and family room. There, Hailu, their cook, produced a fine dinner of roast beef, roast potatoes and beans all, I was told, from the farm at Nyala. There was fresh pineapple to follow, also from Nyala – this time from down in the valley. My curiosity about Nyala Farm grew steadily.

I asked about its history, and what the Stanfords did there, and was told once again, from a different perspective to that of Cousin James. The whole development was fairly recent, but already the Brig and his wife had established a sort of model village for the local people, with a school, a clinic and a model farm, to which they had introduced pedigree cattle from Kenya to improve the local stock of scraggy Zebus. Isabel had grown up with the place, and had helped with the school and farm. Her views on improvement and 'development' in an African context were most interesting.

Everything, she said, had to be done by consensus, as a result of long discussions with the elders of the tribe. Any innovations that were simply imposed would not survive. This was the problem with so much Western development aid – it was imposed from above, without any process of consultation or study as to how it would affect the daily life of the people. Most people here, she said, had no conception of Western-style 'progress'. They were happy with a static, cyclical view of life, and we should think very carefully before setting out to disrupt that.

I found this all most interesting, and said so. I was on the point of contributing some rather sententious, gin-sodden views of my own about the problems of Western intervention in native societies, but just then conversation was halted by the sound of powerful motor engine driving up the compound. It seemed to stop outside my bungalow.

"Now who could that be?" said Graham.

He rose, calling to Hailu to bring us coffee in the drawing room, and we went back into the front room to have a look out the window. We arrived in time to see a small red sports car stopped in front of my bungalow, and an Ethiopian man in some kind of uniform returning to it down the path from my front door, having found no one at home.

Before we could intercept him, he had got back into the driver's seat, and the car drove off.

Graham peered at it closely through the glass.

"Very strange," he said. "You don't know anyone attached to the royal family, do you, Luke? That car has special imperial number plates. Has to be someone at least in the extended royal family."

I was at first baffled, but then a curious thought crossed my mind. It was not, however, a thought that I was sure I wanted to share at this moment.

"No," I said, "I can't say I do."

What had occurred to me, as an exciting but rather disquieting possibility, was "Yohannis". In particular, I thought I recognised the car. It looked very like the red Maserati sports car in which I'd had a number of alarming but exhilarating drives round the Oxfordshire countryside. But how could he have known I was here?

"Well, that really is very strange," said Graham, scratching his head. Hailu came in with coffee on a tray, and he turned to him.

"Thank you, Hailu. Just put the tray there. And now would you go down to the front gate, and ask the *zabanya* who drove in just now in the car."

Hailu bowed, and glided out. Isabel poured the coffee, and Graham pressed a glass of the local brandy on me.

In a few minutes Hailu was back.

"*Getoich, zabanya* he say, that was driver of Lij Yohannis Tessema. He have message for Mr La Touche."

So the cat was out of the bag. Graham and Isabel looked at me with something approaching awe, not unmixed with alarm.

"Good heavens," said Graham. "Do you know this fellow, Luke?"

"Well yes," I confessed, "I do, actually. We were at college together, just for a year, two years ago. But I'm absolutely astonished he should have tracked me down. I didn't tell him I was coming. I didn't even have an address for him. I was going to try to get in touch when I had settled in. This is a complete surprise."

"And I must say," said Graham, "if you had consulted me, I would have advised you to be take your time about doing that. Lij Yohannis is not a very safe person to know, I'm afraid. He's something of a centre of dissidence within the regime. He's personally more or less sacrosanct, but it can be dangerous to be known as a friend of his. I must confess

I rather wish he hadn't found you. But this reminds you what sort of a show they run here. The arrival of everyone is noted, and even Lij Yohannis has his spies in the establishment. Now that he's found you, it's probably best to be polite, but I would urge you, frankly, to steer clear of him, as far as possible."

"I believe he's a fascinating character," added Isabel, "but it really isn't our business to get involved in their internal affairs."

"I'll certainly bear your advice in mind."

"It just occurs to me," said Graham, reflectively, "there may be a less sinister explanation of how he knew you were coming. He has a younger brother at the school – you'll be teaching him; he'll be in Sixth Form this year – and I sent a circular some time back to all parents detailing changes in personnel and other arrangements for the coming year. He may have latched on to that. In the circumstances, you couldn't have avoided his notice for very long anyhow."

After that, exhaustion suddenly caught up with me, and I excused myself, with many thanks, and an agreement to meet in Graham's office at half past nine the next morning, to run through my duties.

Rather unsteadily, I crossed the open space to my front garden, opened the gate, and tottered up my front path, conscious that I was probably being watched from the drawing room window. On my front doorstep, I noticed in the darkness a bulky, roundish parcel. I bent down and picked it up, and let myself in with my key.

Once in, I felt for the light switch, and then set the parcel down on the coffee table. I sat down in front of it, and looked at it with apprehension. It turned out, when removed from its paper, to be a strangely shaped bottle, with a note attached. It bore an elaborate Amharic monogram, with an address and phone number, and read as follows:

> *Luke, old man, why did you not tell me that you were coming out here? That is not friendly! When can we get together? Contact me without delay at the above phone number, and we'll fix something up. I so much want to hear why you are out here, and what you think you are doing. Meanwhile, here is a little gift, to give you a good Ethiopian hangover. It is a bottle of special tej, brewed on my estates. You will not find tej such as this in any whorehouse in Addis. Be careful with it. All the best, Yohannis.*

I was really in no condition to drink any more this evening, but this intrigued me. I went and found a little glass in the kitchen, and then carefully undid the stopper, which was secured with something like beeswax. I sniffed the contents. A strong aroma of honeyed alcohol arose from it, and I poured a small shot of it into the glass.

It was quite unlike anything I had ever tasted, though it was plainly a kind of mead. The fumes seemed to rise to the top of my head, and my senses began to swim.

I replaced the stopper, and groped my way into my bedroom. Tekla-Mariam had laid out pyjamas, and even turned down the bed. Somehow I undressed, struggled into the pyjamas, and settled down to sleep.

I lay for a while staring at the ceiling, listening to the various sounds of the tropical night – cicadas, frogs, the occasional hyena – trying to take in the events of the day, not least the latter ones. I could formulate no clear thoughts, but a sense of exhilaration, mixed with mild unease, settled over me as I sank into oblivion.

CHAPTER FOUR

I woke up shortly before eight o'clock, to find Tekla-Mariam fussing tactfully around the bedroom, drawing back the curtains, and arranging my clothes more tidily on the back of the chair where they lay.

As I regained full consciousness, I was relieved to find that I didn't feel quite as mouldy as I expected. A little delicate, however. No doubt about that.

Noticing that I was awake, Tekla-Mariam addressed me, shifting a little nervously from one foot to another.

"*Getoich*, you like bath this morning? I turn on water heater last night. Plenty hot water."

I struggled up on one elbow, and rubbed my eyes.

"Well yes, thank you, Tekla-Mariam. That'd be good."

"Okay, *getoich*, I make bath."

He disappeared into the bathroom, turned on the taps, and returned in a moment.

"You like tea? I make tea."

I nodded, much impressed.

"Yes, that'd be fine. Thanks."

"For breakfast, you like scramble egg. I have eggs."

Again I nodded appreciatively, and thanked him. I was not in a mood to argue. I had never been the beneficiary of anything like this level of service before, even from my scout in Oriel, and I felt I might as well enjoy it. One could get used to this.

TM glided out, and returned in a minute or so with a tray, supporting a cup of tea with milk, and a sugar bowl. He set this on the bedside table, and then went to check the bath.

"Bath ready in two-three minutes, *getoich*", he reported. "I go make breakfast."

I was not used, as I say, to early morning tea, but this went down well. Much revived, I headed for the bathroom. As I shaved, and then wallowed, I tried to focus on the day ahead. I looked forward to finding out more exactly what my duties would be, if only to discover how much free time I would have. I had not come out here, after all, I had to confess to myself, primarily to serve my fellow man, but rather to work out certain problems of my own, and to garner some new and interesting experiences in the process. For that, time would be important. I was looking forward, also, to meeting the rest of my colleagues, particularly the rampant and dangerous Simon Blakeney. He sounded as though he could be entertaining.

There was also the problem of Yohannis. Now that he had found me, it seemed to me that there was no way round giving him a call, however much anxiety that might cause either Cousin James or Graham Wiggins. Not to do so would be positively rude, I concluded, and lead him to suspect that I didn't want to see him, which was very far from the case. I wished, though, that he hadn't made himself quite so notorious since we had parted company something over two years ago.

Tekla-Mariam's scrambled eggs proved interesting – curiously aromatic and slightly burned, but still eatable. He stood attentively at my elbow, trying to anticipate my every need, even passing me the salt and the butter, until I reassured him that I could manage, whereupon he returned to the kitchen, slightly crestfallen.

After breakfast, I decided to take a brief stroll around the compound, to let him tidy up, before going over to the administration building to my meeting with Graham Wiggins. Everything was bright in the morning sunshine, and the air was bracing. I poked around the rear of the various bungalows and school buildings, following the periphery fence, and then ventured out onto the road outside the front gate of the compound. Three roads led away from the gate; one into town, along which I had travelled already, another leading away out of town in an easterly direction, round the foothills of Entotto, and a third more or less at right angles to this, leading straight away from the gate in a southerly direction. In all three directions all that could be seen were clusters of native huts, surrounded by groves of eucalyptus, and a scattering of more western-style bungalows, surrounded by wooden fences.

An old lady in native dress, carrying a large bundle and a black parasol, was standing on the opposite side of the road, waiting. As I watched, a little Fiat Millecento came into view, from the southern road, and she flagged it down. After a short discussion, involving much waving of the umbrella and some of the bundle as well, she climbed in, and the little car disappeared in the direction of town. It seemed to be some sort of taxi, such as Cousin James had mentioned. I made a note of it.

I turned, then, and walked back to my house, to pick up my briefcase (in the interests of appearing more businesslike), before strolling over to the administration building. Tekla-Mariam had tidied away the breakfast things and made the bed, and was wondering about lunch. I could see already that there would be at least two drawbacks about having a personal servant: I would have to take advance decisions about meals, and I would almost certainly end up eating too much. For lunch, I agreed, after some evaluation of alternatives, to risotto and fruit, and then I left for my business meeting.

The Headmaster was installed in his office, dealing with the mail, when I arrived. He waved me to a chair.

"Well now, did you sleep well? Tekla-Mariam looking after you all right?"

"Oh yes, sir," I replied. "I did, and he did. He's very efficient and willing, I must say."

"Good, good," he said, "I'm very glad to hear that." Then a slight look of embarrassment passed across his face, and he continued. 'By the way, Luke, old man, you can cut out the 'sir'. We're pretty informal here, as you'll find. Just call me Graham."

I smiled and nodded.

"Fine, sir – I mean, Graham. Sorry for being so feudal. I was just not quite sure how to address headmasters."

"Oh, don't worry about it. You were quite right, of course, but I think it would just cause unseemly amusement. If my staff are really annoyed at me, they may address me as 'Headmaster', but otherwise it's just Graham. Except our Indian colleague, Dr Ratna. He sticks to Mr Wiggins, and I leave him to it. So, now that we've got that settled, let's get down to business."

For the following hour or so we looked through curricula, class lists and lists of textbooks and set books for the Overseas O Level English course. I was to teach English to the three top classes, Fourth, Fifth and

Sixth, and, I learned with surprise, Latin (this new subject had been hastily added to the curriculum, to celebrate my arrival). They would be beginners, a little group of just two, but a most interesting pair: an Irish girl whose name, I learned, was Fiona McHugh, and Yohannis' younger brother, Tewodros. Ras Tessema, it seemed, wished his younger son to become acquainted with the roots of Western culture. This would have to be done after lunch, during the first hour of the siesta, so I would not have much of a chance to develop a taste for that delightful custom.

The details of my duties were now set out for me. I had been given advance notice of the set books, *Pride and Prejudice* and *Twelfth Night*, and had dutifully read them over at home during the summer. The grammar and composition book and the reader for the Fourth Form, I would have to have a look at over the weekend, to be at least one step ahead of my charges.

At around eleven o'clock Graham called for coffee, in best colonial style, and we took a break. While the coffee was coming, the phone rang. It turned out to be Cousin James, ringing from his office in the Ministry. Graham exchanged greetings with him, and then handed me the phone.

"So, how are you getting on? Graham putting you through your paces?"

"Yes. I think we have it all straightened out now."

"Good. Splendid. Now listen. I have arranged for you to see Ato Kebede Degachew, who is Director-General for foreign residents in the Ministry of the Interior, at four o'clock this afternoon. He will sort you out. Remember to bring your passport, and a chit from Graham to say that you are legitimately employed by The English School, and the whole thing shouldn't take very long. Take a Millecento down to the Ministry. Graham will tell you where it is, and how to go about that. And then take another one back. Either I or Wolde will come to collect you for dinner at about six-thirty. Have you got all that?"

I scribbled on a piece of paper.

"Yes. I think so. Thanks awfully. I'll see you later, then."

"Splendid. And do be polite to Ato Kebede. It's very good of him to see you."

"Okay, I will. Thanks again."

And he was gone. I turned to Graham and explained the message. He was pleased.

"Your cousin is a very useful man to know, I must say. These work permits can take ages, and the whole process can drive you up the wall. You could be up and down to the ministry for weeks if you didn't know anyone, and most people, of course, don't. We have a bit of an entrée, in fact, thanks to the Brig, but all his personal friends seem to have retired, as far as I can see, and I don't think we could guarantee results in a single afternoon."

'Well," I said, "I haven't got it yet, of course."

"Oh, you won't have any trouble. Ato Kebede owes your cousin James a few favours, I rather think. All you have to do is get there, with the required documents. I'll just make you out the proper documentation. And after the siesta, about a quarter past three, you come over to the house, and Isabel or I will take you down to the road, and show you how to flag down a Millecento. It's an important skill in this town."

"Fine," I said. "Thanks very much." Then a further thought occurred to me. "By the way, how should I go about getting the phone connected? It seems to have been cut off."

"Oh darn, I'm sorry about that. We did that after poor old John's death. That's not too difficult, though. I'll get Girma to get on to the phone company. They can probably do it on Monday or Tuesday. There's not a great rush for phones. By the way, I must introduce you to Girma. He's officially our librarian, but he's useful in all sorts of ways. He's a good man to give you Amharic lessons, by the way, if you're interested."

"Yes," I said, "I would be, actually."

"Well, we'll go and meet him. He'd be glad of the work, and he's quite good. He should be in his office. He's an interesting fellow."

As we walked over to the library, Graham told me more.

" I found Girma a few years ago hanging around in the Mercato – that's the general town flea-market, by the way – when I was down there looking for a spare part for the Landrover. The place is full of urchins and young men trying to sell you something, and you tend to brush them off, but this fellow who came up to me sounded a bit different, so I listened to him. He was quite shy and diffident, for one thing, which is unusual with these sort of characters. Then he asked whether by any chance I knew anyone who would like a secretary, and this seemed such a funny request that I stopped and thought about it. And then I thought, well, I could do with some sort of factotum in the administration, if he was any good, so I got talking to him, and he told me that his father had been arrested and executed some months before, through being implicated in one of these unsuccessful mini-coups that there have been a fair few of down the years, but which we don't get to hear too much about. I gather that his Dad's Minister was involved in the coup, and his Dad sort of had to go along. It left the family pretty well penniless. Girma has to support them from what I can pay him. The Minister got off with being exiled, I believe."

This story depressed me a little. The darker side of life in this country was once again obtruding itself in a rather immediate way, as in the case of the corpse on the gibbet, but this time a little closer to home.

Girma Assefa turned out to be a slight, diffident young man, with a worried expression (such as he could readily be excused for). Graham introduced me, explained what I would be teaching, and then said that I might be in the market for some Amharic lessons. I confirmed this warmly, and we agreed to talk about it further on Monday, when I had got a better idea of my other commitments. Girma then showed us round the library. This had a rather random collection of books, donated, it would seem, by numerous expatriates who had come and gone, but it also possessed a useful reference library, provided by the British Council, which had taken the school under its wing.

We left Girma to his work, after Graham had told him about my phone problem, and walked back to Graham's office. On the way, I asked cautiously if I might make a phone call. I felt that, if possible, I had better call Yohannis, and face up to whatever complications would ensue. I didn't want to insult him, and I did want to see him, even if wiser heads than mine felt that I should steer clear of him. Graham made no difficulty, and tactfully left me to myself in the office.

Nervously, I dialled the number that Yohannis had given me. It rang for a short while, and then the receiver was lifted. There was a certain amount of clicking and buzzing, and then a rather gruff voice said, in Amharic, "*Abet*?"

"Hello," I said, I'm sorry, but do you speak English?"

"Yes," said the voice, "I speak. Who is this?"

"My name is Luke La Touche, and I wonder if I could speak to Prince Yohannis Tessema."

"Ah!" said the voice, much more warmly. "Mr La Touche! You are most welcome. I am His Highness' private secretary. Unfortunately, His Highness have to go away for a few days. He will return on Monday. But he tell me to tell you he very much like to see you, and will call you when he get back. Do you have phone number he can call?"

"Well," I said, "unfortunately I do not have a phone myself yet, but I hope that I may have by Tuesday. It needs to be reconnected. I can call him again as soon as that is done, and give him the number."

I was really not keen on Yohannis calling The English School, and fortunately his secretary did not suggest that.

"Very good," he said. "In that case, we will wait your call. Thank you for calling, Mr La Touche. His Highness will be pleased. Goodbye."

"Goodbye," I said, and the receiver was put down.

I went out to find Graham, apologising for the inconvenience. He generously brushed this aside, and raised another subject.

"By the way, talking of language lessons, I have a possible job for you, if you want it – though don't hesitate to refuse if you feel it's too much. We've had some Russians up here in the last week enquiring whether anyone might be interested in giving them some English lessons. It's a couple of people attached to the Soviet Information Service. I don't much like messing with Russians, but I thought I'd pass it on. If you do decide to take them on, though, just watch out about being recruited. They're rumoured to have a big spying operation out here, covering all of East Africa. This fellow I talked to seemed perfectly pleasant, but you never know."

I was rather intrigued, having never met a Russian.

"Oh, I wouldn't mind, I think. It might be quite amusing. How much would they want?"

"Oh, a couple of hours a week, I should think. Be sure you charge a decent fee, by the way. Ten dollars an hour would be about right. And, by the same token, you might offer Girma five."

"Thanks. That sounds fine. I'll remember that."

"Well, that's about all then, I think, for the moment," said Graham, looking around the office. "You have those textbooks? You might as well go off and have a look through them. Is Tekla-Mariam making you lunch?"

"Yes, he's threatening rather a large one, by the sound of it."

Graham laughed.

"Yes, you'll have to watch that. You could put on a lot of weight here, if you don't restrain your servants. Do you take any exercise?"

"Oh, I like to walk," I said. "I play squash and tennis a bit, but I don't suppose that'll be possible here."

"On the contrary," he said. "We have two tennis courts here, and the British Embassy has one. Squash we can't offer, I'm afraid. Play any ping-pong, though? We have a table."

"Yes, that too," I said.

"Well, that's great," he said. "I'm sure you'll find willing partners. We usually have a few games of doubles over the weekend, and we can fit you in."

"That would be lovely," I said, and took my leave, thanking him for the books.

I walked back across the compound to my bungalow. It was now somewhat after noon, and Tekla-Mariam was waiting for me eagerly. He had been pottering in the kitchen, but came out when he heard the door.

"*Getoich*, you like lunch now?"

"Okay, Tekla-Mariam, that'd be fine. I'll have a wash. You can serve it up."

It was, as I feared, quite a substantial meal, and not badly cooked, so I ate too much of it, and half an hour later was left staring at the wall in front of me, feeling like a python that had just consumed a goat. I moved rather heavily to the armchair, and TM produced some coffee for me there.

"You like something else, *getoich*?"

"Oh no, thanks, Tekla-Mariam. That was fine."

"Okay, *getoich*, I go now?"

"Yes, that's fine. And Tekla-Mariam, I will go to Sir James for dinner, and I won't be back till Sunday afternoon, okay? So I won't need you till dinner on Sunday."

"Okay, *getoich*." And then something occurred to him. "You like hen, perhaps, Sunday night?"

"Yes, that'd be fine." I could see that choosing the menu was going to be an ongoing problem. I felt a bit like a Victorian housewife dealing with the cook. I would have to find out about shopping, and do some.

TM shifted from one foot to the other.

"You give me one dollar to buy hen?"

"Oh yes, of course!" I produced a dollar, and he glided out.

I sipped my coffee thoughtfully, and took a desultory look at the English grammar book. I probably should take a siesta, I thought, but I don't want to oversleep and miss my appointment with Ato Kebede. However, after reading the introduction and looking through the contents, I went in and flopped down on my bed.

Just on cue, around half past one, the sky darkened, a gust of wind shook the canvas ceiling of the room, and the rain began to fall. Today it only rained for three quarters of an hour or so, but the sound of it drumming on the corrugated iron roof was profoundly soothing, and I dozed off for a while.

I woke with a start, to find the sun shining again. I looked frantically at my watch, but, thankfully, it was only ten to three. I sank back on the pillow, and tried to gather my thoughts, but found it difficult. Too much was happening, or about to happen. It seemed much easier, for the moment, just to let things flow over me. My thoughts focused on Graham Wiggins, and I decided that I liked him. Cousin James's analysis of him was doubtless justified, but he hadn't proved over-sensitive or obnoxious; in fact rather perceptive and humane. I looked forward also to learning some Amharic from Girma, and so penetrating a little deeper into the mysterious essence of this country.

After a short period of half-awake musing, I roused myself, tidied myself up, and, just on a quarter past three, armed with my passport and Graham's chit, made my way across to the main bungalow to present myself for instruction in how to catch a taxi.

In the event, it was Isabel who met me, and offered to guide me.

"There may not be too many millecentos cruising around at the moment," she said. "It's a little early in the afternoon. But there's bound to be something."

Accompanied by the children and the dogs, we went down to the front gate and looked out along the road. I had plainly made a hit with the children. They asked if I was coming back again that night.

"I'm afraid not," I said. "I won't be back till Sunday."

"Well, then," said Isabel, "do join us for supper that evening."

"That's very kind of you," I said, "but Tekla-Mariam is promising to prepare a hen for me, so I suppose I'd better eat that."

She laughed. "Oh, so he offered to find you a chicken, did he? And what did he charge you for that?"

"Just a dollar," I said. "That seemed pretty reasonable."

"Oh, it is, by our standards. But in fact he'll be able to get one for about half that. Still, it's a harmless little racket, so I go along with it. The same with a meal of wat, if he offers you that. It's worth it, though, to keep everyone happy. They like it if they can swindle us a bit. Makes them feel superior."

Just then a Fiat Millecento hove into sight, coming up the southern road. Isabel flagged it down, and began to negotiate with the driver in Amharic. The driver, a rather shifty-looking individual, waved his hands a good deal, but finally nodded. He already had two passengers in the back, Ethiopians in what seemed to be the regulation outfit of khaki suit and *shamma*. Isabel turned to me.

"Now, I've told him where you want to go. It's the Ministry of the Interior, a big white building on Churchill Avenue, just south of the Piazza. He'll put you down outside. The basic fare is twenty-five cents, so just offer that, or they'll try to do you. If you don't have change, I can give it to you this time." And she produced a twenty-five cent piece. "When you want to come back, just stand in the Piazza, at the beginning of Haile Selassie Avenue pointing in the right direction, and flag down Millecentos till one agrees to take you to The English School. They'll understand that, though *ya-Ingliz tamari bet* is better, if you can remember it. You can also mention Siddist Kilo, if necessary."

I thanked her, said goodbye to the children, and climbed into the front seat of the taxi. We drove down Haile Selassie Avenue again, this time in rather more cramped surroundings. The two men in the back seat conversed in Amharic, in subdued tones. When we reached the Piazza, they got out, and the driver, rather grudgingly, took me on a hundred yards or so down Churchill, to the building which Isabel had described. There I gave him my 25c and got out hastily, fearing argument. But another possible fare approached straight away, and they began to negotiate.

A policeman with a machine-gun stood outside the building. I approached cautiously, but he waved me on in. Inside at the reception desk, I asked for the office of Ato Kebede Degachew. The man at the desk looked at me curiously, but told me where to go. I climbed two flights of stairs, as directed, and found the office of the Director-General for Foreign Residents, which dealt with work permits. I entered a largish room, filled with quite a number of bored and dejected persons, both Ethiopian and foreign, occupying every available chair, and leaning against the walls.

There was a rather bored and arrogant-looking, though strikingly beautiful, young lady presiding at a desk at the far end of the room. It was almost four o'clock, so I went up to her, and introduced myself, saying that I had an appointment at four with Ato Kebede. She looked incredulous, but got up and headed for the inner sanctum, saying, "Wait here. I will see."

What happened next was impressive. She came back looking much more respectful, and said, "Mr La Touche, please come this way. Ato Kebede is expecting you."

There was a rustle of envious astonishment round the room, and some muttering, as I followed her into the inner office. Ato Kebede was at the door to meet me. He was a small, thin, rather anxious-looking man, with a pencil moustache, but he smiled warmly on this occasion, and waved me towards him.

"Welcome to our country, Mr La Touche," he said. "You are a cousin of Sir James, I understand. He is well, I hope?"

He shook me warmly by the hand.

"Yes indeed he is, I'm glad to say," I replied. "It is very kind of you to see me at such short notice, Ato Kebede. I am most grateful."

"Not at all. Not at all. I am glad to be of any help I can to a cousin of Sir James. Now have a seat here, and I will call for some coffee. You will have coffee?"

"Yes, many thanks." I was not going to refuse, though I thought with a pang of the host of impatient customers in the outer office, some of whom looked as if they had been there for weeks. But I was excited also at the prospect of conducting my own Ethiopian negotiation for the first time.

Ato Kebede called a boy for coffee, and then relieved me of my documents. He studied them briefly, simply commenting on the Irish passport, of which he did not see very many.

"But there are some. Some people working with the UN, and also some nuns." He complimented me on my passport photograph.

"You are a handsome young man, Mr La Touche, if I may so – and not unlike your distinguished cousin in appearance!" Then he called a subordinate from an adjoining office, and gave him the document, and some orders concerning them.

He settled down then in his chair, and rubbed his hands.

"So, you will be with The English School? That is a good place. Brigadier Stanford is a good friend of this country. I'm sure you will have a happy time there."

"Thank you, sir, I'm sure I will." I said.

"So why have you come to our country?"

I pondered briefly. I did not want to start in on my real reasons, as they really sounded rather neurotic. I decided to sound a more positive note.

"Well, I have become very interested in your language and culture, and since Sir James was out here, I thought I would take the opportunity to come out and study for a while. I am hoping to learn Amharic, and also perhaps *Ge'ez*."

Ato Kebede seemed most impressed. He asked whether I had studied Amharic at the university, and I replied that, unfortunately, this was not possible. I had done Classics, and explained that this involved Latin and Greek. This prompted him to tell me that even in the days of the Greeks and Romans Ethiopia had been a great empire, and that they had trading relations with the Roman Empire. He seemed very well informed on this point.

"Some day," he said, "You should go to visit the old port of Adulis, on the Red Sea coast near Massawa. It is now being excavated by French archaeologists, and they are finding much of interest."

The coffee arrived, thick and sweet, and Ato Kebede discoursed on the history of the kingdom of Axum, and gave me advice on what to visit, until his underling returned with the work permit, duly filled out, and my documents. Ato Kebede inspected the work permit, and then signed it with a flourish, and handed it over to me. We parted with many mutual expressions of esteem, and renewed good wishes for Sir James' health. I passed out through the outer office, past the wondering and envious eyes of the waiting throng, in something of a daze, but I was beginning to see how things worked in this country. It was certainly helpful, it was now abundantly clear to me, to know someone.

Once outside the Ministry, I strolled back up to the Piazza, enjoying the scene. I had not yet had a chance to walk in the streets of this strange, disjointed city, and I proposed not to hurry back to The English School compound, since I had about an hour and a half to spare before Cousin James was to pick me up.

The citizens were going about their multifarious errands, and a very mixed lot they were. There were, of course, many Ethiopians in basic native dress, bearing a variety of burdens, sometimes carrying black umbrellas, occasionally riding mules. But there was also a great variety of other races, Arab, Indian, Mediterranean and Northern European, especially when one reached the Piazza itself. Even among the Ethiopians, there were many different ethnic groups, such as the *Amharas*, the *Gallas* and others much more Hamitic in appearance.

A cloud of beggars and hawkers, many of them young boys, beset the passers-by, offering for sale combs, cigarette-lighters, shoelaces, Durex, or engaging to shine one's shoes or watch one's car. Some wretched figures, leprous or with missing limbs, flapped feebly from the pavement at the passers-by. I made a leisurely circuit of the Piazza, looking at the shop fronts, studying the faces of the people, while managing to avoid all solicitations. I paused at the window of Giannopoulos' Bookstore, and studied the enticing polyglot offerings. I always found it difficult to resist a bookshop, but for the present I stored it up as a future pleasure. I dragged myself away, and strolled on, past the Post Office.

I decided I might just have time for a beer, or something stronger, in the Ras Makonnen Bar before going to look for a taxi. I felt I had somehow earned this after my transaction in the Ministry, though really I had to concede all credit, once again, to James. I crossed the square, mounted the steps of the fine old French-style building, and found a vacant table on the verandah, looking out over the public scene. A waiter bustled up.

"*Abet, getoich?*"

I settled for a local beer, a Melotti. While he was fetching it, I took out my work permit and studied it with satisfaction. In English and Amharic, it attested to the right of Mr Luke La Touche to work as a teacher with The English School until further notice. I put it away carefully in my inner pocket, with my wallet and passport, and turned to study the passing scene. The waiter returned with the beer, pleasantly chilled. It tasted not at all bad.

One could get used to this life, I decided. I looked forward to meeting the rest of my colleagues, and hoped they would be congenial. It would be important to the quality of life to find a group of like-minded bachelors with whom to go out on the town. Various plans formed in my mind as I sipped my beer. I would make an effort to learn Amharic. I would keep a diary. I would try to do some serious writing. I would explore the countryside. A variety of exciting possibilities opened out before me. The one issue I did not address, pushing it into the back of my mind, was the basic one. What on earth was I doing here, and how did this adventure relate to what I intended to do for the rest of my life? This question I pushed resolutely aside because I knew I had no answer to it. I could only hope that somewhere along the line an answer would emerge. Meanwhile, the prospects looked pleasing, and I proposed to enjoy them.

But just then my musings suffered an interruption. As I looked out across the Piazza, I noticed a European girl hurrying along the pavement, coming towards me. There appeared to be a young man of rather swarthy complexion following her. It was not quite clear whether they were together or not. I was just observing that she was quite young, and distinctly attractive, when she looked up, saw me leaning on the balcony of the bar, and swerved up the steps towards me. Panting and wide-eyed, she slumped into the chair opposite to me, and said loudly, "Gosh, darling! Sorry I'm late. I got delayed. I hope you haven't been waiting too long?"

I gathered my wits sufficiently to look welcoming. Plainly there was some emergency here.

"No," I said, cheerfully, "no problem. I've only just got here myself, actually."

The swarthy young man seemed rather taken aback by this. He hesitated at the foot of the steps, pondered for a moment, and then sloped off down the street, glancing back once or twice. He looked, on closer inspection, a rather nasty piece of work.

The girl looked at me anxiously and apologetically.

"I'm so sorry for doing this to you," she said. "I really appreciate your backing me up. I had to get rid of that guy somehow" – she gestured down the street – "and I just grabbed my chance. You looked as though you might speak English, and fortunately you did!" She spoke with an accent that, I noticed with some surprise, had a slight but discernible Irish intonation.

"Don't worry at all," I said. "I'm delighted to be of help, if only by just being here! Could I offer you something to drink? A beer perhaps, or a coffee?"

"Oh no, thanks! I really mustn't disturb you any longer. I'd just like to make sure that he's given up, and then I'll go."

I looked at her, intrigued, and rather attracted. I decided to introduce myself.

"Well, my name is Luke La Touche, and I've only just arrived in the country. Have you been here long yourself?"

She shook her head

"No, not very long. We only came in at the beginning of the summer, in June. My father's seconded here with the United Nations, to help reorganise the civil service. My name is Fiona McHugh, by the way. Sorry, I should have introduced myself. I'm just a bit upset at the moment."

She reached out a hand, and I clasped it, across the table. The name sounded vaguely familiar, but I couldn't quite give it a context.

"That fellow was bothering you, was he?" I said.

"Oh yes, he started up a conversation, and I was silly enough to reply, and that encouraged him. Then I just couldn't get rid of him. He wanted my address, my phone number – would I come out with him this evening? I think he's Greek or something. He was really slimy."

"Yes, he looked a pretty nasty specimen, I must say, but I think you've discouraged him. By the way – I hope you don't mind my asking – are you by any chance Irish?"

She looked at me with mild astonishment.

"Yes, I am, in fact, but I don't think I have much of an accent left, do I? I've been in so many schools abroad."

"No, you're right, you don't. I probably wouldn't have noticed, except that I'm Irish myself.'

Her eyes widened. "Are you? But that's extraordinary. You don't sound it, though, I must say."

"No, well, I've been at school for most of my time in England. That corrupts one's accent pretty thoroughly, I'm afraid."

"Oh no, I didn't mean that!" she said in distress. "Actually, now that you mention it, I can hear a sort of Irish intonation."

I smiled. "It's very kind of you to say so."

"No, really, I can! And what have you come here to do?" she asked. "Or are you here just on a visit?"

"No, not really." I said. "I've come here to work. I'm going to teach English, in a place called The English School."

She stared at me in astonishment.

"Crikey!" she said. "That's where I'm going. My Dad enrolled me when we arrived. I'll be in the senior class, I think, We still have to settle that with the headmaster. Oh, but this is so embarrassing ! Of all the people to throw myself on the mercy of! My future English teacher!"

I looked at her, and laughed. But at the same time, certain conversations from the previous day now came back to me rather vividly. Fiona could not have been be more than seventeen. And she was very likely to be facing me in class on Monday.

"Well," I said, judiciously, "we'll just have to behave as if nothing happened, won't we? There's certainly nothing to be embarrassed about. I'm just glad to have been able to help. Are you going to be all right now, though? Are you sure you wouldn't like something to drink, after all?"

"Oh no, thanks. I'm not really allowed to drink yet, anyhow. And I should be getting home."

"Well, so should I," I said. "I need to catch a taxi back to the school. You could join me if you live in the same general direction."

She looked pleased and relieved.

"Yes, actually, we live out near Arat Kilo. If you wouldn't mind, that would be great."

So I paid the bill, leaving a generous tip (I intended to come back often), and we walked up to the beginning of Haile Selassie Avenue, as Isabel had recommended, to catch a Millecento. Fiona was in fact much better at this than I was, marching boldly out into the street to flag down drivers, and within minutes we had captured an otherwise empty cab which was ready to go to Arat Kilo and The English School.

Her travels had made her unusually sophisticated, I noted. Her father had served a good deal abroad in the last ten years, and she had attended English-language schools in various Asian and African countries. She plainly knew how to manage in the Third World, despite her untoward adventure of this afternoon. And even that she had got out of pretty boldly and imaginatively. I told her something about myself as we drove towards Arat Kilo, though trying to maintain what seemed a suitable reserve. In due course we reached one of the pleasant modern bungalows I had noticed on the road beyond Arat Kilo leading towards the school. As we came to a stop, a thought seemed to occur to her.

"Won't you come in for a bit?" she said. "I'm sure my Mum and Dad would like to meet you, and thank you for rescuing me. My Dad can run you up to the school in a moment."

I looked at my watch. It was almost a quarter to six. Something told me that this was not a good idea, but on the other hand it was an adventure, and I had half an hour in hand.

"Well," I said, "I really don't like to disturb your parents. And I do need to be back around a quarter past six. I'm being collected to go to dinner at half past."

"Oh, no trouble. I know they'd love to meet you. And I'll see that Dad runs you up in good time." So I accepted graciously, and paid off the taxi.

The spacious bungalow was fronted by a verandah adorned with bougainvillea and wisteria. Fiona let us in the front door, and called for her parents. Her father replied from his study, and she went in to bring him out, telling him rather breathlessly of her adventure, and explaining who I was. He followed her out into the hall, hand outstretched to greet me. Mr McHugh was a smallish, thick-set man, with a friendly, open, weather-beaten face, and close-cropped, greying hair, which stood up in a shock from his forehead.

"Dad, this is Mr Luke La Touche, who I think will be teaching me English at The English School."

He shook me warmly by the hand, with a firm grip.

"Well, well, Mr La Touche, very pleased to meet you. I'm Frank McHugh. It sounds like you were in the right place at the right time from my daughter's point of view. Thank you for looking after her!"

He spoke with a soft Northern Irish accent.

"Oh, not at all," I said. "I was only glad to be of help."

"Well, come inside, would ye not, and have a glass of something."

"Mr La Touche can't stay very long, Dad," interposed Fiona. "He has to be back up to the school at a quarter past six, and I was wondering if you could run him up."

"Oh surely, surely. But you'll have time for a glass of something first?"

"Well, thanks, I think I would," I said, "but I don't want to disturb you."

"Ah, no trouble at all. We're very pleased to meet you." And he led the way into a large room to the left of the hall. "Where's your mother, Fiona? I'm sure she'd like to meet our visitor."

Fiona went out to find her mother, and Mr McHugh poured me a generous measure of Jameson's whiskey, which he proudly displayed to me beforehand. Strangely enough, I had brought over just such a bottle for myself, but I felt no need to mention that.

"Well," he said, "so you're Irish, Fiona tells me." He said this without malice, but with a certain curiosity.

"Yes," I said, feeling a little defensive, as I always did when having to explain my nationality, "but a rather strange sort of Irishman, I suppose. I was born in Malaya, and sent to school and university in England."

"But you live in Ireland?"

"Yes, my home is in Wicklow." I did not elaborate on this.

"And you feel Irish?" He looked at me quizzically, but kindly.

"Yes, I must say I do."

"Then you're Irish. And don't let anyone tell you any different."

He raised his glass to me. I warmed to Mr McHugh. I had felt distinctly nervous about confronting what I regarded as a 'real' Irishman, expecting to have my claims to nationality at least tacitly rejected, but here I was confronted by a sudden blast of benign common sense, and I was grateful for it.

"Our Fiona is almost in the same boat as yourself, you see. Been out of the country so long she doesn't hardly sound Irish any more. But I always tell her, it's what you feel. That's the important thing."

I was a little stuck for a reply to that. What did I feel, after all? At that moment, however, Mrs McHugh, wiping her hands on her apron, was ushered in by her daughter. She was a large, motherly, friendly – looking woman, who plainly liked to preside personally in the kitchen, servants or no servants.

"Well, Mr, La Touche, it's very nice to meet you. I've just been hearing Fiona's story. You're sure you can't stay for a bite of supper with us?"

"No, thank you very much," I said, "but I'm afraid I can't. I'm expected at my cousin's for dinner." I glanced at my watch. "Indeed I probably should be going."

"Well, well!" said Mr McHugh. "You have a cousin here?"

"Yes, he's attached to the Department of Justice here – Sir James Mallory. I don't know if you've heard of him."

Mr McHugh raised his eyebrows.

"Heard of him? I should say I have heard of him. One could hardly avoid hearing of Sir James Mallory in this town. I haven't had the pleasure of meeting him yet, though. So he's a cousin of yours, Mr La Touche? Is he Irish as well, then?"

"Well, yes," I said, "he is actually, but his branch of the family have lived in London for a generation. But they came from Tipperary originally. I'm not sure that he feels very Irish, though." And I smiled.

"Ah well, we'll leave him to be English so," said Mr McHugh, with a laugh. "We can't deprive them of all the talents."

He waved me to a comfortable cane chair, and we sat for a short while, while I gave some account of myself, and my first impressions of the country – though I omitted any reference to the corpse on the gibbet. Then Mr McHugh took a look at my glass, which was nearly empty.

"Well, if you drink up the rest of that, then, I'll just run you up in the car, if you like. Mustn't keep Sir James waiting."

As I thanked him, Mrs McHugh interjected:

"But you must come down and have dinner with us another time, soon – if you'd like to, that is."

"I certainly would," I said. "That's very kind of you."

"That's grand, then. We'll send a message with Fiona, sometime next week, perhaps, or the week after – when you're settled in."

"I'll look forward to that."

Fiona said goodbye quietly, and expressed the hope of seeing me on Monday. Once in the car, as we drove out onto the road, Mr McHugh turned to me.

"She's a great girl, Fiona," he said, "but she's needs watching. I hope she won't give you a bad time. She's very bright, but she tends to get bored in class, if the teaching is not to her liking. I'm sure she won't have any complaints on that score from you, though, from the sound of you."

"Well now," I said, "I'm not so sure. I'm only starting out in this business, after all, and I'm not absolutely clear that this is what I want to do for the rest of my life. But I'll do my best not to be boring, at least."

Mr McHugh laughed.

"I'm sure you won't be boring." And then he asked me the inevitable question, why on earth had I chosen to come out to Ethiopia. I simply gave the non-complicated answer – to search for a bit of adventure before settling down, and so on. To my relief, he gave it his complete approval.

"I've been spending the last five or six years in various parts of what they call the 'third world', and I'd recommend a year or two in this sort of place to any young fella who can manage it. It's frustrating, certainly, a lot of the time, when you're trying to help out, but for a fella in your situation, that's not so much of a problem. The main thing is that it brings you closer to what life on earth is all about." He beat his hand gently on the steering wheel. "It helps you to appreciate your own culture, and its advantages – gives you a perspective on life that'll stand to you in the future. Ah yes, I'd recommend it to anyone. I think you'll have a great time here – as long as you don't get into any crazy mischief, of course. And I'm sure you wouldn't be one to do that."

"Well, I certainly hope not," I said.

"And you have your cousin to advise you. That's a great thing."

We turned in to the gates of The English School, and he drove me up to my bungalow. As we parted, he thanked me again for rescuing Fiona, and looked forward to seeing me again soon. I tottered up the path to my front door, beginning to feel the cumulative effects of the afternoon's adventures and a large whiskey. It was just a quarter past six.

CHAPTER FIVE

I had just put a few overnight things into a bag, and was sitting waiting to be collected, when I heard footsteps coming forcefully up the path. Then a boisterous voice called out.

"Hello! Do I hear we have a Paddy on the compound? Anyone at home in there?"

I was intrigued, and went to open the door to this strange manifestation. I was met by a cheery, broad-faced, red-haired young man, somewhat taller than myself – nearly six foot, in fact – holding a bottle of beer in each hand, and grinning wickedly.

"'Ello, 'ello !" he said loudly. "You the new boy?"

"Yes," I said with a smile, "I suppose I am. Will you come in?"

"Thanks very much. I will." He spoke with quite a broad Yorkshire accent. He transferred one of the bottles to join the other in his large left hand, and extended his right to me. "I'm Simon Blakeney."

"I thought you might be." I said. "Alan Lonsdale mentioned you yesterday evening. I'm Luke La Touche."

"Pleased to meet you, Luke. So, old Alan mentioned me, did he? Hope he was polite, then!'

"Oh yes, quite polite, on the whole."

"Ha, the bugger. Well, I just thought I'd bring you a little house-warming present, like, in case you wanted to offer me a drink, and hadn't laid anything in yet." And he extended a beer.

I accepted it civilly, though I was once again beginning to reach my alcohol limit, with the evening still relatively young.

"Well, thanks very much. I think I can offer a glass, at least." I went into the kitchen, and found two which looked clean. Blakeney produced a massive Swiss Army knife, and beheaded the bottles with a flourish. At least, I reflected, he didn't take them off with his teeth.

"In fact," I added, as an afterthought, "I could offer you some Irish whiskey, if you'd prefer that. I brought over a bottle of Jameson's."

This produced a guffaw.

"Irish whiskey? You people make whiskey, then? No thanks!" Then he perhaps decided he had gone a little too far. "No, but seriously. Let's 'ave the beer for now. I'll take you up on the whiskey another time."

I offered him a glass, but he waved it aside, and slumped down comfortably into one of the armchairs.

"No, save the glass," he said. "I'll use the bottle."

I poured the Melotti beer carefully into the other glass, and lowered myself into my armchair. He raised the bottle in salute.

"Well, welcome to Cloud Cuckoo Land! What brings you 'ere, then?"

"I just needed a rest from the Western world. Wanted to get away and think. Maybe do a bit of writing. How about you?"

"Oh, about the same. Fed up with Britain. Wanted a bit of adventure. You'll get the same answer from most people you meet here. The married ones are generally escaping from an underpaid, boring rut. Those of us who've so far escaped marriage are in search of a bit of adventure. Fortunately there's quite a little group of those. I'll introduce you to them. It's not a bad place for that sort of thing, really."

"So I've been hearing."

He laughed.

"Well," he said, changing the subject, "and what sort of a Paddy are you, then? Strangest one I ever come across."

I smiled ruefully.

"Yes, not a very convincing one, I suppose. Ex-colonial, English public school Paddy. I don't really belong anywhere much."

He looked concerned.

"Oh, it's not as bad as all that, surely? You are Irish, though, aren't you?"

"Oh yes, I'm Irish all right. I live there. But I don't really belong there, I'm afraid."

"Well, sounds like Addis is just the place for you. It's full of characters who don't belong anywhere – except in the pages of a second-rate spy story. What are you doing this evening, by the way? I've just got back from a little safari, as Alan may have told you, but I wouldn't mind a trip downtown, if you're not doing anything."

That reminded me, abruptly, of my situation. I was about to be collected for dinner. In fact, at just that moment I heard the sound of a car driving up the compound.

"Gosh, that's a most attractive offer, but I'm afraid I'm about to be collected by my cousin for the weekend. I'll be back on Sunday afternoon, though, I think. Perhaps we could get together again then?"

Blakeney raised his eyebrows in ironic astonishment.

"You have a cousin here, do you? Who would that be, then? I'd say this is the world-wide Irish conspiracy at work!"

I laughed deprecatingly. "I don't think he can count as Irish, actually. He's been out here for a while now, as legal advisor to the Emperor. His name is James Mallory."

"Well, well. I've heard of him, all right. Can't say I've met him, but I've seen him at embassy parties. Pretty much of an *eminence grise*, I understand. No, I wouldn't have thought of *him* as a Paddy. You're right."

Just then there were steps in the path, and a knock on the door. I went to open it, and found Wolde.

"Good evening, *getoich*. Sir James send me to bring you."

"Oh fine, Wolde, thanks. I won't be a minute."

Blakeney was plainly rather impressed. I hoped it wouldn't put him off. It didn't seem to, though.

"Well," he said, cheerfully, "I'll be going, then. When you get back on Sunday, give me a shout. I'll be around, if you're not too late."

"Fine," I said, I'm sure I won't be. It was good to meet you. Thanks for the beer.' He waved and was gone.

When we got back to James's bungalow, I left my bag in the hall, and was ushered out onto the verandah, where I found him in conclave with two other dignified figures, one of them, as it turned out, the President of the Supreme Court, the other the Minister of Justice, Ato Abebe Retha. This distinguished company rose to greet me. The President was none other than Dr Willy Buhagiar, the old friend of James's whom he had told me about yesterday, and whom, I learned later, he had recommended to this position, when the Emperor wanted to reform his judiciary. He was a stout, jolly, olive-skinned figure, with horn-rimmed glasses, and he shook my hand warmly. The Minister, on the other hand, was a thin, spare Amhara, with a fine, aristocratic face, like a saint on the wall of a Byzantine chapel. He spoke English carefully and accurately, with a somewhat guttural accent.

As James made me a gin and tonic, I made positive noises about how interesting I was finding everything, and pleased the Minister by saying that I looked forward to learning about Ethiopian culture and history. He assured me that there was much to be learned, and urged me to visit Gondar and Axum and Lalibela, and if possible the monasteries on Lake Tana, where many ancient manuscripts and other relics were preserved.

It turned out that the President was staying for dinner, while the Minister was not, so Ato Abebe took his leave after a short while. Cousin James saw him to the door, leaving Dr Buhagiar with me on the verandah.

"A really excellent man," said he, in reference to the Minister, as soon as he was out of earshot. "The best sort of Ethiopian intellectual. One can only hope that he survives. He has a tendency to speak his mind to his Imperial Majesty, and he does not tolerate gladly either fools or rogues, of which there are unfortunately all too many in high places in this country."

I was intrigued by this plain speaking. Dr Buhagiar seemed as if he would prove entertaining.

"Yes," I said, "he certainly seemed a very interesting man."

Dr Buhagiar now changed the subject rather abruptly.

"Talking of interesting people, Sir James tells me you're acquainted with young Prince Yohannis?"

Again I was intrigued. This was plainly somewhat on James's mind, if he was discussing it with his friends.

"Well, yes, I was up at college with him for a year. I liked him a lot. Cousin James tells me, though, that he's a rather controversial figure here."

Dr Buhagiar smiled. "Yes, you could say that, I think. In fact, I'm afraid that he may be getting himself and a lot of other people into rather more trouble than he's bargaining for. I must say that I would keep him at an arm's length, if I were you."

"Yes, that's very much what Cousin James said. I'll bear that in mind, certainly, but I have the problem that I don't want to be rude. He's already found out that I'm here, and he's been leaving messages."

"H'm," said Dr Buhagiar. "No, one does not want to be rude, certainly. But you should just try to ensure that you don't become involved with him. I really would advocate that."

A small knot of anxiety began to form in my stomach. But just then Cousin James came bumbling back.

"Well now, how's your drink?"

I assured him that I was in no need of a refill.

He asked then how I had got on with Ato Kebede. I described that very satisfactory meeting, and thanked him for setting it up.

"He's a very cultured and pleasant man, as far as I can see, and certainly quite a fan of yours."

Dr Buhagiar laughed at this.

"Been pulling strings again, have you, James?."

Cousin James smiled contentedly, but said nothing.

Wolde came out to announce dinner, and we filed inside to the dining-room. It was once again an excellent meal, this time featuring kebabs. My impression was that Cousin James was a fairly demanding master in the matter of food, but he also gave credit where credit was due. Conversation round the dinner table was fascinating, but not all of it could I take in adequately. There was a certain amount of gossip about the ministry and the judiciary, but then Willy Buhagiar turned to me, and began to explain some of his problems in setting up a Supreme Court (he was intended, of course, only to be an interim figure). He was having difficulties with one old Ras whom the Emperor had entrusted with the role of liaising with him, who was inclined to maintain that there should be not one, but three Presidents of the Supreme Court, on the model of the Blessed Trinity, a proposition which Dr Buhagiar found it very difficult to argue against without seeming irreverent.

Would it matter that much, I wondered.

"Well," he said, "it might not seem to, but the three old duffers that would be appointed would probably argue so interminably that no decisions would be handed down before the decease of the litigants. Still, it's not my problem, I suppose. I won't have to live with the consequences."

He enjoyed being here, he explained, but he was looking forward to retiring to Malta, after many years in various parts of the Empire. He and James had known each other in Malaya, it seemed, where they had both been judges.

The conversation turned then to the Amharic language, and to Classical *Ge'ez*, and Dr Buhagiar discoursed on the number of words common to *Ge'ez*, in particular, and Maltese, which he claimed, grandly, to be descended from Carthaginian. This was all fascinating, but my head was beginning to swim, since wine at dinner was added to the various other things I had consumed during the afternoon and evening. We rose to return to the verandah for coffee, which I was glad of, but when Cousin James produced the brandy and cigars, I decided that the time had come to retire.

I excused myself, explaining that I had been drinking on and off since the late afternoon, and in my defence I told the story of my rescue of Miss Fiona McHugh. This amused James greatly, and Willy Buhagiar even more.

"Ah, young Luke," he said as I took my leave, "there are now two dangers I have to warn you about. Steer clear of radical princes and of precocious schoolgirls, especially if you are going to be teaching the latter in class. Otherwise your stay in this beautiful country, though interesting, may prove to be rather short."

I smiled weakly, and staggered off to bed, warned by Cousin James that we would have to be up good and early in the morning, in order to reach the Awash before the midday heat.

I was too tired to give the events of the day the reflection they deserved. As soon as my head hit the pillow I was asleep.

I woke up, however, some time in the middle of the night, in the grip of a curious, semi-nightmarish dream, only snatches of which survived waking, but which involved hurrying down interminable corridors in vast buildings, searching for somebody or something, late for some appointment I had made. No doubt, I reflected, the mixture of drinks, but the dream nonetheless left me with an unpleasant, though unfocussed, feeling of panic, as I stumbled out to the bathroom to relieve myself of some of the previous day's drinking.

It took me some time to get to sleep again after this. I lay on my back, listening to the sounds of the night, in a state of misery, overwhelmed, suddenly, in the blackness, by waves of loneliness and bewilderment.

CHAPTER SIX

I was wakened by Wolde tactfully drawing back the curtains. I was still feeling a bit mouldy, but at least my previous night's state of mind was only a memory, and I found myself looking forward to whatever new adventures the day would bring.

Willy Buhagiar had in fact stayed the night, and he and Cousin James were waiting for me at the breakfast table when I appeared. After an excellent breakfast of fried eggs, toast and honey, we piled into the Mercedes for the journey to the Awash. Wolde had plainly been hard at work, and the car was loaded both with provisions and with picnic furniture. The boot was full of boxes giving off interesting smells, and there was a folding table and chairs tied onto the roof. Dr Buhagiar and I got into the back, and James joined Wolde in the front.

Another car-load, it seemed, would be joining us at the Awash, from the British Embassy – the First Secretary, Ewan Hardiman, and his wife, and the British Consul-General in Eritrea, who was up for a visit and was staying with them. All these would then be coming back to dinner. The round of entertainment seemed endless.

"Hardiman's a very interesting fellow," said James over his shoulder, as we drove off. "I hope he'll take to you. He's made a deep study of the history and language of this country, and he could teach you a lot, if he would. Really the best sort of foreign office product. His wife is delightful too."

"Sounds great," I said. "I certainly hope he takes to me."

"Oh, I think he will," said James. "You're a likeable lad, when all's said and done."

We passed through the Piazza once again, and down the grand boulevard leading south to the airport. Again I had an opportunity to observe the extraordinary mixture of modernity and traditional chaos that characterised the city. One might have a fine new road flanked by modern buildings but no pavement, or a modern road and pavement bordered by *tukuls* and shacks, or a fine modern building with a dirt road and no pavement, but very rarely all three together.

Once past the airport, we were out into the open country. The landscape was still green after the rains. In contrast to what I was familiar with in Europe, the countryside presented an impression of infinite openness. No fences, no hedges hemmed in one's view. Rolling hills stretched to the horizon, punctuated only by occasional clumps of eucalyptus, sheltering clusters of native *tukuls*, and the odd isolated thorn tree. At intervals, in the middle distance, naked children, armed with short spears, tended herds of goats or hump-backed zebu cattle. The land sloped gradually downwards towards the south, in the direction we were going, though a number of impressive volcanic peaks punctuated the southern and western horizons.

James turned round to me again.

"We're heading gradually down, you see, from the Ethiopian highlands towards the Rift Valley, though we won't get there today. The Awash flows into that. Actually, it never reaches the sea at all. It just gets swallowed up in the Ogaden Desert. But it's quite a fine river where we come across it."

I nodded, taking in the varied scene. In front of us, a stately personage on his mule, holding an umbrella, and followed by his wife on foot with a bundle on her head, moved aside begrudgingly from the middle of the road to let us past.

"A local dignitary," remarked Willy. "You can tell by the magnificence of his umbrella, and his wife's gold ornaments."

The landscape began to become repetitive, but its very breadth gave an inkling, at the same time, of the mysterious vastness of Africa. One felt that one could turn off the road at any point and vanish into an endless expanse.

The road itself, after about ten miles, changed from a rather battered tarmac to hard-packed red dirt, or *murram*, so that the car raised a cloud of fine red dust after it, and occasional traffic coming the other way covered the windscreen with more of the same. Wolde ploughed on down the middle of the road, blowing the horn lustily at any potential obstacles, such as men on donkeys or children driving goats. Cousin

James dozed. Willy Buhagiar discoursed on Ethiopian politics. I tried to listen, but began to be lulled into a pleasant coma.

Suddenly we drove into a ramshackle town – no more than a wide main street, with a few rudimentary side-streets leading off it. The buildings were mainly of mud-brick, with corrugated iron roofs, but there were one or two more substantial Italian-style buildings, one of which proclaimed itself 'Hotel'. Quite a number of the humbler buildings had the familiar red fluorescent light above their doors. If one reckoned brothels as pubs, I thought, this would be the equivalent of many a small market town in Ireland.

"Bishoftu," said Willy, seeing me peering at it. "At least that's what the natives, and most of us, call it. It's the *Galla* name, though. The official Amharic title is Debre Zeit – a piece of cultural imperialism which few pay much attention to. There are some hot springs here, a bit off the road, and a rather nice resort hotel, which is a good place to spend a weekend." And he pointed at a road leading off to the right, over a low hill.

The open country resumed. We passed through one or two other small towns, and then suddenly the road dipped sharply, and began to wind down into a sort of gorge. Cousin James woke up.

"Splendid," he said. "Almost there. Well done, Wolde. Made very good time."

Wolde inclined his head in acknowledgement, and the Mercedes cautiously negotiated the remaining mile or so of road, the surface of which, being on a sharp incline, had now become noticeably worse.

We slowed to a crawl, but now, round a bend, there came into view a welcome vista – a broad, rather turbid river, pleasantly shaded by clumps of acacia and other trees. Some quite steep cliffs rose up on our side of the river, but on the other the trees and scrub stretched away into the distance.

"The Awash," exclaimed Cousin James, "great, green and greasy! Now I hope that no one has occupied our favourite spot."

Wolde manoeuvred the car carefully down to the river, and along the bank a short way, to a grassy patch between some trees. No one else appeared to be in sight.

"Well, the others haven't got here yet," said James. "No matter. We can set up shop in any case. At least there are no unwanted intruders."

We climbed out. I was slightly stiff from the drive, and glad to be out of the car. The air was distinctly warmer, and the atmosphere smelled different from Addis. I remarked on this.

"Ah well," said James. "We've come down a couple of thousand feet, you see. You would only have noticed the last bit, perhaps, but we've been in fact descending all the time. We're at below five thousand feet here. It makes quite a difference, at this latitude."

Willy Buhagiar stretched and yawned.

"Yes, you'll notice that the air is a bit thicker. Quite difficult to stay awake after a good lunch!"

Wolde began to unpack provisions from the boot. Chairs were unhitched from the roof, and set up under the trees by the bank. Cousin James took out a large straw hat, placed it carefully on his head, and made for one of the chairs.

"Now," he said, "Willy and I will take our ease under the trees until the others arrive, since we are old gentlemen, but you might like to take a little walk of exploration. There is some wild life to be observed, if you're interested. Hippos in the river, down a bit from here. They like to congregate on a mud bank opposite a hot stream that flows into the main one. Watch out for that, as it will scald you quite badly if you step into it. A bit of a shock if you think you're going to cool off! And there are baboons up on the cliffs. They'll just be working their way up at this time of the morning. They spend the day up at the higher altitudes, and then come down again in the evening. Don't get too near them, though, or the males will start throwing things. They're very protective of their territory – and their ladies. You may also see a few buck. And watch out for leopards."

"Leopards?"

Willy Buhagiar chuckled.

"He's just teasing you," he said. "There are leopards, but you won't see them. They'll all be fast asleep at this time of the day, tucked up cosily on some convenient branch of a tree."

Still, a pleasant tingle of excitement remained with me as I began to make my way cautiously down along the river. There was a sort of path, beaten either by animal or human feet, which followed the river bank down to the left. The trees overhung the river, and provided a pleasant shade from what was beginning already to be an oppressively hot sun. I made my way cautiously along, watching out for jutting roots, leopards, and snakes (which had not been mentioned, but must, I felt, be around). For the moment, however, nothing stirred, though there was a background of varied birdsong, and always the cicadas. After about a quarter of a mile, though, the path led round a corner, following a bend in the river, and I emerged into a broader panorama.

There was a clearing in the trees, the river widened out, and the cliffs receded somewhat. In front of me, a small stream flowed into the main river. As I looked at it more closely, I could see wisps of steam rising from it. This, no doubt, was the hot stream. I came up close to it, and looked out across the river. There, out some distance from the bank, more or less opposite the stream, there seemed to be a pile of smooth logs or barrels floating in the water. Then one of them moved slightly, and I saw that they were in fact hippos, five or six of them, almost entirely submerged, but with their eyes and noses, as well as the great curves of their backs, protruding above the surface. I stood and watched them, fascinated. I felt suddenly in the heart of Africa. Behind me the cicadas set up a wall of noise, drowning out any other sounds there may have been. I seemed an intruder on this peaceful scene – just an ordinary day like any other in the life of these hippos.

In a sudden access of lightheartedness, I raised a hand to my mouth, and called out, "Hi, boys!" One of them turned slowly and looked at me, rising slightly out of the water. Then suddenly it gave an enormous yawn, showing its cavernous mouth, adorned with a few massive molars, and subsided again. I felt somehow that I had been dismissed, and turned to look back at the cliffs, in search of baboons.

Sure enough, there they were, dotted about half way up the cliff face, a number of big, stern-faced males with imposing ruffs standing guard, while females, often with young, pottered about among the shrubs that covered the cliff. I walked a little way towards them, following the hot stream. It was fairly open country, with just a few scattered thorn trees, and after about fifty yards my presence was observed. One great male rose from his perch, showing an expanse of red bottom, and gave a loud bark. Instantly the whole troop was on alert, and began to move faster up the cliff face. I stopped, and began to step backwards. As I retreated, I noticed one or two clods of earth and stones landing quite close to me, and realised that I was being bombarded. I found this amusing, but also slightly worrying, and made my way back without delay to the river bank.

When I came in sight of our camp, I observed that the others had arrived. A large, pleasant-faced young man, whom I presumed to be Ewan Hardiman of the Embassy, a slim, dark-haired young woman in white blouse and khaki shorts, who must be his wife, and a small, wiry older man, were in conversation with James and Willy. Behind them, Wolde was setting up the materials of a copious lunch.

They all turned towards me when I approached.

"And here's young Luke," said James, "back safe from his adventures. Did you find the hippos?"

"Yes," I said cheerily, "just where you said they would be."

"And no leopards?"

"No leopards. But I did say hello to the baboons."

"Splendid. All is well in God's universe. Now come and meet Ewan and Susan Hardiman, and Nigel Lloyd, our consul in Asmara."

I came over and was introduced. Ewan Hardiman directed his attention very amiably to me.

"You've just arrived, I gather?" he said.

"Yes, just last Wednesday. It seems a lot longer, I must say."

"Ah yes, it always does. How do you find it all?"

I was beginning to prepare a set reply to this sort of question, but something about Hardiman made me feel that he deserved, and would repay, a little more than that.

"Well," I said, "it's a strange thing, but I alternate between seeing the strangeness and the ordinariness of everything. I mean, I was standing just now looking at the hippos, and I had first a sensation of utter strangeness. 'Here I am', I said to myself, 'close to the heart of Africa. I'm in a totally alien world.' And then I thought, 'But of course, for the hippos, this is just an ordinary day like any other – except, I suppose, that I've turned up to look at them'. There they were, wallowing happily on their mud-bank, in a totally banal environment – for them. And this has been hitting me ever since I arrived – the ordinary in the midst of the bizarre."

Hardiman laughed, and looked at me narrowly.

"Yes, precisely," he said. "I know what you mean. I've got some way past that now myself, but I can remember thinking very much the same when I first arrived. This is, after all, one of the strangest places on earth that one could find oneself in. I don't say the strangest – I've been in a few weirder spots in my time – but one of the strangest. I gather from Sir James that you're quite interested in the language and the history."

"Well yes," I said. 'I can't claim I came here for that reason, but now that I'm here, I'm keen to learn as much about it as I can."

"And why did you come here?"

Once again, something in Hardiman's attitude made me feel that no superficial answer would be adequate, but I was at a loss for anything really satisfactory.

"I don't know any longer if I have an answer to that. I think I'm just a casualty of the times, really. The Cold War and the arms race just began to get to me, and the prospect of graduating into that sort of world suddenly seemed appalling." I waved a hand, and continued feebly, "I know this isn't a solution, and even Ethiopia is caught up in the general madness, but at least there's something pleasantly absurd about the whole scene here."

Hardiman smiled and shook his head. We had moved away slightly from the rest of the company, and were standing by the river bank, looking out over the broad reach of the Awash to the savannah beyond.

"I can sympathise with a lot of that," he said, "but don't for Heaven's sake imagine that this is some sort of comic opera regime. It has its absurd aspects, certainly, but it has its serious side, and its nasty side, as well, and the Emperor undoubtedly means business. He's also deeply involved in the Cold War, I assure you – though in his own very devious way. So there's really no escape. I'm afraid. Not," he continued, "that I don't think that it's an excellent idea to do what you're doing, just for the present. But then I think you really have to head back and take your place in the real world. I mean, let's face it, if the Third World War breaks out, there will be nowhere to hide. You might as well be right in the thick of it. The only thing worth doing, it seems to me, is to try and do one's bit to change people's minds. I know it seems a hopeless proposition, but every little helps. And there may just now be no alternative to this sort of confrontation. I'm afraid the Russians will just have to grow up a bit, get a bit flabbier, more prosperous, more corrupt. Then maybe we can do business."

I laughed. "You subscribe to Macmillan's thesis, then?"

"Yes," he said, "I think I do, frankly. 'A fat Communist is a happy Communist'. Isn't that it? I think there's quite a lot in that."

"I agree there may be," I said, "but are they getting any fatter?"

"Oh, I think so," said Hardiman. "Yes, a little, certainly. In fact, I know the Russian cultural attaché here quite well, and he's quite a fat and happy Communist. He certainly doesn't want war. I rarely escape from his company without drinking many toasts to world peace, alternately in vodka and whiskey, which can be very troublesome. I must introduce you to him."

But just then we were summoned back by Cousin James to the groaning picnic table which Wolde had laid out under the trees, to take a pre-luncheon drink.

Cousin James had provided the wine, but the Hardimans made a special contribution from the resources of the Embassy in the form of a large flask of Pimms, complete with slices of cucumber and lemon. Both parties had brought ice. We sat down on deck chairs in a loose circle under the acacias, facing the river, and sipped our Pimms. In a way, this produced an even stranger sensation than had the contemplation of the hippos half an hour earlier. The capacity of the British to maintain the trappings of civilisation in the most unlikely surroundings was something that I had often read about (I was too young, of course, to appreciate it in Malaya), but to experience it first-hand, and to observe the absolute naturalness with which it was done, fascinated me so much that I was unable to attend properly to the conversation. I wondered idly what Wolde thought of all this, but he was bustling about setting out the lunch, and gave no indication of sensing anything unusual.

I was recalled from my musings by the consul from Eritrea, a pleasant, low-key businesslike man, who was sitting next to me.

"Well," he said, "You're a cousin of James, I understand."

"Yes," I said, "once removed, I should say. He's a second cousin of my mother's."

"Ah!," he said. "But you yourself are Irish, I believe. Do your parents live in Ireland?"

I hesitated, not wishing to cast a shadow on the conversation.

"Well, yes, my mother does. My father's dead, actually."

"Oh," he said, suddenly embarrassed, "I'm very sorry to hear that."

"Well, he died a long time ago, in fact, when I was about two. I never really knew him, I'm afraid. He was an engineer in Malaya. Cousin James was out there too, in fact. It was just at the beginning of the war. My father was captured at Singapore, and died in a camp not long after that."

"Yes, a very nasty business that. The Japs have a lot to answer for. Well, I am sorry to have brought that up. It's an interesting story, though, if a sad one. You don't really remember your father at all, then?"

I did not often think or talk about my father, which made it that much odder to be discussing him with a total stranger under an acacia tree beside a river in the middle of Africa. But it is easier to talk of some things with total strangers, and especially with an unobtrusive man like Mr Lloyd.

"No, I don't, I'm afraid. Sometimes I think I can remember him, in a white suit, coming in to say goodnight to me before he and my mother went out to dinner. But I may be just imagining that. Otherwise I only know him from photographs. Cousin James has really been the nearest to a father that I've had. He's my godfather as well, you see."

"Well," he said, "that explains a lot."

I noticed Susan Hardiman, who was sitting to the other side of me, listening to our conversation with interest. Now she intervened.

"That's really an awfully sad story," she said, with sympathy.

"Oh," I said, "it all happened a long time ago. I didn't even know what was going on at the time."

"But still it's sad," she said. "It must have been very hard on your mother."

"Yes, I think it was. She's got over the loss of my father, of course. At least I think she has. But it's a lonely life."

"She never thought of marrying again?"

I hesitated, glancing in the direction of Cousin James. He was deep in conversation with Ewan Hardiman and Willy Buhagiar, but he might have been listening to this nonetheless. Susan Hardiman noticed the hesitation and the glance, I think, but did not remark on it.

"Well no," I said, "not to my knowledge. We just don't meet very many suitable people where we are. We're rather buried in the country, you see."

In fact, now that I thought about it, there were a number of reasonably suitable people around on the Wicklow scene – middle-aged, prosperous, retired businessmen and Indian Army officers – whom Mother was glad to play bridge or tennis with, cooperate with in organising Church fêtes, or to sell cream or brussels sprouts or raspberries to, but whom she was not willing to encourage further than that. I thought of poor Colonel Parsons, for one, the decentest of men, and great fun, really, even if he did tend to tell the same stories again and again, but who was constantly rebuffed, and even ridiculed behind his back. Come to think of it, it was odd how she erected a barrier round herself, such as even I could only partly penetrate. And I had to come away, and sit on the banks of this river in the middle of Africa, to see how odd it all was.

Susan Hardiman gently pursued her questions, and once again I found that I was uncovering layers of myself to a perfect stranger that I had left untouched for as long as I could remember. It suddenly seemed to me now, as we talked, while addressing the delights of Wolde's curried chicken salad, that I was after all a very odd bird, and I began to feel slightly sorry for myself. This may have had a certain amount to do with the Pimms I had consumed, followed now by some very passable white wine from Eritrea, but it came over me powerfully nonetheless.

I belonged nowhere, really. I had some claim to being Irish – I carried, proudly, an Irish passport – but it did not serve to bring me any closer to my countrymen. Nor could I really feel comfortable with the English, in whose company I had spent most of my life, and from whom, inevitably, most of my friends were drawn. I had always made a point of differentiating myself from them, of being slightly alien, and they accepted that cheerfully. They were generally pleased, I think, to feel that they knew a reasonably 'civilised' Irishman – like knowing a cultured black man. They even came to stay, occasionally, and delighted in the state of dilapidated grandeur that they were faced with.

But to live in dilapidated grandeur can be depressing after a while. If one is extremely rich it does not so much matter if one is odd (though even the very rich, no doubt, have their problems), but to be rather poor and rather odd can become troublesome. Of course, being Protestant doesn't help – a little island of righteousness and rationality in a sea of Roman Catholic superstition! I had not been brought up to feel very strongly about religious differences, and would not have had much objection, after all, from a theological point of view, to becoming a Roman Catholic, if it would increase my sense of identity.

But my family was not just Protestant. It was Huguenot, and that meant something. We had not just changed our religion to acquire some advantage (or avoid some disadvantage) from the British regime. We had personal cause to know what unbridled Roman Catholic intolerance could do when it was unleashed, as it had been at the revocation of the Edict of Nantes. That was what had driven my remote ancestor, first to Holland, with all his worldly wealth sewed into the seat of his trousers, and then to Ireland, in the train of William of Orange. I did not feel inclined to give up my traditions just in order to fit in better. And anyhow, it wouldn't have worked. My accent was wrong. My experiences were different. I was, let's face it, irremediably odd.

Susan Hardiman seemed to notice my rather elegiac mood, and moved to change the subject. We were getting through a fruit salad composed of various exotic species, helped by thin fingers of shortbread. She praised the salad, and pointed out passion fruit and kumquats.

"What are you two finding to talk about?" Ewan Hardiman called over. "Is she pumping you, Luke? She does that, you know. Don't tell her anything you don't want to. You have the right to remain silent."

I laughed. Susan Hardiman and I glanced at each other, and as our eyes met it suddenly struck me how very attractive she was. I looked away again in momentary confusion.

"No, I wasn't giving too much away," I lied. "We were just talking about Ireland."

"Ah yes," said Ewan, "that most distressful country!"

I looked at him in surprise, not expecting a reference to an Irish patriotic song from such a source. He noticed my surprise, and responded.

"Oh yes, I know Ireland quite well, actually. My father used to like to go to Connemara on fishing holidays, and I liked listening to ballad singers in the local pubs when I was small. I have quite a repertoire, in fact, of Irish and Scottish rebel songs, which I will deliver after a few pints – or indeed a few vodkas, as my friend Alexei has cause to know. It confuses him very much."

"You're better off than I am, then," I said. "I listen to them mainly on records. I used to play them quite a lot in Oxford, just to remind myself that I was Irish. But I'm not much good at singing them."

Lunch being now over, James and Willy Buhagiar once again resorted to the ploy of being old gentlemen, and declared they were going to take a nap, but that the younger folk could do what they wanted.

"Well," said Ewan, "I think we might take a walk. What do you say? Just along the river. Stay out of the sun."

"You've just been along there, though, haven't you, Luke?" said Susan.

"Yes," I said hastily, "but I don't mind going again."

Mr Lloyd too was happy to join us, and we took a pleasant stroll, once again, down to the hippos and the hot stream. Now, in the mid-afternoon heat, the hippos had subsided further into the river, only a number of noses showing above the surface. On the cliffs behind, the baboons also were sheltering under the rocks. All nature had taken cover, and the world was given over to the white noise of the cicadas. Otherwise, silence. Even under the trees, the heat enveloped us like a blanket.

"Can one swim in this?" I asked.

"Not advisable," said Ewan. "It's fairly fast-flowing and muddy, and there are crocs."

"Crocodiles?" I said.

"Yes, why not? You're in Africa, remember. You won't see them, generally, but just wait till you get into the water!"

"Gosh," I said, "That's a pity. I could have done with a swim."

There was a reflective pause. We looked at the river.

"Oh well," said Ewan, "maybe the old folks were right. I think we should just go back and lie down for a while."

He led the way back, followed by Lloyd, with whom he was discussing the problems of Eritrea. I padded along behind Susan, trying to keep my eyes off her pleasantly swaying hips.

We lay on rugs spread on the rough grass, and dozed until the early evening, when the heat subsided a little. James had unfolded a large white handkerchief, and had draped it over his head, knotting two of the ends. It rippled gently as he snored. Under a separate tree, Wolde also dozed. I tried for a while to order my thoughts, but gave up, and soon slept.

When I regained consciousness, I found that we were packing up. Wolde had got most of the things into the back of the car, and was beginning to load the roof. I got up to give him a hand, bringing folded deck-chairs as people vacated them. He thanked me gravely, and arranged them on the roof, securing them with ropes.

The Hardimans and Nigel Lloyd left first, with warm expressions of thanks, and promises to see us later that evening. When Cousin James had inspected the fastenings on the roof, and checked around under the trees for anything that might have been left behind, we began our progress back.

It was now getting towards five o'clock, and the sun was beginning to slant towards the horizon, lighting up the cliffs beside the river with a golden glow. As we climbed back onto the plateau, I could feel the air becoming a little cooler and fresher, and remarked on this.

"Yes," said James, over his shoulder, "that's a pleasant feature of this country. You can change the climate by going relatively few miles to the south or east, and up or down a few thousand feet. You'll find that in Nyala, when you visit it. Go down into the valley, and you're in the tropics. Up where the farm is you're more or less in the temperate zone."

But in general very little was said on the way back. Willy Buhagiar dozed. We were generally poleaxed by heat, drink and food. How we were to face dinner this evening, even if Wolde had the energy and ingenuity to prepare it, was quite beyond me. The pace of life suddenly seemed overwhelming.

CHAPTER SEVEN

Late the following afternoon, I sat in my armchair in the front room of my bungalow writing a letter home. I had decided to snatch a few minutes before going over to call on Simon Blakeney as agreed, since I had a sinking feeling that I wouldn't be in much shape to write letters after a night on the town with him.

I wrote Mother a brisk account of the previous few days, highlighting my establishment in the school, complete with personal servant, and James's overwhelming hospitality. I described in particular the picnic at the Awash, the dinner that followed when we got back, and then being roused at what seemed an unmerciful hour to go to the service at the English Church. There, dear old Padre Matthews gave rather a long sermon, but promised to help me with my Amharic. Following church, I walked on Entotto with James, Dr Buhagiar, and Mr Lloyd – after which there was another copious lunch, followed by a siesta.

To round off, I commented on how I was not sure if I could keep up the pace, but at least it kept me from brooding as to whether this is a crazy adventure or not. "Everyone I talk to is very positive," I wrote, "and congratulates me on my choice, but I do feel, when I have a chance to think, a bit like Ming up the palm tree." This was a reference to my mother's new Siamese kitten, who tended to get himself into inextricable positions in trees, and then miaow piteously and penetratingly until rescued. "Still, I'm here now, and I'll have to make the best of it."

I sucked the end of my pen, thoughtfully. Not a good idea to sound too lost, or she'd be worrying. And I wasn't, really. I couldn't complain.

I was about to go on to give an upbeat report of my adventures in getting my residence permit, when I heard emphatic footsteps on the path approaching the door. I put down the letter, to be finished later.

Seconds later there was a thunderous knocking, and I rose to admit an indignant Simon Blakeney.

"Hey!," he said, "I thought you were going to call over to me when you got back?"

"Yes," I said, "sorry! I was just about to, but I thought I'd take a moment to catch my breath, and start a letter home."

I indicated the unfinished letter on the coffee table.

"Ah," he said, mollified, "fair enough. Sorry to rush you. Do you want some more time? I could come back, or you could come over to me when you're ready. I just thought we should get going around six-thirty if we want to get in anywhere, and I was going to offer a drink at my place first."

"Oh no, fine. I'm all set now. We might as well go on.'

"Okay," he said briskly. "Over to my place, then, for a quick gargle, just to get us going, and I'll fill you in on the possibilities."

We strolled across the compound to Simon's bungalow, which was very similar to mine, except that it had no garden to speak of – a bit more modern, in fact, but a good deal more chaotic. He apologised for this with a wave of the hand, scooped some books and a dirty shirt out of the spare armchair, and gestured to me to sit in it. I looked around the room with interest, wondering if my own bachelor pad would manage to stay any tidier than this after a few weeks. That would largely depend on Tekla-Mariam, I felt.

Simon got us two bottles of Melotti beer, decapitated them, and we sat drinking them by the neck.

He enquired ironically after my weekend, and I described briefly the main events. Simon grunted sarcastically at most of what I had to say, but he commended the Awash.

"I must take you down to Bishoftu some weekend," he said. "There's some hot springs just outside the town, and a resort hotel. It's a good place. You nearly always meet some interesting birds down there."

"Yes," I said. "That was mentioned as we drove past. No mention of interesting birds, though."

"No, I imagine not. Well, let me tell you what I have in mind for this evening. I thought I'd introduce you to my favourite sink of iniquity. It's quite a ways off, though, out the other side of town, so we need to get going pretty smartly. It's worth it, though. Called the 'Bella Napoli' – though generally known to its supporters just as Anna's Place. It's run by this fantastic old cow Anna. Never learned her last name. Originally from Naples. Been here since before the war. It was apparently a favourite place for Italian officers during the occupation, but she managed to survive the collapse – I suppose, through doing more or less the same favours for the new regime as she did for the old one. Anyhow, it's a great place. Good booze, good food – she does a great *pollo alla diavola*, for one thing – and great girls. I must fix you up with one."

"Yes," I said cautiously, "that sounds great."

"Okay then," he said, stirring in his chair, "we'd probably better get going. Finish up that – or leave it. There'll be lots more at Anna's."

I took another swig, and put the bottle down on the table. Then I followed him out to his car, an impressive old blue Citroen, with wide running boards and a good deal of chrome. It was kept in a good deal better order than his bungalow. I congratulated him on it, as we took our seats.

"Yes," he said complacently. "She's a good old bus. Mileage is not great, but she runs well, and she's very comfortable. If you want to get a car, by the way, I can introduce you to my garage man. Marco's a crook, but he's a good-natured one, and he'll stand over what he sells you."

"Yes," I said, "I suppose I had better think about getting a car."

"Well, you can get around pretty well in the city with millecentos, but it's awkward late at night, and then if you want to go out into the countryside at all – or even out to a place like Anna's... Not so easy to get a Millecento to take you out from the Piazza."

We drove back along Haile Selassie Avenue towards the centre of town, through the Piazza, and out the other side, towards the western suburbs of the city. As the sun went down, girls were appearing in front of the multitude of red-lighted shacks that lined the avenues, and the bars and little shops were doing a lively trade. The business of the evening was getting under way. I felt an anticipatory tingle.

We passed undistinguished suburbs for a while, and then, just as the African night was coming down, in its sudden rush, out into the countryside. For ten or fifteen minutes we bumped along into the gathering dusk.

Then Simon pointed ahead. "That's it!" On the horizon I could see a clump of eucalyptus near the road, and some neon lighting. "As you can see," he continued, "it's quite isolated, which has the advantage, from Anna's point of view, that no one, whether police or anyone else, can come up on her without her being ready for them. She always has a *zabanya* on the watch. Not of course," he added, grinning, "that Anna would think of doing anything *illegal* – and anyhow, she's on very good terms with the cops – gives them complimentary drinks, and lets them have a free screw now and then – but you never know. She likes to know what's coming, in any case."

As we approached, a large, rather battered sign announced *BAR-RISTORANTE LA BELLA NAPOLI* and a design of grape clusters and wine glasses.

"You may as well know," said Simon, "Anna has a single price – all drinks one dollar. Quite a reasonable idea, really. You can have beer or wine or cognac or even *tej* – or if you're a strict teetotaller who has accidentally wandered in you can have a lemonade, but it doesn't matter a damn. All one dollar. No cover charge. Girls, by the way, cost five dollars – or if you want to be really nice, and you're really pleased with the service" – and he grinned wickedly – "you can give ten. That'll be much appreciated. Frankly, I'd advise, if you find one you like, to start off with a ten, and you'll have a friend for life."

I didn't dare show it, but the idea that we would automatically end up with a girl frankly terrified me. The awful truth was that I had never yet had sex with a girl. I thought I knew what to do, but the furthest I had ever got was a certain amount of heavy petting with a girl I knew rather well in Oxford. The summer before, in fact, while on a holiday in Crete with a friend from College, we had stayed (initially by mistake) in a brothel near Heraklion for a few days, and had made friends with a number of the girls, who were plainly fascinated by our innocence. One of them, very young and good-looking, actually offered to give us a free ride, but my companion, who was more cautious than I was, was worried about contracting the clap or worse, and persuaded me that we must politely decline. She had been rather hurt, and I had been much disappointed. That had been my best chance so far.

"Any problem with disease?" I asked, lightly.

"Well, there's always *some*, I suppose," said Simon, "but the thing to do is wear a rubber. I can give you one if you haven't stocked up. I did get a dose once, shortly after I got here, when I didn't wear one, but I got a shot in the hospital, and that sorted me out. Anyhow, the girls will mostly insist on you wearing one. They don't want to get pregnant, after all."

We drove through the gates to the compound, parked the car under the trees, and made our way to the front doors, which were invitingly open. We climbed up the rather rickety wooden steps onto the verandah. Just inside, curving away to the right, was a long, chrome-ornamented bar, with a copious collection of bottles on the shelves behind it. Presiding at this, and giving us a searching once-over, was a large lady of about sixty, dressed in black, with a fine array of ornaments adorning both neck and wrists. Her hair, which was a flaming red, was done up on her head in a sort of topknot. Beneath a generously accentuated mouth, her chins descended symmetrically towards her bosom.

"Ah, Signor Simon," she exclaimed goodhumouredly. "Where you been, eh? I no see you some weeks now. I thought maybe you sick, or dead, or something."

"No, no, Anna. Nothing like that. I was away on safari for a bit. Up north, around Gondar. You missed me?"

"Oh yes, we miss you. Frewet miss you too. And who's your friend here? He looks nice young man. I hope you not teach him evil tricks now."

"Anna, this is Mr Luke La Touche. He's just arrived in Addis. He's going to teach in the Stanford School as well."

"Ah. Signor La Touche, you are very welcome to my little place. I hope you have very good visit here. You be careful of this Blakeney, though. He have many bad habits." And she grinned broadly, revealing an array of gold teeth. "What kind of name is that, Signor La Touche? You not Italian. French, perhaps?"

No, Anna. This man is Irish. Irlandese. He doesn't look it or sound it, but that's where he's from, Irlanda."

The signora's eyebrows went up.

"Irlanda? Ah, that is quite unusual. I not meet many people from Irlanda. You like Irish whisky? I have good whisky here."

"Don't touch it," whispered Simon. "It's disgusting stuff. Made locally, in Dire Dawa. Anna, we're looking for dinner, if that's okay. Could we eat outside?"

"Oh sure," she said. "You go find a table. I send you out menu."

"Great," he said. "Is the *pollo alla diavola* on tonight?"

"Yes, you like? Okay, you go sit. I send someone. You like something to drink?"

"Oh, two beers, please, to start. Okay?"

And we went back out to find a table under the trees. Little lights were strung from tree to tree, and on the tables aromatic tapers smouldered, to keep away the bugs. We chose a table, and seated ourselves. The night was still warm, but not oppressive. Simon stretched, and linked his hands behind his neck.

"Ah, this is the life, eh? Beats Wallasey, I can tell you. After a few months you'll wonder how you ever could have survived back in the dear old UK"

"Wallasey? That's where you were?"

"Yeah, stuck in a secondary modern in Wallasey. Can you imagine that?"

I laughed. No," I said, "not really."

Simon looked at me narrowly.

"No," he said. "I don't imagine you can. I think you've probably lived a pretty privileged life, La Touche, is that so? Pretty privileged for a Paddy, anyhow."

I considered this. "I wouldn't see it like that," I said.

"No? And how would you see it, then?"

"Oh, I don't know," I said. "Not privileged, certainly. Pretty deprived, in many ways. We've never had much money, for one thing."

"Ah no, perhaps not. But you had expectations. You would expect to move in the right circles, to get to the top, now wouldn't you?"

"Well, where am I now, for instance?"

It was Simon's turn to laugh.

"Well, this is not too bad, is it?" He leaned forward. "No, I'll tell you what you're doing. You're goofing off, aren't you? You've just dropped out of the race for a year or so, but then you're going to go back and take up where you left off, and slip effortlessly into some plush job."

I looked at him. Simon was obviously a man who liked to start an argument, just to keep the conversation going, but I was not sure that I wanted to oblige him.

"I wish I was as clear as you seem to be as to what I was going to do after this. Just at present, my mind is a complete blank."

"But it certainly wouldn't include teaching in a secondary modern in Wallasey."

"No, I grant you that. It wouldn't. But how about you? You wouldn't go back to that either, would you?"

"No, bloody right I wouldn't. But my point is that my range of choices is a lot more limited than yours."

"I really don't know what you mean," I said. "I don't have any more choices than you have, so far as I can see."

But just at this moment a strikingly beautiful girl appeared, carrying a tray with two glasses and two chilled beers. Simon's attention was abruptly diverted by this.

"Hello, love," he said. "Who are you, then? I don't think we've met. You new here?"

The girl smiled, and put down the glasses and beers in front of us. She was quite tall, with delicate features and light coffee-toned skin. Her eyes were particularly notable, bright and intelligent, though with a slight sadness about them. She raised a quizzical eyebrow at Simon's question, and answered in halting English.

"Yes, I come last week. My name is Berhane."

"Berhane!" said Simon. "That's a lovely name. Berhane. My name is Simon, and this is my friend Luke. Where're you from, then, Berhane?"

She looked at him a moment, and then at me, before replying.

"I am from Tigre. From Makalle. You know it?"

"Ah yes," he said, "Very nice. I was driving through there just a few days ago."

Her face clouded a moment.

"No," she said. "Not so nice. That is why I am here." She changed the subject. "You like to eat now?"

"Yes, fine," said Simon, slightly chastened. "You like some soup first, Luke? They've got a really good *zuppa alla pavese*."

I waved my hands defensively.

"Some other time," I said. "I've been eating far too much these past few days. I'll just take the pollo."

"Okay then, Berhane. We'll just have the pollo alla diavola. I told Signora Anna. And salata, okay?"

"Okay," she said, and glided away with an aristocratic swing of her shoulders.

Simon watched her go.

"Wow," he said. "There's something for you, my lad, unless she's been snapped up already. I'd grab her myself, but I'm stuck with dear old Frewet. I can't drop her, or she'd create bloody murder. And anyhow, she's good fun. I wouldn't be too sure about Berhane. But isn't she a stunner? Those Tigrean girls have very fine features. She's *interesting* – what d'you think?"

"Yes," I said cautiously. "She certainly is. But I can't just grab her, surely, can I?" I had a nasty feeling that Simon was going to propel me into something.

"Well, yes, you more or less can. The thing is to ask Anna, though. She's the boss. She'll mark your card. We need to check that she hasn't been bagged already by some favoured customer. We don't want to muscle in on an army officer, or a secret policeman."

"Let me get this straight," I said. "You are proposing that, after dinner, we should, ah, get together with some girls?"

Simon laughed loudly.

"Yes, as you so quaintly put it, that's what I would propose that we do. We can digest our dinner over a coffee and brandy, and then we can 'get together' for a while. You see that row of rooms out the back there, by the compound fence?" And he pointed past the restaurant and bar, to where I, on turning, could see a long low building, with a series of doors opening straight off a long verandah. "They contain very comfortable facilities for getting together. We just need to check with Anna that Berhane's available."

"Doesn't Berhane have any say in this?"

"Not much. I mean, she's joined the establishment. She has to obey the rules of the house. Anyhow, she has no reason to refuse you. You're young, good-looking, civilised. Sometimes the girls can complain, if they get stuck with a known pervert, or someone hideously old and fat, but there's no problem here. No, the only question is whether she's already booked. And I have a sort of idea that Anna sent her out precisely as a present for you – a sort of introductory offer. So you're probably okay."

"Hey, wait a minute," I said. "I'm not so sure about this."

Simon looked at me with raised eyebrows.

"You don't mean to tell me that you'd turn down the chance of fucking a girl like Berhane? You scared or something?" He grinned broadly. "You're not a virgin, are you?"

I hoped that my blushes were obscured by the darkness.

"No, no," I blustered. "It's just that I wasn't, sort of, thinking in those terms."

"Well, start thinking! You're in Ethiopia now, remember. It's the custom of the country. Anna would be quite offended if you left without sampling her girls. She'd conclude you were some sort of a poofter. The honour of Old Oireland is at stake!"

I laughed, and decided to relax. What the hell, I thought. You are in Ethiopia now. You came for new experiences. This is one of them – and not at all a bad one, by the look of it.

Berhane came back, quite promptly, with a basket of bread, and I studied her with new interest. Her white *shamma* showed off her shapely figure, firm and muscular, but not too thin. As she walked way, her hips moved invitingly.

The *pollo*, when it came, turned out to be delicious, grilled over a charcoal fire, seasoned with red pepper and herbs, and accompanied by fried potatoes and green beans. There was a salad of sliced tomatoes in oil and some sort of greenery on the side. We attacked it with enthusiasm.

Berhane came back with a pitcher of red wine and two glasses. Simon poured. I tasted it. Rough, but not bad. Seemed like some sort of chianti.

"Where does this come from?" I asked.

"Oh, Eritrea, probably. They produce quite a lot up there. Not bad stuff, either."

For dessert there were just grapes, but big, juicy ones. With coffee Simon called for some local brandy. He pulled out some cheroots, offered me one (which I declined), and lit up, and leaned back in his chair.

"Now seriously, La Touche," he said, expelling a stream of smoke in my direction, "what are your purposes in life? It seems to me you aren't too clear just what you want out of all this."

I considered this challenge. Simon, it seemed to me, was someone one could get annoyed with or not, as one pleased. It pleased me not to. I looked at him.

"Do I have to have a purpose? Do you have a purpose?"

He took a pull on the cheroot.

"Do I have a purpose?" he repeated, slowly, as if thinking it over. "No, okay, you've got me. I'm not at all sure that I have. My only purpose is to have a reasonably good time for as long as I can get away with it. But you, now, you look the sort of fellow that just might have a purpose tucked away somewhere, waiting to pop up and reveal itself. And I would like to know what that purpose is."

And he stabbed the air with his cheroot.

I in turn allowed myself a pause, taking a slow mouthful of the cognac, and letting it trickle gently down my throat. On top of the wine, I found it pleasantly fuddling to the wits.

"My purpose," I said, enunciating each word carefully so as not to slur it, "my purpose right now, at this point in time," – and I allowed myself to slip into a pseudo-American drawl – "is to enjoy the rest of this brandy, and then to get laid. "

This diverted Simon from theorising to action. He gave a delighted whoop, and sprang to his feet.

"Okay, La Touche. That's the right spirit. Let's go and get laid! But we'd just better go check with Anna first."

He sprang up the front steps ahead of me, and plunged into a confidential discussion at the bar with the Signora. After a brief exchange, she emitted a deep, throaty chuckle, and slapped her hand on the counter.

"Okay, no problem. I send her along. You boys go out, make yourselves comfortable. What rooms I give you? Let me see."

And she turned back to study a row of keys, and selected two adjacent ones. She turned back to Simon, and handed them to him.

"Okay, you boys go and have fun. You have fun now, Signor La Touche!" She waved an admonitory finger in my direction. "You very welcome to my place."

And she chuckled again, broadly, her chins rippling.

"Yes, thank you, Signora," I called, and waved a hand.

We walked towards the row of rooms.

"What's the drill, then?" I said.

"Oh, you just go in, make yourself comfortable. Berhane'll be along in a moment. Here's your key. You're in number five. And here, take one of these."

Simon reached in his pocket, and took out a packet of Durex. He extracted one and handed it to me.

"I suppose one'll do you," he said, with mild irony.

I accepted it with a nod, and headed for number five.

Once inside, I examined my surroundings. The furnishings were pretty simple. Just a bed, two chairs, a chest of drawers, and a long mirror at the head of the bed. I began to undress, and as I did, I was conscious of a rising tide of panic. Perhaps I wouldn't be able to perform at all. I would disgrace myself. It would be all over the compound. Simon would be the first to know. I sat on the bed, in my underpants, feeling like a condemned criminal, waiting for the moment of reckoning.

In a little while, I heard footsteps and giggling, and the girls came over together. In the event, I needn't have worried. Berhane, despite being new to Signora Anna's, was superb. She may have sensed, with female intuition, that I was hopelessly inexperienced, so she guided me gently and authoritatively from one stage to the next. First she slipped effortlessly out of her *shamma*, revealing just a pair of very skimpy black knickers, and no bra. Her breasts were small and firm, her body perfectly proportioned. She slid down beside me on the bed, and turned me towards her, and gave me a long, wet kiss.

I was clutching the Durex foolishly in my right hand. Seeing it, she prised it loose from me, undid it, and reached down to put it on. To my great relief, I had an erection by this time of impressive dimensions. My only fear now was that I might go off too soon, if she fondled me for too long. She seemed to realise even this, though.

"Oh," she said teasingly, "you very big. Big and fierce. You like to come in to me quick?" And she drew my hand down between her legs, slipping off the knickers in one expert movement. I had not really explored this area of a girl before, and found it soft, wet and yielding. She moved herself against my hand, rhythmically.

"You like?" she said, dreamily.

"M'm," I nodded, almost afraid to speak.

"Okay, you come in. Come on. That's right. That's good. Yes."

And gently, smoothly, she guided me in.

It did not last long, but it was utterly satisfying, at least for me. As for Berhane, she did all the right things, wriggling and moaning, extracting the last bit of value out of me. I looked up, and there we were in the mirror, pressed together, brown against white. A shudder of pure joy passed through me. I looked down at her again.

"Oh Berhane," I said, gently. 'That was wonderful. Thank you. You are very kind, as well as very beautiful."

She looked up at me, and smiled.

"You like?" she said. "You like me?"

"I like you very much."

I lay down beside her, and stroked her cheek. She reached up and took my hand, and laid it against hers. She looked at the hands, side by side.

"White, black," she said. "*Nechh, tugur.*"

"*Nechh, tugur,*" I repeated, obediently. But the delicate hand beside mine was more golden brown.

"That is Amharic," she said. "You learn some Amharic?"

"Not yet," I said, "but I want to."

"I speak Amharic," she said, "Tigrinya. Little Italian, little English."

"Oh, your English is very good," I said gallantly.

"No no. Just little. But I learn. I want to learn. You teach me, perhaps?"

"Oh yes," I said. "But then you must teach me some Amharic."

She nodded, and smiled.

"Okay, I teach you. That was first lesson – *nechh, tugur.'*

As I lay there gazing at her, I became aware of sounds of heaving and groaning through the wall, which appeared to be quite thin. Simon, it seemed, was coming to a climax. There was giggling and squeaking from Frewet, and then a great roar, and silence. Berhane and I looked at each other. Then she grinned wickedly.

"Come on," she said. "We show them".

Slowly she began to bounce up and down on the bed. The springs began to rattle obligingly. Then she began to groan and shout. "Ooohhh. Aaahhhhh. Oh, yesss. Very gooood!"

I got the idea, and helped with the bouncing.

"Oh, oh," I shouted. 'Oh, Berhane, this is fantastic!"

We bounced faster and faster, and then ended with a combined shriek.

From the other side of the wall there was a stunned silence. Then an indignant shout from Simon.

"Hey, steady on in there. Some of us are trying to get some rest."

We collapsed in muffled laughter.

"Oh sorry," I called out. "I didn't realise these walls were so thin."

There was a confused grumbling from beyond. I lay again, looking into those deep eyes, in a swoon of various emotions. This is a remarkable girl, I told myself. I mustn't fall for her, though. That would be silly. She is very good at what she does, that's all. She has to do this sort of thing with a lot of people. She can't afford to get sentimental about the customers. And yet, she handled me so very well. That was a touch of genius, too, putting the great stud Blakeney in his place like that. Truly, an unusual girl.

Simon shouted through the wall again.

"Come on, stir yourself in there. We'd best be getting back."

"Righto," I called, and rolled off the bed.

Berhane even provided an after-sales service, bringing a bowl of water and a towel, and deftly removing the durex. I dressed quickly. Then I reached for my wallet, extracted a ten dollar bill, and pressed it gently into her hand. She glanced at it, and then kissed me, a little shyly, on the cheek, and slipped out the door ahead of me.

On the drive home Simon was somewhat pensive.

"You certainly seemed to enjoying yourself in there," he said after a while, a little grumpily.

"Oh yes, sorry about that," I said, airily. "She really is a fantastic girl, Berhane. That was a great experience. I'm most grateful for that, Simon. I really am."

He grinned, mollified.

"Yeah, she seems a good ride, all right, young Berhane. I think you've fallen on your feet there."

"But Frewet's obviously good fun as well," I said.

"Oh yes, she's grand, really. A very affectionate little thing. And she'll do anything you want."

"Oh yes?" I said.

"Oh yes. You must explore a few possibilities with Berhane next time."

"Yes, I must." I didn't ask him to expand on that.

We were driving through the Piazza.

"Well, you want any more excitement," said Simon, "or have you had enough for one night?"

I raised my hands in surrender.

"No, for God's sake. I need to get to bed. Are you seriously suggesting more?"

"Well, sometimes we stop off for a nightcap at the Ras Bar, for instance. But I agree, not tonight. We've got to face into the beginning of term tomorrow, after all."

"My God," I groaned. "I'd more or less forgotten about that."

"Yes, my lad," he said, with grim satisfaction. "On parade, bright and early, tomorrow morning, nine o'clock in the Assembly Hall."

The old Citroen got us home safely, and we parted quietly outside Simon's bungalow.

Later, I lay on my back in bed, staring at the ceiling, my senses tingling with the memories of the evening. I could still feel the pressure of that lean young body straining against me, and hear Berhane's delighted giggle as she played her trick on Simon. Even that, I thought, she did with consummate tact, covering up for my inadequacy. Truly, an unusual girl. I must not become involved with her, though. That would be silly. Very silly.

And so I dozed off.

CHAPTER EIGHT

The following morning reality sank in fast, as I awoke to the realisation that it was the first day of term. Tekla-Mariam had brought my morning tea and was pottering around, drawing the curtains, and rearranging my scattered clothes. I pulled myself up on my elbows, and gazed around me. I seemed to still discern a faint scent of Berhane, and glanced at Tekla-Mariam with a sudden pang of guilt, as if he might pick it up as well. But he gave no sign of any such suspicion.

"You take bath, *getoich* ?"

I raised a hand in assent, and he went into the bathroom and turned on the taps, causing the immersion heater to flare into life. Then he retired to his kitchen, to work on the breakfast.

I sank back on the pillow with a sigh, but then pulled myself together, and rolled out of bed. After a bath and shave, and a plate of Tekla-Mariam's scrambled eggs and toast, I felt somewhat more able to address the challenges of the morning, such as facing my first class. But Simon had been pretty reassuring about the kids being no problem – well behaved and generally keen to learn, or if they weren't that keen, as in the case of many of the Ethiopian aristocracy, at least polite about it.

First, however, there was School Assembly, at nine o'clock sharp. I left the bungalow a little before that, clutching a briefcase with what I hoped were all the books I would need, hoping to catch Simon on the way. Instead, I ran into Graham Wiggins himself, sweeping across the compound. He was kitted out this morning in a sweeping academic gown, with a bulging file under his arm, and looked every inch the headmaster.

Indeed, as I was to learn, this was for Graham one of the high points of the day. He greeted me briskly.

"Well, good morning, Luke, old chap. How are we feeling this morning? All ready to go, then?"

"Oh yes, I believe so," I replied brightly, successfully repressing the instinctual 'sir'.

"You're in good time, I see, anyhow. That's a promising start. Not like some I could mention. Seen young Blakeney since he got back?"

"Oh yes, actually. We were out together last night."

"Good grief! Been leading you astray already, has he?"

"Oh, I wouldn't go so far as to say that. Just a pleasant evening of dinner and chat."

This seemed to satisfy him. He grunted. We reached the door of the Administration Building together.

"Well, you go on in, then," he said. " You'll find most of your colleagues in there already, I hope. I just need to pop into the office for a moment."

And he dived down the corridor towards his office. I went forward into the assembly hall, where already a large number of students had gathered, with more flowing in all the time. There was a lively buzz, as friends greeted each other after the holidays. A number of enquiring faces turned in my direction. I looked for my colleagues, and saw Alan Lonsdale signalling to me from a group of them, drawn up at the front of the hall, near the podium from which Graham would shortly be addressing us.

I went over to join the group. I did not see Simon amongst them. Alan made the introductions, and I met a number of colleagues whose names I immediately forgot, and would have to recover later. Then the hall suddenly fell silent, as Graham swept regally up to his rostrum.

He set down his papers on the podium, and then paused for a moment, allowing his gaze to range over the assembled crowd, as the hush gradually prevailed throughout the hall. Then he spoke.

"Good morning all, and welcome to The English School for another academic year."

There was an answering murmur of 'Good morning, sir' from the assembled students. He beamed out at us confidently, stroking his moustache.

"I am sure that it is going to be another very good one, and it is you, both students and staff, who are going to make it so." Just as this point the door behind him opened furtively, and a rather bleary-looking Simon slid into the hall, and edged himself along the wall behind the rostrum until he joined the rest of us. If Graham was aware of this intrusion, he gave no sign. He was not going to have his beginning of the year speech disrupted by any such diversion. He carried on without a pause.

"As those of you who are returning will see, there have been a few changes. The gymnasium has had a much-needed coat of paint. The library has been reorganised, under the direction of Ato Girma, and I hope that you will all find it much easier to use. Remember that developing a habit of reading is one of the best helps towards your education that you can give yourselves. We have tried to provide a good selection of books in Amharic as well as in English, and I am most grateful to the British Council for helping us with the latter.

I would like to welcome to our midst a new member of the staff, Mr Luke La Touche, who comes to us directly from Oxford University, to fill the position left vacant by our much-loved colleague Mr John Davies, whose sad death while on holiday in Cyprus over Easter left such a gap in our senior English instruction. Mr La Touche will take over Mr Davies' classes with the Fourth, Fifth and Sixth, and he will also, since he himself read Classics at Oxford, offer Latin in the afternoons to anyone interested. I have already sent round a circular to parents announcing this, and some interest has been expressed. If any more of you want to avail of this opportunity, speak with your parents, and be sure to let me know without delay."

It was a shock to hear myself announced in this way. It brought home to me to an extent that had not quite sunk in up to now that all this wasn't just a game. I had a job. I was filling a position. And in just a few minutes I would have to start acting the role I had been put into. I liked the touch about 'straight from Oxford'. Graham was making the most of that. And fair enough, though I wondered how many of the multi-cultural audience looking up at him had actually ever heard of Oxford University.

The diversity of the school did present itself rather dramatically in a gathering such as this. As well as a strong representation of plainly Ethiopian faces, I could see Arabs, Indians (even a few Sikhs in turbans), dark Mediterranean faces, which could be Greek, Italian or

Armenian, a fair scattering of ruddy well-scrubbed British complexions, as well as others that looked clearly American (in that indefinable but unmistakable way that Americans look), and others again that seemed distinctively Slavic – I had heard that we had a number of Yugoslavs, in particular.

All these now were being summoned by Graham, at the end of his address, to join in a prayer and a hymn. He explained the position firmly for the benefit of new pupils, who might be unfamiliar with it.

"Now I would like to call upon you all to bow your heads briefly in prayer, and then we will sing a hymn together, to begin the school day. This may seem strange to some of you who are new, but I would remind you that this is an English school, and this is the way we do things here. I am not asking or expecting you all to conform to Christian practices, much less to those of the Church of England. By all means pray to whatever divinity you feel comfortable praying to. The main thing is to start the day by committing ourselves to the care of some power greater than ourselves, who will guide our thoughts and actions throughout the day. And I would ask you, out of courtesy, to join in the singing of the morning hymn, which today is 'All Things Bright and Beautiful'. You should all have a copy of it."

The students inspected and rustled papers all round the hall. Then Graham bowed his head, and uttered a brief prayer to his very British God, to which most of the company seemed to answer Amen. Only now did I notice that Isabel Wiggins was seated at the piano in the corner of the hall, ready to pound out the tune. Graham announced the hymn, and raised his voice in song. We joined in valiantly, and so – miraculously, it seemed to me – did at least a considerable majority of the hall. They seemed to like the idea, and in fact, I reflected, there is a lot to be said for starting the day with a good hymn, lustily belted out. The roof-beams seemed almost to vibrate as we ended – "the good Lord made them all."

We faculty stood around for a few minutes, allowing the students to filter out and find their classrooms. I went over to Simon.

"You're not exactly at your liveliest this morning, I should say," I remarked.

He grinned ruefully, and rubbed an eye.

"No, blast it, I'm not. Great way to begin the year! Had a little nightcap after I got home, and it didn't agree with me too well."

"My God," I said. "That was pushing things a bit, wasn't it?"

He groaned. "I suppose it was. I hope old Wiggers didn't notice me slipping in late."

"I wouldn't count on that," I said. "He doesn't miss much, I think."

"No, he doesn't, blast him."

Just at this moment, the man himself, who had been greeting some senior pupils, came over to us.

"Ah," he said, smiling blandly, "Good morning, Simon. Glad you could make it!" Simon bowed acknowledgement, rather shamefacedly. "You know where you're meant to be, I presume? I just want to introduce Luke to his classroom."

"Yes, Graham," said Simon, hastily, "I'd better be getting over there. See you later," he said to me, and sloped off.

"Well now," said Graham. "It's English with the Sixth to begin with, is it not?"

"That's right, sir. I think I have the right books for them."

In the stress of the moment, I forgot not to call Graham 'sir', but he let it pass. He was doubtless feeling at his most headmasterly this morning.

"Oh well, today will be just introductory, you know. Call the roll, try to memorise faces, and then talk a bit about the course, and how you plan to organise it. You know the sort of thing."

This, of course, was just the sort of thing I did not know, but I nodded bravely. Graham rooted amongst his papers, and produced the class list. I looked at it with apprehensive interest. There were just twelve names on it.

"You'll find them a nice lot, I think. A few jokers in the pack, but no one really troublesome or malicious. One fellow to look out for a bit is your friend Prince Yohannis' younger brother Tewodros. He's a bit of a lad. Will talk the hind leg of a donkey if given a chance. And there are two new people – one girl, who is actually, I believe, Irish, as I think I mentioned before, which should interest you, Fiona McHugh. Her father's over here with the U.N. Seems bright enough. And there's a lad from Yugoslavia, son of the new ambassador, Slavko Milosevic. He may have a bit of trouble mixing in, so keep an eye out for him."

We walked across the compound to a mud-walled, tin-roofed building, which housed a row of classrooms. It suddenly occurred to me, rather irreverently, that if each of the doors had a red fluorescent light above it, the building could easily be taken for one with quite another purpose.

Graham led me in, and presented me to the class, introducing me in much the same manner as he had in the assembly. It was a small room, and the desks were arranged in three rows of four, spaced at a distance from one another. Straight away I noticed, just in front of me, a dark, round-faced boy with a cheeky, self-confident expression, whom I guessed might be Yohannis' kid brother, and behind him, to my left, the figure of Fiona, smiling. Having introduced me, and having warned everyone to behave themselves, Graham swept out purposefully, his gown billowing behind him, and left me to it.

Facing one's first class cannot be very high up on anyone's list of favourite experiences. I looked out at the twelve pairs of eyes boring into me, and tried to get a grip on myself. Basically, I thought, they don't mean me any harm. They only want to size me up, and to be told what I want them to do. They want, if anything, to be taken in hand. So I looked out at them with all the confidence I could muster, and greeted them warmly.

"Good morning," I said. "My name is Luke La Touche, as the Headmaster has just said, and I'm here to teach you English. I hope that we'll get on well together. I would certainly like to. I would also like to be able to give you all the help I can. I must warn you, though, that I am rather new to this business, having just stopped being a student myself, and I may need a bit of help from all of you, especially at the beginning. At least I have not forgotten what it is to be a student, so I hope that I'll be reasonably sympathetic to your problems."

I hoped this was the right line to take, confessing my total inexperience. In the event, it seemed to be. Their expressions softened and lightened somewhat, and they seemed to relax.

"By way of starting, then, I think I will just call the roll, so that I can begin to get to know who you are."

I spread out the roll sheet. At first sight, it was a most interestingly varied group, covering most of the ethnic elements represented in the school as a whole. I began to go down the list.

"Mikias Assefa."

"Sir." A tall good looking Ethiopian answered me in a deep voice from one end of the front row. This was a good start. I greeted him.

"I hope I pronounced that correctly," I said.

"Yes, sir."

"Good. You must all correct me if I make mistakes."

I passed on. There was Iohannis Bisrat, another fine-looking Amhara; Gabriela Cocchinone, a rather glamorous Italian girl, who put me in mind of Alan's adventure of the previous year; a clean-cut American, David Crosson; another Ethiopian, Berhanu Gabrewold; a large and gloomy-looking Greek, Manolis Hadjidakis; then Fiona, who answered her name with a bright smile; then an Armenian boy, Vartan Malkhassian; then a Slavic-looking lad, the Yugoslav Ambassador's son, Slavko Milosevic, who looked, indeed, rather serious and lost; an Arab, Ahmed Osman; then came the cheeky-looking lad in the front row, who turned out to be, as I had suspected, Tewodros Tessema; and finally a charming-looking Indian girl, Margaret Shillong

They seemed a most interesting lot, as I looked out on them, trying to fix their identities in my consciousness. After the roll-call, I spent the rest of the class introducing them to the set books for the Overseas 'O' Level, which was what they were meant to be working towards. This year they were *Pride and Prejudice* and *Twelfth Night* – both entertaining enough, but each posing problems of interpretation for a very multi-ethnic audience in the middle of Africa. I set out my plans for doing grammar and syntax, and promised to distribute some detailed course plans when I could get them copied. Nobody said anything yet, but everybody watched me closely, and most took notes – everyone, indeed, except young Tewodros, who continued to survey me with arrogant curiosity, making no effort to write anything down.

At the end of my exposition, I asked for questions, hoping to stir up some audience participation. There was, as might be expected, a lengthy pause. Then suddenly Prince Tewodros put up his hand. I was unsure how to address him. It seemed absurd to say 'Your Highness' to this young twit.

"Yes?" I said.

"Sir," he said, in an almost perfect public school accent, "I wonder if you'd agree with me? I must say I'm surprised that London University couldn't come up with anything more suitable to this part of the world than *Pride and Prejudice*."

I laughed, and there was an answering titter from the class.

"Yes," I said, "that's a very reasonable complaint, I think. I suppose all one can say is that the world of Jane Austen is almost as strange to modern English schoolchildren as it is to all of you, but on the other hand her brilliant observation of that world is something that we can all respond to. Or I hope we can. I'll do my best to help in that, anyhow. Shakespeare as well, of course, is very alien in some ways, but I think one can relate to him as well, because of his superb powers of characterization, if we can get past the initial language barrier. Thank you for that point, Tewodros. Does anyone else have views on this?"

He had indeed started the ball rolling, if only because, as I suspected, he was not the most popular of figures. Various voices were raised in disagreement.

The large Greek, Manolis, raised a massive hand.

"No, sir, I do not agree with this complaint. It is important to study other cultures and other points of view. Otherwise, we are all stuck in our own particular culture."

"Yes," pitched in the American, David Crosson, "great literature is great literature. We've gotta relate to it, right? We can't always expect it to relate to us."

There were murmurs of assent from round the room.

"Right," I said. "These are important points. One of the things education should do is to take us out of our own time and place, and confront us with issues of timeless value. But we have to recognise that there will be problems of comprehension. One idea that occurs to me," I added, "is that it might be possible to get films of both these works from the British Council. I'll ask them, and then, if they can get them, we could have a showing some evening."

"Yes, that would be lovely," said one of the girls, the young Indian, Margaret Shillong, and again there was a general murmur of assent. Fiona, I noted, said nothing, but looked interested and amused.

"Okay," I said, "I'll see if I can fix that up. Now I think that's all we have time for this morning, but if you think of anything before tomorrow, we can discuss it at the beginning of the next class."

And with that I rose to leave. I had a free period then, which I was glad of, since I was feeling thoroughly talked out. I gathered up my books and papers, said that I looked forward to seeing them tomorrow, and glided out with as much dignity as I could muster.

I crossed the compound, feeling rather pleased with myself. That had not been too bad. At least we had broken the ice, thanks largely to his Highness's intervention. I felt better able to face the Fifth and Fourth after the break, especially with an extra bit of time to myself now. I was planning to extract some coffee from Tekla-Mariam, but a voice from behind me brought me up short. It was Alan Lonsdale, also making for home across the compound.

"Well, Luke, old man, how did that go, then?"

"Oh, not too bad, I think. They listened to what I had to say, anyhow."

"Oh yes, that's all they'll do at first. They're just sizing you up. They'll open up pretty soon. They're a lively, intelligent bunch in the Sixth." He waved a hand in the direction of his house. "Like a coffee, or are you busy?"

"Well, no," I said. "I was just thinking of that myself. But how are you fixed?"

"No trouble to me at all. Come along. There should be coffee waiting. There's not much time at the break, since we're really meant to do a little patrolling at that time."

So we went back to his place, and settled down in the living room, where indeed there were coffee and biscuits waiting.

"Well," said Alan. "What are your impressions? Did you come across Prince Tewodros, by the way?"

"I did indeed," I said. " In fact, I'm really quite grateful to him. He got a discussion going at the end of class by complaining about the irrelevance of a work like *Pride and Prejudice* to modern African reality. This provoked almost everyone else in the class to disagree with him. I got the impression that they might have done that no matter what he had said."

Alan laughed.

"Your impression would not be wrong," he said. "Prince Tewodros is generally regarded by his comrades as a bit of a pain in the arse."

"I imagine he's something of a handful, is he?"

"Like his big brother. Actually, he's good value. And he'll like you, of course, as one public school man to another."

"Oh?" I said. "How is he a public school man?"

"Well now, that's quite a story!"

And Alan proceeded to tell the saga of Prince Tewodros. His father being quite an Anglophile, Tewodros was sent off, like his elder brother, to Harrow, at the age of sixteen, to round off his education. Alas for his father's plans, however! Tewodros was discovered towards the end of the Winter Term of his first year *in flagrante delicto* with a barmaid in a local pub which was itself off-bounds to all but prefects and sixth-formers (one of whom had, indeed, discovered him), and was asked to leave. He spent the remainder of the spring pleasantly in Chelsea, sampling the various pleasures of London, and returned to Addis, in mild disgrace, to complete his studies, and ideally gain a few 'O' Levels, at The English School, joining the Fifth Form in time for the beginning of the Spring Term. Back home, his father limited his allowance severely, but left him enough to run a modest Jaguar sports car, keep a couple of polo ponies, and support at least one mistress, who could be seen from time to time on the Jan Hoy Meda, cheering him on during polo games.

"Well, well," I said, "I can see that that would be enough to set him off from his colleagues – or I suppose it would?"

"Bloody right it does," said Alan, with a laugh. "And he doesn't exert himself much to become popular. I remember him strolling up to me at the end of class one day last term as I was tidying up my stuff. He saw my watch still on top of the desk, and pointed to it. 'I wouldn't leave that behind there, sir, if I were you,'" says he. "Oh?" I said. "'No,'" he said, "'you can't trust these natives, you know.'" And I don't think he was having me on. As far as I could see he was quite serious. The gall of him!"

I laughed. "Lord," I said, "between young Tewodros himself and his big brother, I can foresee having a pretty lively time with that family."

"Well, let's hope it's not too lively," said Alan. "To change the subject slightly, though – sorry if I seem to be sticking my nose into your business, but it's all meant well, I assure you – you've been out on the town with old Simon, I think?"

"Yes," I said, a little cautiously. "We had a pleasant evening together yesterday."

"Well, I'm glad to hear that. But I do think I should warn you about Simon. He's a great lad, of course, and I like him a lot, but he does have a bit of a weakness for getting into scrapes, especially after he's had a few drinks. He's had a few fairly serious brushes with the police before this, and he's actually under threat of being sent to the provinces, or even of being sent home altogether, if he gets into any more trouble. It's just that he becomes a bit exuberant and argumentative after a few pints, and one thing seems to lead to another. And this is really not a country to do that in. I just mention this, not to put you off Simon completely – he's very good fun most of the time, after all – but so as you can be on your guard. Try not to get sucked into anything untoward."

"Right," I said, a trifle coolly. "Thanks for the word of warning."

It was becoming somewhat comical, I noted, how one was solemnly drawn aside, sooner or later, by almost everyone one met, and warned about almost everybody else, but I supposed that this was par for the course in any colonial environment.

I finished my coffee and rose to go, thanking Alan for his hospitality. Outside in the compound, the sun was hotting up, though it was not yet eleven. I strolled back to my quarters to dump my books, before facing into the break. Tekla-Mariam stuck his head out of the kitchen, and asked about lunch. He offered spaghetti or *Kedgeree*. After a little thought, I chose *Kedgeree*. Then the bell rang, and I wandered back across the compound to see what I should be doing.

Almost immediately bodies began to pour out of classroom doors, and the compound began to fill up with a babel of voices, speaking what seemed a representative sample of the world's known languages. Most seem to know each other, but quite a sprinkling of new kids stood around initially on their own, looking a little bewildered.

Graham emerged from his office and called me over to explain what I should be doing during the break, which was simply to patrol about, either alone or with another of the staff, to see that nothing got out of hand – no excessive horseplay, or smoking behind the classroom buildings, or anything of that sort – and to be available if any of the students wanted anything. One would not be expected to be on duty more than once or twice a week normally, it seemed, but he hadn't worked out a roster yet, and wanted everyone on hand for the first day or so anyway.

"Fine, sir," I said, "I'll just stroll about, then."

"Everything okay otherwise?"

"Oh yes, thanks," I replied. "Up to now, anyhow. I've only seen the Sixth so far, but I'll be seeing the others after the break".

"Jolly good," said Graham, in brisk, headmasterly fashion. "I'll leave you to carry on, then." And he headed for his bungalow.

I looked around, hoping to come upon Simon, and caught sight of his bluff and cheery form bearing down on me.

"Care for a stroll around the compound?" he said.

I nodded enthusiastically, and fell into step with him.

"How did it go, then?" And he eyed me ironically.

I told him about the class, and in particular about young Tewodros.

"Ah yes," he said, "they're a good bunch, even that cheeky young turd Tewodros. I think you'll enjoy them."

"I was thinking of inviting them to coffee in my bungalow once or twice a week during break," I said. "How do you think that would go down?"

He laughed. "I should say they'd be tickled pink," he said. "Old Wiggers might raise an eyebrow, though. It would have to be a day when you weren't on duty yourself, of course."

"Yes, though I suppose I could go in and out, if it came to that. It's more for them to have a special sixth form place to go and talk to each other. They don't really have that, do they?"

"No, they don't, I must say. That's not a bad idea. Increase their self-respect a bit. Good thinking, La Touche. You'll go far."

The rest of the morning passed off well enough. I introduced myself to my fifth and fourth year classes, took the rolls, talked about the books we would be reading, and gave them course plans. They watched me silently, and the more industrious took notes. For the moment, they were just a jumble of white, black and brown faces, frequently with tongue-twisters of names – and no doubt many with interesting histories. Time and circumstance would gradually sort them out.

By one o'clock I was more than ready for Tekla-Mariam's excellent *Kedgeree*, followed by fruit salad and Nyala Farm coffee, and by two o'clock I was stretched on my bed with the blinds drawn, observing the siesta.

The rains were not yet quite over, and just as lunch was ending the sun had vanished and ominous clouds had built up, bringing, in fact, a welcome degree of cooling. Now I lay contentedly on my back, staring at the *abujadid* ceiling whiffling gently in the breeze from the open window, and listening to the rain beating on the corrugated iron roof in a steady, soothing roar. I had now more or less seen what was in store for me, and I felt that I could handle it. I even came to the conclusion that it might all turn out to be rather fun.

I understood from Graham that in general I was not going to get much chance of a siesta, since Latin classes were going to be scheduled three days a week at two o'clock, just after lunch, if there were any takers, but this was not yet fixed up. I knew already that Fiona was one, but my impression was that Graham was hoping for one or two more, to make it worthwhile. I hoped that the rains would have tailed off, though, before we got down to anything serious, because in this sort of downpour communication would be quite difficult.

In fact, though, the rain did not last long at this time of the year. I must have dozed off, lulled by the downpour, because when I came to my senses again it was almost a quarter to four, the rain had stopped, and the sun was again beating down. Normally, I gathered, there would be games in the afternoon, and then another hour of classes or prep, but not today. I was just beginning to consider how I might occupy myself for the evening, when a loud knock came on the front door.

"Hey, La Touche," came Simon's voice through the door, "are you there? Are you conscious?"

Tekla-Mariam had gone home for the afternoon, so I swung myself off the bed rather blearily, and came to the door in my socks.

"Ah," said Simon, "there you are. Fancy going down to the Piazza for a beer?"

That sounded an excellent idea, and I said so. Simon waited, pacing around and picking books off the shelves, while I put on my shoes and jacket.

"Old Davies left you quite a nice collection of reading matter, I must say. Some good records too. I might borrow some of them some time, if you don't mind."

"Oh no, fine," I said. "He does have some good stuff, doesn't he?"

Simon didn't wish to bring the car into the centre of town, so we headed down the compound to the front gate, to catch a Millecento.

"By the way," said Simon, "did I hear you saying you'd like to get hold of a car?"

"Well yes, I was thinking about it. Is there any chance of picking up an old banger, though? I don't think I can afford anything else."

"I'll tell you why I mention it," said Simon, with a laugh. "It just occurred to me that about this time of the evening, in or around the Ras Bar, we just might come upon one of the greatest old crooks in Addis, who happens to be a good friend of mine, Signor Marco Benedetti. I think I mentioned him to you yesterday. He likes to take an early evening *arak* around this time, if business is not too heavy, so we might be lucky. If so, I can probably fit you up with an old car more or less on the spot – if you're sure you want one. You can drive, I suppose?"

"I've been driving for a few years now," I said.

"And you have a licence?"

"I have an Irish licence, for what that's worth."

"It'll do for a bit. You'll have to get an Ethiopian one, though, and that's the usual hassle – unless, of course," Simon added ironically, "you can get your cousin James to help."

We caught a Millecento without much delay, and as we drove in to the Piazza, Simon filled me in on his friend Marco. Marco ran a garage near the Piazza, where he marketed and repaired old and new Fiats – and other makes, at a pinch – and he had done this since well before the war. Prior to that, he allowed it to be known to his friends, he had spent some time in Chicago, during the Prohibition Era, engaged in some unspecified business, and had known a lot of interesting people, including Al Capone himself, but he had thought it advisable at a certain stage to leave in a hurry, and instead of going back to his native Naples, he had headed out here in the wake of the Italian occupation. Since he was a skilled mechanic, he had set up a garage, and had done well with it. He formed an alliance with an Ethiopian girl he had found in a *tej-bet*, and they now had five children – the oldest two sons were already able to help him in the shop. When the World War started, he was conscripted into the Italian army to repair lorries, and did that for a year or so, but when the Italians collapsed, he simply went back to his garage, and resumed trading. Despite a little unpleasantness just after the Liberation, he had continued there ever since.

"He's a genius with old cars," Simon concluded, "and if he likes you, he'll fix you up with something pretty good, for almost nothing – maybe a thousand dollars. And he'll let you pay by instalments."

This sounded fine. I calculated that I could put a few hundred down, then pay out about a hundred a month. Simon thought that should do.

We paid off the taxi outside the Ras Bar, and headed for an empty table on the verandah, overlooking the Piazza. A waiter hurried over to take our orders, greeting Simon by name.

"Ah, Wolde! Two beers, please – that's okay for you?" he looked over at me. I nodded. "Wolde, this is Mr Luke, a good friend of mine. He's just arrived here, but I'm sure you'll be seeing quite a lot of him in the future."

Wolde bowed. "You are very welcome, *getoich*," he said gravely. "I hope you will be very happy in our country". And he glided away to get the beers.

Simon leaned back luxuriously in his chair.

"This is really the best time of the day," he said, stretching. "You've just got rid of the little buggers for the moment, the whole evening is in front of you, and you can sit here for a while on the verandah of the Ras, sip a beer or a raki, and watch the world go by. And somebody or other interesting is almost bound to turn up. I'll keep an eye out for Marco."

Wolde returned with two ice-cold Melottis, and we settled in to them, while keeping an eye on the outside world.

It was not Marco who was the first to turn up, however, but a lugubrious and humorous Frenchman called Maurice Hugot. Simon pointed him out crossing the Piazza from Giannopoulos' bookstore, sidestepping the traffic in a dignified manner, a cigarette hanging out of the corner of his mouth.

"Hey, there's old Maurice. I haven't seen him in a couple of months. I think he headed for the Yemen at the beginning of the summer. He's crazy. You'll enjoy him. He's been checking out the bookstore. He's quite a literary type, in fact. Written a couple of novels himself, and some travel books. Not bad either, if your French is up to it. Mine's a bit rocky. I have one of the novels, though, and I'll lend it you if you like."

"Fine," I said, and watched Maurice ponderously ascend the front steps of the bar and lurch over to our table. He slumped down without preamble into a vacant chair, and looked first, balefully, at Simon and then, interrogatively, at me.

"Well, Maurice, you old dog," Simon greeted him. "How has life been treating you, then?"

"Ah, mon vieux, not too bad. I cannot complain. So you are back from your travels, hein? How are things? And who is your friend?"

Simon introduced me, and explained my situation and background, with various satirical details. Maurice's eyebrows wiggled.

"And what is this French name?" he said. "La Touche? That is most interesting."

'Well," I said, "that goes back a bit. My family are Huguenots. They left France at the end of the seventeenth century, and ended up in Ireland."

"Ah yes," said Maurice. "We behaved very badly to the Huguenots. It is great foolishness to fight about religion. But your family found Ireland agreeable?"

"Oh yes," I said. "They did pretty well there, on the whole."

"Ah, Ireland," he said, "the land of Joyce. For Joyce I have great admiration. And also Shaw, of course. But always you have to leave your country to become great. Perhaps you also? And do you know Samuel Beckett?"

Fortunately I had seen a production of *Waiting for Godot* before coming out, so I was able to tell him that.

"Ah yes," said Maurice, "that is indeed an excellent play, but also his novels are remarkable – *Molloy, Malone Meurt.* You have read them?"

"No," I had to confess, "I'm afraid I haven't."

"Ah, you must, you must. I do not know if they are translated. You can read a bit French, though?"

"Yes, I can, a bit," I said.

"Ah good, good. This savage Blakeney, he know no French. He could not even get himself a fuck if he come to Paris."

"That's a lie, Hugot, and you know it! And anyhow, all whores speak English."

Maurice shook his head lugubriously.

"No, not the French whores. No, no, you will be stuck, Blakeney. You will have to play with yourself."

At this point, however, Wolde returned, and Maurice ordered a pastis.

"Well, anyway," said Simon, changing the subject, "how was the Yemen? That was where you were headed when I last saw you, I think."

"Oh, the Yemen!" Maurice rolled his eyes to heaven. "That is truly a crazy place. The Yemen makes Ethiopia seem absolutely normal."

He proceeded to expand on this in most amusing terms. He had dined and engaged in disputations with sheikhs and mullahs. He had ridden a camel all the way to the Saudi border. He had even been kidnapped by bandits, but had persuaded them in broken Arabic that he was just a penniless pilgrim and a good Muslim, and they entertained him royally for three days before letting him go. We did not know how much to believe, but it hardly mattered. He was in the process of writing it up for a French magazine.

Maurice finished his pastis with a flourish and looked out across the square. His gaze fixed on something unwelcome and he frowned.

"Ah," he said, "merde! I will leave you, I think. There is your friend Hirschhorn coming to join you. I am allergic to that fellow." He glanced at Simon as he rose to go. "I will see you at Anna's perhaps, before too long?"

"Oh yeah," said Simon. "I'll give you a ring."

"And so, I bid you au revoir, Monsieur La Touche. I am sure we will meet again soon."

And he slipped gloomily away, avoiding a breezy and boisterous, distinctly American-looking figure, who was making his way to us across the square, waving enthusiastically.

Jack Hirschhorn (the 'Jack', as it turned out, did not represent John, but was short for Jackson) was a member of the recently formed U.S. Peace Corps, and a graduate of Yale. He bounded up the steps, slapped Simon on the back, expressed himself delighted to meet me, slumped down into a vacant chair, and called for a beer from Wolde. Jack was very much of an activist, as I rapidly discovered, with a propensity for enrolling one in projects of his own devising. At the moment, it emerged, he was trying to organise a modern jazz group, to play gigs in a number of Addis night clubs.

Simon incautiously asked him what he was up to these days, and the response was a detailed description of this latest scheme of his. When he asked if either of us played an instrument, I, even more incautiously, admitted that I had played the trumpet in a group at school (though rather more Swing than strictly Modern), and that was enough for Hirschhorn to engage me for a work-out at his place that very Wednesday. I was unable to think of any good reason to refuse. Simon intervened.

"Come on, Jack, for Christ's sake, give the lad a break. He's only just got here. He doesn't know what he's getting into."

"Oh now, Simon, don't be like that! I'm not pressurising you, am I, Luke? You just come along on Wednesday and see how you like it. I can get hold of a horn for you. It'll be cool. You'll see."

"Well," I said, cautiously, "just bear in mind that I'm bound to be a bit out of practice."

This was waved aside.

"No problem, no problem! We'll soon lick you into shape."

After some further chat, Hirschhorn downed his beer and rushed off about his business, having given me his address and phone number, and giving instructions how to get to him. He urged Simon to come along as well.

"Oh hell," grumbled Simon, after he had gone, "maybe I will. He's pretty good value, old Jack, if you can keep him under some sort of control. Things tend to happen round him. Do you really play the trumpet, anyhow? There's no end to your accomplishments, it seems!"

"Well, I used to," I said. "But I'm sure I'm pretty bad by now. Your lip tends to go, for one thing, if you don't keep practising, which I haven't been. We had a little group at school. I hardly played at all at College. So I'll probably disgrace myself in the work-out, and get out of things that way."

Simon now decided that we were not going to come upon Marco this particular evening by sitting in the Ras Bar.

"The bugger must be working late. We'd better go round to the garage, and see if we find him. It's just up the back of the Piazza, in fact."

So we paid for our drinks, and headed across the square, and into a maze of little streets to the west of it. After five minutes we emerged into an open space (one could hardly call it a square), along one side of which there was a complex of rather dilapidated sheds, and a lot full of cars. Over the entrance to the car lot was a rusty and battered sign proclaiming Benedetti Motors. And sure enough, in the recesses of one of the larger sheds, deep in consultation with one of his native mechanics, was a large, burly, villainous-looking figure which turned out to be Marco Benedetti himself.

'Ah, Signor Simon," he beamed, flashing a number of gold teeth, "how are things? What can I do for you today?"

Simon shook his outstretched hand, submitted to an embrace, and then introduced me. "Actually, Marco, I've come round on behalf of

132

my friend Signor La Touche here. He's just arrived in Addis, and he's looking for a nice, inexpensive old car to run around in. Something for around a thousand dollars, maybe. I told him you were just the man to fix him up."

"Oh yeah," said Marco, in a fascinating Neapolitan Chicago drawl, "you betcha. You come to the right place. I fix you up with something real nice. Any friend of Signor Simon is a friend of mine."

He gave some final orders in Amharic to his assistant, and we walked across to the lot.

Marco surveyed his holdings reflectively, scratching his week's growth of beard.

"Now let me see what I have you like to look at," he said. "Simon say about a thousand bucks. Well, I think there is no too much problem." He led us over to a rather elderly silver-grey Fiat Millecento, and patted it on the hood. "Now this car just come in recently, from a fella he had to leave the country. Is old, but not too bad the mileage. Is good condition. I do still a few little things to it, I can let you have it Wednesday. Okay? I guarantee everything six months."

Simon prodded a tyre with his foot, peered in the driver's window, and walked round it.

"I can't see too much wrong with that," he said. "You give it your special gas-saver treatment, Marco?"

"Oh yeah, I fix it up good."

Simon turned to me. "Marco's developed this great gizmo for saving on petrol. He tunes it so it's sucking in a much higher proportion than normal of air to petrol. Gets you about fifty miles to the gallon, which is quite a saving. Only problem is a bit of loss of power. Not too good going up the hills, eh Marco? But it gets there in the end."

Marco beamed proprietorially.

"Yes, I look for patent for this world-wide. Meanwhile, is special to all my customers."

I was fascinated.

"Well, I'll take it," I said. "Would you like a deposit now, Signor Benedetti?"

Marco patted me on the arm.

"You just call me Marco," he said. "No, no deposit. You are friend of Signor Simon. You pay me Wednesday, when you take her away."

"Oh" said Simon, "another thing, Marco. Signor Luke has not got much ready money. He was wondering if he could pay you in a few instalments."

Marco waved a hand. "Is no problem. We fix up on Wednesday. However you like. We fix it then."

So we shook hands on that. Simon asked after the wife and family, and the state of business, and we strolled back towards the Piazza.

"Well, thanks for that," I said. "I presume Marco can be relied on."

"Ah yes, you needn't worry about that," said Simon. "Marco's an old bandit in many ways, but he looks after his friends. The old banger will go, and if it doesn't he'll fix it. I wouldn't go on a trans-African safari in it, but it'll get you round Addis, and down to Bishoftu or the Awash – that sort of thing."

We got a Millecento back to the school compound, and on the way Simon told me some more of Marco's story. When the Italian army collapsed in face of the onset of the British expeditionary force, Marco – like many old-time Italian settlers – declined to leave with the troops. He was a little nervous though, as the Fascists had committed some pretty nasty atrocities, not least in Addis itself. Anyhow, when the day of liberation arrived, and the Emperor was led back into his capital, Marco, like the rest of the Italian community, stayed home and lay low. To his alarm, though, about the middle of the morning, he heard a commotion outside his front gate, and looked out to see his foreman and all his workers marching up the path to his bungalow, armed to the teeth with old rifles and spears, and looking very fierce.

His foreman knocked on the door, and Marco went out to face him, feeling that his end had surely come. But his foreman saluted solemnly and said.

"*Getoich*, it is not safe for you today. We have come to protect you."

And his whole workforce formed up in the front garden and guarded him for the rest of the day. After that life continued as usual.

I liked that story. There was something vaguely Irish about it.

We parted in the middle of the compound, feeling that an early night was indicated. Back home, Tekla-Mariam was waiting with a tasty roast hen, the bird I had cancelled the previous evening. But he also presented me, reverently, with an ornate envelope, on which, with a flutter of anxiety, I recognised a familiar monogram and hand.

It was a note from Yohannis, brief and to the point.

> *Luke – I am having a little party on Saturday night, around*
> *nine onwards. There are a few people coming that I thought you*
> *would like to meet. I very much hope you can come. Give me a*
> *ring as soon as you can to confirm.*
> *Cheerio, Yohannis.*
> *PS If you would like to bring a friend, please do so, if you think*
> *I will like him (or her!)*

Well, hell, I thought, that's that. This is an offer I really can't refuse. I'll see if I can't drag Simon along, since Yohannis makes the offer. It'll be good to see him again, this time in his own environment.

CHAPTER NINE

The first week of term passed in something of a blur. A great deal happened, but I was mainly preoccupied by the new routine. Not that my duties were very arduous – just the three senior English classes in the mornings, and some supervision of breaks, lunch, games or prep – but it kept me busy. I launched the Sixth on *Pride and Prejudice*, introduced the others to their readers and grammars, and got them all started on writing essays.

On Tuesday afternoon, almost as good as Graham's word, my telephone was reconnected, and I was able to phone Yohannis' number to accept his invitation for Saturday. Once again, I got his secretary, His Highness being out, but he was most charming, and recorded my acceptance, and my intention probably to bring a friend (assuming that I could rope in Simon). That evening I also phoned Cousin James, to let him know that I now had a phone – and, if the truth be told, to see if I might scrounge Sunday lunch or dinner. In this I was successful, though I had to fudge a bit as to what I was doing on Saturday. An invitation to dinner with colleagues was my explanation, and that fortunately satisfied him. I was simply not prepared to go over the issue of Yohannis again. I was resolved to go my own way on that. In the event, I was invited to church, a walk on Entotto, and lunch. I accepted with thanks, hoping that I would be in reasonable shape on Sunday morning, when I would be collected at half past nine.

On Wednesday my duties were added to, and my chance of a siesta destroyed, by the inauguration of the Latin class, which was to be held three times a week, on Mondays, Wednesdays and Fridays. The oddly matched pair of Fiona and Prince Tewodros assembled in the sitting room of my bungalow (I had decided to hold the classes there) at two o'clock, just after lunch, and I launched them on the mysteries of the Latin language. Right from the outset it became apparent that Tewodros was not going to be the easiest man to teach. He was much more interested in discoursing himself on things that concerned him, or that he knew something about. In trying to explain the relation of Latin to various modern languages, I was incautious enough to make a comparison between the relation between it and the Romance languages and *Ge'ez* with Amharic. Tewodros reacted with interest. Did I know any *Ge'ez*, he enquired first. I had to confess that I didn't, but that I was reporting what I had been told.

That resulted in a disquisition from Tewodros on the nature of the *Ge'ez* language, and its connexion, or alternatively non-connexion, with the various modern languages of Ethiopia. This was all very interesting, but could have gone on indefinitely. I tactfully directed his Highness's attention back to Latin, by turning to look at the book that we were faced with, something called *Latin for Today*, of which some copies had been obtained through the British Council.

Fiona listened to all this with quiet amusement. As it turned out, she was well prepared for Latin, as she had done quite a bit of French in her various schools, and also knew Italian pretty well, having gone to school in Rome for a couple of years, while her father had been posted to FAO headquarters there.

"That's great," I said. "I think you'll find both that Latin is not too difficult after Italian, and that it's interesting to see the reasons for the connections between Italian and French."

We established the general characteristics of the language, and looked at the first exercise, by the end of the hour, despite a few other attempted diversions from Tewodros, and my odd little class dismissed, leaving me somewhat unsettled.

I was distracted, though, shortly after four o'clock, by Simon calling to collect me, to go downtown and collect the car. We caught a Millecento to the Piazza, and walked up to Benedetti Motors. In fact, Marco was as good as his word, if not better. He seemed even to have given the old banger a lick of paint in the interval, and he had attended to all such matters as oil and water, brakes and lights. The Fiat was standing proudly in the middle of the lot, surrounded by a wild assortment of vehicles in every stage of dilapidation, and looking very well.

By arrangement, I paid Marco two hundred dollars down, with

further instalments of a hundred to follow for the next eight months. She was taxed till the end of the year, and he had spoken to an Armenian friend of his who would give me insurance at a reasonable rate. My driving licence was good for three months, which gave me easily enough time to get round even the most recalcitrant Ethiopian bureaucracy.

We shook hands on the deal. Marco handed me the keys, and a tax book. I climbed into the driver's seat, and Simon into the passenger seat. Marco leaned in the window and showed me the gears and other controls. Cautiously, I inserted the key into the ignition and turned. She started up like a bird.

"Ebbene," said Marco, "she go just fine now. But anything go wrong, you bring her right back, okay?"

I promised to do that, and with a final pat on the hood, Marco stepped back to watch me take off. I reversed carefully round the yard, and faced the front gate. With a final wave, Marco headed back to his workshop, and I crept shakily forward to the public road.

"Okay," said Simon. "Where shall we head for?"

"Oh God," I said, "I just want to get back to the compound."

"Hey now," protested Simon, "you can't do that. That's not the right attitude at all. We've got to go and celebrate this great new car. Let's at least head out to Anna's for a celebratory drink, just to baptise it!"

I groaned.

"You're trying to destroy me, Blakeney! I need to get used to this thing first. Anyhow, I don't know the way."

But Simon was not to be diverted from his purpose. He directed me firmly, first right, then right again, and so out of the city by the road we had gone on Sunday evening. I gripped the wheel in a state of frozen panic, as Simon urged me past donkeys, herds of goats, and elderly dignitaries with umbrellas, out into the country, until the welcoming archway of La Bella Napoli came into view, in the midst of its eucalyptus grove.

"Okay," I said, " one celebratory drink, but nothing else. I'm really not up to it."

'Fair enough," said Simon, grinning. "We'll just show Anna the car, and maybe she'll stand us a drink. I wouldn't count on it, though – tight-fisted old broad!"

In the event, he was right. Signora Anna was very pleased, if slightly surprised, to see us – early, and in the middle of the week, and she was pleased to inspect and admire the car, but she did not offer to stand us a drink.

"That is good you get a car from Marco," she told me. "He look after you good. If he say she go, she go."

So we ordered beers, and went out to sit under the wisteria in the courtyard to enjoy them, as the sun was still hot. The beers were delivered by Berhane, who also seemed pleased to see me. When she had set down the beers, she looked at me with a slightly shy smile.

"You boys like to come out the back with us after?"

I began to demur, much though the thought of Berhane's body stirred me, being quite determined on returning safely to the compound, and getting some corrections done.

"I don't think so today, Berhane, thanks. We're a bit in a hurry at the moment. Maybe on Friday, though? How about that?"

Her face fell, and she looked down at the ground.

"Friday not so good," she said. "Friday may be very busy. I don't know."

It occurred to me then, as it should have before, that after all Berhane was not at my disposal. She had a living to earn, and no doubt other admirers to deal with, and Friday might indeed be a busy evening. It was not a thought that pleased me, but I had to accept it. I looked over at Simon, who was grinning wickedly.

"Oh hell," I said, "I see her point. Friday must be the rush hour in this business. I suppose we could take a little while?"

"Okay with me," said Simon, cheerfully. He looked at Berhane. "Is Frewet around?"

She smiled sweetly. "Yes, Frewet is here. I will get her. You come over when you ready."

So we finished our beers in a state of anticipation , and in the event we had another delightful session. This time the girls chose rooms some way separate from each other, so there was no opportunity for competitive groaning. After I came, she caught me expertly in her *shamma*, and lay with me for a while, stroking my hair and saying a few things to me softly in Amharic. I kissed her on the forehead and the eyes, and ran an appreciative finger down her flank.

139

"I don't understand a word you're saying," I said, "but I really like the sound of it. You must teach me."

"Yes, but you teach me too. I want to speak English good. For example, you tell me what's a nice word for what we do now? I don't like 'fuck-fuck'. Is a dirty word."

"Yes, it is, isn't it," I said, "I don't like it either. It's a nasty, rough word. We could say 'make love'. We were making love."

"'Making love!'". She rolled it round her tongue. "I like that. I like to make love. We make love."

"Yes". I stroked her cheek. "We make love."

I really must not become attached to this girl, I thought. She does not belong to me, and I don't really want to acquire her, even if I could. I began to feel like one of those fatuous young men in Greek New Comedy, madly in love with a courtesan, and bent on milking his old father for all he was worth to support his obsession, having, perhaps, to steal or bamboozle his beloved away from the grip of some Braggart Soldier or other pest. I might very well find, I reflected, that I was having to compete with precisely such a person – soldier, policeman, or government official, as it might be. I would have to watch my step.

We tidied ourselves up, dressed, and went to rouse Simon and Frewet. I tactfully slipped ten dollars into Berhane's hand, and kissed it. She kissed me back demurely on the cheek. When her knock on the door was not acknowledged, she boldly opened it and stuck her head in. I caught just a glimpse of Frewet's chubby bottom up in the air above Simon, before Simon roared gruffly to Berhane to bugger off, and they'd be through in a moment.

I went back to sit under the pergola, and reflect in a contented daze on the events of the day. Berhane offered me another beer, but I prudently declined, and chose a coke instead.

In due course, Simon emerged, complaining about the cheek of Berhane, but looking pretty pleased with himself. We paid for the drinks, and set off on the return journey. As we drove back into town, though, I suddenly remembered, with a shock, that we had an engagement with Jack Hirschhorn, and we were already a little late.

"Oh God," groaned Simon, "I've actually had enough. You really do get yourself talked into things, don't you? I don't think I can face old Jack this evening. We'd better drop in on him, though, or we'll be very bad news. Let's just tell him we're shagged out, and you'll join in next Wednesday, or whenever, okay?"

"That's fine with me," I said. "I've certainly had enough action for one day."

So Simon directed me to Jack's bungalow, a pleasant modern building out on the airport road, which he shared, he had told me, with another Peace Corps volunteer called Chuck, who played the drums. When we arrived, there was already music sounding from the open window of the front room, so we stepped right in.

"Hey," shouted Jack, "where you guys been? We started without you! Let me introduce the group."

And he did, before we could get a word in. Apart from himself on tenor sax, he had Chuck on the drums, a guitarist called Mervin, and a young Ethiopian called Haile Mariam, whom they were training as a bass player. What they badly needed, Jack emphasised, was a trumpeter. And now, from behind the sofa, he produced a gleaming trumpet – courtesy, he announced, of the US Information Service. I was stuck. Simon groaned.

"Look, Jack," he said, "we're wrecked today. We've just been buying this car from Marco for Luke, and then we took it out for a spin to the Bella Napoli ... "

"Oh yeah," said Jack derisively, "and then you had to have a few little drinks, and then a little fuck-fuck, and now you're too tired to do what you were meant to be doing in the first place."

"Okay, okay," said Simon, raising his hands in surrender. "Let's do one number, anyhow. Let's just see if this man can play the trumpet at all. I don't believe he can."

This put me on my mettle. I was not going to be trifled with by Blakeney. I reached out for the trumpet, and put it tentatively to my lips.

"I haven't actually played in a while," I warned. "My lip's not in very good shape."

Jack waved a tolerant hand.

"No problem. Take it nice and easy at first," he said.

I blew, and to my relief produced a clear middle C. Then I ran up and down a few scales.

"Well," I said, "what do you play?"

"Whaddya know?"

I thought. As a trumpeter, though I had, as I say, played mainly Swing, I was a humble admirer of Miles Davis and the cool tradition.

"Does anyone know, say, 'Round Midnight'?" I said, "or 'Straight, No Chaser'? Or maybe 'My Funny Valentine'?"

They looked suitably impressed. Simon looked nonplussed.

"Hey, man," said Chuck. "That's cool. Think you can do one o' those?"

I nodded.

"I could give 'em a go, anyhow."

"Okay," said Jack, "Let's try 'Round Midnight'. Everyone happy with that?"

They nodded. So we launched into that Thelonious Monk favourite. Jack led off after the riff, then Mervin on the guitar, and then I came in. To my relief, I found I could do more or less what I had in my head. I hadn't forgotten too much.

The truth was, I had always wanted to be a trumpeter. It was a way of escaping, at parties, from the weary struggle of trying to get girls to accept you for a dance. If one could get up and join in with the band for a few numbers, I found they came up to you of their own accord. There is something about a musician that attracts girls. But over and above that, I loved to lose myself in the music, to get inside the music and blow my way out of it. That is something you can do with jazz, and not with anything else that I know of. Now I threw in a few Davis-like special effects, and handed over to Chuck for a solo. Young Haile Mariam hung in there bravely. He was certainly talented. All in all, we actually sounded pretty good.

"Okay, that's it," said Simon, when we had finished. "I give in. The bugger can play the trumpet. But now I want to go home."

So did I, though this experience had revived me somewhat. But on the other hand I was glad to quit while I was ahead. As for Jack, he was ecstatic. He had his group. He didn't want to let me go, but he yielded, on the promise that I would come next Wednesday for a proper rehearsal. He wanted us in the Club Paradiso the following Friday and Saturday. I had to make clear to him that I couldn't commit myself for weekend after weekend, but that didn't bother him. He just wanted me to come when I was free. On those terms, then, I accepted, and Simon dragged me away.

As we drove up towards the Piazza, Simon shook his head with grudging respect.

"Well, La Touche, you are a bundle of surprises, and no mistake. I would never have thought you could do that. You are definitely one weird Paddy. You got any other tricks up your sleeve?"

I grinned.

"No," I said, "that is about it, I think. That's about my only trick, after all, and I'm not very good at it. Just enough to enjoy myself a bit."

He grunted discontentedly.

Happily, we made it back to The English School compound without anything worse than the near miss of a native dog on Haile Selassie Avenue, and I parked the Fiat round at the rear of my bungalow.

As I parted from Simon, however, I just remembered Yohannis' postscript invitation.

"Oh, by the way," I said. "I forgot to mention this earlier, but I wonder if you'd be interested in coming along to a party of Prince Yohannis' on Saturday. He's asked me if I'd like to bring a friend – if I thought he would like the friend!"

"Hah," said Simon, "you swanky bugger! You got a royal invitation already, have you? Well, thanks for the thought. I think I wouldn't mind coming along – though I don't know if it'll be exactly my scene. And how do you know he'll like me?"

"I don't," I said. "It depends on how you behave. But I'll take a chance on it."

Simon poked me in the stomach.

"Now don't get above yourself, La Touche. Just because you're a car owner, because you've got laid, because you can play the trumpet, and because you're a friend of royalty – just don't get above yourself! See you tomorrow." And he swaggered off across the compound. I turned and went in to see what Tekla-Mariam had prepared for me.

That evening after dinner, Isabel called to the door, to relay an invitation from her parents to spend a weekend at Nyala Farm. I excused myself for the coming weekend, but wondered if I might accept for the following one, and she was quite sure that that would be fine.

"Even better, in fact," she said. "The rains will be well over, and everything is at its best. Did I see you coming in with a car this evening, by the way?"

"Yes," I said. "I managed to pick up an old Fiat, with Simon's help. It seems fine."

"Well, if you feel safe driving it, you can drive yourself out. It's only about thirty miles out of town. But it's a pretty rough road. It might be better to come with us in the Landrover this time. We'll be going out anyway."

"Well," I said, "if you don't mind, I would prefer that, at least the first time. I'm not *that* confident about the capacities of my car. It's said not to be very good going up hills."

"No, that's perfectly fine," she said. "I think you're wise." Then another thought occurred to her. "By the way, do you know that it's Maskal on Friday – that's their New Year festival here? The school has a free day, and we usually go up to the Jan Hoy Meda to watch the festivities. It's all quite colourful, if you'd like to join us for that."

I was intrigued. 'That'd be great," I said. "I'd love that."

"Right then. Graham can confirm that with you tomorrow."

Isabel wished me good night, and strode back purposefully to the headmaster's bungalow. I watched her go with a feeling of affection. There was something comfortable and eminently sensible about Isabel, born, no doubt, of having to make do all her life with the easy-going chaos of a colonial existence.

Thursday at break Graham caught me in the compound, and called me over to his office. I thought that perhaps it concerned arrangements for the next afternoon, but in fact it was something else. The Russians had returned, and wondered if I would be interested in tutoring them.

They were standing rather awkwardly in the office. Graham introduced me, and read their names to me off the cards that they had handed him. One, a pleasant-looking broad-faced man, was called Safar Abdolov, and turned out to be the Director of the Soviet Information Centre. The other, younger, sharper-faced one was a construction engineer seconded to some project near the capital which the Russians were financing, who needed to brush up his English before getting down to his job.

I had never met any live Russians before, and I was most interested to do so. I said that I would be glad to take them on, and offered them a cup of coffee in the bungalow, since I had a free period after the break.

They accepted gratefully, and I took them off Graham's hands, to his palpable relief.

"Well, that's fine, then," he said, rubbing his hands. "Mr La Touche will look after you. I'm sure he'll be just what you need." He shook hands with each of them, and they thanked him warmly.

"Oh by the way," he said to me as I was leaving, "Isabel was saying you'd like to come up with us to Maskal. We'll be going up about three in the afternoon, so we can come and collect you. Things don't really get going till the early evening, but it's good to get there early."

I thanked him, and led my charges across the compound.

Tekla-Mariam was somewhat taken aback to find three for coffee, but he rose to the occasion, with coffee and a selection of biscuits. I established my guests on the sofa, and sat down to face them. Safar Abdolov did most of the talking.

They would like help, he explained, with English conversation and reading. It was always difficult to understand the idioms. The engineer, whose name was Yuri Alexeivich Prigogine, was worried about communicating with his Ethiopian colleagues on the project. He had studied English in a special school in Moscow, but he was still rather nervous about it. Abdolov himself was plainly much more comfortable with English, but wanted to read some literature under supervision. He came across as a bit of an operator, but I found myself warming to him. He seemed an outgoing and cheerful character. He suggested that perhaps we might begin by taking issues of The Ethiopian Herald, the local English-language newspaper, and going through that for suitable material.

I complimented Comrade Abdolov on his English, which was actually very good. We fixed up a weekly lesson for Tuesdays at five o'clock, which would cut into my drinking time, but would be no harm at all for just that reason. We agreed on a fee of ten dollars an hour per head, which I recalled was just what I gave to Berhane for a rather shorter but more intense session, and parted with the warmest expressions of regard.

Also that day I made the acquaintance of George and Teresa Barnes. They were another pleasant, youngish couple, of very much the same background and nature as the Lonsdales, except that George was larger, slower, and more staid than Alan Lonsdale – not at all the sort of man, I reflected, to commit any indiscretion with a student, however beautiful. George taught Science and Maths, and Teresa helped to look after the very junior ones. It was they with whom Simon had been on safari in the North just before term began.

Once again, as I had come to expect, I was in receipt of gentle warnings, especially in respect of Simon.

"A grand chap," George emphasised, "a grand chap, but you've got to watch him. You've got to know what your own limits are, and stick to them." George looked like a man who knew what his limits were, and stuck to them. Teresa nodded in support. I tried to look suitably concerned and responsible.

"Ethiopians like to have us foreigners around, so long as we're useful and behave ourselves, but basically they don't much like foreigners. They're an old and proud people, you know, and they don't forget that. They'd much prefer to be able to do everything for themselves. So if you're not being useful, or not behaving yourself, you're out – or worse!" And he looked ominous.

"Oh?" I said.

"Oh yes," said George. "Fellows have been known to disappear altogether. No British, I must say, that I know of, but Indians, y'know, and even Scandinavians. Probably in some prison camp down in Gamu Gofa, if they're alive at all. No, this is a great country if you behave yourself, and mind your own business, but it's got a dark side to it, mark my words."

George and Teresa had been out five years now, and ranked almost as old-timers. They seemed to be enthusiastic travellers, and had covered most of the country, except for Gamu Gofa and the area down towards the southern Sudan, which was really out of bounds to foreigners, it seemed. They'd also been down to Kenya and Tanganyika on two summers, to escape from the Rains. They had a sturdy old Landrover, which preserved the marks of its many journeys. George issued a firm invitation to come out with them on their next weekend expedition. My weekends were beginning to fill up.

CHAPTER TEN

Friday was the Maskal holiday, so I decided to lie on in bed for a bit. Tekla-Mariam obligingly served me breakfast there, and I propped myself up with Ullendorf's *The Ethiopians*. Out of curiosity, I looked up what he had to say about Maskal, and found the following:

> There is a prodigious number of feasts in the Abyssinian Church... The New Year and Maskal feasts display distinct Hebraic affinities. The dates, 11 and 23 September respectively, corresponding clearly to the Hebrew season of the yamim nora'im. With the introduction of Christianity it became necessary to transform the celebration of the New Year into a Christian feast – without undue interference with the religious practices then in vogue – and in this way the Christian feast of Keddus Johannes, St. John the Baptist, was superimposed on the ancient Judaic structure.
>
> Maskal, the feast of the finding of the True Cross, appears to have received its Christian sanction at the end of the fourteenth century, but the pagan and Hebraic rites associated with it point to a more ancient and more complex origin. The earliest meaning of these feasts – as was also the case in Israel – was no doubt seasonal: the month of Maskaram (= September) marked the end of the rains, the resumption of work, and the reopening of communications.

This was all most interesting in its way, and yet frustratingly uninformative as to what I might expect that evening. I became absorbed in the book, however, and was only recalled to reality by a loud knock on the front door around eleven o'clock. Tekla-Mariam was pottering in the kitchen, and opened the door to Simon, who had come over to see if he could scrounge some coffee. I set Tekla-Mariam to working on that, and then climbed out of bed and got dressed, as Simon harangued me from the sitting room.

"I forgot today was Maskal, when we were thinking of calling out to Anna's for the evening," he shouted. "But it's okay, she'll be open as usual. It just might be a bit crowded."

"Well, actually," I said apologetically, "I think I'm probably going to be tied up. I accepted an invitation from the Wigginses to come up with them to watch the Maskal celebrations. Do you know anything about Maskal, what goes on?"

"Oh, shit, I don't know," said Simon, a trifle petulantly, "I've never bothered with it. It's just a colossal piss-up, as far as I know. A lot of dancing and singing, and I think the Emperor lights a bonfire, and then all hell breaks loose."

I came out and joined him in the living-room for coffee.

"I suppose if they're bringing the kids they won't want to stay very late," I said, tentatively. "Maybe I'd be able to slip away afterwards and join you."

"Well, I wouldn't count on it," said Simon. "I think you've got a nice family evening on your hands. No, I'm going out for a nice gloomy Gallic booze-up with Hugot and whoever else turns up. Discuss the state of the world and that sort of thing. We may take in Anna's, but I think it'll be rather too crowded. It'll probably be more of a pub-crawl. We might drop in this night-club that Jack Hirschhorn claims to have a gig in. That could be amusing. By the way, that was pretty impressive on Wednesday night. Jack was really fired up. You'll never get rid of him now."

"Well," I said, "I've always wanted to play modern jazz, though, if I ever had the opportunity."

Simon chortled malevolently.

"Well, you're fookin' well going to get the opportunity now," he said in his broadest Yorkshire. "Ol' Jack's got his hooks into you, and no mistake!"

He hung about a while longer, talking of this and that, and then pushed off to organise the rest of his day.

As Simon predicted, I did not get any real chance to escape from my family entertainment – nor, in fact, did I really want to. I was going to have a hard enough night the following night, I felt. We went up, in the late afternoon, packed into the Wiggins' Landrover, with their servant Hailu and a picnic supper, and occupied a piece of high ground looking down on the Jan Hoy Meda, a kind of public park and parade ground, where the ceremonies were to take place. We were joined by another couple, a lecturer in Physics at the University, Jack Harris and his wife Sheila. They had a young son, Hugo, who had been brought along to play with the young Wigginses.

The Harrises had only been out in Addis for a year, and had thus never attended Maskal before, so it had to be explained to them as well as to me – as far as Isabel, who was the only authority, was able to do so. She was used to these events from her childhood, but plainly had never gone into the background of them very deeply. Still, it was better than nothing. Gradually, as the evening wore on, more and more people flooded onto the great ceremonial plaza, singing and dancing in groups, and taking copious draughts from bottles or flasks, containing *tej* or *talla*, or perhaps something stronger. A series of bonfires were prepared, one huge one in the centre, before which there was a platform, and various small ones around the plaza, but none was yet lit. As Isabel explained, no fire could be lit until the Emperor himself appeared and lit the big one. Then things would really get going.

We turned to enjoy the supper that had been prepared, together with a choice of beer or Eritrean red wine, of which I chose the latter. After an hour or so, a sound of music and chanting arose from the direction of the cathedral in the distance, and an extraordinary procession came into view – first a long line of gorgeously dressed boy deacons, and then a phalanx of priests, also elaborately dressed, and carrying ceremonial umbrellas. In their midst they carried a large receptacle of some sort, which Isabel declared was a repository for a fragment of the True Cross, and from time to time groups of them would form up on either side of it and dance a dance in its honour, to the accompaniment of discordant chanting.

The procession gradually neared the reviewing stand and main bonfire, and then formed up round it in a ragged circle, still chanting. In a while there was a commotion, and excitement throughout the crowd, and the imperial Rolls Royce came into view, preceded by a large motorcycle escort, and followed by three or four other cars. As the Emperor emerged, the whole crowd fell to its knees and bowed down, until he and his party had taken their seats on the podium. I had a chance to study him, and the rest of the royal party, through the Wiggins' field-glasses, in the gathering dusk.

He was a neat, severe little man, with a finely clipped beard and piercing eyes. He looked out over the assembly with authority, every inch an emperor. I cast an eye over the rest of the party, but could make no identifications, and appealed to Isabel. She pointed out to me Crown Prince Asfa Wossen, his sisters, Princess Tenagne Worq and Princess Tsehai, his two young sons (pupils at The English School), and his nephew, the Emperor's grandson, Prince Alexander Desta. I continued to study the group, and, casting my eye over the back row, I was interested to pick out the figure of Yohannis, looking extremely solemn and respectable, with young Tewodros beside him, and to the other side a large older man, who was presumably his father, Ras Tessema. So, despite all the rumours, he was not that far out of favour with his formidable relation.

After a pause, the Emperor rose and advanced to the bonfire. He uttered a short prayer in Amharic, broadcast over loudspeakers, and was then handed a flaming torch, which he set to the base of the great pile of wood and brush. It went up with a spectacular whoosh of flame.

Bonfires began to spring into life all round the plaza, and singing and dancing broke out again, more enthusiastically than before. It was shortly after this that the Wigginses decided that it was time to go home. The children had been very good, but they were beginning to tire and squabble, and moreover, things, it seems, could begin to get rough. When the locals had had a certain amount to drink, Graham confided to me, they could turn nasty. It was better for foreigners to make themselves scarce. So we left the increasingly wild scene, and drove back down the hill for a nightcap in the headmaster's bungalow.

Once again, I was prevailed upon to read a story to two very sleepy little persons, and then rejoined the adults for a stiff brandy and soda before retiring. Jack Harris was a large, jolly, bearded man, whose main concern at the time seemed to be the organising of a Christmas production of Gilbert and Sullivan. It was to be The Pirates of Penzance, and I inevitably found myself enrolled in the chorus, an honour I was not inclined to refuse. It sounded good fun. Not for the first time since my arrival, I reached my bed somewhat the worse for wear.

Isabel kindly promised to take me shopping next morning, to introduce me to a good European grocery store, so at about ten I was collected and taken out in the Landrover to a market not far from the Piazza. I allowed Tekla-Mariam to do the necessary shopping for the first week, giving him a few dollars at a time, but now I took the opportunity to stock up on both necessities and luxuries, and came back loaded with parcels, and considerably poorer.

Mr Florides, the Greek proprietor of the general store, to whom Isabel introduced me, was most hospitable, and insisted on our taking a coffee and a glass of raki, with sweets for the children. This was good salesmanship, of course, as I became rather openhanded in consequence. Staple items were cheap enough, but anything imported or in a can was actually very expensive, and I had not yet quite got the feel of what an Ethiopian dollar was worth. Isabel warned me off a few things, but others slipped through. What, for instance, possessed me, I wondered as I unpacked my acquisitions later, to indulge in a tin of Italian asparagus, or indeed a Scottish fruit cake?

Suddenly I realised that I was going to have to go rather easy till the end of the month. Tekla-Mariam helped me unpack the things, looking with a worried frown at such items as the asparagus, and then prepared me a chicken sandwich and coffee for lunch (I had persuaded him that I could not generally eat a lunch on the scale that he had been serving me, if I was to eat dinner as well – and function in the afternoon before that). While I was enjoying this, Simon pushed his head in the door, looking a little bleary, and wondered if I wanted to come shopping with him.

"I've just come back from shopping," I said. "Isabel took me in with her this morning."

"Oh she did, did she?" he said, somewhat huffily. "We are privileged, aren't we?"

"Well, she offered last night, as I was leaving, and I took her up on it. And she's a good guide. She's lived here all her life, after all. You've only just got up, I take it?"

"M'm," he said. "Pretty rough night last night. I don't remember the latter part of it any too well, actually. Where did she take you?"

"We went to Florides' grocery, and then to a rather nice bread shop."

"Ah yes, Florides is the man, all right. Well, I'll leave you, then. I've got to stock up. Unless you want to come for the ride?"

I excused myself from this. I wanted to be alone for the afternoon. I pleaded exhaustion.

"Okay, then," said Simon, "I'll check in with you when I get back. I suppose we should leave for your noble friend's party around eight-thirty or so. It's bit of a drive."

"Oh?" I said. I suddenly realised that I had no idea where Yohannis lived; nor did his note carry any address – just the monogram. "Do you happen to know where to go?"

"Well," said Simon, "I would presume that he has a place in Ras Tessema's *ghibbi*. That'd be the normal thing, until he starts a family of his own, which I presume he hasn't done. And I know where *that* is. It's big place out on the other side of town – on the way out to Anna's."

"Okay," I said, "we'll try that. I suppose I could phone up and ask, of course. It's a nice piece of arrogance on his part, I must say, just assuming that everybody knows where he lives."

Simon laughed.

"Yes, I think it just wouldn't occur to him that someone mightn't. Anyhow, phone if you like, but I think that's where he is. I'll see you this evening."

And he disappeared. Left to myself, I first of all had a short siesta, and then settled down to read. But I soon became restless. The afternoon was fine – slightly overcast, so not too hot – and I felt a sudden urge to go out and explore a little on my own. Give the old car a bit of a workout as well. After some thought, I decided to try just to follow the road past the school out of town, to see where it would go. I wouldn't go too far, just till I could find some open countryside.

With some apprehension, I edged the Fiat out of the gates of the compound, waving to the *zabanya* on duty, and turned left. The road in fact led upwards, over a spur of Entotto, so I found myself after a mile or so near the top of a ridge overlooking the city. The regular clusters of huts faded out, the road turned to dirt and became rather bumpy, and I was on my own. As the climb got steeper, the old Fiat began to labour a bit, and I remembered the drawbacks of Marco's famous petrol-saving device. I decided not to test its capacities to the limit, and after a short while pulled in and parked at a bend in the road near the summit, where a rough path led off to the left, up the mountain. I got out and stretched, breathing in the mountain air. An old gent on a mule came over the brow of the hill, and passed me at a trot, heading for the city. He raised his umbrella in greeting, and I returned his salute.

I looked around. The city was a confused jumble below me, half-hidden in eucalyptus. The clouds had dispersed, and the sky was blue. Far off on the southern horizon rose the impressive bulk of Mount Wuchacha, closing off the plain below the city, flanked by a range of lower hills. I decided to follow the path for a while, since it seemed to offer fine views, while providing at least intermittent shade as well. There was a great silence, broken only by snatches of birdsong, and the occasional distant tinkle of cow or goat bells. It was pleasant to stroll along and think things over. I found myself somewhat more sure now than I had been a week earlier that I had basically done the right thing. I had badly needed to get away from western civilisation. Admittedly, I was still enjoying the fruits of it here, but in a satisfyingly zany mode. Ewan Hardiman, at the Awash last Saturday, had no doubt been right in maintaining that there was really no escape from the Cold War madness, but somehow this felt like one. Maybe it was the altitude, but one felt up here that one could look down fairly dispassionately upon the world, and sort out one's thoughts at leisure.

After a stroll of about twenty minutes, following the contours of Entotto towards the west, just as I was wondering whether anyone lived up here at all, I rounded a bend in the trail, and found myself suddenly facing a remarkable scene. There was an indentation, a sort of bite taken out of the mountain, and in a clearing, at a distance of about a hundred yards, I was confronted with an extraordinary square rock-cut church, with, on the one side, a little group of huts, surrounded by the usual eucalyptus, and on the other a largish communal building of some sort. One or two monkish figures, and a scattering of boys, were moving around between the huts and the larger building.

I was not at all sure that I wanted to intrude on this scene, but I was spotted by a number of the boys, and they ran over towards me, waving their arms in a friendly greeting. They gathered round me, and chattered at me, but I could only spread out my hands helplessly, and tell them in

English that I couldn't understand. This did not deter them, and a few of them took me by the hands, and drew me, with shouts and laughter, towards the settlement. "*Na, na, getoich*," they called out, pointing to the main building. I followed along with them, feeling somewhat helpless.

In fact, however, in the main building we found a stately old monk who spoke some French, the preferred foreign language of the older generation. My French was of not much more than the schoolboy level, but we could communicate. He explained that this was a monastery, dedicated to St. George, with an elementary school attached to it, and the children who had captured me were the pupils, and also deacons in the church. The church itself, he explained, was very old, and was not built, but cut out of the rock. We went out to look at it more closely, and this was so. It did indeed seem to have been laboriously cut out from the living rock, which surrounded it on three sides. He showed me into the murky, smoky recesses inside, and I could dimly make out rich hangings, silver ornaments, icons, and finely carved wooden furnishings. The walls were covered in frescoes, now unfortunately very grimy, but still impressive. He pointed out various scenes, such as the Baptism in the Jordan, and St. George and the Dragon.

Then I was invited to one of the huts, to take coffee. A number of other monks gathered round and greeted me, but none except this one old man, who seemed to be the abbot or head of the community, could speak any European language. A sort of honey-cake was produced. They looked very vile, but I felt that I must try one, and in fact it tasted not unpleasant, though very aromatic. I told the Abbot that I was a teacher, and that I had just arrived, and was hoping to learn all about the country. This pleased him, and he tried to explain to me the curriculum of their little school. It sounded very strange. Basically, the children had to learn off by heart one of the four gospels each year, and that was about all.

This was all fascinating, but I realised that I should be getting back. I finished my coffee, and pointed at my watch. I excused myself to the Abbot, and thanked him for his hospitality. He clasped my hands in his, and urged me to come back whenever I wished. I was accompanied to the edge of the clearing by the same boys who had captured me in the first place. They didn't beg, or seem to want anything, except to shake my hand. It was a thoroughly happy scene.

I made my way back to the car in a rather exalted state. I had not expected this encounter. I had actually wanted to be alone with my thoughts; but this was better. I had made contact with a little corner of the 'real' Ethiopia – if anything in this extraordinary land could be regarded as real. I made a mental note to ask Willy Buhagiar more about the Ethiopian church, when I next met him. He seemed to be a man who knew about such things. I drove back down the hill, the Fiat going much more happily downhill than up, and got back to the compound some time after six, just as the sun was beginning to sink into the west, and the smoke of ten thousand fires of eucalyptus leaves rose to hang in a fragrant cloud over the city, as evening meals were prepared outside more or less every tukul.

I treated myself to a generous measure of my precious Jameson to fortify me as I read a little more Ethiopian history. Tekla-Mariam served me a modest meal, and by half past eight or so, when Simon came over to collect me, I was fully ready to go out and sample another facet of the real Ethiopia, though how 'real' this was going to be I was much less certain.

I hadn't bothered to call after all, but in fact Simon was right. We drove across town, and up to the gates of an imposing, fortress-like estate which he identified as Ras Tessema's *ghibbi*. A guard emerged when we drove up to the gate, armed, not as in the case of The English School *zabanya*, with an aged rifle, but with a modern-looking machine-gun, and looking as if he meant business. I was profoundly glad that I had my invitation, which I handed to him through the window. It occurred to me that his English might not be quite up to deciphering it, so I said at the same time, "Lij Yohannis's – party," and this did the trick. He handed me back the invitation, and opened the gates for us, waving us through, and pointing up to the left, where a large old French-style bungalow stood by itself, about a hundred yards away, in a clearing of the eucalyptus groves which covered the estate. There were lights on in the front rooms, and a number of cars already drawn up in the driveway.

"Well, well," said Simon, as I pulled away from the gates and the guard, "this is impressive, all right. There's some serious firepower there, I should say."

"Yes," I said, "I suppose they have to be careful, but I'm not very clear where the danger is meant to come from."

"Ah well, things are not that secure, after all," said Simon. "There are always rumours of coup attempts, and you've got to remember they just had a real one recently."

I pulled into a space between one car with diplomatic number plates and another with some sort of official ones, and we got out.

The front door was slightly open, but as we approached a servant came out to meet us. Again I had my invitation at the ready, but I didn't need it.

"Mr Luke La Touche," I said, firmly, "and Mr Simon Blakeney."

"*Eshe, getoich*". And we were led into the front hall, where Yohannis himself, who was just passing from one room to another, happened to spot us.

His face lit up. As I saw him now up close, after the interval of two and a half years and a half, he was recognisably the same old Yohannis, but somehow more solid and authoritative on his own ground. He was dressed in a remarkable blend of Western and native dress, a white polo-neck, very sharp pink Italian-style jacket, and a richly embroidered *shamma* thrown over it all. He looked every inch the playboy intellectual.

"Luke, old man," he exclaimed, coming over to embrace me. "This is great! It's been a long time! I am so glad that you could come. It's so good to see you! And this is your friend?"

"Yes, this is Simon Blakeney, who also teaches at The English School."

He clasped Simon by the hand.

"Simon? How are you, Simon?" Then he turned back to me, reproachfully. "And how are you anyway, you dog? Why did you not tell me you were coming to Ethiopia? It was a complete surprise for me."

I spread out my hands apologetically. I did not want to have such a conversation on the doorstep, but I had to say something. It came out rather lamely.

"Yohannis, it sounds silly, but first of all I actually forgot you would be here, and then I didn't have your address ... "

"Anyhow, never mind, I have found you. Come in and meet some people, and I'll get someone to give you a drink."

And he steered us into the room on the right, where he had been headed. We were met with a remarkably varied scene. The guests made up a splendidly multinational gathering, sporting both Western and traditional Ethiopian dress, as well as a scattering of military uniforms. I did not expect to know anybody, but one unexpected person who caught my gaze was my recently-enrolled pupil for English, Safar Abdolov, Director of the Soviet Information Centre. He was over at the other side of the room, deep in conversation with a young Ethiopian in a military uniform. He stood beside some french windows, which gave out onto a lawn illuminated by fairy lights and did not, for the moment, see me.

Yohannis led Simon and me over to a small group centring on a rather striking stoutish middle-aged man of somewhat effete appearance, who was holding forth on some subject, plainly in a most amusing way. Most of the group, men and women alike, were dissolved in laughter.

"Now," said Yohannis, "if I may interrupt what is obviously some very wicked and amusing story by John, I would like to introduce my friend Luke La Touche, just out here from Oxford, and his friend, Simon Blakeney."

I noticed Simon stiffening somewhat, and regarding the figure at the centre of the group with some distaste.

"Luke, this is John Langdon. He teaches English at the University. Also an Oxford man, but a few years before us." He then ran expertly through the rest of the group, but I took in no more than the first name, that of Langdon, and the last, a Miss Wendy Thesiger from the British Embassy. I liked the look of her. She was somewhat plump, but most attractive, and had an intelligent, humorous look about her.

"I'll be back to you in a little while," said Yohannis, patting me on the back. "I just have to have a few words with some people over there."

Langdon looked at me with interest. He was dressed with fastidious neatness, and wore on his fingers a number of ornate rings.

"Well, well," he said, with something of a drawl. "Welcome to the other side of the looking glass! So you're a friend of Yohannis, eh?"

"Yes," I said, "we met in Oxford when he was there."

"That was Oriel, wasn't it?" said Langdon, a little disdainfully, I thought. I was always a bit sensitive about Oriel, conscious that it was not one of the most fashionable of colleges.

"Yes," I said. "And what was your college?"

"Oh, I was at Magdalen, but some years ago now. And you've just arrived?"

Just then, a respectful figure appeared at my elbow, offering a tray of drinks, and another with various interesting morsels to eat. Simon went for a Scotch, but I thought I discerned a sample of Yohannis' proprietorial *tej*, and chose a glass of that. Langdon observed this.

"Ah, I see you've chosen *tej*. I hope you know what you're doing."

"Well, I'm not sure that I do," I said, "but Yohannis sent me over a bottle on my arrival, and I found it interesting, so I thought I'd try it again."

This little piece of oneupmanship put Langdon slightly on the defensive.

"Yes," he said, "you could describe it as interesting, but I would approach it with caution. I can't say I care for it much myself."

I took a sip, and nodded.

"I'll be careful." I turned to Miss Thesiger. "You're from the British Embassy, did I hear Yohannis say?"

"Yes," she said brightly. "I'm the second secretary. And I know all about you, from Ewan."

"Oh yes," I said. "We had a very pleasant picnic together, last Saturday, at the Awash."

Just then, Yohannis returned and grasped me by the arm.

"Sorry, Wendy, but can I take this man away for a little while?" he said. "I have not seen him for a long time. I will bring him back to you."

Miss Thesiger smiled sweetly, and Yohannis steered me away, leaving her to Simon.

"Let's go out into the garden," he said, importantly. "I want to talk to you."

We passed out into the relative cool of the garden, the darkness of which was illuminated fitfully by the multicoloured lights draped from various trees. As we passed Mr Abdolov, he glanced in our direction, and registered mild surprise. I lifted a hand in greeting, and passed on.

'Well, Yohannis," I began, "It is great to see you, I must say, and I'm really sorry for not announcing myself in advance, but I didn't want to impose on you, and my cousin James, you see, was fixing me up with a job, so I was all right. How did you find out that I was here, after all?"

He laughed. "It was a great surprise, I can tell you, but don't forget that you're teaching my younger brother Latin! But who is this Cousin James of yours? Do you have a cousin here?"

"Yes, Sir James Mallory. He's acting as legal adviser to your revered uncle-in-law. Have you come across him?"

Yohannis stopped in astonishment.

"Oho! Sir James Mallory is your cousin? What an extraordinary thing. Of course I know about him, but I haven't met him very often. I don't think he would approve of me very much, actually."

I laughed. "No, actually, I don't think he does. In fact, he rather warned me against you, to be perfectly honest."

Yohannis looked at me in wry amusement.

"So you haven't taken his advice?"

"Well," I said, "let's say I've noted it. And in that connection, what are you up to, Yohannis? Why would my cousin James be displeased with you?"

He grinned. "Well, I think it is because your cousin James is a rather conservative fellow. In fact, I do not think that he is a very good influence on my revered uncle-in-law, as you call him."

He paused, and looked out into the darkness. Then he began to speak, in a much more serious tone.

"You see, Luke, this country of ours, as I see it, is approaching a crisis. The Old Man, my uncle, is a very great man, no question about that, but he has his limitations, and he is getting old. What's happened is that he has himself provided the conditions for the overthrow of his regime, and if someone does not try to produce some changes from within, I'm afraid the whole situation will blow up." And he spread out his arms expressively.

"You see, he has encouraged progress and development, because he likes the idea of that. He has sent a lot of bright young people away to study, not just to the West, but even to the East, to the Soviet Union, and they have been coming back, and getting more and more frustrated, because he still wants to run everything himself in his own way. He still keeps these useless, conservative old friends and supporters of his at the top of most ministries and enterprises. He has trained up a very intelligent and efficient bunch of young army officers, and yet he's not giving them enough promotion, because he won't fire the old fools that he has at the top. So you see, it's a dangerous situation, and what I want to do is to see that change comes about in an orderly way. Because it's going to come in one way or another, and frankly, I want to save my own skin, as well as his, if I can. I'm not being particularly altruistic in all this, just realistic."

I listened, fascinated. I had heard Yohannis hold forth along these lines before, back in Oxford, but here, in his own back garden, what he had to say took on a much sharper edge.

"Jesus," I said. "You make things sound pretty serious. But I gather from Cousin James that you don't exactly see eye to eye with the Emperor on this."

Yohannis laughed.

"I think you could say that! He's got so used now to running everything himself that he can't accept help from anyone. And of course he doesn't take me seriously at all, because of the way I live."

"Oh?" I said. "And how do you live?"

"Well ..." Yohannis waved a hand. "I do like to have a good time. But that doesn't mean I'm not serious about what I believe in. I think it was Trotsky who said that just because one is a socialist, it doesn't mean that one shouldn't enjoy oneself."

"It's a good principle," I said, "but I somehow doubt that that's one of Trotsky's. He always struck me as a rather austere character."

"No, no," said Yohannis, "I think it was Trotsky. But it doesn't matter. It is a good principle, and I live by it." He put his arm in mine. "So let's go back in and have a good time. You shouldn't have to concern yourself with all this, anyhow. It's not your country, after all. You're just a visitor. And I hope you have a *very* good visit!"

I was much impressed. Yohannis had developed significantly since I had last seen him, both in the direction of serious purpose and of frivolity. It was hard to judge which tendency really had the upper hand. Then he steered me back through the previous room, across the hall, and into an inner sanctum, which seemed to be his study. A number of aristocratic-looking young Ethiopians were sprawled about, taking up the armchairs and the sofa. On the desk there was a dish containing white powder, and some dark, tobacco-like stuff, with cigarette-making apparatus beside it.

"Now," said Yohannis, advancing to the desk, "let's take a little cocaine. This is really excellent stuff. Have you ever tried it, Luke? I don't remember there being much around in Oxford in our day."

"No," I said, suddenly appalled, "there certainly wasn't. And I honestly don't think I would, thanks, Yohannis. Your *tej* is quite exciting enough and I have to drive."

Yohannis was quite put out.

"Oh, come on!," he said. "You should at least try it! But at least try a joint of marijuana. I grow this myself on my estates – in America they call it pot. There was a little of it around in Oxford, I think."

"I don't remember coming across any," I said, suspiciously.

"No? Oh well, you may not have been with me at the time. But you must try some now. It is not at all a violent thing, and it produces a most pleasant sensation – especially when combined with my *tej*!" And he grinned. He began to roll me a cigarette of the stuff, while I watched him cautiously.

When he had done, he handed it to me, and gave me a light.

"This is called a joint," said Yohannis. "You must smoke it all, slowly. And remember to inhale."

I took a cautious draw. Smoking was a habit I had never taken up – at school the group I mixed with had decided that smoking was vulgar, and had turned to taking snuff, which I dutifully tried, but had never much enjoyed. The only smoking I had done was the occasional Gauloise or cigar, for the smell of it, and I did not inhale.

"You must inhale deeply," ordered Yohannis, "and hold the smoke in. Otherwise it is no good."

I obeyed, holding in the sweetish, aromatic smoke for as long as I could.

"Good! Now breathe out, and try again! Oh by the way," he added, gesturing towards the recumbent figures, who had obviously been partaking of the goodies on the desk for some time now, "these are various friends of mine. I won't confuse you with their names, but this is my cousin, Alexander Desta" – and he pointed to a tall, fine-looking young man in the nearest armchair, who was conscious enough to raise his hand in friendly greeting. I thought I recognised him from the reviewing stand the previous afternoon. "Alexander, or Skinder, as we call him," added Yohannis in a low voice, "is actually commander-in-chief of our navy, improbable as that seems at this moment. But he's a good man," Yohannis continued in a hoarse whisper. "I really think he should be the next emperor, if this country is to be saved."

I looked with interest at Cousin Alexander, and took a second puff on my joint. And gradually now it began to take effect. Yohannis rolled one for himself, to keep me company, and beckoned me over to a sofa on which there were two places free. We sank down comfortably, and he began to ask me about my first impressions of the country.

From this time on, however, my memories of the evening become somewhat hazy. I can remember colours and shapes becoming extremely pronounced, and seeming to hear snatches of conversation with preternatural clarity. Sometimes it seemed to be me who was speaking, but I heard it as if the voice was coming from somewhere else. I had another glass of *tej*, and then another joint. I can remember laughing immoderately, and delivering utterances of great wit. I even have a dim memory of wandering back into the main room, and addressing Comrade Abdolov in Russian, although I know no Russian.

Finally, Simon caught up with me. He was reasonably sloshed, but in better shape than I was. He decided it was time to go home. Yohannis protested, but Simon was quite firm. He got the keys from me, and steered me out to the car, protesting mildly, as I was having what seemed to me to be very jolly time. However, I was in no shape to resist, and I was more benign than belligerent.

Once in the car, Simon fiddled around a bit with the gears, but got the car started without any trouble, and we drove carefully out of the compound, returning the salute of the heavily-armed guard.

"Sorry," said Simon, when we were safely on the open road, "but that is just not my scene. From the moment I saw Langdon I was turned off. I really don't like poofters, and he's a pretty aggressive specimen, I have to tell you. Had to leave the UK in a hurry, by all accounts, and managed to fix himself up here. And I can't say I found too much else of interest, except maybe that Thesiger girl, but I don't think you'd get much change out of her, really. A bit too cautious. She seemed to like you, though."

He turned to look at me more closely.

"But what the fuck have you been drinking? You are really in a weird state. And where did you get to, anyhow?"

I composed myself with dignity, and spoke slowly and carefully. The words, though, felt curiously disconnected, as if they had a life of their own.

"It's not so much what I've been drinking. It's what I've been smoking. Yohannis took me off for a walk in the garden, and then brought me back to his study, and gave me some stuff called marijuana. Have you heard of it?"

"Yes, I've heard of it, all right. I've even tried it a few times, out here. Never came across it back home. Your friend Yohannis is into serious stuff!"

"He also had some cocaine in there," I said, ponderously, "but I turned that down."

"Shit!" said Simon, looking at me with eyebrows raised. "Coke as well, eh? You were bloody right to turn *that* down. That's serious stuff. There's not too much harm in pot, I think, as long as you don't make a habit of it. But cocaine! I would say Yohannis spells trouble. And I don't like his friends – especially those fellows in uniform. There was this one guy, who introduced himself just as 'Tamrat', and tried to chat me up. He was a fishy piece of work. He was far too interested in who we were and what we thought about the country and the regime. He smelled like some kind of policeman to me. I wonder what in hell he was doing there."

I shook my head.

"No, didn't come across him," I said. I was not in the mood for doubts or complaints. I was still in something of a beatific state – though my head was swimming slightly – and I wished to believe only good of the world. Simon got us home safely, parked the Fiat behind my bungalow, and piloted me to my door. He stuck the key in the lock, and turned it.

"You going to be okay?" he said.

I was really only half drunk, and half in a preternaturally alert state. I nodded, and thanked him.

"Yes, Simon, old man," I said, rather ponderously, "I am quite sure that I will be okay."

In fact, I was far from sure of this. My stomach and my head were both feeling distinctly mobile. But I now wished above all to be alone.

Simon looked at me speculatively for a moment, and then gave in.

"Fine," he said. "See you tomorrow, then. And thanks for the invitation, even if it was a weird scene."

I woke up next morning quite early, feeling rather less hung over than I expected. Marijuana and *tej* turned out not be as lethal a combination as had seemed likely at the time. I was in reasonably coherent form when Cousin James collected me for church at a little after half past nine. The service was (or at least seemed) rather long, and we had to have a chat with Padre Matthews afterwards, and after that we had to go across to his bungalow so that he could give me the Amharic grammar he had promised me the previous Sunday.

Then we went for our walk on Entotto with Willy, who joined us after his Roman Catholic service. The scent of the pines was soothing, and the air bracing. I was able to remain non-committal and vague about the previous night, pretending it was just a dinner with my immediate neighbours on the compound and some friends of theirs, and hoping that the truth would not come out in one way or another. I had certainly had an insight into what could be the problems involved in associating too closely with Yohannis, but I was still inclined to take things as they came. After all, as Yohannis had himself remarked, it wasn't my country, and there was no reason for me to get myself involved with his various conspiracies, whatever they were. As for cocaine and suchlike, I felt that I could steer clear of that, and stick to good old-fashioned booze – and, well, after all, maybe the occasional joint.

Willy Buhagiar did enquire over lunch whether I had heard anything more from Prince Yohannis, but I replied, blandly, that I hadn't. I even expressed mild disappointment at that.

After a nap of an hour or so, Cousin James got Wolde to run me over to the school. Simon was waiting around when I got back to the compound, wondering about a short visit to Anna's. Sunday evening seemed a pretty good time for catching Berhane at leisure, so to speak, so I was very willing to go along with that, cancelling Tekla-Mariam's dinner preparations just in time, and taking just an hour to prepare my classes for tomorrow. I had to admit to myself that I was becoming more than a little addicted to Berhane's embraces – and indeed she was as delightful as ever, and seemed pleased to see me. I suppose, I told myself, it may keep me out of even greater mischief, getting involved with nubile students, or – the great colonial temptation – other people's wives.

Only one disturbing detail cast any shadow over the evening. As we strolled into the Bella Napoli to greet the Signora and order some dinner, Simon suddenly froze. The room was largely empty at this time of the evening, but over at the far side of it, near a window, there was a group of men in uniform, having a drink. When we were seated out at our table under the vine trellis, Simon told me what had bothered him.

"Did you see that group across the room?" he said.

"The fellows in uniform? Yes, I did. Why?"

"Well, the fellow on the left, is that spook from last night – who was really interested in finding out who you and I were, and how we knew his Highness. He kept on trying to draw me out about my views of the country, obviously seeing if he could get me to criticise the regime in some way, suggesting that he was some sort of a dissident himself. I smelled a big fat rat, I must say. He had agent provocateur written all over him. So I just stayed very bland and positive. Said I really enjoyed the country, but didn't really understand the political situation – that sort of thing – and that you had only just arrived. So he finally gave up and slunk away, saying how very pleasant it was to meet me, and how he hoped we could meet again soon. Not if I can help it!"

"Good grief," I said, "I don't like the sound of that. I didn't come across him at all. You didn't mention him last night."

"Yes I think I did, but you were obviously too stoned to remember." He looked at me austerely. "I must say, though, that your friend Yohannis may know what he's doing, but I'd say that this mixture of playboy and socialist revolutionary is a pretty explosive combination in a country like this. He may be able to get away with it himself, but people around him are very likely going to get hurt."

I scratched my head.

"Yeah, I know, I know. I agree with you, actually, but ... it's silly, probably, but I just don't want to offend him if I don't have to. And I do find him interesting. I'll just take things quietly, and be sure not get involved in what doesn't concern me. That's all I can do." I meant it, and as I said it, it seemed to me a reasonable position. Yohannis surely didn't need me for his plans, whatever they might be.

On Wednesday, as promised, I went back for another band rehearsal, and enjoyed both the playing and the company. It turned out that young Haile Mariam, or Hailu, was one of Jack's senior pupils, but also the son of the owner of the nightclub where we proposed to perform, the Paradiso.

Not that his father ran the place – that was done by a local Greek. Jack explained the situation to me as we went out to the kitchen in search of more beer. Hailu's dad was a major property owner in the city, and this was just one of his minor properties. Ethiopian aristocrats, I gathered, like Classical Greek aristocrats, did not generally sully their hands with trade. So Hailu was of some strategic importance. He was also very keen on modern jazz, however, and not at all bad on the bass – a genuinely useful member of the rhythm section. I was not going to be able to join the group this weekend, but I promised to leave myself free the following Friday and Saturday.

So it was a reasonably eventful week, and that was without reckoning in my growing acquaintance with my classes. The teaching was settling into a rhythm, and seemed to be under control.

My plan of initiating a coffee morning for my sixth form class on Thursdays proved a great success. They were a little nervous at first, but settled happily in to my sitting room, taking up all available seating, and cushions on the floor, while a slightly baffled Tekla-Mariam served them coffee and biscuits. Graham was somewhat sceptical about this mollycoddling, as Simon had thought he would be, but Isabel was most supportive. She lent me extra cups and cushions. I wandered in and out, not wanting to put a damper on things, but in fact they were quite pleased to chat to me, and not at all shy. It gave me a different perspective on everyone to meet them outside of a classroom situation, and they plainly found the same with each other. It was intriguing to see how the class came together as an organism in the wake of the first coffee morning. Even Tewodros was on better terms with his peers. They took to teasing him instead of cold-shouldering him, and he responded with arrogant good humour.

CHAPTER ELEVEN

On Saturday afternoon, around half past two, I found myself heading out for Nyala in the old Fiat. Isabel had given me careful instructions to take the Debre Birhan road in a north-easterly direction for about twenty-five kilometers, and then look for a sign to Nyala, pointing off onto a dirt road to the left. If I followed that for a further fifteen kilometers or so, I would come, first to the model village, and then, going on through that, to the Stanford residence, Nyala Farm itself.

The car laboured a bit on the way up over Entotto, but it gave no trouble on the main road after that, since it was a good surface and relatively flat. I found the sign for Nyala Farm without any trouble – it was the only landmark for many miles – but after about ten kilometers of toiling along on the rutted murram surface of the track leading to it, I became disturbingly aware of a hissing from in front of me, and an ominous wisp of steam began to rise from the radiator. I pulled over quickly and stopped the car. Damn, I thought, this old bus is a bit of a wreck after all. I'll have to remember to bring a jerrycan of water with me on future journeys. But for the moment there was nothing for it but to let the radiator cool down. I reckoned, anyhow, that there was not too much further to go, and I was in good time (I had been asked to arrive for tea, and it was not yet quite four o'clock), so I felt that I could afford to give the car a rest.

I got out and looked around me. I was in the middle of a fairly flat plateau, plainly somewhat higher in altitude than Addis itself, In every direction, though, there were visible blue intimations of mountains, rising behind each other, in ridge after ridge, punctuated by some fairly spectacular peaks. Not much sign of life around, but clumps of eucalyptus on the skyline in various directions indicated the presence of native settlements of some sort. I sat down in the shade of the car, and breathed in the clear air.

Suddenly from nowhere there appeared an elderly man on a mule, adorned with a fine tassled umbrella and a handy-looking spear. He reined in the mule, and contemplated me with amusement.

"*Machina mbi alle* ," he said, with a grin.

I could make nothing of this, except that it probably concerned the car, but I nodded cheerfully, and pointed to the radiator, hoping that this would satisfy him. It did. He made some further good-humoured observation, and rode on, in the direction of Nyala

In the event, after a good twenty minutes of rest, the car seemed ready to move again, and I continued, slowly and cautiously, for the remaining five kilometers or so, until I reached the village, a very neat and cheerful collection of European-style buildings grouped round a little square, with rows of *tukuls* stretching out in various directions. I saw a man crossing between two of the buildings, and called out to him, hoping he could understand some English. He came over to me, and fortunately proved to know a little. I asked for the Stanford house. He broke into a grin, and directed me on through the village in the direction I was going. I thanked him, and drove on through the square, past a row of *tukuls*, and then up a slight rise, for a further half-mile or so, when I rounded a bend in the road and the house came into view.

It was a lovely old thatched bungalow, with a deep, low-slung verandah, covered in climbing roses and bougainvillea, and a little flower garden in front, on either side of a stone-flagged path. I parked the car in front of it, beside a large and rather battered-looking Landrover, and got out. The house looked out, towards the west, on a most spectacular panorama of mountains and, in the middle distance, a slashing gorge, which ran from south to north. Between the house and the lip of the gorge a few hundred yards away there was nothing but a few flat-topped acacia trees. It seemed a little piece of Old England set down in the middle of an African wilderness.

I was not left long to contemplate this glorious panorama, however. The front door opened and an imposing old lady in a voluminous flowered robe advanced slowly down the path to greet me. Her face was tanned, weather-beaten by the African sun, and her snow-white hair was swept back in a severe bun. Her piercing eyes surveyed me.

"Well, well, Mr La Touche, is it? How clever of you to find your way. Did you have any trouble? Here, Mammo will take your bag."

And a boy hurried out past her to relieve me of my overnight bag. She advanced towards me with hand outstretched.

"I'm Louise Stanford. You're very welcome to Nyala."

I grasped the outstretched hand. "Very good to meet you," I said, "and very good of you to have me. Everything went pretty smoothly, thanks. Isabel's instructions were very accurate. Just a little overheating of the radiator some way before I reached the village, but I took a short break, and it cooled down."

"Well, that's lovely. Come on in, and we'll fix you up with some living quarters. Tea won't be for a little while yet. We do everything very late here, as you'll discover. But I can introduce you, and show you around a little."

Mrs Stanford struck me, at first viewing, like a motherly version of Queen Victoria. I could see where Isabel got both her profile and her great aura of good-humoured competence. I should have been overawed, but instead felt immediately at home.

"It really is a beautiful place you have here," I said. "I've heard quite a bit about Nyala from Cousin James, and I was really looking forward to seeing it. It certainly lives up to its reputation."

"Well," she said comfortably, "we like it. It suits us very well. And how is your Cousin James? "

"Oh, he's very well," I said, "and sends his best wishes, of course."

"Well, you tell him, when next you see him, that we expect him down to visit us without delay. We always need him at the bridge table, for one thing. Now come in and meet my husband." She waved me forward through the front door into a capacious but low-ceilinged living-room, and directed me towards an armchair near the fire. "Andy dear, this is young Mr La Touche, James's cousin. "

Brigadier Stanford had been in his chair, snoozing. He now struggled to his feet, and shook my hand very hospitably.

"Glad you could come, my boy. Hope you won't find it too boring. We live a pretty quiet life here."

"Oh, I'm sure I won't, sir," I said. "Absolutely everything is exciting for me at the moment."

"Good, good, that's the spirit. Play any bridge?"

Fortunately I was able to reply in the affirmative, and this pleased him exceedingly.

"Take a seat there for a moment, and tell me about yourself."

I settled myself, rather nervously, into the voluminous armchair opposite him, and he sank back into his appraising me with amusement. I ventured to study him in return. The Brig, I decided, looked even more like a British bulldog than Churchill. His face was lined and weather-beaten, with two twinkling eyes looking out over a turned-up nose and a pugnacious chin. He was not fat, even in old age, just very solidly built. He looked, indeed, as if he could stop a tank single-handed. I was glad that I had not had to face him in battle.

"So," he said, "you've come out to this part of the world for a bit of adventure, I suppose?"

I told my tale in the form that I had been developing it over the last week or so, and to my relief he approved it thoroughly. It occurred to me that it was perhaps not unlike what he had done himself almost half a century ago.

"Splendid!" he said, when I had finished. "It's just what I would recommend every young chap to do who has the opportunity. Of course, whether you ought to stay for any length of time is quite another question. I did, and then I found I couldn't go home even if I wanted to. You get spoiled, you see. When I had to go back to the UK after those damned Italians arrived I was miserable. Yes, quite thoroughly miserable. Couldn't wait to get back. Fortunately I got the chance. But I wouldn't recommend it these days, I'm afraid. Things are beginning to get a bit dicey. You could get chucked out at any time. Better not to get too dug in, I should say."

He looked about him, and changed the subject.

"But you should find your quarters, and meet my grand-niece Caroline. Where is the girl? She's come out here just for a little while, but rather more for a rest than for adventure. She's had enough adventuring back home, by all accounts."

Mrs Stanford intervened, rather crossly.

"Now, Andy, don't be indiscreet. Mr La Touche – or may I just call you Luke?"

I nodded enthusiastically.

"And you must call me Louise. Come and let me show you your

room. And then we may find Caroline. I think she's sunbathing in the courtyard."

I rose and followed her out, marvelling at my surroundings. The front room looked well lived in and splendidly comfortable. It was filled with well-padded old furniture, and adorned with all kinds of Ethiopian ornaments, paintings, rugs, spears, ancient guns, wood-carvings. Behind this room we came out onto a sort of cloister, running round an open courtyard, off which there was a series of rooms. In a corner of this courtyard, partly shaded by a flowering tree, there lay a girl in a deck-chair, reading. Before I had any chance to look at her more closely, however, Mrs Stanford ushered me forward to my room, which led off the cloister to the right.

Like the living room, it was low-ceilinged, but bright and cheerful, its window opening out onto what seemed to be an orchard, with a view of distant mountains. There was a large and comfortable-looking wooden four-poster bed, and a chair and desk by the window. Mammo appeared to have already unpacked my bag. The bed was folded down, and my pyjamas laid out on the fold, while other articles were arranged on shelves.

On a bedside table, there was a candle in an ornate candlestick, with matches beside it, and hanging from the ceiling an old-fashioned hurricane lamp. Only then did I notice that there was no electric light. Mrs Stanford noticed my glance at the lighting arrangements, and laughed.

"Yes," she said, "no electricity here, I'm afraid. Too damned unreliable. We have a generator in the village, but we don't bother with it ourselves, except for the farm. We like the old hurricane lamps. And for cooking and water heating we use gas cylinders. So you can have a bath before dinner, if you want. By the way," she added, confidentially, "the Brig likes to dress a bit for dinner, so if you've brought a tie ... "

"Oh, absolutely," I said, having been warned previously by James. "This is lovely." I waved a hand. "I feel quite at home, I must say."

"Splendid, splendid! That's just what we want you to be. And now, you must come and meet Caroline. Ah, but I almost forgot!" She led me next door to a capacious bathroom, with a fine old free-standing tub and wash-basin, and next door again, to a lavatory, of equally heroic dimensions. "This is the guest bathroom, so you only have to share with Caroline. We have our own."

From there she led me back to the figure reclining under the tree.

"Caroline, my dear, let me introduce you to our guest, Luke La Touche, the cousin of Sir James Mallory, of whom you've heard me speak so often."

The girl sat up, removed her sunglasses, and directed at me a somewhat clouded gaze – slightly sulky, but also inquisitive.

"Hullo," she said, and extended a hand, which I took, returning her greeting, and her gaze. She had a fine figure, fully revealed by her bikini, and a delicately-etched, rather elfin face, which I found intriguing. It was not obviously beautiful, but it could grow on you, I felt.

"Now, my dear, I think you should rouse yourself, stick some clothes on, and take Luke for a little walk – just show him the surroundings – before tea. How about that?"

Caroline nodded, and pulled herself to her feet.

"Okay," she said, with an unexpected smile. "If you'll hold on a sec, I'll just put on a robe, and some shoes."

"Fine," I said, and she headed off to the bedroom on the other side of the bathroom.

"Splendid," said Mrs Stanford. "I'll leave you two young people to your own devices for a while. I have to finish bottling some plums before tea." She swept off regally in the direction of the kitchen, on the other side of the courtyard.

I sat down on a rustic chair near the tree, and waited for Caroline to emerge, in the meanwhile letting my spirit embrace the clear, crisp air, the mixture of flower-smells, and the varied birdsong.

In a few minutes she came out, wrapped in a striking yellow beach-robe, and waved to me to follow her. There was a gate at the back of the courtyard, leading out into a garden, and she went before me out through that. We walked along in silence for a short while, along a path lined with fruit trees, in the direction of the setting sun. I thought I would let her be the first to speak, and after a brief battle of wills, this she did.

"Well," she said, "so you've come out to teach in the school, have you?"

"That's right," I said.

"And how long do you think you'll stay?"

"Oh, maybe a year, maybe two. It all depends."

"Depends on what?"

"Well, how much I like it, for one thing. And then..." And I paused, uncertain quite how to go on.

She glanced at me, interested.

"And what else?"

"Oh," I said, hesitantly, "it depends also on how quickly I sort out certain problems in my head."

"Oh Lord!" she said, looking at me derisively. "Don't tell me you've got problems too?"

"Oh," I said, "do you have?"

"Oh, I have loads of problems. My parents sent me out here in the hopes that the old folks here might sort them out."

"And are they?"

"Well," she said, "it's a bit early to say. I've only been here a couple of weeks."

'What sort of problems do you have?" I said, boldly. "Or is it anything you want to talk about?"

"Oh, I don't mind," she said, smiling, "but I think you should tell me yours first."

"Well, mine aren't very interesting," I said, "but I'll run through them if you like."

"Carry on," she said. "I'm listening."

I sighed.

"Well," I said, "my main problem is really the Cold War, I think. I got quite involved in anti-nuclear protests and in the disarmament movement in Oxford, you see – Aldermaston marches and so on – and as a result I really got pretty alienated from the whole system. The problem was that we weren't having any effect on the situation at all. I just couldn't see myself settling into any ordinary sort of job while the world was in such a crazy state of mind. Quite a number of my friends felt the same way, but they didn't get as far as Ethiopia. They dropped out nearer home. One of them has headed off to Greece, to teach English in Athens. I actually called in on him on the way out here ..." I tailed off rather lamely.

Caroline looked at me with amused contempt.

"You must be a total nutcase," she said. "You call that a problem? Of course the world is crazy. And Ethiopia is just that bit crazier than anywhere else, if you ask me. Don't you have anything more serious to worry about than that?"

I paused, and smiled ruefully. My other problem, I reflected, was really about personal identity – who on earth was I, and where on earth did I fit? – but I had a strong feeling that this would go down even worse than my first attempt at explanation, so I decided to downplay it.

"Oh, not really a problem, I suppose. Just a vague feeling of unease about where I fitted in. I'm Irish, in fact, but I don't fit in very well there, because I've lived mainly out of the country. I was born in Malaya, you see, and went to school mainly in England. But I don't feel I belong in England either."

To my relief, she didn't jeer at that, but took it quite seriously.

"Yes, I can see that being a bit of a problem," she said, reflectively. "But then how is this going to solve it?"

I laughed. "I don't know," I said. "I don't suppose it will, really. And now, what about your problems?"

We had reached the end of the orchard, and stopped and looked out together over the vast expanse of Africa that surrounded on all sides this little patch of English order. The sun was just beginning to go down in the west, lengthening the shadows of the acacias, but the air was still warm.

"My problems?" she said, smiling to herself. "Now there we have something more serious."

"Oh?" I said, looking at her with interest. She was looking into the incipient sunset, with a wistful expression that made her elfin face that much more attractive.

"Well yes, you see, I was all set to go up to Oxford this autumn – St. Hilda's – to do English. I even got an Exhibition, good little swot that I was. But there was a problem" – and she turned towards me, with a gaze that was both tentative and provocative. "You see, I had become *involved* with someone" – this uttered with heavy irony – "and he wasn't at all suitable."

I looked at her, not knowing quite what to say.

"Oh?" I ventured. " In what way was this person unsuitable?"

She smiled. "This person was not just slightly unsuitable. He was *very* unsuitable. He was middle-aged and married. In fact, he was the father of one of my best friends."

I opened my mouth, and then closed it again. Now I really did not know what to say. Caroline was, I think, rather pleased with the effect she had produced.

"It wasn't something I wanted to happen," she continued, "and nor did he, I think. But he's an English lecturer in the local college near us, and he helped me with a few projects I was working on, and one thing led to another, I suppose. His wife is a bit of a bitch, actually. He says they don't sleep together any more."

Jesus, I said to myself. This girl is eighteen, going on thirty.

"So your parents found out?"

"Yeah. Well, first she found out – I think the silly sod must have *confessed*, in a moment of weakness – and she phoned my Mum. So there was something of a showdown with parents, and their best solution was to ship me out here to Uncle Andy and Aunt Louise to let things cool off, and get the College to grant me a year's postponement, which they decently did. So here I am. Now you're quite sure you don't have an unhappy love affair lurking in the background? I got the impression that more or less everyone who headed out to Addis was running away from something like that."

I shook my head ruefully. Conducting a rapid survey of my emotional life at Oxford, or back in Wicklow, I could not come up with anything, despite some moments of brief excitement at dances – and one of my English cousins whom I rather liked – that would cause me to cross the road, never mind head for Africa. It was a sad record.

"No," I said. "I've had a rather boring life, in that way. But I don't think that anyone that I've met so far has been running away from an emotional crisis. It's more just the boredom of everyday life in Britain that seems to have driven people out here, as far as I can see. A good many of them are married, after all."

"Well," she said darkly, "you look more carefully. You'll find that most people here are running away from *something*. At least those that aren't married. Anyhow, that's my story, since you asked. Now let me show round the rest of the place."

We wandered round to a kitchen garden, then to an enclosure with hens and ducks, well-wired to keep out the hyenas, and on to a cluster of huts, roofed with corrugated iron, where the servants lived, and so round to the front of the bungalow again. In the brief period of our circuit of the farm, the sun had sunk noticeably down in the sky, and was now poised, like a great orange, to slip below the rim of the western mountains into the swamps of the southern Sudan.

"We might as well go in now," said Caroline, after a short pause. "It should be tea time."

And so it proved to be. Tea, like most meals at Nyala, was served late – in this case, around six o'clock. Dinner, I learned presently, was customarily not served until after the nine o'clock news on the BBC World Service, to which the Brig liked to listen in full evening dress, whiskey and soda in hand, while he commented, with varying degrees of outrage, on the course of world events. Now, however, a buxom girl in a gleaming white *shamma* brought in tea and cucumber and egg sandwiches and fruit cake, which we took in an alcove away from the fire, in front of a set of french windows open to the west, as the sun disappeared.

Having given an account of my situation and my ancestry to the Brig, I ventured to ask him in turn a little about his history. As Cousin James had suggested, he was quite willing to talk, if one could show him that one had an interest in, and some knowledge of, the subject.

"Well," he said, leaning back in his chair with a second cup of tea, "as I keep telling young Caroline here, this is a country which can easily get a grip on you, if you allow yourself to take an interest in it. After all, I came out here as a junior officer in the diplomatic corps back in 1914, just before the outbreak of war, and I was stuck here for the duration, apart from a brief excursion down to Tanganyika, to help to root Jerry out of there. So I set myself to learn something about the country, and the language and the culture. Well, of course, it's an endlessly fascinating place, as I'm sure you're already finding out, and after the war, when they wanted to move me, I just wasn't willing to move. So I resigned from the service, and went into business – import-export, that sort of thing – and managed to scrape a living at that until the Italians invaded in 1935. Fortunately Louise was prepared to join me out here after a few years – otherwise I might have been tempted to go native!"

He looked over at his wife with a comfortable chuckle, and was rewarded with an affectionate smile from that quarter. Mrs Stanford had settled down a little apart from us, and was topping and tailing gooseberries into a large bowl, aided by Caroline.

I nudged him a little further.

"And at what stage, sir, did you get to know the Emperor? Was he around when you first came out here?"

"No, no. He just gradually appeared on the scene. When I came out here first in early 1914, there was a pretty confused situation. Old Menelik had died back in 1912, you see, and had left the kingdom to his grandson Lij Yasu. But Yasu was just a kid, and he was a bit of a playboy and a fool as well – declared himself a Muslim, for one thing, which didn't go down too well – and then proposed to marry a series of wives, which outraged everybody. So they deposed him, and set up his mother, Zauditu, who was Menelik's daughter, as Empress. And this is where Haile Selassie comes in. He was just Ras Tafari Makonnen then, of course. His father, Ras Makonnen, had been Menelik's right-hand man, and Menelik had actually wanted him to succeed him – Makonnen's father Sahle Selassie had been King of Shoa, which is the area round Addis, so he was of royal blood – but Makonnen unfortunately died, and that's how Menelik came – in some desperation, I think – to settle on the wretched Yasu.

Anyhow, young Ras Tafari got himself appointed Regent to the Empress Zauditu in 1916, and over the next fourteen years he gradually came to take over the real power in the kingdom. By the time the old girl came to die in 1930, he was ready to be crowned emperor."

I was nodding all through this, but in truth my head was beginning to swim. The coronation, though, rang a bell, as I had read Evelyn Waugh's rather wicked account of it in his travel memoirs before coming out. I rashly mentioned this. The Brig's face darkened.

"Ah, that fellow Waugh! I came across him when he was here, I remember, and I can't say I much liked him. He's clever enough, I grant, but he gave a very superficial and slanted account of things, I must say."

"He was only here for a few weeks, I suppose," I ventured.

"Yes, of course. Like all these newspaper chappies. They blow in, get an instant impression of the situation, and then write about the place authoritatively ever after. It's just not as simple as that. I've been here damn near forty years by this time, after all, and I don't think I feel competent yet to write properly about this place."

"So you're not inclined to write your memoirs, sir?" I said.

The Brig snorted.

"Not on your life," he said. "I'd have to be rude about far too many chaps who are still around! They'll have to wait a while longer, I'm afraid." And he chuckled again.

The sun had by now definitely disappeared, and the room was suddenly becoming dark. The Brig heaved himself to his feet. "Time to light the lamps," he exclaimed. He toiled laboriously about the room, and, one after the other, a series of hurricane lamps hanging from the ceiling glowed into life. In a little while, a mild light suffused the room. The lamps swayed gently in the evening breeze, emitting a slight hiss. It was a most soothing light and sound – infinitely more expressive than brash electricity.

The Brig settled himself down again.

"So," I said, "when did you first get to meet the Emperor, then, sir?"

"Oh, not till much later, really. I met him first on a delegation of foreign traders some time in the early thirties. They asked me to lead it, since I could speak some Amharic, and, although the Little Man speaks French quite well, and certainly understands English, it was thought, quite rightly, that it would be appreciated if one could address him in Amharic. He liked the fact that I could speak the language, even if not very well, and asked me where I learned it, and a bit about myself, and he gave the delegation what it wanted. I liked him then, I must say. He came across as very shrewd, but fair. He wanted what was best for his country at all times, but he was prepared to encourage anyone that he felt showed goodwill – and if they wanted to make a bit of profit for themselves as well, that was fine by him.

"Still, I didn't really get to know him well until we were all back in the UK, when he was in exile in Bath. I got seconded to liaise with him, as did your Cousin James – that's where I met him – and we got on very well. And then when the war broke out, I was rounded up by Wavell and shipped out to Cairo to plan an invasion. The Emperor himself came out in June 1940, and that winter Orde Wingate and I mounted the invasion which brought him back to power. So we've been pretty good friends since that – though I don't see too much of him these days, I must say. He's become a bit less accessible since this last coup attempt, and anyhow I'm out here most of the time now. But your Cousin James tells me that even he finds it more difficult to get a hearing with him these days."

"Yes," I said, "I seem to remember him remarking on that."

"Well, it's natural, I suppose. He's getting old too, of course, like the rest of us. It's exhausting, and at times pretty discouraging, to have to run this country single-handed, and that's basically what he's doing. If he doesn't keep his eye on a given project, it tends to just grind to a halt. If they make an effort at something, they do it for him, not generally because they want to do it, or see the point of it. You see, these people in general don't really yet have any concept of progress, such as we would take for granted. They can't see why things shouldn't go on more or less exactly as they were. It's the same here in Nyala. We've introduced all sorts of improvements in their lives – always after consultation with the elders, of course – but still I'm damned sure that if we disappeared tomorrow they would just let everything slide right back to where it was before. And sometimes you begin to wonder if they aren't right. It may be we who are crazy, after all, with all this relentless so-called progress."

The Brig gazed out reflectively at the darkened expanse of Africa beyond the french windows. Then he roused himself, and rose to his feet.

"Well, almost time to change for dinner, I think. You feel like a bath, my boy? You may be a bit sticky after your journey. The boys can fix it, if you want. Plenty of water."

"Oh, well, I'd love one, if it wasn't too much trouble," I said, delighted. I had in fact been feeling rather sticky.

"No, no, not at all. I'll just find Mammo. By the way, dear" – he turned to his wife – "were we not planning that the young folks might take a trip down the gorge tomorrow morning? "

Mrs Stanford looked up, and then over at Caroline.

"Oh yes, we were, weren't we? How about that, Caroline? Would you like to take Luke down the gorge to the lower farm? Of course, we'll send one of the boys along, to look after the mules."

This sounded rather alarming, but Caroline looked enthusiastic.

"Yes, that'd be great," she said. "Shall we bring a picnic?"

"Of course," said her great-aunt. "We wouldn't send you down there without provisions. I'll notify cook this evening."

"That sounds lovely," I said rather cautiously, "but will we get back in time for me to drive home before dark?"

179

"Oh yes," said the Brig. "Don't you worry about that. You should be back up by about four at the latest, even if you have a bit of a siesta. That should get you back into town before six. That all right?"

"Oh yes," I said, "that should be fine." The idea of plunging over the edge of the gorge on a mule didn't in fact attract me enormously, but I felt that it would be both ungrateful and fainthearted to turn down the idea.

"Splendid!" said the Brig. "That's settled then. And now let's see if we can get you a bath."

In fact the bath was quite a production. The taps produced cold water, but the hot water had to be carried in by the servants in a series of large containers. It was for some reason brownish in colour, but seemed clean enough. In any case, it felt delicious, since the evening had by now become rather cool. I lay luxuriating there for quite some time, pushing a large sponge reflectively around with my toe, and mulling over the events of the day.

When I finally emerged, adorned in white shirt, blazer, and college tie, it was almost time for the nine o'clock news. The Brig, resplendent in dinner jacket, offered me whiskey or gin. I chose a gin and tonic. Caroline had dressed herself most attractively in a rather clinging long gown, with a plunging neckline, from which her small but prominent breasts threatened constantly to escape. I was just getting Mrs Stanford to give me a full account of the various types of fruit she produced when it was time for the news.

It was an odd experience to listen in that living room to humdrum news of the home country and the rest of the world, with the lamps swaying and hissing gently above us, while a succession of exotic bugs banged blindly into them, and the scent of various tropical flowers floated in from the garden. The Brig gave close attention to everything, but for the rest of us, I think, it was as if all this was happening on another planet. It was all I could do to make intelligent noises of assent to his trenchant comments on the various items.

Then we adjourned, for dinner, to a smaller room off the living room, where Mammo and others served up a splendid meal of roast lamb, raised on the farm, adorned with a wide selection of homegrown vegetables, and gooseberry fool to follow. And so, in due course, we filtered back, stuffed, into the living room, first for coffee, and then, the coffee things cleared away, for bridge.

The bridge game was quite a challenge. The Brig, like many long-time bridge players, took the game pretty seriously – a commitment that his wife, who was partnering me, plainly did not share. About me he was not yet sure. I would have to prove myself. Fortunately, bridge was a skill that I had acquired at school, and had had some occasion to use at home in Wicklow when Mother was short of a fourth, so that I was able to keep my end up. This evening Caroline had to make up the four. The Brig had very little hope for her as a bridge player, but at least she was willing to concentrate and try.

In spite of Louise Stanford's frivolous approach to the game, she and I had won the first rubber, which made everything worse. The Brig was now determined on a comeback. He had bid four spades, and he was meditating his lead.

Fortunately for domestic harmony, the Brig made his four spades, Caroline supporting him adequately, and, after a few further setbacks at the hands of Mrs S and myself, the rubber. He proposed another hand, but fortunately without much real conviction, and, after a brief nightcap of the local brandy, it was possible decently to retire to bed.

I was barely able to walk as I made my way to my room, but once I was lying down, I found myself strangely wakeful. Perhaps I was just overtired, but my conversation with Caroline before tea came back to disturb me. Specifically, it had stirred in me a memory of something I had wanted to suppress. As I lay on my back staring at the ceiling, listening to the night noises, something floated back into my mind.

It was in my second year, just around the time of my Mods exams, that I formed a friendship with a rather attractive girl from Somerville who attended a number of the same lectures. In particular, we were both doing a special subject in Comparative Philology, and I gained some mileage after one lecture by being able to explain to her more or less what a laryngeal was. So on the head of that I asked her to coffee, and she came. Her name was Jenny Danziger. She was half-American, which made her, I suppose, more forthcoming and self-assured than the normal English undergraduette, and her dark, Jewish good looks made her stand out in any company. Her father, as I recall, was an executive with some large American company in Britain, and a scientist by background, but she had become attracted by Classics, and had insisted on taking Latin and Greek at whatever expensive finishing school she had attended.

We got on rather well. She was very smart, but I had acquired a slight temporary advantage over her in the matter of laryngeals, and managed to keep my end up after that, though with difficulty. Anyhow, one thing led to another, and after a number of coffees together, I asked her along to a party given by the university newspaper, *The Cherwell*, for which I was writing a few things at the time. There we fell in with a flamboyant acquaintance of mine called Julian, who was, at the time, the Literary Editor. Julian set out deliberately to make an impression on Jenny, which he quickly succeeded in doing. He was, it must be said, a rather striking figure, with long flowing locks, and a rather intriguing hooked nose. After about a quarter of an hour and a couple of glasses of plonk, she was fixing her eyes on him in a thoroughly mesmerised way, and laughing at all his *bon mots*, which the beast was uttering at a most remarkable rate.

I did manage to get her away in the end, but not before they had exchanged addresses and phone numbers, on the pretext that she had written a poem or two that she would be glad of his opinion of. She thanked me most heartily for having introduced her, and on the way home to her digs expatiated on his various excellences.

So, to make a long story short, I lost Jenny to this Julian fellow, but that is only the background to the real point of the story, which is why it came back to me now. Despite becoming infatuated with Julian (who was really only concerned to add her to his collection of conquests – in a way, I suppose, exercising what he conceived to be his *droit de seigneur* as Literary Editor), Jenny wished to remain 'good friends' with me, so we continued to meet for coffee from time to time. This, however, became eventually more than I could stand, and shortly before the Mods exam I wrote her a note, saying that really I found it too much of a strain continuing to see her in this way, in view of her relationship with Julian.

Jenny was quite distressed by this, and summoned me to lunch to explain myself. And there, over spaghetti and a glass of wine, she said something that was presumably well intended, but which cut me to the quick.

"You see, Luke," she said, "I like you a lot, and I really value your friendship, but, you know, you're just not the sort of person that a girl *kinda falls in love with.*"

I had sat back in my chair then and looked at her, speechless with misery. She seemed to sense that this had not gone down too well.

"Oh come on, Luke," she said, "I didn't mean it like that! I just meant ... "

"But what do you mean?" I responded faintly.

"Oh, I don't know." She spread her hands in confusion. "It's just that you're so sort of cool and self-contained. You just don't, like, seem to *need* love. Oh hell, I don't know what I meant. All I can say is that I don't feel about you in that way."

I had to make my excuses and leave. She wanted me to promise to still be friends, but I knew that that had to be the end. The trouble was that Jenny had struck a nerve. This was very much what I had secretly feared for quite some time, that, while I could strike up acquaintances with people of either sex, I was after all not someone who could ever inspire love. She had confirmed that suspicion. I can remember walking aimlessly around the streets of Oxford, and then around Christ Church Meadow, for hours, just mulling over this fact, before I could face going back to my rooms, turning on the gas fire, and settling down to some work.

I got over that. One does. Fortunately, I had the exams to worry about. But that conversation had struck home, and now, having forgotten about it for quite some time, I dredged it up in the middle of the night, here in the middle of Africa. Perhaps, after all, I thought, I am not doing anything nearly so grand as withdrawing from the Cold War and the Arms Race; I am running away from a much more personal problem. I am a cold fish. I do not inspire love. And the hope would be, presumably, that, in a more tropical climate, and at an altitude of six or seven thousand feet, I might somehow be able to shake off this curse.

Facing up to this new revelation, then, was something that I did not find as depressing as might have been expected. Instead, I found myself fired with determination to break away from my fate, to lighten up, to behave recklessly, to see what I could squeeze out of life before it strangled me. And on that note I fell mercifully asleep.

I was woken only by a knock on the door, which I answered with an inarticulate mumble. It turned out to be Caroline, checking on me.

"It's me," she called through the door. "Are you decent?"

I sat up suddenly.

"Oh yes, fine. Come in."

She stuck her head in the door.

"Sorry to barge in, but I though I'd better just check. I think we're meant to get going around ten, so as to be down the valley before it gets too hot. Did you sleep well?"

"Oh yes," I said, raising myself on an elbow. "Rather too well, if anything." I looked at my watch, which told me it was a little after nine. 'Thanks for calling me. I'd better get out of this."

"Well, the bathroom's free, if you want to use it. I'll see you at breakfast." And she vanished.

I staggered out to the bathroom, and got myself up in ten minutes or so. When I reached the dining room, breakfast was in progress. Once again, there was a remarkable spread of homegrown and homemade produce set out before us. I was reasonably used to home produce from our life in Wicklow, but that did not include bacon from one's own pig, bread from one's own wheat, coffee from one's own beans, nor yet a selection of one's own tropical fruits.

I remarked on this to Mrs Stanford, and she beamed.

"Well, my dear, I'm glad you appreciate it. We do like to aim at virtual self-sufficiency here, and it's nice to know that we could survive pretty well indefinitely if we were cut off from the outside world, because in these times, after all, you never know..."

Then, as she poured me another cup of coffee, she directed a searching look in my direction, and changed the subject.

"You know," she said, reflectively, "you do have a remarkable resemblance to your cousin James, now that I come to look at you properly. I got an impression of that yesterday evening, but now this morning I'm much more struck by it. It's something about the eyes, in particular. Has anyone ever told you that?"

I was taken quite by surprise.

"No," I said, " I must say they haven't. But then, after all, we haven't been together very often. This is really the longest I've been in his vicinity, really, since I was quite small."

"Well," she smiled, "It's nice that you'll have this time with him, at last. I know he was looking forward very much to your coming – though of course James is not very demonstrative, at the best of times. I could tell, though."

"Well," I said, "it's certainly very pleasant for me to be out here with him. He's been enormously hospitable – and useful, of course."

Caroline had been listening to all this with some amusement, but now moved to break up the party.

"I think we'd probably better be going, Aunt Louise. I think I saw Mammo bringing round the mules to the front."

Mammo had indeed led a string of three mules round to the front door, one for either of us, and a pack-mule, loaded with supplies. He himself would go on foot, loping along ahead of us, leading this mule, with the effortless stride of the Ethiopian highlander. Mrs Stanford accompanied us out, and checked the supplies, which seemed to satisfy her, and which certainly looked pretty copious. Mammo gave Caroline and me in turn a leg up on our mules. The Ethiopian saddle looked rather cumbersome, but felt comfortable enough when one was in it. I looked nervously at the back of my mule's head. He had his ears back, but otherwise seemed mild enough. I hoped he was. Mammo gave his animal a tug on the reins, and the expedition began to move off. Caroline followed, digging in expertly with her knees. Mrs Sandford gave my mount a brisk smack on the rump, and he jerked into motion as well.

We headed off on a rough path leading between two acacias, straight towards the lip of the gorge in the middle distance. The sun was already warm on our backs, though the air was pleasantly crisp. There was a feeling of vast spaces.

"Have you ever ridden one of these animals?" shouted Caroline over her shoulder.

"No," I shouted back, "never a mule. I've had to ride horses back home a certain amount, but I can't say I'm a great enthusiast. I never went in for hunting, or anything."

"Well, they're not bad if they're in convoy, as long as you're not the leader. In this case they'll just follow Mammo and the pack-mule. Remember, though, when we get to the path down the gorge, to lean in well towards the edge of the cliff, and don't look directly down.

Otherwise it gets pretty scary. There's no real danger, though. They're very sure-footed animals."

"You've done this a few times, then?" I said.

"Oh, just twice, actually. But it makes you feel like a veteran."

Caroline's advice was well chosen. In about ten minutes we reached the lip of the gorge, and faced a truly awesome spectacle. I tried not to look directly down, but gazing out ahead of us I saw what appeared to be an almost sheer drop of two thousand feet to the valley floor below, which seemed to be luxuriant with vegetation of all kinds. A stream flowed down the middle of valley, and raising my eyes towards the head of the gorge to the south, I could see where it came from, a splendid waterfall, spilling over the lip of the gorge, and descending in two stages to the valley below.

The ride down could not be described as pleasant. One had to grip the flanks of the mule hard with one's knees, and lean backwards and inwards, keeping one's eyes either on the wall of rock beside one, or occasionally on the middle distance. It took nearly an hour of slow and laborious zigzagging to reach the bottom. However, there was a great sense of achievement when one finally got there. "It's actually not so bad coming up," Caroline assured me at some point in our descent. "It's a smoother ride, and not so dizzy-making." I was glad to hear it.

The difference in climate made itself felt as soon as we collected our senses. It had been getting warmer as we descended, but now I realised we were in the tropics. The air was thick and steamy, and full of exotic smells and noises. In the tops of the tall trees, eucalyptus and other, one could see black and white colobus monkeys chasing each other around. On the ground ahead of us, a couple of buck scampered away through the undergrowth as we advanced, and there were other anonymous crashings in the bush to either side of us, which Caroline guessed were probably pig.

We were heading, in fact, for a sort of summer house or hunting lodge, set in a clearing, for the use of those who were down supervising work on the lower farm. There was a native village down here as well, the *tukuls* of which we saw in the distance, inhabited by those who worked at the tropical level of the farm. Here there was a coffee plantation, and bananas, and oranges, and even pineapples beside the river. Further down the valley, Caroline said, they were experimenting with cotton.

With great relief we slipped off the mules, and left them in the charge of the faithful Mammo. The summer house was most attractive, simply furnished with two beds, a table, a dresser and some chairs, and a little paraffin stove, the windows protected only with light bamboo blinds, which provided, as did the overhanging eaves, a maximum of shade and circulation of air. We looked in on it, but then Caroline suggested that we take a walk through the plantation, down to the river, before lunch. That seemed a good idea to me.

After a short walk through the forest, we came to a fence and a carefully shut gate, tied together with various bits of wire. "Got to keep the damned pig and deer out," explained Caroline, proprietorially, as she undid the various bits. "They'd wreck everything." We walked first through a grove of orange trees, the fruit of which was still unfortunately green, and then through the coffee plantation, down to the river. Caroline quizzed me about Oxford, on which I could tell her quite a lot, and then about my origins in Malaya, about which I could tell her almost nothing. She was natural, unaffected, and not at all shy – conscious, I thought, of her own attractiveness, and happy with that. The affair with her friend's father, I thought as I studied her profile surreptitiously, must have contributed to this. It did indeed contribute greatly to her subtle attractiveness. At one point, as we strolled along beside the river, our eyes met, and she smiled almost conspiratorially.

"No hippos or crocs in this, I suppose," I said, stopping to study the stream as it burbled through the plantation. It was still shallow and fast-flowing at this stage of its progress. On the other side, I could see, there were pineapples; on this side, just in front of us, coffee. I reached out idly to one of the bushes, and caressed the small, hard, green beans. Caroline stood close beside me, so that our arms touched lightly. I imagined I could feel a certain friendly warmth pulsating from her arm to mine which stirred in me a disquieting tingle.

"Let's go back," she said, slightly huskily, as if she too had felt something. "I'm sure Mammo has got the lunch set up by now."

Again, I was in no mood to argue, and we retraced our steps to the lodge in the clearing, once again displacing a few buck on the way, when we got out of the plantation and back into the forest. And always there were the monkeys, playing tag in the tops of the trees.

The lunch was in fact set out for us, including a very welcome flask of cool home-made lemonade, with Mammo standing guard over it patiently. He had laid a table on the verandah of the little house, in the shade, and having seen that we had everything, he retired tactfully to the shade of a huge sycamore about a hundred yards away, near where he had tethered the mules, and, wrapping himself in his *shamma*, prepared to enjoy his siesta.

We rather picked at our lunch, excellent though it was. For one thing, the tropical noonday heat tended to sap the appetite, but for another, a strange electricity had been generated between us that seemed to supplant any need for food. Caroline kept glancing at me speculatively, and I at her. I felt something had to be said, but I could not bring myself to say it.

Suddenly, she sat back in her chair, raised her eyes defiantly to mine, and made a most extraordinary statement.

"I don't mind admitting it," she said. "I'm feeling distinctly sexy. It must be the weather. Do you want to make love?"

I stared back at her, temporarily speechless. A charge of adrenalin coursed through my stomach, leaving me weak, but very happy. I had interpreted the vibrations correctly, but I would never have had the nerve to act on my intuition. Now that she had brought it out in the open, though, the tension suddenly dissipated.

"Gosh, Caroline," I gasped, "I was really hoping that something like that was on your mind, but I wouldn't have dared say anything."

She giggled delightfully.

"I could see you weren't going to say anything," she said, derisively, "so I supposed I would have to. This is the nineteen sixties, after all."

I laughed in turn, a trifle shamefaced, but defiant.

"Yes, I am a bit inhibited, I suppose. But you have to admit that you're far less likely to be turned down on a proposal like that than I am."

She looked at me, and grinned. "Yes, I suppose you're right."

She paused thoughtfully for a moment, and then continued.

"By the way, I'm not necessarily saying that I want to get *involved*, you understand. In fact, I think I've had enough of that for a while. I just want to *fuck*. That's all there is to it. Is that okay with you?"

I gulped.

"Oh, absolutely," I said. "That's fine with me."

"Right!" she said, briskly. "You got any thingummies?"

Again, her businesslike directness temporarily took my breath away. I groped hopelessly in my trouser pockets.

"God, sorry," I said. "I did have a few in my coat, but I left that in the house."

Well, that's okay." She reached for her bag. "I think I have one or two in here. It's just a habit I got into, fortunately. You can't rely on men to think of these things."

"No, I suppose not," I said, faintly.

She rose from the table, and I followed her into the house, mesmerised by the undulation of her hips under her tight shorts.

In the green shade of the room we slipped out of our clothes in a moment, and stood facing each other. Her breasts, as I had observed earlier, were small but prominent, and her body was lean and lithe as a panther's.

"What about Mammo?" it suddenly occurred to me to ask.

"Oh, Mammo won't disturb us for the next hour at least. He's far too tactful."

And she turned her back on me, and made for the right-hand bed. I followed her. There was just a *shamma* spread over it, so we slipped under that, and into each other's arms.

In its way, it was one of the most extraordinary experiences of my life so far. Fortunately I had been initiated into the mysteries by Berhane, and that was great, but after all she was hired to do the job. This was different. Caroline was offering herself to me quite freely, and she was proposing to get just as much enjoyment out of it as I was.

This she plainly did. She strained her body against mine, wrapped her legs round me, and seemed to come, violently, more or less just as I did. We collapsed together in a flurry of shrieks and groans. Then we looked at each other in horror and began to giggle uncontrollably.

"Sshhh," I hissed urgently, temporarily assuming an Irish accent. "Mammo will think I'm after murdhering the young mistress!"

Caroline buried her face in my shoulder and went on giggling for a while. Then she looked up at me.

"That was really fun," she said. "You're a pretty good lover."

"Oh, thanks," I said. "You're not so bad yourself."

"We must do this again sometime," she said, grinning wickedly.

I stroked her cheek gently, tidying back a damp strand of hair.

"By all means," I said.

We were sticky under the *shamma*, so we threw it off, and lay for a while side by side in the warm gloom, with a slight breeze ruffling the bamboo blind. Then Caroline stirred.

"Come on," she said, "we'd better get ourselves out of here. There'll be enough gossip in the servants' quarters as it is." She looked at her watch, and I looked at mine. It was just before two o'clock in the afternoon. "We might just have time, I suppose," she added, "to take a short skinny-dip in the river, if you liked. It's a bit chilly, but it's refreshing."

This idea sounded good, so we dressed quickly, and crept cautiously out of the cabin, Caroline bringing along the *shamma* for use as a towel. Mammo, thankfully, was still wrapped up under his tree. If he had heard or noticed anything odd, he was giving no sign of it. So we tiptoed across the clearing, and dodged down the forest path. I disposed tactfully of the evidence in the bushes as we went.

The river was indeed a bit of a shock, and it was hardly possible to submerge, but, as Caroline had predicted, it was most refreshing. We were in and out pretty quickly, and dried off sketchily with the *shamma*.

The idea was to start back up the trail at about three, and this we achieved with time to spare. When we got back to the lodge, we found that Mammo had roused himself, and had already almost finished tidying up the lunch things, leading one to suspect that he had not been as fast asleep as he had appeared to be. He then repacked the mule, and we were ready to set out.

As Caroline had said, the journey up was a lot less alarming than the journey down, and not much longer, so by shortly after four we were once again on the high plateau, amid cooler, crisper air.

Mrs Stanford was waiting for us in front of the house as we rode up, having no doubt seen us from the living room window. The Brig had still not risen from his afternoon nap, but she arranged an early tea for us, and he appeared before the end of it to see me off.

I left Nyala shortly after five, with warm invitations to return ringing in my ears. Caroline and I were able to do no more than look at each other meaningfully. We shook hands politely, and I thanked her for a most interesting expedition. Then I drove off on the slightly precarious journey home, with my nerve-ends tingling and an ache in the pit of my stomach.

I took things pretty easy on the way out to the main road, and the old car did not let me down. As I came over the rise of Entotto, the lights of Addis twinkled welcomingly below me in the twilight, and I coasted down the hill to The English School compound.

The ache and the tingling stayed with me for the rest of the evening, as I tried to put a shape on the events of the weekend. I couldn't complain. I came out to this country in search of new experiences, and there certainly had been no shortage of those. But how much more in the way of new experiences could I take? It is all very well to agree to make love with a rather beautiful girl, on the spur of the moment, without any strings attached, but the heart doesn't understand these eminently sensible arrangements. It tends to attach itself, despite whatever the head may have agreed. Caroline had done me the enormous favour of neutralising, at one stroke, the baneful legacy of Jenny Danziger. True, she did not actually declare that I was lovable, but she had at least made plain that I was not physically repulsive, and for that I felt very grateful, apart altogether from the pleasure she had given me.

It was a strange thing, I reflected. Sex is a most intensely physical pleasure, but the most attractive aspect of it in the end is actually the intellectual experience. The real fascination of it is relating in this peculiarly intimate way with another intelligent human being, I thought. And this was an intelligent human being – endowed, admittedly, with a very attractive body – I had come upon that afternoon. Despite her warning, I had a feeling that it would be a serious challenge to avoid falling in love with her.

CHAPTER TWELVE

The following morning, the ache in the pit of my stomach to which I have referred was supplemented, when I woke up, by a profound stiffness in the arse. I had not been on a horse for some time, and this told. I had been gripping on to that mule for dear life, especially on the ride down. I creaked across to Assembly – to the amusement of my colleagues when they learned the reason.

Isabel was most anxious to learn how I had got on, and waylaid me as I was returning to my bungalow during break. I complained of stiffness from the mule-ride, but emphasised how much I had enjoyed the whole experience, and how greatly I appreciated the hospitality of her parents.

"And how did you get on with Caroline?" she asked, with a smile.

"Oh, very well," I replied blandly. "She was excellent company on the trip down the valley."

"I'm very glad to hear that," said Isabel. "She must have liked you. The old folks are rather stuck to know what to do with her, actually. Perhaps now they'll send her into town for you to squire her around!"

I maintained my composure with some difficulty.

'Well, I'd be glad to take her around, certainly, if they would like a bit of a rest. But of course she'd have to stay with you, wouldn't she, and that would be a nuisance."

"Oh well, we wouldn't mind for a couple of days at a time. It would certainly be a relief to the aged p.s, and to Caroline herself, I'm sure. We'll see."

Complications! I thought, with a sigh. I could not deny that I had something of a longing to see Caroline again, but at the same time I rather dreaded the consequences. Suppose it came out that I was another unsuitable liaison?

I spent, on the whole, a relatively quiet, studious week, though I still had not managed to get down to any serious writing, such as I had promised myself to try. My classes were under control, even beginning to be fun, as I learned more about the personalities of my pupils. In my first Amharic lesson from Girma, we looked at the mysteries of the Amharic alphabet. Amharic, along with its ancestor *Ge'ez*, is the only Semitic language that is written from left to right, but this is balanced by the fact that of every letter of the alphabet there are seven distinct forms, corresponding to the variety of vowel that may follow it. I was not sure how far I was going to get with this. It would need a lot of work – certainly get in the way of any sort of creative writing. Meanwhile, however, I was learning a few words and phrases from Tekla-Mariam and from Berhane.

I wrote a long letter home, trying to describe to my mother the beauties of Nyala (apart from Caroline). I was finding it progressively more difficult in my own mind to give a coherent account of my adventures. It was all too strange and difficult to communicate. Still, I owed it to her to write. On her side, she was writing regular bulletins from Wicklow, detailing the little problems and triumphs of life at Bellevue. Granny had been by no means well, and Dr Salter was a frequent caller, though fortunately very broadminded about his fees. Gerry Walsh had been persuaded to fix the fence into the back haggard, and had put twenty head of cattle into the Long Field. The hens were laying well, and there had been a good crop of apples. Reading over her letters, and lying back in my chair, I seem to get sudden whiffs of chill autumn mist, and the pungent scents of dead leaves and cowdung.

Looking at my mother's life from this remote perspective, I was overcome by a deep sadness. What had induced me to abandon her there? It was selfish and heartless of me. But then, let's face it, I can't really join her there in any case, in Bellevue. I would have to earn my living, sooner or later, perhaps in England – probably in England – certainly at least in Dublin. Why on earth, it occurred to me, could she not have got together with Cousin James? They really did love each other, in some strange way, I was convinced of that. But they were two inhibited and obstinate people, and there was really nothing I could do about this.

My Russians were warming up. One week Safar brought along a bottle of vodka, and some delicious little meat pies, and we had a party. I supplied the coffee and cake, as before, and I offered some Irish whiskey, to match the vodka, which went down very well. Indeed, they dangerously depleted my supply. I began to see the Russians, once they managed to drop their official, stonefaced facade, as being remarkably like the Irish. We drank to world peace, and to Irish-Soviet friendship, and really became quite silly. Nikolai even sang a sad Russian song, and the others joined in as a chorus. When we finally got down to business, many of the stories in the Ethiopian Herald suddenly struck us as very funny indeed.

That evening I had another rehearsal at Jack's, and we worked out a repertoire for the coming weekend. I had been trying to practice a bit every evening, using a mute to muffle the racket, and my lip was gradually coming back, as was my pleasure in improving my technique.

By the following Friday, I was ready to play my first gig at the Paradiso, and by five o'clock, after classes, was warming up at the Ras Bar with Simon. We were wrapping ourselves around the first ice-cold Melotti of the day, and waiting to see who would turn up to join us, when a red sports car with its roof down pulled up at the steps of the bar. A familiar figure, in dark glasses was at the wheel of it, and beckoned to me imperiously. A number of faithful subjects, having recognised a member of the royal family, were already engaged in prostrating themselves on the pavement.

'Sorry," I said to Simon, in astonishment. "It's Yohannis. I'll just go and see what he wants." I hurried down the steps to the car, and Yohannis greeted me exuberantly.

"Luke, old man! I'm very glad to have caught you. This is most fortunate. I was just going to phone and see if you'd like to come down with me for the weekend to the country, but I happened to see you here. I'm going down to my hunting lodge on Lake Langano for a couple of days, and I wondered if it would amuse you to come along."

I had to think fast. "Gosh, Yohannis, that would be delightful. My only problem this weekend is that I've promised faithfully to play in a jazz group tonight and tomorrow, and I really can't stand them up."

"A jazz group? This is remarkable! I didn't know you played jazz."

"I play trumpet," I grinned. "I wasn't playing much at Oxford when we met, but I've been persuaded to take it up again by this American fellow I met."

"Well, well," said Yohannis, undaunted, "I'd love to hear this. How about I come along to your session this evening, and then we can drive down to the lodge after that. It's only about an hour's drive at that time of night. We can have a bit of hunting tomorrow, and I can get you back again for tomorrow evening. We can take a longer trip some other time."

"Well, I mean, that'd be great. "

"Where are you playing, and when do you start?"

"Well, it'll be from around nine to at least midnight, I'm afraid, and it's at a place called the Paradiso."

"Oh yes," he said, "I know it well. Belongs to a good friend of my father's."

"Well, we have his son in the band, in fact."

Yohannis laughed loudly.

"Well, this I absolutely must hear. Look, I'll see you there, some time after nine. Bring an overnight bag, and we'll go on straight from there."

And he drove off, to the bows and salutations of his subjects, which he acknowledged with a series of regal waves.

I tottered back up the steps, slightly dazed, and reported these developments to Simon. He raised his hands to heaven.

"All I can say, La Touche, is that you are in danger of getting in way out of your depth. How do you know what goes on in this hunting lodge of his?"

"Okay," I said, " you're right. I don't. I admit it. But what can I do? Yohannis is a hard man to refuse. Anyhow," I added, "I came here for some new experiences, and I'm really not in the mood to turn them down when they present themselves, especially in this form."

"Aha!," said Simon, his eyebrows rising derisively. "So we came here for new experiences, did we? I thought we were withdrawing from the capitalist rat-race and the madness of the Cold War."

"Well," I said defensively, "that too, of course. But also new experiences – within reason."

At that point we were joined, almost simultaneously, from different directions, by Maurice and by Marco, and the conversation turned in other directions.

"Ah, Signor Luke!" Marco greeted me warmly. "How is she going, your auto?"

"Oh, just fine, in general, Marco," I said, but I told him, then, about the overheating on the way to Nyala, and he was suitably concerned.

"You bring her in to me when you can, and I fix her up. She need a bit of tuning, perhaps."

I promised to do that, and the gossip turned in other directions. We were joined in due course by a colleague of Maurice's, a large and cheerful Viking called Knut, and then by a most learned and talkative Indian physician, Dr Ranjan Ratna, who served as doctor to The English School. "The right man to go to," Simon introduced him, "if you get a dose of the clap." Dr Ratna had served, before becoming established in Addis, in various rather remote parts of the provinces, and had many curious stories to tell.

Suddenly, though, I realised that it was half past seven, and that I had to get back and pack a bag before we went out to find something to eat, so Simon and I excused ourselves. Maurice was disinclined to come on to the Paradiso, by reason of his abhorrence of all things American, including jazz, but Knut was keen, so it sounded as if he might grumblingly attend for a while, and we agreed to see them there. Dr Ratna had to return to the bosom of his family.

Simon drove me to the compound, I put a few things into a bag, and we headed off to Addis Ababa's only Chinese restaurant for some Szechuan delicacies, washed down by a couple of flagons of rice wine. We managed to arrive, slightly sloshed, at the Club Paradiso shortly after half past eight, giving me some time to warm up.

The place was still fairly empty when we got there, but someone was tinkling away on the piano to the few punters who had arrived. Simon picked a table near to the band, and got himself a beer. I left him, and disappeared out the back, following the sound of instruments warming up. I found the band assembled in one of the dressing rooms, which also, to judge from the bed and selection of mirrors, served as a refuge for any customer who wanted to retire with one of the girls. There was a full corridor of such rooms. Jack was already in something of a fuss, and bitched at me a bit for being late. I just smiled beatifically, and reached for the trumpet.

Our repertoire for this weekend was distinctly 'cool', with just a scattering of up-tempo numbers. We ran through the riffs of 'Round Midnight', 'April in Paris', 'Embraceable You', and then 'Straight, No

Chaser'. I was feeling happily in command of my instrument, and tried out a few Milesian quarter-tones and rills, until it was almost nine o' clock, and Jack's equilibrium was restored.

"Okay, guys," he said, "that should do it. Let's get out there and slay 'em dead."

"Oh, by the way," I said, turning in particular to Hailu, "I think we may be going to have a distinguished visitor tonight, in the person of Lij Yohannis Tessema. I saw him earlier this afternoon, and he seemed really keen to hear us play. He said he'd be along."

"Oh wow," said Jack, excited. "Good work, Luke! I remember you saying you knew this guy. If we give a good performance tonight, maybe we'll get a commission to play at one of his parties."

"Yes," I said, "we might indeed, come to think of it. That's worth working for. He was looking forward particularly to hearing you on the bass, Hailu."

Hailu grinned in some embarrassment.

"Oh," he said, "I think he will come just to tease me. That is what he usually does."

We were announced by the Greek manager, Mr Efstathiadis, and filed out onto the stage to the accompaniment of scattered applause. I looked out across the saloon, now almost full. Simon was at his table, joined now, I was amused to see, by Knut and a grumpy-looking Maurice. No sign yet of Yohannis, but I was not expecting him to be prompt. I hoped there would be room for him, but in fact there seemed to be a large table reserved near the stage, and it occurred to me that it might be for him, if he had phoned ahead.

We launched into our first set. It was a satisfying experience. The audience, mostly expatriate in appearance, but with some young Ethiopians mixed in, was not too demanding, fortunately, since our ensemble work was a little ragged, and my solos, at least, contained a multiplicity of missed and half-missed notes. But we played with expression and verve, and soon we had the open area in front of the stage full of dancers, while those still in their seats applauded enthusiastically.

It was around a quarter to ten when Yohannis arrived, accompanied by a party of five others, one of whom was his cousin Alex Desta, and another young man whom I remembered from his inner sanctum at the party, and three glamorous-looking girls, with the delicate bone-

197

structure of the Amhara aristocracy. I had been right about the table. Immediately on the party's appearance, waiters bustled round them and ushered them to it, with much bowing. I was just beginning my solo in 'Straight, No Chaser', as it happened, and I pointed the trumpet at him cheerfully. Yohannis removed his dark glasses, and raised a hand in salute, then turned to ordering drinks. Mr Efstathiadis himself hurried over and greeted him, and then all of the party in turn. He was plainly very pleased to see them. I reckoned this would help to endear us to him. A number of bottles of champagne were hastily brought to the table, and corks began to pop. Various members of the group got up from time to time to dance, but not Yohannis himself. He just lay back in his chair, champagne glass in hand, and grooved on the music.

At the end of the set, I came down off the stage, followed by Hailu, and went over to greet the company.

"Well, Luke, old man," shouted Yohannis, grinning, "I had no idea you could do this. This is really impressive! And Hailu too, plucking away like a real professional!"

He introduced me round the group, but apart from Alex Desta, I didn't get the names. The girls came across as simply *woizerit* this and *woizerit* that. They smiled sweetly as they shook hands. Jack was hanging back, so I waved him forward to be introduced. Yohannis greeted him, and congratulated him on the band.

I noticed Mr Efstathiadis in the background, gold teeth gleaming and eyes popping. Then we left them to it, and retired backstage, pausing at Simon's table on the way to exchange a few insults. Maurice was still hanging in there, though looking very sceptical. Knut, though, was plainly enjoying it greatly. He shouted a compliment as we passed, which I valued, remembering the great jazz tradition of Sweden.

We came out for the second set, this time to much warmer applause, and launched into a lively rendition of 'Summertime'. I may have been too drunk to make a fair assessment, but I thought we were sounding better and better. I was rediscovering what a joy it was to make music, to lose oneself in the rhythm, to participate, even to this minor extent, in the act of creation. About half an hour into the set, however, my exaltation was doused somewhat by noticing suddenly, standing at the bar, a figure in policeman's uniform and dark glasses; the mysterious Colonel Tamrat, apparently. His gaze rested on Yohannis' table. Then he finished his drink, and turned and left. Of course, I reflected, he may be seconded to serve as Yohannis' bodyguard, and so it would be simply his business to be here. But it was no concern of mine, in any case, so after a while I dismissed him from my mind, and submerged myself once again in the music.

It was shortly after midnight when we signed off. The club was by no means closing yet, but they would have to make do with their resident piano player after this. Simon came up and slapped me on the back, and said that he and Knut would go off and have a nightcap somewhere else, and find themselves a couple of girls. Maurice, I noted, had finally bowed out sometime during the second set. Only now did I explain to Jack that I had accepted an invitation from Yohannis, which both impressed and disappointed him, but I promised to be back tomorrow night, and then we would have a drink after the show.

I took my bag, leaving the horn with Jack, and came over to Yohannis' table, where the party was just breaking up. Yohannis had arranged for his cousin Alex to take the rest of the party home, and he and I would leave in his Landrover (since the road did not really suit the Maserati). We all shook hands with Mr E, and then, outside, with each other. Yohannis spoke briefly to Alex Desta in Amharic, kissed each of the girls in turn, and then steered me over to the Landrover, where his driver was waiting patiently.

Yohannis and I climbed into the back seat, and the car pulled out of the club car park onto the main drag, Adowa Avenue, heading south out of town. Yohannis started off by repeating his praise for the performance, but then slumped back in his seat, and looked over at me, lowering his voice to a whisper.

"By the way, better not to say anything important in the car. I'm not quite sure of this driver. He's been given to me by the Ministry of the Interior. He pretends he doesn't know English, but I think he does."

I raised my eyebrows, and nodded.

"Lots of time to talk when we get there, though," he continued. "And we should get in a little hunting tomorrow, though we'll have to get up pretty early if we want to have any luck."

'What sort of game do you hunt?" I asked.

"Oh, there's pig, and various kinds of buck, and ducks on the lake.

We might even see a leopard if we're lucky – though I don't like to shoot them if I don't have to."

We continued to gossip as the car left the city along the airport road, in the direction of Bishoftu. It was not till we were well out of town that it became apparent to me that we were being followed. The lights of a car had been steady behind us for about a quarter of an hour before I began to notice it. Though we were not travelling particularly fast, this car made no attempt to pass, and indeed came no nearer, nor yet did it drop back. I turned round to look at it a couple of times, and then turned to Yohannis.

"Yohannis, do you think it's possible that someone is tailing us?"

Yohannis looked round, and then shrugged indifferently.

"Yes," he said. "I'm afraid it is entirely possible. My uncle seems to like to know where I am, and who I'm with, these days. But I wouldn't worry about it. Once they see we're headed for Langano, they'll probably leave us alone. And I'm sure they won't be worried about you. If it were the Soviet military attaché now, that would be another matter." And he chuckled.

"Doesn't this sort of thing bother you at all, though?" I asked, bewildered.

He shrugged again. "It does a bit. Or it used to, certainly, when it first started. But my feeling now is that I don't have anything to hide, so they can watch me all they want." Then he lowered his voice again. "But I forgot. Better not discuss anything serious in the car."

We relapsed into a sleepy silence. I began to feel a little anxious. Were we, then, going to discuss serious matters when we were out of the car? And what serious matters?

The Landrover was not particularly comfortable, nor was it, as I have said, particularly speedy, and it was almost two in the morning by the time we turned right off the main road, having driven through the largely sleeping town of Bishoftu, and began to bump along a rather irregular track. At least we had lost our tail, which disappeared when we passed through Bishoftu.

In a little while, a large lake came into view on our left, gleaming dimly in the light of a nearly full moon. Reeds lined the shore, and out in the middle of it there rose the bulk of an island. It was a wild and beautiful scene. After about ten minutes of lurching along the track we came to a set of formidable gates. The driver blew the horn, and a *zabanya* staggered out of a hut just inside, and challenged him through the bars. Once he was satisfied as to our identity, the man set to work to unlock and throw open the gates. As we passed, he saluted, and I noticed that, as at Ras Tessema's *ghibbi* in the city, he was armed with a pretty useful-looking automatic weapon.

In another minute or so a rather splendid lodge came into view, looking out over the lake. Lights began to come on in various parts of it, as the servants stirred themselves to welcome their master.

"Gosh, Yohannis," I said, impressed. "This is a really beautiful place you've got here."

He looked pleased.

"I like it," he said. "I had it designed, actually, by our best young Ethiopian architect, Abebe Worqu. He's a friend of mine. It's a creative adaptation of traditional architecture. You'll see it better in the morning."

But as we climbed out, I could already see that the building combined, in an interesting way, features of a Scandinavian-style hunting lodge, using a lot of wood, with a curved native thatched roof. We had driven round the back, where the main door appeared to be. Facing the lake there was a raised verandah, the ground sloping down from the house to the shore. A boy hurried out to take my bag, and Yohannis waved me inside.

"I'll show you to your room," he said. "And then how about a little night-cap on the verandah before we turn in?"

It was very late, especially if we were to go hunting in the morning, but the idea of a drink looking out over the lake in the moonlight was too attractive to turn down, so I made no objection. My room was delightful, not unlike that at Nyala, low-ceilinged, wood-panelled, but looking out, this time, not on an orchard but on a rather splendid swimming-pool, which gleamed dimly in the moonlight against a background of forest.

"Hey," I said, "you have a pool."

"Yes," said Yohannis, "you can have a swim now if you want."

I laughed. "Gosh, it'd be sort of pleasant, but I think it's a bit late. Let's just have a little drink, and then bed. I've had a hard night. Maybe tomorrow, though?"

"Yes," said Yohannis, "we can have one after hunting. Come on up to the verandah now, and we'll find a drink."

And five minutes later we were ensconced in two capacious cane chairs, looking out over the lake, each with a generous glass of Scotch and soda in hand. Yohannis had also produced a joint, explaining that it was of particularly good quality, and we passed it back and forth in the approved manner. The combination was remarkably soothing. I looked out over the waters of the lake, and let flow over me the multitudinous noises of the soft, warm darkness.

"Well," I said, "this is certainly some spot. It's got a great feel to it. Seems a bit warmer than Addis, or am I just overheated?"

"Yes," said Yohannis, "we're actually about a thousand feet lower. You feel the difference."

"Mm." I sipped my drink. "I must say, you know," I ventured, "when you're surrounded by all this, Yohannis, it seems very noble of you – or very rash – to involve yourself in the sort of political activities you seem to be involved in." And I looked over at him.

He was gazing out into the darkness. I could only see the outline of his face.

"Well," he replied, "as I've said to you before, it's not really a matter of altruism. If I thought I could just sit back and enjoy this way of life for the indefinite future, I might just be tempted to do that – though I really think I'd get pretty restless after a while, anyhow. I'm not really cut out to be just a playboy. But I think I can see the writing on the wall. Then he resorted temporarily to Marxist jargon.

"The contradictions within this society are just too great, and they're growing, hand in hand with development and prosperity. But they could be controlled, if the proper steps were taken. It's just unfortunate, though, that my uncle has been running this place so long he has become convinced that he always knows best, and that only he can run it."

"But," I said, "if he's so definite about that, isn't it better just to let him get on with it? From what I've heard, he's a dangerous man when crossed."

Yohannis sighed, and sipped his whiskey. Then he took a drag on the joint, and passed it back to me.

"Yes, that is true. He does not welcome new ideas. And that means that it may become necessary to save him from himself."

I did not much like the sound of this.

"But it's plain, isn't it, that he's watching you pretty closely? I mean, let's face it, that car tonight only gave up when we went through Bishoftu, and it was reasonably obvious where you were going. But he knows you're down here, for example. And when you go back to town, he'll know that too. And if you get in contact with anyone, he knows that, I presume.'

"Ah well," said Yohannis, slowly, "he doesn't know everything. I have ways of getting round his surveillance. But in any case, as I've said before to you, I'm not involved in subversion or in revolution. I'm actually trying to avoid that. I'm trying to bring people together, to make them feel they all have a place in this regime."

And then suddenly he froze, and laid a hand on my arm.

"Keep absolutely still," he whispered, "and look out there." And he pointed with his glass.

I strained my eyes out into the darkness. I had no idea what he had seen.

But then I saw. Padding down the path to the lake from the surrounding forest came a magnificent leopard, its muscles rippling under its spotted pelt. It paused a moment as it passed in front of the verandah, and looked around, its fierce, intolerant eyes glinting in the moonlight. It occurred to me that we were by no means out of range of his leap if he chose to attack us. But in fact, if the leopard sensed our presence, he showed no interest in us. He had come for a drink in the lake, and that is where he turned.

I watched him lower his muzzle to the water's edge and drink. He lapped like a cat, pausing after every few laps to look around him. Muzzy as I now was with both Scotch and pot, I was conscious suddenly of an extraordinary sensation. It seemed to me, as I watched the leopard, that I was there at the water's edge, inside his pelt. For a moment I became the leopard, looking out of his eyes as I raised my head from the water. My eyes scanned the surrounding bush with preternatural penetration. I felt the savage exaltation of the predator.

And then the moment passed, leaving me suddenly exhausted. We sat there in frozen silence till the leopard turned and padded back into the bush. For a short while neither of us said anything, and then I suggested that we really had better get to bed. To my relief, Yohannis made no objection, and saw me down to my room. As we parted, he laid a hand on my arm.

"Sleep tight," he said, "and don't dream about leopards!"

CHAPTER THIRTEEN

The incident of the leopard did unsettle me somewhat, certainly, but if anything in a rather positive way. It seemed like a brush with the essence of Africa, a reminder that there were dark, savage forces out there of which I knew little, which could strike at any moment. But fortunately I was by now so exhausted, and the bed so comfortable, that I fell asleep quite easily and did not dream about anything.

The next thing I knew, Yohannis was shaking me awake. It was barely daybreak, and we couldn't have slept more than four hours or so. My initial feeling was that my limbs would not obey me, even if I wanted them to. I blinked at him blearily. Presumably his servants had woken him. He was still enveloped in a richly embroidered dressing gown, but looking pretty lively.

"Okay?" he said anxiously. "Think you can make it? We need to get going pretty early if we're going to have any chance with pig, especially."

I groaned, rolled over, and sat up.

"Right," said Yohannis, "I'm just going to have a quick shower, and I'll see you for breakfast on the verandah in about a quarter of an hour. We can grab some coffee and maybe an egg before we go. The servants will bring us a good lunch, in any case."

"Okay," I said, "I think I'm awake."

I looked at my watch. It was just after six. Even this, I supposed, was pretty late for serious hunters, but it was quite early enough for me in the present circumstances. There was a bath in the bathroom attached to my suite of rooms, but I somehow couldn't quite face it. I looked forward to a swim in the pool later. A dash of cold water on my face served to get me going, and I began to feel quite excited. This was a new dimension to life. I had really been too tired last night to appreciate my surroundings much, but now my situation began to sink in, and I had to say it looked pretty good. The mixture of modern luxury and unspoiled wilderness appealed to me, as did the prospect of going pig-hunting with the most dangerous man in Ethiopia.

I got to the verandah first, in fact, and found coffee and rolls laid out on a low table, flanked by the two cane chairs that we had occupied last night. An early morning mist hung over the lake, which lay there glassy, undisturbed by any breeze. In the middle distance, to the left, I could discern a large flock of pink flamingoes, moving slowly close to the shore, their heads down, puddling. The air, though cool, held within it the promise of a hot day to come. There were scents of pine and eucalyptus, and other things too exotic to be identified. I poured a coffee, and a servant appeared with two fried eggs on a plate. I took up a fresh roll, buttered it, and dipped it in an egg, scooping it together with a fork.

The appearance of Ethiopia's most dangerous man, a few minutes later, reminded me that I was by no means properly dressed for the occasion. He had togged himself out in a sort of light-weight military camouflage material, of a greenish-brown colour, and looked very well in it. I looked at myself ruefully. I had on a white shirt and grey slacks – reasonably suitable for night-club wear (Jack had decided on a sober appearance for the band, at least until we established ourselves), but not for wandering around in the bush. Yohannis studied me with amusement, and scratched his head.

"We're going to have to tone you down a bit, old man, or we will scare the pig. Maybe I can find you a brown shirt, at least. I think we are more or less the same size."

I nodded. "Sorry," I said. "I wasn't thinking about hunting. I just brought a toothbrush and a change of underwear, really."

"No problem," said Yohannis. He called for a servant, and gave some commands in Amharic, gesturing expressively with his long, delicate hands. The servant nodded, bowed, and hurried off. Another servant appeared, with eggs for the master.

We gulped down a little more breakfast, and a fine military brown shirt was brought. I tried it on, and it fitted adequately. My white shirt was taken away by the servant. I felt suddenly more suited to the expedition.

We assembled outside the front door, where a small platoon of support staff were waiting. There were bearers to carry the guns and the provisions, and beaters with spears and machetes, presumably to roust out the pig and whatever else we might encounter. It was an impressive line-up. Yohannis inspected them, and then gave a signal, and we moved off along a trail leading into the forest, working our way round the lake to the west. As we went along, he gave me instructions in a low voice.

"First of all," he said, "how are you with a gun? Have you done much shooting?"

I had to confess that I hadn't. I had been out a few times in Wicklow with neighbouring farmers, who were being nice to me for my mother's sake, hunting rabbits, and once or twice ducks along the coastal marshes, and had had some practice shooting tin cans off posts with a .22, but I was really pretty incompetent.

"I think, Yohannis, I'll leave you to do the shooting. I'd hate to bag one of the servants."

He grinned.

"Okay, maybe you're right. Not worth taking any risks. Once the pig starts coming at you, it's important not to panic. If you're not used to a gun, anything might happen."

Then he gave me my instructions. We would take up our position in a pre-arranged hide, and wait. We must remain absolutely still. The boys would work their way round in a wide arc, and then close in on a thicket where there were usually pig at this time of the morning. We might come upon some buck as well, feeding in the meadows beside the lake; gazelle or oribi.

We padded along the forest path, in single file, for perhaps half an hour, Yohannis pointing out birds and flowers along the way in a most knowledgeable manner, though in most cases he could only give me an Amharic name, which produced no impression on my memory. All I could do was enjoy the birdsong, and take in the exotic scents exhaled by the earth, as the day became warmer. The most notable items were the marvellous constructions of the weaver-birds, in the trees by the shores of the lake. These hung like child's cradles from the branches, fine, symmetrical confections of reeds, twigs and mud.

We came then, to the edge of a clearing, and stopped. Yohannis motioned me to the left, where I saw now a small opening in what had at first appeared to be an impenetrable bush. I went towards it, bent down, and began to climb cautiously in. Yohannis followed. The boys headed off in the opposite direction, keeping to the cover of the forest.

We settled down on a bed of dry leaves in what turned out to be quite a sophisticated hide. Through gaps in the foliage in front of us we had a clear view of a meadow, with what seemed to be further impenetrable jungle beyond. Yohannis checked his rifle, and laid out some extra bullets on the ground beside him.

I pointed across, and whispered.

"There are pig over there, are there?"

Yohannis nodded.

"Yes, we usually expect to find a few families of them snoozing in the bushes over there. When the boys get round behind them, they'll drive them in our direction. And then," he crooked his finger and pulled an imaginary trigger.

We sat looking out at the meadow. It was a peaceful scene. Just the rattle of the cicadas, and the calls of many birds. We were near enough to the lake, invisible to our left, to hear it lapping gently, as a morning breeze stirred it. For nearly ten minutes nothing at all happened. Then, suddenly, in the middle of our field of vision, quite near the edge of the clearing, there appeared a large male oribi. He stood alert, sniffing the wind, his beautiful tapering horns sweeping back from his brow. Then, satisfied, he bent to nibble some grasses.

I glanced at Yohannis, I hoped to God he did not intend to shoot this magnificent animal. Fortunately, he did not. What he wanted was pig. Interpreting my glance as an enquiry on that very point, he raised his hand in a negative gesture. We returned to watching. The big buck grazed for a short while, and then something alerted him again. He raised his head, and listened intently. Then, not being satisfied this time, he turned and trotted off smartly out of our range of vision to the right, away from the lake.

"I think he got wind of the boys," whispered Yohannis. "They have extraordinarily sensitive smell and hearing. They need it, of course."

And sure enough, a short time later all hell broke loose on the opposite side of the clearing. First, a burst of shouting and hallooing and cracking of branches, then a loud cacophony of grunts and squeals, and finally there crashed into the clearing a confused jumble of pigs, of various shapes and sizes. One big boar headed off like a rocket towards the lake, but what presented themselves directly across our line of vision was a mother pig and a number of half-grown piglets. Yohannis had his rifle to his shoulder, and was taking aim. Oh Lord, I thought, not the mother and the piglets. I'll never be a hunter.

But indeed that was his choice. He brought down the sow with one barrel, and one of the piglets with the other. The rest fled screaming, as did the rest of the herd. Yohannis ejected the shell in one swift movement, and reloaded furiously. Run, you wretched animals, run, I prayed, but at the same time I hypocritically applauded him.

"Good shooting!" I shouted. "That was impressive. You've got two."

Yohannis peered frantically through the foliage.

"Yes," he said, "but we could do with another suckling or two. They're very good eating."

He tried another shot at the retreating herd, but missed, to my secret relief. Still, we had something to show for our morning's exertions. The boys now broke cover, and headed for the prostrate pigs, with shrill whoops. Yohannis and I also emerged from our shelter, and went to meet them. The mother pig was still kicking, so Yohannis put another shot into her, and she lay still.

The boys quickly rigged up a carrying frame for the sow, and soon she was slung on two poles, being carried along by four of them, while a fifth carried the piglet by the back legs.

"Okay," said Yohannis, "roast suckling pig for lunch. Let's get back and have a swim before it gets too hot for you."

"That sounds great," I said, "but can they prepare a pig that fast?"

I felt slightly queasy, if the truth be known, at the idea of having for lunch something I had just seen running about a few minutes previously.

"Oh, no problem. Actually, game is very tender if you can prepare it immediately, within the hour. Otherwise, it toughens up, and you have to hang it. So they need to move fast."

"Ah," I said. I seemed to remember something of the sort from hunting back in Wicklow. So we marched home in triumph, the boys singing, and Yohannis in excellent spirits, telling me stories of his hunting expeditions with his father, which involved far more formidable prey than a mother-pig and her piglets.

The rest of the morning passed very pleasantly indeed. We got back to the hunting-lodge at a little after ten. I had brought no swimming togs, but used a spare pair of underpants. The water of the pool was pleasantly cool, as the sun was by now beginning to assert itself. We swam up and down a few times in a leisurely way, until the butler (as I characterised Yohannis' senior houseboy) brought the gins and tonics that had been ordered. Attracted by these, we climbed out, dried off a bit, and slumped into deck chairs partly shaded by a large tree, facing out towards the lake, the drinks between us on a low hardwood table. This, I thought, was just about how I would always like to face the untamed wilderness – gin and tonic in hand, in the shade by the side of a pool. I was ready to subside into a pleasant stupor.

Yohannis, however, was in a philosophical mood.

"Luke, old man," he said, when we were properly settled, "tell me something. Do you ever wonder what you will be doing in ten, or twenty, years' time? I mean, do you ever think about being a middle-aged, important person, running some business, say, or ruling somewhere?"

I sipped my drink, and endeavoured to consider the question seriously.

"Well," I said, "I'm hardly likely to be ruling anywhere, I shouldn't think, for a start. There's not much British Empire left, for instance, even if I wanted to get in on that, and the little there is going fast. But apart from that – no, I can't honestly say I've given it much thought. I mean, one of my problems, Yohannis – and it's one of the main reasons I headed out here – is that, especially in my final year in College, I found that I couldn't focus on the future at all. I couldn't conceive of what I might do for a living. Everything seemed equally futile."

Yohannis looked at me in astonishment.

'Do you really mean that?" he said. "I find that difficult to believe. I am just constantly planning about the future, and imagining what my role in it will be. It's really my main concern. In fact, all this playboy stuff that people criticise me for is really just to distract myself from this. Otherwise I think my head would burst from all this planning and worrying."

I turned to contemplate him. He was staring out over the lake, his brow creased in a worried frown. I realised that I had never really taken Yohannis quite seriously before.

"Well," I said, judiciously, "I can see that it's more natural for you to think that way. After all, you can reasonably expect to take part in ruling this place - if you can stay out of trouble long enough, that is - and it's an exciting situation, to be able to help in building up a country. I just don't have that sort of situation facing me. I mean, my relationship to Ireland is rather tangential. It's my country, in the sense that I don't have any other, but I don't really feel I belong there, and I certainly can't summon up much interest in how it's governed. I might conceivably get a job there doing something, maybe in law, but it's much more probable that I'll end up somewhere in England - though I can't imagine what I'd be doing there either."

"But I find that terribly sad!" exclaimed Yohannis. "Don't you see, Luke? That is sad!" He seemed genuinely distressed. "One must be concerned about one's country. What else is there?"

He paused, and sipped his drink, and frowned. Then he continued, on a new tack.

"I suppose one reason I feel so much more strongly than you seem to do on this is a kind of inferiority complex we Africans have - it's not so much true of Ethiopians, I think, but I found it very obvious in other chaps from newer African countries that I met in Oxford, and I picked it up from them - I mean, that, let's face it, here we have all sat for all these centuries, just as long as you have, if not longer, and we haven't really made very much progress - or not in the way that Western Europe defines progress. And now suddenly all this development is being imposed on us from outside, and our peoples find it very hard to take in."

"In this country," he continued, "it's the responsibility of people like me, who've had the opportunity to look at this so-called progress a bit and understand its implications, to introduce it to the people, and to try and control its invasion. That's a problem that you in Ireland just don't have."

I waved a hand in demurral, spilling a little gin and tonic on the tiles of the patio surrounding the pool.

"Well, I mean, it's not as if Ireland has no problems. I think it has serious problems, actually. It's just that I don't feel personally implicated in them in the way that you plainly are here. I see what you mean, though. There is a sense in which European-style progress has passed Africa by, and that, I suppose, needs some explaining."

Yohannis turned to me with a provocative twinkle in his eye.

"And what would be your explanation, Luke, old chap?"

I looked at him austerely.

"Now that is what I call being put on the spot," I complained. "I don't have an answer to that. I haven't ever given it much thought, actually. But it might have something to do with the fact that life is rather easier down here. At least, the weather is. I mean, you don't have to make any great effort to stay alive, or to scrape a livelihood. You can pretty well sit in the shade and watch things grow. In Northern European conditions, one really has to try harder, or one would just perish."

"But that would just explain Northern Europe, though," said Yohannis. "Not the Mediterranean – which is, after all, where Western civilisation came from, if I'm not mistaken. Nothing much wrong with the weather there, surely."

I thought for a bit.

"Well," I said, "as far as civilisation is concerned, I may be prejudiced, but I would see the other key factor, apart from the weather, as the Greeks. I mean, all round the Middle East there were great civilisations – the Babylonians, the Egyptians, the Hittites, and so on – but so far as we can see there was something static about them. They progressed technologically, up to a point, but intellectually they got stuck. Only the Greeks had the sort of open, enquiring minds that we would recognise as properly intellectual. And it was from the Greeks, via the Romans, who were great organisers, but not great intellectuals themselves, that all the rest of Europe acquired whatever civilisation they now have."

Yohannis thought about this for a moment, and then laughed.

"The Greeks!" he said. "That, I must say, is amusing. If you look at the Greeks we have here in Ethiopia, you'd never think of them as the originators of anything, never mind Western civilisation. Their minds are totally fixed on how to squeeze a few extra dollars out of any deal – nothing more exalted than that. I don't think you'd find an intellectual among them."

"Yes, well, there's Greeks and Greeks, after all. The Romans didn't have a great deal of respect for the Greeks they knew either. There was really only a period of about two hundred years during which all this happened with the Greeks, and then they rather lived on the credit of that ever after. But they did start things off, I think. I mean, the Irish, for example, if left to themselves, wouldn't necessarily have got much further than the average African nation. But the thing is that they weren't left to themselves. First there was Greco-Roman culture, together with Christianity. And then there were the British."

"Yes, well, I suppose we're just getting the same thing now. But it's annoying to think that, as far as I know, the human race began somewhere in Africa – so they are saying – and yet now we have to learn things from far more junior races!" Yohannis smiled, but a little sadly.

"But at least Ethiopia can claim a long and distinguished civilisation, surely? I've just been reading up on it, in fact."

"Ah yes," said Yohannis, smiling, but still sadly, "that is true. But the problem there is that that civilisation, such as it is, is basically Semitic – as we know, the Amharas came over originally from southern Arabia, and they brought the civilisation. I am a *Galla*, as you know, so I can't really claim it as mine. So I am still left with the problem."

I looked at Yohannis with some admiration, as I listened to him formulating all this in his rather clipped, but virtually perfect English public school accent. We'd had a number of discussions like this in our rooms in Oxford in times past, but they had somehow lacked the immediacy of this one. Here he was in the midst of his own country, and speaking from a position of leadership – if only he were allowed to exercise it. That was a basic difference between us, I reflected. It was not the fact that he was a few years older than I was, since even that only put him in his middle twenties. It was rather that he naturally thought in terms of administering his country, whereas I could only look on mine from the point of view of an irrelevant outsider. What was to be done about Ireland was simply not on my agenda. I was fully engaged in wondering what was to be done about myself, and even to that I had no solutions.

"Look," I said, "Yohannis, I wouldn't worry about it all too much. I mean, the way the world is going at the moment, the pace of development is so fast that, in another generation, this country will probably be thoroughly modernised even without anyone worrying about it, and in another generation everyone will have forgotten whose civilisation it was anyway. There'll be a sort of general, homogenised, world civilisation, and everyone will be wishing there were still a few primitive places left."

He shook his head.

"No," he said, "I don't think it's going to be that easy. You see, in a country like this, first of all, there's a lot of resistance to change, from older people at the top – like most of the old *rases* and *dejazmatches* around my uncle – and then there's still a great mass of people who just have no understanding of progress. They can only imagine things happening in the same way as they are now. And if you have no concept of progress, it is very difficult to make progress. No, I'm afraid that if there is not very careful planning, there will be chaos here before there is any progress. We could lose even what we have. That is what is bothering me."

At this point, however, philosophising was interrupted by more practical concerns, as the butler approached to tell us that lunch was served – and indeed this announcement had been heralded for some time before by a range of very attractive aromas rising from the kitchens, preeminently that of roast pork.

Yohannis sprang from his chair, we pulled on shirts, and he ushered me round from the pool-side back to the verandah where we had eaten previously. Here there was now a magnificent spread laid out, with as its centre-piece our piglet of this morning, now well roasted on a large platter, dripping in its own fat, and surrounded by yams and potatoes.

It was by now almost too hot to eat very much, but the pig, carved for us expertly by the cook, certainly tasted excellent, washed down by some of Yohannis' special *tej*, chilled for the occasion. This was followed by fresh pineapple, exquisite Greek pastries, and coffee. Within a little over half an hour I was stuffed and torpid, fit only for the siesta which Yohannis mercifully proposed. The idea was to sleep till around half past four, have another swim, and perhaps another little drink, and then set off for town to keep my engagement at the Paradiso.

Once in the bedroom, I stripped off my shirt and still slightly damp underpants, slid under the light bed-cover, and lay for a while on my back staring at the ceiling, where an old-fashioned fan turned soothingly, conspiring with the light afternoon breeze to make the curtains ripple gently. I brooded briefly on the contrast thrown up by our recent conversation between the degrees of purposiveness of Yohannis' life and of my own. Admittedly, it was all too probable that his ambitious plans for his country would come to little or nothing, frustrated by the obstruction of his uncle's trusted advisers, but at least he had a clear aim in life. Compared to him, I felt like a jellyfish afloat on the tide, quite without a purpose, waiting for something to turn up. This was a depressing reflection, but before long, thankfully, the murmuring of the fan had lulled me into a dreamless sleep.

I was awakened by a respectful knock on the door. It was an elderly servant, bringing the message that Lij Yohannis wondered if I would like to swim. I told him yes, rose, reassumed the underpants that had to do duty once again as togs, and shuffled out to the pool. Yohannis was already there, floating on his back.

"Well now, how are you feeling?" he asked.

"Pretty stuffed still," I said, "but otherwise fine. That was a great lunch, I must say, but it's more than I'm used to."

"Oh yes," he said, "I don't generally eat that sort of lunch either. But just once in a while it's good to go out and hunt something, and then eat it. Sort of reconnects one to one's roots, you know. Anyhow, get in the pool, and you'll feel better."

I did, and he was right. The water was cool enough to be refreshing, and after a few lengths I was feeling somewhat restored.

The sun was still fairly high in the sky when we climbed out for another drink, this time a beer. He had not returned to our weighty topics of the morning, but instead we reminisced about Oxford. He told me about a working-class English girl that he had met in a pub down near the station, whom I had known nothing about, and with whom he'd had a brief affair, until her brother and a couple of his friends had waylaid him one night and warned him off with dire threats. He had been more amused than angered by their ignorant racism, and it gave him an excellent excuse to break off the relationship, which had begun to bore him. The girl had entertained him, though. Apart from being quite good in bed, she had given him interesting insights into the basic English mind, which he was grateful for. He had found her remarkably ignorant, not only about Africa, but even about other European countries, and the history of her own country. She had lived in a one-dimensional world, and found that quite satisfying.

"I don't think," said Yohannis, thoughtfully, "that you would find anyone quite that ignorant in the whole of Ethiopia. I mean, even peasants in the depths of the countryside, who knew nothing about Europe or America, would know a lot about their own history and traditions. I don't think you would find here anyone quite so empty as Mavis was. And yet she was a nice girl. She was not prejudiced, like her brother and his friends. She was quite keen to learn things, but she knew nothing, nothing. It was quite extraordinary. Just pop songs, film stars, football – that sort of thing."

By the time the sun began to slip below the tops of the pines, Yohannis suggested that we had better think about getting back. We left the pool. I put my bag together, smoothed the bed, and joined Yohannis in the hall. The Landrover and its driver were waiting outside. We drove back, so far as I could see, anyone tailing us. Yohannis left me in to the compound, and climbed out and embraced me as we parted, promising to get in touch soon.

"Thanks a million again," I said. "That was a great adventure. I had a really superb time."

He raised his hand in salute from the window.

"We'll do it again," he said. "Only longer next time."

As he drove away, I noticed faces at a number of windows around the compound. I headed hastily up my front path. It was now nearly seven o'clock, getting towards sunset, and I wanted a little rest before heading off for my gig.

CHAPTER FOURTEEN

Tekla-Mariam was there to greet me, emerging from the kitchen with a slightly anxious frown.

"Ah, Tekla-Mariam," I said, apologetically, "I'm sorry. I was away for the night with Lij Yohannis. I would have told you, but it all happened rather suddenly, and you weren't there when I came in yesterday evening."

He nodded.

"That is no worry, *getoich*. I was not expecting you for dinner. But I was worry only this morning, when policeman call."

I looked at him in astonishment.

"Policeman? When? What on earth did he want?"

"He no say, *getoich*. He only ask where you are, and I no know. So he go away again."

I thought for a moment.

"This policeman," I said, "what did he look like? Was he small, a bit fat, with a small moustache, like this?" And I drew a line with my finger across my upper lip.

Tekla-Mariam looked surprised, and nodded.

"Yes, he like that. You know this policeman?"

"Yes," I said, "I think I do."

It sounded very much as if I had received a call from the mysterious Col. Tamrat. I could only assume that this was somehow linked to our being trailed down to Lake Langano last night, and that I was being checked up on. In that case, Colonel Tamrat would have known the answer to his own question. To Tekla-Mariam I remained cheerful and unruffled, but I was both disturbed and annoyed. Plainly the authorities were even more concerned about Yohannis, his movements and his contacts, than he thought they were. It seemed so perverse and unfair, in view of his patent desire to help his country, and even to preserve the existing regime, but there it was.

"It's nothing to worry about," I reassured Tekla-Mariam. 'This policeman is a friend of Lij Yohannis. I'm sure it is nothing serious."

Tekla-Mariam nodded, but he still looked worried.

"*Getoich*, " he said, "you like dinner now? I have *wat*."

"Oh yes, thanks," I said, "if you can do it in half an hour. I have to go out at eight o'clock."

He nodded. He disappeared into the kitchen, but in a moment returned, holding a piece of paper.

"Oh, *getoich*. I forget. Miss Caroline call, and then she write this and leave it for you."

"Miss Caroline?" My heart gave a jump.

"Yes, Miss Caroline here for weekend. She staying with Mr, Mrs Wiggins. She want to know where you were too."

I laughed. "Like the policeman? You have been having an exciting day, Tekla-Mariam."

"Yes, *getoich*."

He returned to the kitchen, and busied himself with pots and pans. I made myself a whiskey and soda, slid into an armchair, and addressed myself to Caroline's note, in a mood of both excitement and apprehension. On the one hand, my body was fully ready for another encounter with Caroline's naked body; on the other hand, my mind said that it could do without further complications. I unfolded the piece of paper. It read as follows:

> *Hullo, Luke. Where the hell are you? Tekla-Mariam said he didn't know. I am down here for the weekend (and maybe a bit longer). If you get back, would you call over to Isabel and Graham's? Love, Caroline.*

I looked at this epistle narrowly, trying to interpret it. It was not the most romantic of documents, certainly, but what did I expect? But she had ended it with 'love', which was encouraging. I tried to think what I could propose to her. I was tied up tonight – unless she wanted to come

217

and listen to some jazz – and I was committed to Cousin James for the usual Sunday lunch, with church and a walk before that – unless I could wriggle out of it. I could get away for Sunday afternoon, certainly, but that now seemed rather long to wait. I stood up with sudden resolution. Maybe she would like to come down to the Paradiso – if Graham and Isabel had no objection. I wasn't sure how protective of her they were meant to be. I would go over now and propose it, and we could take things from there. I put down my drink on the side-table, and walked out of the house, straight over to the Wiggins'.

Isabel herself answered to my knock.

"Ah, there you are," she said. 'We were wondering where you had got to. Come on in. Caroline's visiting us for the weekend, and was asking for you."

"Yes," I said, stepping into the hall, "Tekla-Mariam gave me the message. I was just staying overnight with a friend, and we went for a bit of a drive today. Sorry, I wouldn't have barged in on you like this, but I just wanted to see if Caroline would like to come out this evening. I'm playing trumpet tonight with a jazz group in a night club, so I thought that perhaps she might like to come down and listen – that is, if you felt it was suitable."

Isabel's eyes opened wide, and she laughed.

"Well, you are full of surprises! Jazz trumpet, indeed. I'm sure she'd be delighted, and I don't think we have any objection, unless it's a very seedy place."

"Oh no," I assured her, "it's quite respectable. It's called the Club Paradiso. I don't know if you've heard of it."

Isabel thought for a moment, and then shook her head.

"No, doesn't ring a bell. But if you say so – and at least it isn't notorious, or I would have heard of it!"

But at this moment Caroline herself appeared, from the direction of the sitting-room. She was wearing a rather attractive white frock, which suited her very well, and she had put her hair up. She looked, if anything, rather more beautiful than I had remembered her as being, and her sudden appearance in the doorway caused a constriction in my throat.

"Hello," she said, her eyes boring into me. "Where have you been?"

"I'm sorry," I said. "I wish I had known you were coming to town. I went for a drive in the country – but this evening I'm going to play jazz in a night club. I was just wondering if you might like to come down and listen."

"Wow," she said, her face lighting up. "Of course I would! Jazz in a night club! I had no idea you did that! I didn't even know that there were any night clubs in this town. Would that be okay, Isabel, do you think?"

Isabel nodded, smiling.

"I was just saying to Luke that I can't see any objection, as long as he can look after you. I suppose you'll be fairly late."

"Well, we might be," I said. "I think the group likes to go for a drink afterwards. But I won't want to be too late, in any case. I had quite a tiring day. Shall I call over around a quarter past eight?"

"Oh yes," said Isabel. "We can get some food into her by then, I think."

I went back to my bungalow in a state of some exaltation. I was not at all sure how this evening would end, but I had some preferred outcomes. It occurred to me to see what Simon was up to. I imagined that he was long gone for the evening, but on taking a look out my front door I saw a light in his front room across the compound, so I went in and phoned him. There was a short delay, and then a rather muffled, shaky voice was heard on the other end.

"You don't sound too good," I said solicitously.

"Oh, that you, La Touche? Where the hell have you been?"

He was plainly somewhat the worse for wear.

"I've been hunting pig with the aristocracy," I said. "What have you been up to?"

Simon groaned.

"Christ, I'm not sure I can remember very well. You'd need to ask Knut. By God, those Swedes can drink. We got in a fight with some Arabs, I can't remember why. I got back here somehow or other, and I've been resting for the day."

"Oh Lord! Well, you presumably don't want to come down to the Paradiso again, then, this evening." He groaned again. "It's just," I continued, "that this grandniece of the Stanfords I think I told you about, Caroline, is down for the weekend, staying with the Wigginses. I've asked her out to listen to the jazz, and I was sort of hoping for someone to chaperone her. I'll be on stage most of the time, after all. But I expect she'll be okay."

At this, Simon seemed to perk up a bit.

"Oh?" he said. "What's she like, this Caroline? She a bit of all right, then?"

"Well," I said cautiously, "she's not bad. Quite lively, actually. But of course she's very young."

"H'm," he said. "Well, maybe I'll pull myself together, and come down for a while. But not another late night, mind. I don't think I could take it."

"Oh no," I reassured him, " that's suits me. I didn't get much sleep last night either. And of course Caroline has to be back at a reasonable time."

"Well, okay then."

"I'll be over to you in about half an hour, okay?"

Tekla-Mariam served me a fairly fiery chicken wat, which I washed down with a cool beer. I was just on the fruit and coffee when Simon presented himself. He seemed a little pale and hollow-eyed, but otherwise in reasonable shape. He accepted some coffee, and demanded to be told about the trip to the hunting lodge, so I gave him a somewhat edited run-down, describing the setting, and concentrating on the hunting expedition and the swimming-pool.

"Lucky bastard," he lamented. "It sounds fantastic."

"It was pretty impressive," I agreed. "And what impresses me even more is that, with all that going for him, Yohannis still wants to get himself into trouble by dabbling in politics."

"Oh, I don't know," said Simon. "Maybe it's a kind of guilt complex. He knows he shouldn't be living like that. I think it does him some credit, in a way."

"Oh yes," I said, "but still ... I mean, we were actually followed down there. A car tailed us all the way to Bishoftu. I pointed it out to him, but he didn't seem too worried."

And then I thought of Colonel Tamrat's visit this morning, but for some reason decided to suppress that. I didn't want Simon to fuss, and start in on me. I felt I was in receipt of enough warnings by now, and I was prepared to take the consequences of my decision not to avoid Yohannis. At least I was clear in my own mind that I was doing nothing wrong.

We decided to take my car, since Simon claimed still to be feeling not very well, and I went over to the Wigginses to collect Caroline. She came downstairs looking, if anything, more attractive than before. She had now thrown a light cape over her dress, and had obviously put on some makeup. I explained to her about Simon, and she seemed pleased that she would not be left alone while I was playing. I introduced them at the car. They shook hands, and I could see Simon looking her over appreciatively. Caroline climbed in the front, beside me, while Simon sat in the back, leaning over both of us. He was clearly rather impressed, and engaged her in conversation all the way to the club, wanting to know where she lived, why she had come out here (she didn't tell him the whole story, I was glad to note), and how she liked it.

Caroline chatted with him over her shoulder, glancing at me ironically from time to time, when she was not telling the whole truth. When we reached the club, I guided them in and got Mr E, who was most solicitous this time, to give them a good table, and then disappeared backstage to meet up with Jack and the group, and we had time to run through one or two of our numbers. We decided to bring in Rogers' and Hart's 'My Funny Valentine' this time, as a vehicle for me, and we ran through the riff of that.

When we came out, I noticed to my displeasure that Caroline and Simon were laughing together very heartily about something, but she applauded us enthusiastically as we lined up, and waved. I acknowledged her with a bow, and a flourish of my horn. The club was full, and buzzing. We launched ourselves into our set, rather more smoothly than the night before, and the audience responded well. Towards the end of our first set, I started into 'My Funny Valentine', and to my alarm observed Simon and Caroline get up to dance. Shit, I thought, could she possibly be about to take a shine to the bugger? But then I told myself firmly not to be childish. It is perfectly reasonable that they should dance. We are playing danceable music. Caroline is simply here for a good time, and both Simon and I are part of that scenario. She herself declared that she is not interested in commitments, and I have no business getting possessive. But still, I ached a little.

When we reached the interval, I came down off the stage and joined them at the table for a beer. Caroline was full of compliments, her eyes shining.

"That was really terrific, Luke. I really admire people who can play an instrument."

It was Simon's turn now to look slightly sick, but he chimed in gallantly in support.

"Yes, that was pretty good, lad, I must say" – this in broadest Yorkshire. "He's full of surprises, is our Luke."

The rest of the band, led by Jack, filtered over, and I introduced them. Caroline was fascinated by Hailu, and showered him with compliments, which pleased him very much. We agreed to have a drink or two afterwards, though specifying that we didn't want to be very late.

Simon and Caroline danced a few times during the second set, but I noticed nothing further untoward, and when we ended she was liberal with compliments once again. Mr Efstathiadis came through with a fee of a hundred dollars per night, which was not princely, but very welcome, and left us all twenty-five dollars richer – Jack divided it equally.

Armed with that, we decided to go downtown, to the bar of the posh new Africa Hotel in Adowa Square, just for a nightcap. When we got there, Jack began to make a fuss of Caroline, kidding her that she shouldn't waste her time going to Oxford, but should come over to Yale, and asking if she had ever done any jazz singing, which she had not. This suited me fine, and the evening ended towards midnight with my equilibrium largely restored. I chatted a bit to the taciturn Chuck, who was from Chicago, and had majored in Anthropology. We had brandies or beer. Caroline chose a gin and tonic. I'd had to give an account of Yohannis' hunting lodge and our activities of the morning, to exclamations of envy and astonishment from Jack, and ribald comments from Simon, while Caroline expressed sympathy for the poor little pig, and was glad that at least I hadn't shot it.

We got back to the compound in pretty good humour. Simon said goodnight, hoped he would see Caroline around, and headed off for his bungalow. I was relieved that he didn't try to kiss her. I escorted Caroline to the front door of the Wiggins' bungalow, a trifle disconsolately now. I felt that I really had thrown a spanner into the works by bringing Simon in on the expedition. That had blown my chance to steer Caroline in the direction of my own lair. When would we get together?

However, as she reached the front door, she turned and whispered.

"You go back to your place, but don't lock the door. I'll be over in a few minutes, when the coast is clear."

My heart leaped, and I kissed her on the cheek. She smiled at me.

"Okay," I said. "See you in a little while. I just hope nobody's waiting up for you."

She looked up anxiously at the darkened house front, but there seemed no sign of life.

"I'll be very quiet," she whispered. "I'll just open the door quietly and close it again – from the outside."

I strolled back to my bungalow. At the front door, I looked back cautiously towards Simon's place, but he had gone in. I left the door slightly open, and headed for the bedroom, to make sure all was tidy. It was in good shape, thanks to Tekla-Mariam, and I began to undress, quivering with anticipation.

I was just down to my shirt and shorts when I heard the door open and then close, and Caroline stood before me.

"Hey now," she said, "you're getting away on me."

I paused and looked at her. She seemed to shimmer in front of me.

"Gosh," I said, rather breathlessly, "I've been missing you."

"M'm," she replied, nonchalantly. "Me too, a bit."

Then she began to undress, swiftly and efficiently, first the cape, then, over her head, the dress, then the shoes, kicked off unceremoniously, then, over the head again, the slip. I watched her, unbuttoning my shirt. She was down now just to bra and panties, and came over and presented herself to have the bra unhooked. I took off my shirt, threw it onto a chair, and fiddled clumsily with the catch of the bra, finally getting it undone. I kissed her on the back of the neck.

"Sorry," I said, "I don't have much experience of these things."

"Why am I glad to hear that?" she said, looking at me over her shoulder and smiling.

I put my arms round her and hugged her to me. The feel of her small, firm buttocks against me produced an erection and she wriggled voluptuously.

"Oh, Caroline," I groaned, "I know you don't want to get involved, and I'm trying not to, but it's difficult."

"Oh," she said, impatiently, "don't let's worry about that now. Just don't get all silly on me."

Trembling slightly, I reached down and began to slip off her panties. In response she turned round to face me, and, smiling, pulled down my shorts with one swift movement. We clung together for a short while, naked.

Then, suddenly, she jumped up and wrapped her legs around me. I staggered forward momentarily, righted myself, and, locking my hands together under her bottom, steered her towards the bed. My one fear at the moment was that, under this ferocious provocation, I would go off too soon and spoil everything. Fortunately, we reached the bed intact, and I lay quietly beside her for a while, stroking her hair, and kissing her gently on the mouth, the nose, the eyes. Her eyelids fluttered under my lips. Gently I reached down and massaged her between the legs, and found that she was quite ready.

In the event, it was a close-run thing, but Caroline seemed to have a satisfactory orgasm before I was utterly spent. We lay for a while in silence, blissfully clamped to one another with perspiration. I initiated pillow-talk.

"Well," I said, "you seemed to get along very well with old Simon."

I tried to sound suitably light-hearted, but it didn't work. She raised her eyebrows in amusement.

"Oh," she said, "we're not getting a little jealous, are we, by any chance?"

"No, no, of course not. I'm just glad you liked him."

"Yes, I did like him. We had a good time. But we talked about you, mainly. You amuse him a lot. You don't fit his image of an Irishman at all."

I laughed.

"No, I know. I'm afraid I wouldn't fit most people's image of an Irishman. It makes life difficult sometimes. In fact, when I'm with Simon, it sometimes occurs to me that it's he who fits better the image of an Irishman, but I wouldn't dare say that to him."

Caroline giggled. "I must tell him that."

"No you bloody well won't! He'd be furious."

"I will too."

"You will not !"

I pinched her on the bottom, and began to tickle her. We wrestled for a while on the bed, and then fell into a long kiss. Then she recollected herself, and reached out and took my arm to look at my watch.

"Hey, it's after half one. I'd better get back, or we'll cause a dreadful scandal." She rolled over me, and off the bed. "By the way," she added teasingly, "don't you know it's bad etiquette to wear your watch while making love?"

"Oh Lord," I said, despondently. "I suppose it is. I didn't think of that!"

"Never mind," she said, gaily. "Just remember the next time!"

And she made off for the bathroom to clean up. The sight of her retreating back roused me again, but I controlled myself sternly.

I lay back in a haze of satisfied lust. Even the sounds of the water running and the loo flushing took on an erotic tone. In a little while she was out again, and slipped into her clothes, while I admired her from the bed. When she was ready, I sat up, and swung my legs to the floor. She came over to be kissed, and I clung to her for a moment.

"Oh God," I groaned, "I could almost do it again!"

"Forget it," she said sternly, "I've just tidied myself. You can go to sleep and dream about me. I'll let myself out."

And so, smiling sweetly, she went. The front door clicked shut. I went to the bathroom myself, and then tried to settle down. I turned off the light, but found myself watching the patterns made on the *abujadid* ceiling by one of the lights in the compound flickering through the trees, as they rustled in the night breeze.

Damn and blast, I thought. This is marvellous, but it's certainly a complication. And she doesn't want to get tied down either. She just wants a good time. For God's sake, cool it, I told myself. I would have to try and stand back from it, not to get too serious too fast. And with such thoughts as these I subsided into sleep, a sleep in which, fortunately, I did not dream.

CHAPTER FIFTEEN

Sunday morning proved somewhat frustrating, glad though I always was to see my cousin James. There was certainly no way I could get out of it, since James very much wanted to hear how I had got on at Nyala Farm. I thought I would be separated from Caroline by having to go to church, but that was not so, as Isabel decided that, in Caroline's honour, the whole family should go to church. So when James came to collect me, the Wiggins family followed along in convoy.

Church was plainly not Caroline's favourite place. She looked disgruntled, fidgeted a good deal, and tried to catch my eye across the aisle, seeing if she could trap me into some indiscretion. Seated as I was beside Cousin James, I resisted these attempts firmly. We all met up briefly before leaving the compound, and James had had a few words with her (she looking thoroughly demure and girlish). Then afterwards we gathered outside for a while, chatting to Padre Matthews, and I managed to have a few moments alone with her.

Yes, she had got safely into bed without being noticed. Yes, she expected she would be around if I got back in the early afternoon. This suited, since Cousin James would go for his siesta at around half past two.

"How about a drive this afternoon, to see a few things, if you like?"

"Yes, that *would* be fun." she said, with a twinkle.

"How long will you be staying in town?" I asked.

"Oh," she teased, "I thought I might stay on till the middle of the week, actually – Wednesday, perhaps. I might sit in on a few classes, to improve my mind."

"Not mine, anyhow," I hissed. "I'll never be able to concentrate."

"Oh, come on, I'll just sit quietly at the back. I might as well learn something while I'm here."

I looked at her sternly.

"That's a terrible idea."

"I don't see what's so terrible. If you won't let me, perhaps Simon will let me sit in on some of his. I've always wanted to know more about physics."

At that I relented.

"Oh well, I don't mind, really, I suppose. Of course you can sit in, if Graham doesn't mind."

At this point Graham intervened, strolling over from the main group.

"What mightn't Graham mind?" he said, with goodhumoured suspicion.

"Oh," I said, "Caroline was just saying she was thinking of staying on in town for a few days, and sitting in on some classes. I wasn't sure what you'd think of that."

"It's all right with me," said Graham cheerfully, "so long as she behaves. By the way, would you like to drop over for dinner this evening, Luke, since Caroline's here? We might play a game of Monopoly or something."

"Oh fine," I said, glancing at Caroline. "Thanks very much."

"Good, excellent. About six-thirty or so, then, for a drink?"

And he wandered back to communicate this to Isabel.

"Monopoly, " Caroline mouthed. I giggled.

"How about Strip Monopoly?" I suggested, and she responded with an unseemly cackle.

But we were attracting attention, and had to rejoin the group. Soon after James led me off to meet up with Willy Buhagiar for our walk on Entotto. This Sunday, to his annoyance, James was finding himself somewhat short of breath, and had to take a number of rests on convenient rocks, while Willy and I waited around him. Finally he told us to go on to the top of the rise, and come and collect him on the way back.

I was a little concerned.

"Is Cousin James all right, do you think, Willy?" I asked. "Has this happened before?"

Willy waved a hand dismissively.

"Oh, he has his good days and his bad days. It partly depends on how much brandy he's consumed the previous night. But he wouldn't want you to be worrying about him, so not a word about it when we get back."

During the walk I was able to tell of my trip to Nyala Farm, but both then and over lunch I was conscious of an increasing degree of constraint, as I tried to give an account of myself during the past week. I had to downplay the Caroline factor severely, and to say nothing at all of my excursion with Yohannis. Willy actually put me on the spot by asking if I had seen anything of His Highness, but I simply lied. To make things more plausible, I reported that Yohannis had sent a message asking me down to his hunting lodge for the weekend, but that I had been unable to accept, through being tied up with previous engagements. That pleased both of them. I was strongly urged to go nowhere near the hunting lodge. To distract them I told of my incipient night-club career, which greatly surprised James, and amused Willy Buhagiar vastly.

"Indeed," he chortled, "you are a young man of many talents. Would an old codger like me be allowed to attend this club, and learn something of jazz?"

"Of course, Willy," I said. "You could both come down, as honoured guests of the management. It would be quite a sensation."

"Well, I'm not sure I want to cause a sensation," said Willy, "and I'm quite sure that your Cousin James would not wish to."

"No," said James, "a jazz club is definitely not for me. But I salute your enterprise and versatility. By the way, have you heard yet from Mimi Boghossian? I would have thought that an invitation to a playreading would have been made by now."

"Yes," I said. "I'm actually invited round next Wednesday. I hope to God it doesn't go out of my head."

"Good," said James. "I hope you can go. I know I did rather warn you off Mimi, but that was just à propos of being overwhelmed by excessive playreading and so on. I do think in fact that you should foster relations with the Boghossians. They really are a delightful couple, and, as I told you before, Nuri can be a very helpful man to know. In any case, I'm sure that you would enjoy yourself there."

"Well, I accepted promptly," I assured him. And indeed I was looking forward to it, even if some evenings of playreading were involved.

Cousin James then changed the subject.

"That young Caroline seems a pleasant girl," he said, "though I believe she was been sent out here under something of a cloud. So I gather from her great-aunt, anyhow. How did you find her?"

"Oh," I said, casually, "very friendly. We went down to the lower farm together on Sunday, as I think I told you, and she was good company. I think she's probably a bit lonely out there, though, nice as the Stanfords are, so she's happy to get into town for a bit. I've promised to take her for a bit of drive this afternoon, before dinner."

James raised his eyebrows.

"Just a word of warning, though, my boy. I don't want to keep spoiling your fun, but I wouldn't get too involved with young Caroline, if I were you. Louise did suggest that she was somewhat disturbed, even if she doesn't seem so. It might not be wise to form an attachment."

Willy listened to this with amusement.

"Oh come now, James," he interposed. "Can't the boy be allowed any indiscretions? We're warning him off practically everything that turns up!"

"Well," said James, a little huffily, "I am the boy's godfather, and I feel it is my duty to say these things. And besides, you entirely agree with me about Prince Yohannis, do you not?"

"Oh, about Yohannis, yes, certainly. And about not getting involved with one's pupils also. I admit that. But at a certain point we have to let him live his life, do we not?"

I listened to this debate in respectful silence. Cousin James harrumphed.

"Oh well, I suppose so. I just thought I would put in a word."

I moved to reassure him. "I rather got the impression from Caroline that she doesn't want any attachments herself just at the moment. She seems to be recovering from an unhappy love-affair, though of course she didn't give me any details. But I'll certainly be duly cautious."

I said this with a sinking heart. I knew that I had been far from cautious, and that I was now more deeply involved with Caroline than I had ever intended, led astray by her own carefree attitude into thinking that I could be the same. But I had covered my tracks pretty well for the moment.

After coffee on the verandah, then, Wolde was summoned to drive me back, Willy went off home for his siesta, and James prepared to retire for his. I was invited to dinner the following Saturday, if nothing else turned up, as James was having a few people round. And so I took my leave.

Wolde dropped me at the compound, and I first of all checked in to my bungalow to alert TM to the fact that I would be out to dinner, so that he could go about his business. Then I went over to the Wiggins', to see if Caroline was at home. In fact she had been having a siesta, and appeared, slightly rumpled and sleepy, from the downstairs guest bedroom.

"Well," I said, "do you feel like coming out somewhere?"

"Oh yeah," said Caroline, yawning. "I suppose so. Where were you thinking of?"

"Well," I said, "we could just go down to the Piazza, if you liked, and hang about, have a coffee or a beer or something – or we could take a drive up into the hills and go for a walk."

Caroline though for a moment.

"Addis itself is pretty boring, really," she reflected, "unless you want to shop. And shopping with a man is not a good idea!"

I laughed. "So how about a walk in the hills?"

"Okay," she said. "Do you have anywhere in mind?"

I thought for a moment about the monastery I discovered, but then decided that this wasn't quite suitable. They mightn't much welcome women, for one thing. On the other hand, though, Willy Buhagiar had told me of another old rock-church which was not far off the route of our Sunday morning walks, of about the same vintage as the one which formed the centre-piece of the monastery, but deserted, so I suggested that. Caroline shrugged, and agreed. Ethiopian antiquities were plainly not one of her enthusiasms; but, as it turned out, she had other things in mind.

We drove though the city, and up Cousin James's road, which led up over the hill in the direction of Debra Markos, and ultimately Gondar and the north. As I drove her past the park above the Piazza, I told her about my arrival in Addis, and being presented with the corpse on the gibbet, which suitably revolted her. The old car carried us up past Cousin James's villa, which I pointed out, and onto the crest of Entotto, to the point where our Sunday walks usually began, without too much protest.

I pulled over, and we got out, and started off up the trail, admiring the fine views of the city between the pines and eucalyptus. After about half a mile we turned off to the left, over the crest of the hill, in the direction which Willy had indicated.

This church, it seemed, like the one at the monastery, was a smaller, isolated version of what one would find at Lalibela to the north, a building excavated out of the solid rock, created some time in the late Middle Ages, far earlier than any other type of building surviving in this region. I was quite keen to have a look at it, but after we had been walking about half an hour in the afternoon heat without coming in sight of it, Caroline declared that she had had enough.

"I don't really care if I ever get to this damned church," she said. "Let's just sit here for a while, and have a rest, and enjoy the view."

So we sat down side by side on the rough grass, after first checking for ants or other nasty things, and looked around us. We were by this time out of sight of Addis, without having yet come over the other side of the hill, so all we could see around us was rolling scrubland, dotted with acacias and clumps of eucalyptus. There was no sign of human occupation, though a largish clump of eucalyptus on the horizon probably concealed a few *tukuls*. The noise of birds and insects filled the air, but nothing else, not even the sound of cattle or goats. We seemed to be quite alone.

Caroline turned to look at me.

"Well," she said, with a wicked grin, "how about it?"

"How about what?" I said dimly, and then caught her meaning. "Oh no, you can't mean here, out in the open! And besides, I don't have a —"

"Well, I do!" she said. "And what's wrong with this place? There's no one around, and anyhow, if someone appears, we'll see them before they see us."

Attractive as the idea was, I hesitated. I began to wonder if Caroline was somehow obsessed by sex. Certainly my hesitation appeared to act as a stimulus to her. She pushed me down, and rolled over to sit on top of me, at the same time reaching down to unzip my fly.

I went along with this, but I found myself somehow mildly shocked. It was almost as if I was being raped. Caroline pulled down my trousers, slipped off her own panties, and mounted me, in full view of the whole countryside. It was on the one hand enormously exciting, but on the other somewhat unsettling. Almost in revenge, I dug my nails into her thighs, feeling her muscles rippling as she pumped the energy out of me. If I had any thought of punishing her, though, it was a failure. It only seemed to please her further.

In the event, I came violently, to her great amusement.

"Wow!" she said. "Control yourself! They'll hear you back at The English School. Now, that wasn't so bad, was it?"

When I had recovered a little, I rolled her over on her back and kissed her fiercely.

"My God," I gasped, "you really are dangerous. That was good, though. Must have been the funny angle. But suppose some old boy had ridden up on his mule – or even did now?"

"Well, we'd just make his day, wouldn't we?"

But nobody did appear, then or later. The countryside seemed empty. It was probably just the time of day, or the fact that it was Sunday, but we had this corner of Entotto to ourselves.

We rearranged ourselves, and sat once again side by side. I looked at her with admiration, but also a touch of bafflement.

"Caroline," I said, "you are an extraordinary girl, you know, but you worry me a bit. What do you want out of life, really?"

She looked over at me with contempt.

"Oh Lord," she said. "You're not going to go all deep on me, are you?"

"No, no," I said defensively, "I know you don't want to get involved, or anything, but, with all this, I just can't help getting a *bit* involved."

She turned on me with surprising fierceness.

"Well, just don't. Please! Can't we just enjoy ourselves without getting all tangled up? Sex is free – if you have the sense to take the proper precautions – and it's fun. Let's just make use of it while we can."

I shook my head mournfully.

"I just wish I could have your attitude. I do tend to get too serious, I suppose. And yet I don't want to get involved either, in fact, officially. But don't you ever, sort of, develop an ache ?"

"An ache!" she snorted. "Of course I develop an ache from time to time. I know all about aches. And I've just had enough of that. Now if I develop an ache, as you call it, I just relieve it as soon as I can. That's the way to deal with aches. Otherwise they turn into obsessions, and the next thing you know you're what they call 'in love'. I've been though all that, and I've had it. It's a total illusion. It's simply the result of denying yourself sex, and that's a trap I'm not going to fall into again if I can help it." She spat out these words with such passion that I didn't dare argue with her any further.

It did serve to explain things to me a bit, though. Caroline had been badly hurt, plainly more than she would ever admit, by her relationship with this philandering lecturer – a gentleman whom, on reflection, I conceived a strong desire to see hung up by his balls – and this was her response to that. It all made a good deal of sense, in a grim way, but it was also a recipe for further disasters, and I was going to have to watch out if I was not to become one of them.

One thing I was discovering about myself was that sex was *not* free. For me, anyhow, it dragged along a lot of emotional baggage with it. The trouble was, I believed in love – and sex was such a new experience for me that I found it seriously intoxicating. Even in the case of Berhane, I found it hard to resist relating to her as a person – not just a body – and that approaches dangerously near to love.

But Caroline was right, of course – that sort of 'love' in my situation would be simply absurd. Really, the sensible thing was to learn something from Caroline, and shape up, or I would lose her.

"Come on," I said, getting up, and stretching. "Let's make another effort to find this church. If it's not round the next bend, then I give up."

"Okay, I'm sorry. I'm just being silly. Let's leave it at that."

We walked on, arm in arm, in the late afternoon heat. We rounded a bend in the trail, and now the distant sound of cow or goat bells was added to the chatter of the cicadas. Some sign of life, though nothing yet in sight. Ahead of us there appeared a promising clump of eucalyptus, and we agreed to head for that and then pack it in if it wasn't there.

In fact, this turned out to be none other than the little church, in a hollow just to the left of the trail. It was just a more dilapidated version of the square church of the monastery that I had come upon some weeks earlier, but in this case cut down from the surrounding ground rather than carved out of a cliff, so that the roof was more or less on the level of the trail. We climbed gingerly down the side of the trench which surrounded it, and peered inside.

"Yuk," said Caroline, contemplating the murky interior. "It stinks of goat, and cowshit. I'm not going in there."

I peered in after her, and had reluctantly to agree. It was a sad sight. It took some time before my eyes adjusted to the gloom, but when they did, there was nothing to see but the bare walls. If there had ever been frescoes or ornamentation, there were long gone. Generations of goats and cattle had plainly taken shelter there, and generations of herdsmen had lit fires inside. A large lizard sat for a moment on the ledge of the single window, looking at us in frozen disbelief, before suddenly vanishing down the outer wall. It seemed strange to me that what should have been a holy place should have become so utterly disregarded by the local inhabitants. I could only assume that some cultural break had occurred.

"Okay," I said, "you win. There really isn't much to this. It was somewhere to head for, though. And it is a piece of the country's past, I suppose."

"Well," said Caroline, "if that's this country's past, you can have it. Give me Westminster Cathedral any day."

She backed out of the rather noisome gloom, and turned to face the sunlight. I put an arm round her shoulder and kissed her on the neck.

"Sorry about that," I said. "I suppose we'd better be getting back."

We plodded a little wearily back up the trail, past the spot where we had made love, then down main track which led to the car. The view down over the city and the plain beyond from this point was once again spectacular, and we paused a moment to enjoy it. The sun was just going down, causing the eucalyptus to cast long shadows. Below in the city, it lit up the windows of Africa Hall, the pretentious new monument symbolising the Emperor's aspiration to be accepted the Father of Africa, and various other incongruous new structures of glass and concrete dotted about the city.

"You really are quite interested in this country, aren't you?" said Caroline, with a touch of incomprehension in her voice.

"Well, it is an interesting country, after all," I said defensively. "There's really no other African country that has this sort of history and culture."

Caroline sighed. "I suppose," she said, "that if I was here for a bit longer, I might make an effort, but as it is I just find it all rather depressing."

We turned and walked back along the trail towards where I had parked the car.

"How long do you think you will stay, in fact?" I asked, with elaborate casualness.

She shrugged. "Oh, don't know, really. I suppose till after Christmas, at least. That's said to be rather fun. Lots of parties and so on."

I did a quick calculation. We were now just now in the first part of October. That gave some time for things to develop, certainly, but the time would go quickly, as it was even now.

"Is there any particular hurry?" I asked. "You don't have to go up to Oxford till next October, presumably."

She looked at me speculatively, and smiled.

"No, there's no great urgency," she said. "I just think I'll have had enough of this by then. It's not exactly a wild social scene out at Nyala, as you can imagine."

"Well," I said, "You could spend more time in Addis."

"Yes I could. But that's liable to translate into babysitting for Graham and Isabel. It's not that much fun either."

She paused. Since neither of us ventured to mention what else she might do in Addis, we walked on in silence for a while.

"I was thinking I might take a trip before or after Christmas," I said. "Try and see a bit of the country."

'That's a good idea,' she said, evenly. "Where do you think you might go?"

"Oh, I don't know. Alan Lonsdale was talking of driving up to Gondar and Axum, and doing a bit of camping, and asked me if I'd like to come."

"Sounds great," she said. "But what about Simon? Wouldn't you prefer to go with him?"

"Well, yes, I would. But this invitation just came up. It's not definite, though. I'll probably go off with Simon somewhere as well, if he wants to. We just haven't discussed it yet. There's such a lot to see. I'd love to get down to Harar, for example. And of course down to East Africa in the summer, if I can manage it. But that's a long way off."

"What's Harar?"

"Oh, it's an old city down in the south-east, above Dire Dawa. A lot of Arab influence, I believe. Nice old buildings and streets. The poet Rimbaud spent some time there in the last century, so I gather."

"Ah," said Caroline, mildly bored.

We reached the car, and she turned unexpectedly and kissed me, smiling.

"What was that for?" I said.

"Oh," she said, "just for being rather nice. Thank you for the walk. You're chaperoning me very well, I must say."

We drove down the hill saying very little, wrapped in a cocoon of comfortable silence, her arm pressed against mine. Whenever I changed gear, our hands touched. I felt unreasonably happy.

The evening was actually not so tedious as it had promised to be. We had a pleasant dinner, at which we had to give some account of where we had been, and were able to describe our walk to the old rock-church, which shed an aura of respectability on our adventure. And then, after I had read the children another bedtime story (I was unfortunately by now strongly in demand for this), we settled down to a game of Monopoly. In fact, Caroline entered into the game with great aggressiveness, and quickly accumulated quite a bit of slum property, from which she exacted ruthless rentals. Isabel established herself in Park Lane, and Graham and I were preyed on by both of them, until we were finally driven out of business. Then they turned to destroying each other, while Graham and I drank brandy and watched them.

"How's the Latin going?" asked Graham.

"Oh, quite well, I think. Tewodros is a bit of a pest with red herrings, but he can do the stuff when it comes down to it, and young Fiona is very bright and willing. And young Tadesse is doing well. "

Graham nodded approvingly. Tadesse was the son of Cousin James's friend, Abebe Retha, the Minster of Justice. I was impressed, in general, by the aristocratic self-confidence of my Ethiopian students, even when they didn't have much to be self-confident about.

"Seen any more of Tewodros's big brother, by the way?" said Graham, with a smile.

I hesitated, not wishing to confess what I had been up to the previous day, but then it occurred to me that I had been talking about my adventures in Caroline's presence last night, and she might well put two and two together.

"Well yes, actually," I said, as casually as I could. "He found me in the Piazza on Friday, and invited me down on the spur of the moment to spend the weekend at his hunting lodge on Lake Langano. I had to get back for my jazz session, so I went down just overnight, went hunting pig in the morning, and came back here in the late afternoon. It was good fun."

"Well, well," said Graham, amused. "Pig-hunting!"

Caroline looked over.

"Yes, he was boasting about it last night. I'm glad to say he didn't kill a pig himself. But he did eat it for lunch. Who is this Prince Yohannis friend of yours? I didn't get a chance to ask last night. He sounds interesting."

"Well, he is interesting," I said. "Some people" – and I glanced at Graham – "think rather too interesting. He's a friend of mine from Oxford who happens to be a nephew of the Emperor. But he's a bit of a radical, and also a bit of a playboy, and that could cause problems, I suppose, sooner or later."

"Ooh!" said Caroline. "Can I meet him?"

Isabel interposed.

"I really don't think that would be a good idea, dear. We don't even think that Luke should see too much of him, but we do realise that it's difficult to refuse his invitations. One doesn't want to cause offence.'

"No," I said, "that's my problem, really. But I'm not sure that I should introduce you to him, as Isabel says."

"Oh shoot!" said Caroline, pouting. "He sounds really fascinating."

"Oh well," I said, "I suppose he is in a way, if you like the tall, dark, handsome, highly intelligent, and stinkingly rich type."

"Oh, shut up," said Caroline.

Isabel recalled her to the game, where she was anticipating being able to strike a devastating blow. In fact, though, Caroline, throwing the dice with abstracted abandon, slipped miraculously between her properties, and before very long had extracted a number of heavy payments from Isabel. At this point they decided to call it a draw.

Graham and I had another brandy, while the ladies had cocoa. It was obvious to me that there was no way that I was going to sneak Caroline out of the bosom of the Wiggins family tonight, and in fact I'd had just about enough for one day. So when the cocoa and the brandy were finished, I rose and excused myself, thanking Graham and Isabel for dinner and a delightful evening.

Caroline looked across at me meaningfully.

"Thank you for the afternoon's drive."

"Not at all," I replied, hoping to sound just a little suave. "A pleasure. Must do it again some time."

"Sleep tight! Might see you in class tomorrow," was Caroline's parting shot. I managed to make a face at her behind the Wiggins' backs as they escorted me to the front door.

"Good night, then, Luke, old man," said Graham. "See you in the morning. And," he added, sotto voce, "Thanks for squiring Caroline around. I know she enjoyed it."

CHAPTER SIXTEEN

The following day was something of a roller-coaster. I appeared in my senior English class to find Caroline, as good as her word, established demurely in the back row, chatting to nice little Margaret Shillong. I threw a stern look in her direction and she grinned back in defiance. I resolved to ignore her, and turned to a discussion of our prose set book. We had reached the stage where Elizabeth has just turned down Mr Collins' proposal. An interesting dispute on the propriety of this ensued, largely following ethnic lines.

Mohammed Abdurrahman, to whom I had turned first (studiously avoiding the eye and hand of Tewodros, who was dying to intervene), amused me by declaring firmly that Mr Collins seemed to him a good man, and that she should not have refused him. This was greeted with derisive groans by David Crosson, Fiona and others. Mohammed stood his ground, declaring that it was not proper, in any case, for a girl to refuse a man whom her father had chosen for her. I pointed out mildly that in fact Mr Bennet had expressed no opinion in this matter, only Mrs Bennet. But, argued Mohammed, surely Mrs Bennet would not go against the wishes of her husband.

I threw the question open to the floor. David jumped in.

"This is ridiculous," he said. "Of course she's right to refuse him. The guy's a jerk!"

"A jerk?" I said. "I don't think that's reached our side of the Atlantic yet." I looked at Caroline, but she shrugged.

"It's a most expressive word. I like it. It certainly suits Mr Collins. Would that be what we would call a drip, I wonder?"

Now it was David's turn to look confused.

"Yeah," he said. "I guess. Something like that."

"I know what he means," Fiona chipped in, "and I absolutely agree. All this stuff about Lady Catherine De Bourgh, and how she advised him to marry. All he wants to do is suck up to her. He's a dreadful little man."

Manolis Hadjidakis intervened with a typically gloomy comment.

"No, sir, I tell you, this Collins is the best she is going to get. She should take him. Maybe later she can poison him, or something. Then she get back the property."

This provoked a general laugh. Manolis was a very popular figure, despite his gloom – or perhaps because of it.

"Yes," I said, "that's an excellent idea, Manolis, if she just could get away with it. But, in fact, though I don't want to spoil the story, she does get something better in the end. Or so Jane Austen thought, anyhow."

And so the discussion went back and forth. I let them argue, merely steering them back to the text now and again to underpin somebody's point. Tewodros did finally get his oar in, predictably standing up for marriage with Mr Collins, though he suggested, unrealistically, that Elizabeth could always find a lover if she got bored.

Not in middle class Victorian England, I suggested. Only the aristocracy could get away with that. Certainly not wives of clergymen.

Break came while we were still arguing the point, and I joined Caroline on the way out.

"So?" I said, when we were on our own. "How did you find that?"

"I found it fascinating," she said. "The clash of cultures and personalities! And they don't mind speaking out."

"No, they don't," I agreed, "and it makes things entertaining. They're a good bunch. You were talking to Margaret?"

"Yes, she's sweet, isn't she? Shy as a little mouse, though."

"Just a well brought up little Indian girl," I said. "Not like some I could mention."

"Oh, piss off."

We were making vaguely for my bungalow.

"How about a cup of coffee?" I said. "I'm not on duty today, fortunately."

Just as Caroline was agreeing to this, though, Simon appeared from nowhere.

"Hullo, you two," he said. "Interested in a cup of coffee?"

"Oh yes," I said. "You're not on duty either, then?"

"No, thank God. Come over to my place. My boy Wolde will have a pot ready."

"So will TM, of course," I said, "but okay, since you're offering."

We settled into Simon's living room, after the usual clearing of assorted paraphernalia off the chairs and sofa. Caroline chose the sofa. I hesitated as to whether to join her, but then thought the better of it, and took one of the armchairs. Simon took the other one.

"Well," he said, looking Caroline over approvingly, "how are you this morning, then?"

"Oh," said Caroline, brightly, "I'm enjoying myself pretty well. Just spent the last period in Luke's English class, listening to a multicultural discussion of *Pride and Prejudice*."

"Wow," snorted Simon derisively, "that must have been thrilling."

"Yes it was, actually," she replied with some defiance. I looked at her affectionately.

But Simon was not to be squashed.

"Well, come along to one of mine, then, after break. That you'll find really exciting."

She looked at him boldly.

"Yes, I was just thinking I might."

Simon returned her gaze, grinning wolfishly. Something in the interaction of these two was making me uneasy. After all, I could hardly complain. If anything, at the moment Caroline seemed keen on me, but it was just precisely this adventurous streak in her nature that was making me feel uncomfortable. Simon was an attractive fellow, and he certainly had his eye on her – especially since he must have had a shrewd suspicion that something was going on between us, which would act, I suspected, as a strong stimulus.

But no, I beat back such thoughts. If I were to become jealous and possessive, then I would be in a bad way; it could only lead to grief when dealing with someone in Caroline's frame of mind. So I joined in the banter, and thus we finished our coffee pleasantly enough. I went off to struggle with instilling grammar into the Fifth, and Simon escorted Caroline off to his class on something I hoped would be equally boring. I didn't see either of them again until the afternoon.

As usual on Mondays, instead of a siesta, I had a Latin class. That day, however, it was some sort of Ethiopian holiday, which resulted in both Tewodros and Tadesse being absent, so that Fiona McHugh was my only customer. She began by issuing a long-delayed invitation from her parents to come to dinner, delivering a note from her father proposing the following Friday. Mr McHugh apologised that they had not got round to this before, but he'd had various other distractions. All I had lined up for Friday was a gig at the Paradiso, but it was my understanding with Jack that if anything else came up I must be allowed to bow out, so that was no problem. I accepted with pleasure, for half past seven.

Not long before the hour was up, we were startled by footsteps on the path, and a peremptory knock. I called out an invitation to come in, and Caroline stuck her head around the door. She took in the scene with a somewhat intolerant eye. Fiona and I were rather closer than I would have liked on the sofa, sharing a book.

"Oh," said Caroline, with elaborate politeness, "I'm awfully sorry. I didn't realise I would be disturbing something."

"No problem," I said brightly, "just a Latin class. We'll be through in about five minutes."

"Ah," said Caroline. "Latin. Okay. I was just wondering if you were thinking of going downtown later."

"Yes, actually," I said. "I want to do some shopping, if you can stand that. Then we could go to the Piazza, and join the gang at the Ras. Do you want to stick around till we've finished here?"

"No, I'll just go back to the house. You can collect me."

"Right-oh, then." And she disappeared.

After the class, I needed to go down to Florides' to get some supplies. TM had been reporting various basics that we were running out of. I put together a list in a businesslike manner, and then went across to the Wigginses' bungalow to collect Caroline. She was ready when I arrived, so we headed straight back to the car, which was parked behind my bungalow. As we walked across the compound, Caroline glanced over at Simon's place.

"I wonder if Simon would be interested in coming down as well."

"Oh, he probably will," I said, a little shortly, " but I imagine he's still snoozing. He can look after himself, though. We'll find him in the

Ras Bar in an hour or so, without fail, unless he suddenly comes down with the plague."

If Caroline noticed a slight asperity in my tone, she made no comment on it.

As we drove down to the centre of town, she asked me teasingly about Fiona.

"That was a very cosy Latin class I broke in on," she began. "Who's your little friend?"

I bristled.

"Caroline, I object to these insinuations. She's not my little friend. She's not much littler than you, in any case. It just happened that the two other members of the class are Ethiopian, and they were off for some feast day, so there was just Fiona left."

"Fiona? That's a nice name."

I ignored this.

"Fiona McHugh. Her father is Irish, in fact. Over here on secondment with the United Nations." I changed the subject and started to tell her about Mr Florides' shop, grandly styled the Hellenic Market, and then about Marco, who might well be also found later at the Ras. She allowed herself to be diverted, having made her point.

I gathered up my basic supplies at the Hellenic Market, and a few luxuries, bought on impulse, as well – to Caroline's amusement. She kept finding other exotica, and shoving them under my nose, only to have them rejected.

"Ah look, stuffed vine-leaves! You ever had those? They're good, you know!"

"I don't think Tekla-Mariam would understand stuffed vine-leaves."

I turned down a tin of snails on the same principle, passing over the fact that it would have cost the best part of a week's salary.

We greeted Mr Florides himself on leaving, as was the custom, and I introduced Caroline to him. He was at his most charming, and pressed upon each of us a large and excellent piece of *loukoumi* on parting.

"He's rather a poppet, isn't he?" said Caroline, as we walked to the car with the groceries.

"Well," I said, "at the prices he charges, he can well afford to be. But still, I agree, he's a character. So is Marco, as you may have a chance to observe, and Simon always claims he's a total rogue. But he's given me a fair deal with this old bus, so far as I can see."

Caroline laughed.

"It did boil over, though, on the way out to Nyala."

"Yes," I admitted, "but he fixed that for free. Or he says he has. I haven't really tested it since. It got us up the hill, though, on Sunday."

'Yes, it did, didn't it?" And she gave me a conspiratorial and slightly lecherous glance.

We left the bags in the car, and then decided just to walk the short distance to the Piazza. I locked the car, and entrusted its minding to some urchins who were hanging about, and we set out to stroll down the hill, accompanied by a further cloud of urchins offering shoe-shine, combs and Durex. Caroline was amused by the latter item, when shoved under her nose.

"Is this where you get yours?" she said. "I hope they're reliable."

I looked at her austerely, without comment.

We dropped in first to Giannopoulos' bookstore, to check on new arrivals, and see if the *Manchester Guardian Weekly* or the airmail edition of the Times had come in. The papers, as usual, hadn't – Tuesday or even Wednesday was more normal – but I saw a new novel of Durrell's, and some Henry Miller, and fingered them lovingly. Once again, Caroline egged me on, but I decided to be prudent, and wait till the end of the month. My salary was fine for ordinary living, along with a small monthly remittance to Wicklow, but any sort of luxury quickly took a bite out of it. I was largely dependent on my Russian pupils, and honoraria from the Paradiso, for such items as novels from Giannopoulos or sessions with Berhane.

We left Giannopoulos just after five, and crossed the Piazza to see if there was any activity on the verandah of the Ras Bar. In fact there was, but it consisted initially just of Maurice, crouched in his chair with a hunted expression, being harangued on some point by none other than Jack Hirschhorn, who was blessedly oblivious to Maurice's anti-American views. Maurice was disproportionately pleased to see us, and kissed Caroline's hand most gallantly. Jack too was pleased to see us, and tried to nail me down for the weekend. I had to excuse myself for Friday – hoping that he wouldn't question me too closely as to who precisely I was going out to dinner with – but promised to be there on

Saturday. Evenings at the Paradiso were becoming a part of life that I found myself looking forward to. It tied one down in theory, but on the other hand it provided a focus, and could always be got out of if necessary.

We did not in fact have long to wait for Simon, who appeared around half past five, looking rather pleased with himself. He too had been over to Giannopoulos', looking for the papers.

"I thought you two might be down here," he said, sliding into a chair beside Caroline. "I came to look for you, but you'd gone."

"Yes," I said. "I had some shopping to do, and Caroline came along for the ride."

"I barged in on his Latin lesson," she said.

"Oh yes," said Simon, with a laugh. "That's what he gets up to during the siesta."

"I object," I said. "Teaching Latin to the young is a hard and demanding task, especially during the siesta."

"Oh yes," said Caroline, "it was at a particularly hard and demanding stage when I arrived. He was cuddled up on the sofa with Fiona."

"Oho!" said Simon, delighted. "I've warned him about Fiona, repeatedly, but he won't listen, of course. She's really quite a dish."

"I wish you'd stop this," I said testily. "I was merely explaining something that she didn't understand about the perfect tense."

"The perfect tense, eh? I think that young lady understands a good deal more than you think," said Simon.

"Say," said Jack, obtusely, "this sounds pretty interesting."

Maurice was beginning to show an interest too, but fortunately this topic was interrupted by the arrival of Marco, who looked like he had spent most of the afternoon under a lorry, and now badly needed a beer. Jack excused himself for another urgent engagement, embracing Marco, clapping Maurice on the back (to his intense annoyance), and reminding me as he went of the rehearsal on Wednesday. Marco took his chair thankfully.

"*Mon Dieu*, that Hirschhorn," groaned Maurice, raising his eyes to heaven. "You cannot imagine what I have been suffering, until La Touche arrived with this beautiful lady."

"Oh, come on, Maurice," said Simon, defensively, "he's not so bad."

But Maurice just shook his head mournfully.

The talk circulated lazily around for another half-hour or so, and then I decided that I had to get back with the groceries, to give Tekla-Mariam a chance to make dinner.

"Do you want a lift back?" I asked Caroline.

She hesitated, and looked at Simon. Simon rose to the occasion.

"If you want to hang about a little longer," he said, "I can run you back in half an hour or so."

"Okay, then," she said, brightly, "I'll stay on a bit. Dinner's not till seven. Thanks for the ride, Luke. See you later, perhaps."

I surveyed them both, raised a hand to the company, and sloped off, feeling somewhat rejected. But why? It was perfectly reasonable for Caroline to want to hang on a little longer. It was very pleasant on the verandah of the Ras Bar. The company was congenial. I would have hung on longer myself, except that I had things that needed doing. Oh, the hell with it.

I got back to the car, donated some small change to one particular urchin I recognised, and drove back to the compound, where TM was, as I anticipated, waiting for his supplies. He unloaded them straight through the back door into the kitchen, and I set myself to preparing the next day's classes.

Shortly before seven, I heard the sound of Simon's car returning, and shortly after that footsteps on the path. It was Caroline, in a rush. She wouldn't come in, because it was just dinnertime, but stayed on the doorstep, a bit flustered.

"I just dropped over to say"– and she lowered her voice to a conspiratorial whisper – "that I won't be over later. I've got the curse! Sorry about that!"

A quick kiss, and she was gone, barely giving me time to indicate that I quite understood. I hadn't really expected another visit, but this unreasonably depressed me. And yet why? I thought. Too much of this dodging around in the middle of the night would be bound to lead to discovery sooner or later, and consequent unpleasantness. So, no sweat. I had work to do, anyhow.

But that was not quite the end of the evening. I settled down after dinner with some Amharic homework, working away till quite late. I was feeling pleased with myself, at last, that I was making some progress. About half past eleven I was just thinking about going to bed, when I heard a faint noise out in the compound, over and above the usual night noises, that of a door closing quietly.

I wandered over to my front door, opened it gently, and looked out. The compound was silent and peaceful, bathed in the light of an almost full moon. Then, scanning the shadows, I picked out a furtive figure, slipping across from the Wiggins' in the direction of Simon's bungalow. With a blinding shock, I realised that it was Caroline. She paused a moment in front of his door, then it was opened and she disappeared inside.

I suppose I got to sleep that night. I must have, because Tekla-Mariam had to wake me in the morning for my tea. All I remember, though, is lying awake endlessly, going over things in my head, and seething with rage and humiliation.

All right, I said to myself, over and over again, she's a free spirit, she doesn't want attachments, to be tied down. She certainly doesn't belong to me. She can fuck any one she wants. But why did she have to resort to that sort of sneakiness? Could she not have just said, I asked myself savagely, "Look, I want to try out Simon. I'm curious to see what he can do – you know, test his equipment." I could have taken that, I think. Not easily, but I could have come to terms to with it. I mean, I could see that they were attracted to each other, no question about it. And Simon, blast him, was just pissed off at the idea that I had got in ahead of him with this gorgeous chick. It was a point of honour for him to seduce her if he could. But he can't have expected it would be that easy – that, if anything, she would be seducing him.

I tried to persuade myself that perhaps, after all, she'd done me a favour. I really was beginning to fall for this girl seriously, and where would that have led? She had just saved me from making a total fool of myself. Instead of raging at her, I should just learn from her. Now she could screw up Simon's life instead.

But all this rationalising really didn't work very well. My insides were still churning. I was having flashbacks to my experience with Jenny Danziger at Oxford. Admittedly, I hadn't even got to square one with Jenny, but, *mutatis mutandis*, we had the same situation over again. I meet this very attractive girl, and then I introduce her to my very attractive friend, and very attractive girl and very attractive friend find themselves very attracted by each other, and poor old La Touche is left out in the cold, clutching his codpiece, and feeling very sorry for himself.

But not this time, I resolved. I would not hang about on the sidelines, I would move on. There were plenty of other girls around. At least Caroline did something for me – she indicated that I could be physically attractive. Yes, I was grateful for that, and for some moments of pure, exquisite pleasure...

But I determined to put those out of my mind, blast her! The problem that gripped me at that moment was how to avoid her, indeed, both of them, for the next few days. I was sad to think that I would be turning my back on Simon. He was good fun, the bastard, and I didn't want to lose him. But I had a point to make. Or did I? What was this point exactly?

My brain spun like this all night long. One thing I resolved for certain though, was that I would give them both the cold shoulder the following day.

This proved easier said than done. I went from my bungalow straight to Assembly, where I avoided the gaze of a rather bleary-looking Blakeney, and from there straight to class. But then there was the problem of break. I was not on duty, so I could head back home for coffee without hanging about. I glanced cautiously around the compound, and saw Simon standing over near the office. In fact, if he saw me, he gave no sign of it, which I put down grimly to his guilty conscience. But as I crossed in front of the Wiggins', Caroline, who must have watching out for me, came bounding cheerfully down the steps.

"Hi," she said, "are you off home for coffee? Can I join you?"

I looked at her with what was meant to be cold hostility, but it didn't seem to register.

"I'm not sure," I said, somewhat flustered, "I think this is one of the mornings my students are coming over."

This gave her some pause, but not much.

"Oh well, they won't mind me, will they? I have met them, after all. We can chat. If it looks like I'm embarrassing them, I can always go."

"Oh, okay," I said, gruffly, knowing that my guest morning was actually not today, but tomorrow. I was caught.

"You're looking a bit glum this morning," she ventured, as we walked up the path.

"Um," I grunted. "I didn't sleep very well, actually."

"You may be coming down with something," said Caroline brightly. "Just as well I wasn't available last night, in that case."

This was almost more than I could take. Was I going to confront her now, and have a flaming row, or was I going to let it pass? My heart sank. I really couldn't face a row. I looked at her as I ushered her in the door, and I found my anger mysteriously relaxing. What the hell, I thought. She has done me a favour, after all. I was certainly in danger of becoming infatuated with her, up to the previous night, and now suddenly I could look at her with some detachment. I ordered coffee for two from TM, and waved her to a seat.

She slid into the armchair opposite me, and I contemplated her for a moment in silence. She was not, after all, that beautiful, I reflected, with some satisfaction. More of a funny face, really – almost monkeyish, taken at certain angles and in certain lights. Certainly wouldn't win any beauty contests. And where would all this have led to, anyhow? She says she doesn't want any attachments, and I don't either, really. Not just at the moment. So this is just fine.

"Well, I'm off back to Nyala this afternoon," she said, with a sigh. "Aunt Louise is coming down for lunch, to do some shopping, and then we'll drive back, I suppose, for dinner. It's been fun, though. I must wangle another visit to town soon, and you must try to fix up another invitation to Nyala. How about next weekend? Get your Cousin James to invite himself. He's always welcome, I think. And Uncle Andy really likes you. 'A serious young fella', he said, 'and sound on bridge'."

"Well, I don't think this coming weekend," I said. "I'm tied up with various things. I'll talk to James."

"Do that," she said. "I'm going to be bored up there. And remember to bring some rubbers. I think I've run out." And she grinned wickedly.

Tekla-Mariam brought in the coffee before I could make any reply to that, but I frowned. She seemed happily oblivious, though.

"Doesn't look as if your students are going to turn up," she said, derisively.

"No," I said. "This is Tuesday. They come on Thursdays."

"That's fine, then. I won't be disturbing anything."

"No."

She stirred her coffee.

"Oh, by the way," she said, lightly. "I dropped over to visit Simon last night. He asked me over earlier. He said he was feeling lonely."

I looked at her in astonishment, my cup frozen in mid-air. This was at least honest, but it was pretty brazen.

"You went over to visit Simon?" I said frostily. "You mean, after you left me?"

"Yes – oh, relax, I didn't *sleep* with him or anything. I had the curse, after all, if you remember. But we talked for ages – mainly about you, but about England as well. He's had a pretty grim life in some ways, you know. Parents split up when he was quite small. Did you know that?"

"No, I didn't," I said, still rather coolly. "You seem to have found out more than I have about him, in quite a short time.'

"Well, he wanted to talk."

"I should say he wanted even more to get you into bed with him, the beast. He must have been most disappointed. Do I take it that you would have gone to bed with him if you hadn't had the curse?"

She looked at me defiantly.

"I might have," she said, "if I hadn't gone to bed with you first. That's entirely my business. Remember what I said. I like you a lot, Luke my love, but I don't want to belong to you, or to anyone. Simon's good fun, and I wouldn't mind at all going to bed with him, but it doesn't mean that I want to ditch you, and shack up with him. It just means that *I don't want to belong to anyone* – at least for the moment. Can you get that into your thick noddle?"

I raised my hands in surrender.

"Okay, okay, I accept that. I'm sorry. I don't want to corral you as 'my girl', or anything vulgar like that, but this is all a bit fast-moving for me." I must have sounded rather pathetic, because Caroline, leaving her coffee, jumped up and came over to give me a kiss. Then she sat on the arm of my chair, disregarding Tekla-Mariam, who was pottering in the kitchen just out of sight, and ran her hand through my hair.

"Oh Luke," she said, pensively, "you are sweet, but neither of us needs to get involved just at the moment, do we? I mean, I came out here – or was sent out, I suppose – to get out of an entanglement, not to get into one. Let's just try to enjoy ourselves, can't we?"

"Yes," I said, feeling suddenly relaxed and at peace with the world. "Let's. That's fine with me." I reached round and stroked her flank, as it projected over the arm of the sofa. It had a pleasing feel.

"Okay, then." She put a hand on my shoulder, and levered herself upright. "Let's think about the weekend after next. And please don't quarrel with Simon on my account. He likes you a lot, and I think he needs you. He comes on strong, but I think he's actually a pretty insecure person."

Not for the first time I marvelled at the perceptiveness of this girl. She would have had every excuse for feeling insecure herself, after all. And she had the measure of Simon. From being inflamed against him, I began to feel rather sorry for him, and that was a much more comfortable sensation.

So she slipped away, after thanking TM sweetly for the coffee, to his mild confusion, and I was left to put some thoughts together for my upcoming class with the Fourth. Grammar and composition – just the thing to take one's mind off well-turned breasts and thighs.

That was the last I was going to see of Caroline for some time, which was probably just as well. But I still had to face Simon, with whom I was officially not at all pleased. In the event, though, not much came of that. I really had no heart for a fight, over what had turned out to be something of a non-issue. Not that that was any credit to him, of course, but still ...

In fact I didn't have to face him till Wednesday, when he came round at the usual time, after my Latin class, to see if I was on for coming down to the Piazza.

"Come on, get yourself organised. Let's go get a beer."

So we drove down in Simon's Citroen, parked behind Giannopoulos' Bookstore, looked in there to get the *Manchester Guardian Weekly*, and check on the latest consignment of dirty books, and then over to the Ras. Only then, on the verandah of the bar, with cold beers in front of us, did Simon get round to the subject of Caroline. He leaned back in his chair, took a slug of beer, and belched reflectively.

"You know something?" he said. "That girl of yours, Caroline, she's a great chick, but I would suggest you go pretty carefully there. I'd say she would be a load of trouble, in the long run."

"What on earth do you mean, trouble?" I snapped. "And what do you base that observation on, anyhow?"

"Now, keep your hair on," said Simon, adopting a superior tone, and raising a monitory hand. "I'm only thinking of your own good. I had a bit of a chat with her on Monday as we drove home, after you left." (So he wasn't going to admit the midnight tryst!) "What I mean is, she has some pretty weird ideas. She likes you, of course. That's obvious. But she certainly made it clear to me that she doesn't want to belong to anyone. She was pretty frank about what she's after, which as far as I can see is free sex, and the high life generally. There was obviously some trouble back home that she didn't want to talk about, but it's coloured her whole attitude. I'd say she's far too grown up for her own good, frankly."

I looked at him. It crossed my mind to practice oneupmanship by revealing that Caroline had told me her secret out at Nyala Farm, but I drew back from that. Instead, I made a mild reply.

"Yes, well, I think I know that. I mean, she intimated the same thing to me, more or less. And I don't see anything wrong with that. I don't want to belong to anyone else either, after all, and I'm quite sure you don't. So why not Caroline? I admit I'm attracted by her – I don't see how one could not be – but I don't want to own her. After all, I think she rather likes you too," I added, to see if I could provoke him to any indiscretions. Simon took another swig of beer.

"Yes, well," he said, "on the whole, I reckon you can have her. I just think she's trouble."

"Well now, that's very decent of you, I must say," I replied, with sarcasm.

He waved his glass defensively.

"Well, you can't say I haven't warned you."

"No, I suppose I can't."

But then Maurice turned up, and after another beer Simon proposed to adjourn to the Bella Napoli. I was about to agree when I remembered with a shock that I was engaged that evening for my first play-reading with Madame Boghossian. I would have to give my jazz rehearsal a miss as well.

This invitation had taken some time to come, but come it had, in the shape of a finely-embossed and delicately-scented visiting card which had arrived the previous Wednesday, and to which I had responded promptly, though being constantly in danger of forgetting all about it. It sounded like an evening which would be different, and this was a tendency in my world that I was concerned to maximise at the moment. I excused myself, much to Simon's contemptuous amusement ("Play-reading! Fook and stroll abaht! It'll be basket-weaving next!") and caught a Millecento back to the compound, where Tekla-Mariam was ready with a risotto.

The note had specified that the play we would be reading – in my honour, I read with some alarm – was Shaw's *John Bull's Other Island*. No need to bring a text, if I didn't have one, since she had secured a supply. She hoped I would be pleased. It was not a play of Shaw's that I knew, but it was my impression that it was not one of his more fortunate efforts. I hoped that I was not about to be typecast as a stage-Irishman of some sort.

I was expected at the Boghossian residence at eight. In the event, I had no great trouble in finding the compound, on the east side of town as it was, and not too far from Arat Kilo, and got to the front gate at about five minutes past the hour. I gave my name to the well-armed but courteous *zabanya*, who phoned up to the house to announce me, and then waved me on very civilly. Mr Boghossian, I supposed, was a man who did not care to take any chances. As I had rather expected, there was an air of quiet opulence about the well-appointed grounds and the bungalow itself.

I was greeted at the door by a stately old Ethiopian retainer, who ushered me into a spacious living-room, in which there were a number of people already assembled. One of them, I observed with a start, was none other than John Langdon. I had not reckoned on him being among the play-reading fraternity, but, as I came to think of it, there was nothing very strange in that. Cultured, English-speaking Addis was a small enough society, after all, and the Boghossians were doubtless well-placed to know who was available, and to gather them together.

Mimi Boghossian swept forward to greet me. She was a small, pretty, plump woman, with bushy dark hair and flashing teeth, well into her forties, I guessed, but looking younger, and bubbling with vitality. She clasped my hands in hers. Her English was quite fluent, with a pleasant, exotic intonation.

"So this is the young Luke that I have been hearing so much about! It is so good to meet you at last. I wish it had been earlier, but there it is. Somehow this autumn has been very, very busy. But come and let me introduce you. Do you know anyone – or perhaps everyone?"

John Langdon raised a hand in greeting, and smiled.

"Ah," said Mimi, "you have met Mr Langdon, then?"

"Oh yes," I said, "we've met."

She took me round the room, introducing me to several people I had never met before, and whose names consequently flowed straight through my mind without a trace. There was a middle-aged American couple, and a serious elderly Indian. There was a young English couple from the Teferi Makonnen School, and three or four others who were Armenian or Greek. I concluded with some embarrassment that for Mimi eight o'clock must have meant eight o'clock. Only now did I notice that Wendy Thesiger was also among the company. She was sitting slightly in the shadows, not, as I would have expected, near John Langdon, but at the other side of the room, talking to a rather handsome Greek gentleman. I was pleased to see her. She greeted me with a wave and a smile.

"Ah!" said Mimi. "Here is some one else that you know. Good, good! I believe that you are our only Irishman, so you will have to help us with the accents. It is a bit confusing."

"Oh dear," I said, apprehensively. "I'm not sure how much help I'll be there. I don't have a very good Irish accent myself, I'm afraid."

"No," chipped in Langdon brightly. "He's a bit of a fraud actually, Mimi. Thoroughly anglicised, I'm afraid."

"Oh no?" She clasped my arm in mock alarm. "Luke, Luke, you are Irish, are you not? Your Cousin James has assured me of this."

"Yes, I am, of course," I assured her, not liking to be spoken for by Langdon. "It's just that I've spent quite a lot of time out of the country. But I'm sure I can interpret the accents if we need help."

"Good, good. I think we will. Now you sit beside me, and take a glass of wine. I want you to be Larry Doyle, and dear John can be Broadbent. That will be a good combination, I think. I have given the others their parts. Wendy is to be Nora, and I will be Aunt Judy."

She found me a text, and we settled down to business. The significance of Mimi's casting arrangements did not sink in till we were well launched on the play. Doyle and Broadbent are partners in an civil engineering practice in London, and bosom buddies. Larry Doyle is in fact very much an expatriate Irishman, so that no great degree of brogue was required. What I did have to do, however, was to interact at length with Langdon, a situation he plainly rather enjoyed. Mr Chatterji, the elderly Indian gentleman, made a splendid effort as the sleazy Tim Haffigan in Act One, producing, in place of a brogue, an excellent stage Indian accent, which fully served the purpose.

Act Two, staged back in the countryside of the West of Ireland, was more troublesome, but a mixture of Americans, British and Armenians took on the various outlandish male characters required, while Wendy was most impressive as Larry Doyle's abandoned love Nora, and Mimi very plausible as Aunt Judy. Overall, it was surprisingly enjoyable, since everyone was determined to have a good time.

We got no further, in fact, than the first two acts, to the accompaniment of much laughter and jollity, when it was decided to take a break. At around half past nine we were interrupted most pleasantly by the entry of Mr Boghossian himself, carrying a tray with tea, coffee, and an assortment of intriguing Armenian goodies. He plainly was not into playreading himself, but he did not want to remain aloof either, and it amused him to cast himself as the butler.

He greeted me amiably, and asked me how I was getting on. I gave him a reassuring reply, and thanked him once again for his help with the bank account.

"Ah, it was nothing," he said, patting me on the arm. "I was only glad to be able to assist a relative of Sir James. But remember, if ever a more serious problem comes up that I can be of help with, do not forget that I am there!"

I thanked him for the offer, and he changed the subject, asking about the play. I had to confess that I had never read it or seen it before. "But it's great fun, and full of shrewd cracks at both Ireland and England, though inevitably a bit dated."

"Ah," said Mr Boghossian, with mock wistfulness, "I wish that I had time for such things. I hardly have time to read a novel these days. It is most uncivilised."

"Yes," said Mimi, chipping in, and linking her arm in his, "it is really very bad, Nuri. You should relax more."

"Of course I should, my dear. And one day soon I will, I promise you." At which he excused himself, to move courteously round the room.

"I must say, Luke dear," said Mimi, "that you were very good, considering you had not ever seen the play before."

"Yes," I heard Langdon intervene ironically from behind me, "he is, isn't he, Mimi? Something of a natural, in fact, I should say."

"Well," I said, in modest confusion, "I must say I find Larry someone whose situation I can relate to somewhat. And Shaw flows along very well, even when he's being rather preposterous."

So we settled down again, for the latter half of the play. This was more unsettling. What had seemed fairly light-hearted farce, as I discovered, had something of a sting in the tail, as I should have expected with Shaw. Larry Doyle ceased to be a person with whom I had any desire to be identified, while his bumbling friend Broadbent turned out anything but bumbling, and thoroughly odious, and both were incisively, though probably ineffectually, put in their place by the prophetic figure of the 'spoiled priest' Peter Keegan, who was played with remarkable power by the imposing-looking Greek gentleman who had been talking to Wendy Thesiger.

It was well after eleven when we broke up. I thanked our hostess and she booked me in firmly for the next occasion, which she wanted to be *The Devil's Disciple*. As I left, I found myself accompanied, to my slight annoyance, by John Langdon. He paused as we reached our cars, and turned round.

"You wouldn't care for a nightcap, I suppose?" he said, tentatively. 'There's quite a nice little bar near Arat Kilo where we could get a cognac."

I hesitated a moment, but then gave in to the instinctual feeling that had dominated my thoughts on John Langdon ever since the night we had met; I felt I could not be at all sure where such a excursion would lead. I looked at my watch, and excused myself amiably but firmly, though not without having to promise to have drink together before long.

As soon as I reached my trusty Fiat, I got in and drove away. But when I looked back in the rear view mirror, I saw Langdon still standing alone beside his car, gazing after me in the dark.

CHAPTER SEVENTEEN

Dinner with the McHughs on Friday was pleasant, but slightly fraught. Mr and Mrs McHugh welcomed me almost like a long-lost son – they had a son, as it turned out, just about my age, who had recently graduated and was working as an engineer in England. Frank, as he urged me to call him, put a stiff whiskey in my hand, and invited me out to the back porch to help him with the barbeque, leaving the ladies to get on with other things. Once there, as we basted the lamb, he grilled me a bit about his daughter.

"Well now, how's she getting along, do you think? She seems to enjoy the whole thing, from what she tells us – your classes in particular, of course."

"Oh yes?" I said, evenly. "I'm glad to hear that. I think she's getting along fine, actually. She's very bright, of course, so the subject matter isn't a problem – even the Latin, though she likes to pretend she can't understand sometimes!"

"Oh, I think she does find it difficult enough," he said, "in spite of the Italian. It's all the endings. I remember it myself from school. It was one of the banes of my existence, I have to confess to you. I'm glad now that I had to do it, of course, though it's many a blow of the strap it cost me! But that brings me to something I wanted to ask you, Luke – if you wouldn't mind, now. Fiona was wondering if you might have time to give her a few private lessons, just to help her over the difficult bits. Of course, I'd be glad to pay whatever the going rate is. You could come round here after school, maybe, now and again, and we'd be glad to give you your dinner as well, if you like."

I hesitated. Of course I could always do with the money, and some family dinners would be pleasant as well, but I had a suspicion that young Fiona had something more on her mind than Latin, and my life seemed complicated enough already. On the other hand, though, how could I refuse?

"Well," I said, cautiously, "of course I'd be glad to, but I wonder if we could leave it, perhaps, until after the Christmas holidays? It's just that at the moment there seems to be rather a lot going on, and I really don't feel on top of things yet. I'm giving English lessons to some Russians once a week, and I have to work at my jazz trumpet a bit at the moment as well, since I'm playing with a group now at weekends, and I'm a bit rusty. And then we're about to start serious rehearsals for a Gilbert and Sullivan opera that the English community are doing before Christmas."

And then, I thought to myself, there's Caroline and Berhane to be attended to, and Cousin James, and Yohannis, and Mimi's playreadings, and God knows what all else.

"Lord above," exclaimed Mr McHugh, "aren't you the busy fella! I'm glad to see time isn't weighing heavy on your hands, anyhow. But I hardly like to ask you to take on any more in the circumstances. She probably doesn't need any extra lessons, anyway. It was just that she brought the subject up herself, and I was impressed by that."

"Oh no," I said, hastily, "I didn't mean to sound so discouraging. I just feel that things will be a bit slacker after Christmas. I can make time for it in any case – perhaps not every week, though."

"Ah yes, once a fortnight would do fine, I'm sure."

Mr McHugh set me to basting the lamb as it turned on the spit, and went off to refill my glass. I looked around at the neat back yard, in which the McHughs or their predecessors had created a vegetable patch and a rockery. My gaze rested on the clothes line, which bore on it various items of female underwear, and some sheets, and I felt a sudden pang of nostalgia for some semblance of family life – not that I had ever known much of that, really; barely enough to qualify for nostalgia.

"Now then," said Frank McHugh, returning, "take a swig of that and see if it's to your taste."

I took the brimming glass, sipped cautiously, and then nodded appreciatively.

"Grand so." He inspected the carcase. "I'd say that lamb is about done now, wouldn't you? Give it another turn there, maybe, and we'll take it off. They're just ready for us inside."

So we unloaded the fragrant lamb onto a large platter, and I was given the job of carrying it in to the dining room. This ceremony was not to be delegated to servants. I suspected, indeed, that Mr McHugh, despite his periods of foreign service, was not really comfortable with servants.

It was a pleasant dinner, and we talked of many things. I had to give some description of my life at home in Wicklow, which was always something of an embarrassment. In the sympathetic atmosphere generated round the McHugh dinner table, however, it began to sound more romantic than it really was. Mr McHugh himself, it seemed, had grown up on a medium-sized farm in County Monaghan, run now by a brother of his, and he liked to get back there when he could. He wondered had I read *The Great Hunger*, by Patrick Kavanagh, and I had to admit that I had not.

"Oh, that's a grand poem, now. You must read it. It gives a great feel, now, for what it is to be a small farmer up in Monaghan."

I agreed that I must look it up, while reflecting to myself that the poet was yet to be born who would compose a similar celebration of the life of impoverished gentry in County Wicklow. Fiona, who had grown up largely in a variety of foreign cities, listened to all this with amused disdain. I suspected that she had heard all this before from her father more than once.

We gathered back in the living room for coffee, and, for Mr McHugh and myself, a brandy.

"Now," he said, "where I come from, after a good dinner, it would be the custom for everyone to sing a song, play a tune, or tell a story. We weren't really great ones for after dinner conversation, you understand. A pity now, Luke, that you didn't bring along your trumpet, You could have given us a tune."

"Oh," I said deprecatingly, "I'm not sure how good I'd be on solo, unaccompanied trumpet."

"Oh now, Fiona could back you up on the piano, I'm sure. You must bring it along the next time."

"You play the piano, then?" I said, looking over at her.

She blushed. "Oh, hardly at all. I just have a few tunes I can do."

"Oh indeed," said her mother, "she's too modest by half. Get up there now and give us a song."

"Well," said Fiona, provocatively, "I'll do a song if Mr La Touche will join in as well."

"A duet!" exclaimed Mr McHugh, slapping his knee. "That's just the thing. What songs do ye know, Luke?"

I demurred, hopelessly. I didn't really know any by heart, I insisted. I would need a text.

"Ah, sure that's no problem. Fiona has a sheaf of them. She can pick one."

So it was settled. Fiona sat down at the piano, and I leaned over her to read the text. We started with 'She Moved Through the Fair'. Fiona played well, and she had a fine, light voice. I joined in as well as I could, peering over her shoulder. Then she chose a somewhat livelier tune, with which I also joined in, "I Know Where I'm Going". Her parents applauded appreciatively. Frank McHugh then offered to contribute a song himself, and chose a much more rousing number, 'Brennan on the Moor', and we were all able to join in the chorus.

After this, I excused myself, with just another brandy for the road. It was in many ways a delightful evening.

CHAPTER EIGHTEEN

It is remarkable how even the most chaotic life, in the most bizarre of locations, contrives after a time to take on a modicum of pattern and order. After a couple of months in Addis, I found myself falling, not by any means unpleasantly, into something of a routine. The classes were no great trouble. I was slowly learning, on the job, something that in later times special courses were developed for – the art of teaching English as a foreign language. One begins with the naive idea that just because you know the language yourself you can teach it to all comers, but then you find out the hard way that you really need to know at least something about the languages of your pupils as well, on top of the basic techniques of teaching.

As for my pupils, they were all I could wish for, really. With the seniors, many of whom were very little younger than myself, I found myself on terms of growing friendship. The coffee mornings were going very well, and once, as I came back to the bungalow, I even heard, to my alarm, a raucous rock and roll beat. Someone had plainly discovered my Little Richard records, and put one on the record player. Now 'Long Tall Sally' was pouring out all over the compound.

I hurried in to hush them up, before this came to Graham's ears. I was met with mixed apprehension and enthusiasm.

"Hey, sir, this is great! We did not know this guy. Who is he?"

I grinned.

"Oh, he's my favourite man." I said. "He knocks Bill Haley, and even Elvis Presley, into a cocked hat, if you ask me. He's the real thing. He's crazy."

For most of the group, Little Richard was a sensational discovery. They tried 'Tutti Frutti', then 'Rock It Up', then 'Lucille'. Only the American, David Crosson, looked a little disapproving. He plainly did not regard Little Richard as a suitable representative of American culture.

Personalities began to come into focus. I particularly enjoyed the gallows humour of the large Greek, Manolis Hadjidakis, whose family, I gathered from him, left Greece during the civil war. They were now settled on a plantation somewhere down along the railway line to Dire Dawa. Manolis was one of a small number of boarders. He had surprised me one evening a few weeks into the term by coming round after dinner to enquire if he could borrow my car for a few minutes, as there was something he needed to get from the Arab shop down the road. I thought for a moment, and then decided the hell with it, and tossed him the keys, not knowing if I would see him or the car again, and get myself fired into the bargain. But he reappeared, grinning amiably, after about an hour, handed over the keys and thanked me. He had no doubt, I thought, paid a call also on one of the local *tej-bets*, but I reckoned that he could handle it.

After that, Manolis would drop in about once a week, if I was there, either to borrow the car 'for a message', or for a chat. I would offer him a beer, and he would sit and philosophise for a while. Mainly he tried to persuade me that life had no point at all, and I, who felt that mine, at least, had very little point, would feel it my duty to stick up for life in general, and argue the positive case. I enjoyed his whimsical gloom, though I still felt a little nervous about continuing to lend him the car. Some day, he promised, he would repay the hospitality by inviting me down to the plantation.

"You come down, sir, some weekend, and we hunt some pig, or some buck. My father is a great hunter. He like very much to meet you. I tell him that you have been a good friend to me."

"My God, Manoli," I said. "You haven't told him about borrowing the car?"

He grinned wolfishly.

"No, sir, I have not told him everything that goes on. I do not think that he would mind, of course, but is better not to worry him. No, I say only that we have interesting talks together."

So a loose arrangement was made for an expedition. More pig-hunting! Could be fun, though.

My Russian pupils had also become friends, in a way. I was invited to a very jolly dinner party at the Abdolovs, attended by my other pupils, where I succumbed to the custom of drinking toasts in vodka between each course, to the extent of becoming quite reckless. By the time we had toasted World Peace, Progress and Enlightenment, and Irish-Soviet Friendship, I would have been quite ready to disgorge any state secrets to which I was privy. Instead, I contrived to sing, somewhat off-key, some verses of "Finnegan's Wake", the words of which I dredged up from some corner of my subconscious, in response to a haunting Russian lament sung to the balalaika by Safar's pretty and lively wife.

The pressure of my career as a jazz musician, fortunately receded somewhat. To my considerable relief, both Jack and Mr Efstathiadis found that a jazz session every weekend was too punishing a schedule, both for the band and for the public, and we were cut back to a Friday or Saturday every second week, which was about right, actually. Even then, I didn't always make it. The round of drinks and dinner parties had begun to intensify, if that was possible, coming up to the holidays, and I found myself included both in the wide circle of expatriate teachers, and of friends of Cousin James, as well as various people I'd met with at Yohannis' parties and at Mimi's playreadings.

In addition to all these activities, there was the pleasant tradition of film shows in the British Embassy compound down the road, with drinks or even dinners before the show with the Hardimans, who continued to be friendly. And of course tennis parties there at the weekends. I began to get to the stage of having to invent excuses if I simply wanted to stay quietly at home for an evening, and catch up on my Amharic homework.

Yohannis I did not see for some weeks after our weekend at his shooting lodge. As it turned out, he had been sent abroad to represent the Emperor at a rather tedious conference in Geneva on Third World Development. As Yohannis analysed the situation later, his uncle's motives were complex. On the one hand, he wished to give Yohannis something serious to do, and on the other he wished to deliver a mild snub to this conference by sending a rather junior substitute for himself, since he objected to the notion that Ethiopia was part of the 'Third World' – or indeed of any world other than its own. Yohannis found Geneva and the Swiss rather boring, and his fellow-delegates unsympathetic. It was too early to get in any skiing, but he managed to find a few kindred spirits with whom to go gambling just over the border into France, at Thonon, where he came out slightly ahead, he claimed, after an evening at the tables.

He reintroduced himself in a characteristic way, by sending round his chauffeur with a little gift, a carved box of some aromatic wood, which turned out to contain a couple of dozen well-rolled joints of marijuana. An attached note urged me to smoke these in his honour, and to give him a call. When I did that, he asked me round for a quiet evening at home, where I learned what he had been up to. He had picked up some useful ideas on rural development, despite his professed boredom, and he was full of plans for trying them out. One of his girlfriends then came round and we smoked a few joints. I left them together after a while, and on my way back dropped in to a little bar on my way home, where I had a cognac, and then made love, in a rather desultory but relaxed way, to one of the girls of the establishment who had attracted my eye.

Simon and I continued to go out fairly regularly to the Bella Napoli, and on one occasion I brought out a few joints, relics of Yohannis' bounty, to share with Berhane and Frewet, which we found enhanced our love-making considerably. Taking a post-coital Melotti with Simon under the vine-trellis, I found that I was suddenly at peace with myself, in a way that I could not remember being for quite some time.

I was rash enough to announce this, and was rewarded with a snort of derision.

"At peace! He's at peace with himself! Ye daft bugger! Ye'll be accepting the universe next. You're just as high as a kite, that's all. It's good stuff, I have to admit. My compliments to His Highness. And why wouldn't you be at peace? You've had a good fuck. You've smoked a few joints. It's the end of another week. And end of term's just round the corner. Stands to reason, doesn't it? It doesn't mean that you've got any wiser, or discovered the meaning of life, or anything like that."

"No, come on," I said defensively, "don't spoil it. I've got a good feeling here somewhere, and I'm bloody well going to enjoy it. Don't you ever get a revelation like that, or are you just too soulless?"

Simon brooded for a moment. "Yes," he conceded, "once in a while, I suppose. But it usually means that something shitty is about to happen – something I haven't reckoned with at all. On the whole, I prefer to stay half-way miserable, and watch out for life's banana skins."

264

But I was not to be put off. I just smiled at him beatifically, and took another swig of cool beer. Simon changed the subject, maliciously.

"How's your friend Caroline, by the way? We haven't seen much of her recently."

This brought me down to earth a bit. It was true, I hadn't seen anything of her since her rather eventful stay with the Wigginses over a month ago. I still had a rather troublesome ache, which was not entirely worked off by delightful encounters with Berhane, and occasional, more casual partners. As it happened, I was about to go up again to Nyala for a long-postponed weekend, just at the end of term, this time with Cousin James, so we would have to behave ourselves pretty well, or, if we couldn't do that, at least be thoroughly circumspect.

"I don't know," I said, with studied casualness. "She seems to have confined herself to Nyala for the last few weeks. I'm going up there, though, next weekend, with my cousin, so we'll see then. She's probably going home soon, actually. I think she said she was only out here till Christmas."

"Ah," said Simon, thoughtfully. "Well, she's a great girl, I must say, but it's probably just as well she's going back." He looked at me shrewdly. I was not going to be drawn out on this subject.

"Yes," I said, grimly, "you've made that point before, as I recall. You may be right. Anyhow, I'll find out what her plans are at the weekend, I suppose."

A sudden breeze swept under the canopy of vines, blowing a paper napkin off the table. As I watched it pirouette across the compound, a slight chill passed through me, for some reason, dissipating my sensation of peace.

I moved to go. On the way back we talked of other things, mainly plans for the holidays. Simon wanted to take a trip to Harar after Christmas, but I had been invited already by the Lonsdales to join them on a safari up north, to Gondar and Axum, and I didn't feel that I could back out of that. Simon was a bit miffed, but we agreed to do something in the run-up to Christmas, perhaps a weekend in Dessie.

CHAPTER NINETEEN

And so, early on the Saturday afternoon after the end of term, Cousin James and I set off up to Nyala in the Mercedes. Wolde drove us, since he was able to visit his family in the village. It was a considerably smoother ride than in the Fiat, and I was able to enjoy the scenery rather more, through not having to worry about the road. The vastness of the Ethiopian highlands imposed itself on me as never before, range after range of jagged blue mountains stretching out towards the horizon in every direction, with periodic flat-topped *ambas*, as they are called, standing out from the plain in the middle distance.

Occasional clusters of eucalyptus gave evidence of human habitation, and once or twice a herd of goats with a boy in attendance, but there was not much other sign of life in the late afternoon as we bumped and glided gently along the Nyala Farm road in our own little cloud of red dust. Then, suddenly, cresting a rise, we saw the village below us, nestled in a slight valley, and Nyala Farm beyond it, towards the rim of the great gorge.

It was James's purpose to arrive in good time for tea, towards six o'clock. We drove up to the compound, in fact, shortly after five, to a warm welcome from both Mrs Stanford and the Brig. Caroline, I noted, was nowhere to be seen. Mrs Stanford swept forward and folded James in an embrace, before turning to me and giving me a similar welcome. The Brig shook hands vigorously.

"Well, Louise, I must say you're looking blooming," said James. "You both are, indeed."

He contemplated them with affection.

"Oh come, James, it's you who are looking blooming. We are getting quite decrepit. And young Luke looks as if Addis is agreeing with him."

"Yes," I said, brightly, "it does seem to be."

"Putting on a few pounds, possibly?"

She surveyed me critically.

"Oh, very possible, I'm afraid," I said, "Tekla-Mariam just serves too much food, and there are too many dinners out as well!"

Mrs Stanford smiled.

"Well, I'm afraid we won't be helping the cause very much this weekend. You must just keep taking exercise!"

We went in single file up the front path to the verandah, James seeking to deny that he was blooming, and talking of troubles with his stomach. He did in fact, as I recalled now, have quite an array of pills, which he would take unobtrusively after most meals, but it never seemed to cramp his style much.

"Luke," said Mrs Stanford over her shoulder. "Caroline is out in the back, sunning herself, I think. I'm sure she'd like to see you."

"Oh fine," I said. "I'll go and see if I can find her, then."

"Tea will be in about half an hour."

"Ah! Right." I checked my watch. It was just twenty past five. I left them settling themselves into cane chairs on the verandah. Wolde glided past with the bags and I followed him out the back, into the courtyard.

I found Caroline in the same place that I had first seen her, what seemed now a very long time ago, under the big banyan tree in the middle of the courtyard, reading a book. She looked up when I appeared, and her face brightened, but then almost immediately clouded again. She did not, it seemed to me, look particularly well. She closed the book, marking it with a dead leaf, and got up to meet me.

"Hello," she said, attempting brightness. "You got here, then?"

"Yes," I said. "No problems in the Mercedes. A very smooth ride."

I moved forward and kissed her lightly on the lips. She responded rather limply.

I looked at her, concerned.

"Are you all right? You don't seem exactly the soul of jollity at the moment. And where have you been these past few weeks?"

"Come on," she said. "Let's take a walk. I have a bit to talk about."

I didn't much like the sound of this. I followed her out the back gate of the courtyard, into the orchard, and waited until we were well among the apple trees.

"Well, what's wrong then? Nothing I've done, I hope."

She looked round at me.

"Oh no, don't worry. Nothing to do with you. Or not directly, anyhow."

"Oh? With what, then?"

Caroline sighed.

"It was bloody silly, actually. And my fault, in part. I'm more or less gated at the moment. The fact is, Aunt Louise found a rubber in a pocket of a jacket of mine that she was taking out for cleaning. I'd forgotten it was there – thought I'd run out! At first she didn't know exactly what it was, though she obviously didn't like the look of it. She had to ask Uncle Andy. But then she took it very seriously indeed. We had to have a little talk."

"Oh Lord," I said, aghast. "What on earth were you doing with a rubber in your pocket out here?"

She bristled.

"In case you turned up, of course! I can't trust you to remember. And anyhow, I didn't know I had it, did I? Otherwise, I would hardly have handed over the bloody jacket to be cleaned."

I scratched my head.

"So where does that leave everything?"

"Well, you can relax, anyhow. She doesn't suspect you – strangely enough! I suppose she can't conceive of a nephew of her beloved Sir James getting up to any such depravity. No, she assumed that I had met someone else down in Addis on the last trip. If anyone, she suspects Simon, actually. His reputation isn't any too good, you know."

"Yes, I know," I said, looking at her grimly. "And she wasn't far wrong, either, was she?"

"Oh, piss off. Anyhow, I had to swear that I didn't have anyone in mind, but that I'd got hold of a packet just in case. She didn't like that at all, though. It almost seemed worse, I think. Anyhow, I'm confined to Nyala till further notice, except under strict supervision. I think I might as well go home. I'm fed up."

I felt suddenly miserable. This absurd development brought it home to me how thoroughly I was captivated by her after all. I had been persuading myself over the last few weeks that I could take her or leave her, but now my bluff was called.

"Oh, Caroline," I moaned, "this is awful."

"Yeah, well, there it is." A slight pause. She scuffed the earth with a shoe. "Did you bring any ammunition with you, in fact?"

"What?"

"Well, did you?"

I gulped, and was conscious of turning slightly pink. "Well, yes, I did, if you want to know." And my hand moved protectively to my left coat pocket.

Suddenly she grinned wickedly, more in the manner I had become accustomed to.

"Right then, that's good to know. We might have a chance tonight, if we're careful."

"God! Do you think that's wise?"

"No, it's not exactly wise, but I'm horny. Of course, if you're scared ... or maybe you don't want to?" She was well aware of her power.

"Of course I do," I blustered. "You must know that. And it's not a question of being scared. I'm only concerned for you. Will they not be on the watch?"

She shook her head derisively.

"No, like I said, they don't suspect you. And they're not worried about immorality happening at Nyala. It's in the big, bad city of Addis that the trouble is, not here."

"Oh well, okay, if you think so. I'll leave it to you, though, to see if the coast is clear." We had wandered out through the orchard onto the open plain, towards the sunset. A group of vultures had settled on an acacia in the middle distance, and were shifting about restlessly. I looked at my watch. "I suppose we'd better be getting back for tea?"

"Oh, the hell with tea."

"That's all very well for you to say," I replied austerely, "but I'm a guest. Your great-aunt Louise said tea in half an hour, and I imagine she meant it."

Cousin James had in fact emphasised the importance of such rituals as tea in the life of Nyala – like listening to the nine o'clock news on the BBC World Service before dinner – and I had taken due note.

"Okay, then," she conceded in a sulky tone, "tea, I suppose."

But as we turned to go back, she suddenly turned to me and kissed me fiercely. I responded in kind, cupping my hands under her small, tight buttocks and squeezing her to me, but at the same time I found her violence a little unsettling.

After that, we walked back in silence.

Tea was slightly constrained. Caroline and her great-aunt were elaborately polite to each other. James and the Brig discussed political developments, and how the Little Man was handling them, and I listened with interest, though not really following the details.

Jomo Kenyatta, it seemed, was due up on a state visit, and neither of them had a good word to say about him. I kept quiet, but made a note that I would try to go and see him if he held a public meeting. The new Africa was on the move, and the Emperor was trying to control it, so far as he could. He had managed to get the Organisation of African States to establish its headquarters in Addis. I had heard it remarked derisively at a British embassy party that the only interest the Amharas had previously had in black Africans was as slaves, but now they had to treat them as their brothers. Some said that the slave trade still went on surreptitiously, and that a route ran even now from Uganda and Southern Ethiopia, through the Sudan, all the way to Saudi Arabia. But who knew, after all? One heard many things at expat cocktail parties.

This conversation was different, though. Both these old men, I reflected, knew the Emperor personally, and they knew how this country worked, and I was very glad to sit quietly in the twilight and listen to them gossip.

After tea, the custom was to retire to one's room to lie down until the nine o'clock news. I was relieved to stretch out for a while on my comfortable bed, light the oil lamp, and read a bit. I had brought a book of Laurens Van der Post that I had found in Davies' bookshelves, and I was deepening my feel for Africa with the help of it. If I got together with Caroline at all, it would be much later, and meanwhile I was happy to be alone. Nyala Farm cast a certain spell. One wanted to slow down, and adopt a different rhythm. I felt I would have liked a week or so out here, instead of the occasional weekend, but I could see how it might all get on the nerves of a girl like Caroline.

I began to think about the impenetrability of Africa, and the fascination it exerts on the European mind, to which Van der Post is such an eloquent witness. A few weeks before, in fact, I had got the idea of walking into town from the school, instead of taking the car or a Millecento. I just wanted to get the feel of the city. It turned out to be a quite an experience. It was a straightforward stroll down to Arat Kilo, past rows of neat villas, to the University and the Theological College. Then, however, after crossing the square, I set off up Haile Selassie Avenue, and the chaos and complexity of the city struck me far more forcibly. Walking along, instead of driving, really brought home to me both the squalor and the fascination of the place. I realised, from the curious glances I was getting, that I was doing something rather unusual for a *ferenji*, but no one challenged me as I toiled along in the late afternoon sun.

There was a sprinkling of respectable old French and Italian-style buildings on either side of the street, interspersed with little Arab shops, ramshackle car and bicycle repair shops, *tej-bets* (with their red signs already lit, and girls taking the sun in front of them, waiting for business), and of course a profusion of *tukuls*, stretching down into the ravine. I stopped at an Arab shop, to buy a coke and a little paper twist of roasted nuts. The elderly proprietor, in *djellabiya* and skull-cap, roused himself from the chair in which he had been sunning himself, enjoying his chew of *khat*, and greeted me amiably enough. I paid him, and wandered on, munching on the nuts.

The avenue wandered uphill towards the Ras Makonnen bridge spanning the ravine, but I decided to be adventurous, and take a shortcut, following a path that led down between the *tukuls* to the little stream at the bottom of the ravine, where there was a rickety bridge of planks. Suddenly I was in another world, and here I did feel very much out of place. Below the rim of the main road, there was no longer any sign of modernity. Already the women were outside the huts, starting up fires of eucalyptus leaves and twigs to cook their *injera* and *wat*, generating a symphony of fragrant smells to counter the underlying odours of garbage and piss. Again, despite my own sense of intrusion into people's backyards, no one did more than flash me the occasional shy smile. Only at the footbridge was I addressed volubly by an old man, who was resting, umbrella in hand, on a large stone beside the stream. All I could do was to give him a cheery wave, which seemed to satisfy him.

I toiled up the other side, past similar scenes, and rejoined the avenue about a quarter of a mile north of the Piazza, feeling oddly pleased with myself. I seemed to have penetrated some little way into the soul of the city, in a way I had not bothered to do before. I looked with mild contempt at the other Europeans flashing past in their cars. Most of them would never bother to do what I had just done – little enough, in all conscience, but a gesture. The group on the verandah of the Ras, Simon, Maurice and Knut, thought I was slightly crazy when I announced my achievement, but I remained pleased with myself as I addressed the first beer of the evening. And I still felt pleased as I thought over it now. I must do it again some time, I resolved. Good exercise, for one thing – which I needed.

At dinner, Louise announced that the following day there would be an interesting ceremony in the village, to which we were all invited. It was the *Genna* game associated with the Ethiopian Christmas period – also called *Genna* – and being held rather early in this locality. All the men of the village, it seemed, turned out for a sort of wild and chaotic hockey game, the younger generation against the older (around thirty being the cut-off point, though many people were pretty vague as to how old they were), and the game went on until everyone was exhausted, or the village headman called a halt. Louise described it as a kind of ritual battle between the generations – usually reasonably good-humoured, though occasionally heads got broken. The Brig was expected to throw in the ball, and then preside, from an improvised dais, though, fortunately, he wouldn't have to umpire. It all sounded quite entertaining.

After an excellent dinner, featuring a buck that had been killed by the farmhands on the lower farm, all except Caroline settled down to bridge. This time I partnered the Brig, against James and Louise – a terrifying responsibility. Caroline curled up with a book beside the fire, treating me from time to time with meaningful glances.

I did not find it easy to concentrate fully on my hands, since my mind kept straying to the possible adventures of the night, but fear of disgracing myself with the Brig kept me in reasonable order. We lost the first rubber, narrowly, and through no fault of mine, but we won the last two, despite some failures of mine in bidding. The Brig was inclined to go for broke at a certain stage, leaving me to get something like six hearts, and once or twice I chickened out. I was forgiven, though chided.

"Take it from me, young Luke, bridge is very much like life. There come times when you have to take a chance, and then the thing is to go for that chance with everything you've got, and no backward glances. Is that not right, James?"

"Oh absolutely, Andy. Listen to this man, my boy. He's knows what he's talking about."

I took the point. Caution, ducking out of opportunities, I felt was one of my besetting weaknesses. My instinct always was to pull back when things got interesting. I had to force myself to do otherwise. Even this excursion to Addis, I felt, was essentially a negative thing, born of a kind of despair. Since we were at the end of the game, I decided to draw the Brig out by some impertinent questioning.

"And, sir, what was the biggest chance you feel you ever took?"

The Brig chuckled, and leaned back in his chair. James was amused too, and joined in to stir him up.

"Yes, Andy, that's a nice question. What about it?"

The Brig rubbed his nose.

"Oh, I think you know the answer to that, James. The obvious answer would be, I suppose, the decision to lead the Little Man back into the country, but I don't think that's what I would choose. After all, I was a soldier then, under orders. I had some choice, but not an awful lot, really. No, I would say the biggest choice I had to make was to stay on here after the liberation – start up the school, take on the farm, bring up our children here rather than back in the UK. That was a big choice. And yet it wasn't too difficult to make after all, was it, my dear?" And he looked affectionately at his wife.

"Oh no," said Louise. "You could never have fitted into a civilian job back home, Andy my dear. With all of your background and experience, this is what had to happen. You would have been unbearable otherwise."

The two old people beamed at each other. I felt a sudden pang of envy at their certainties.

We had a local koniak as a nightcap, and dispersed to bed. No hurry in the morning, said Louise. Breakfast about ten.

The night was fun, I must say, but not without its excitements. Hardly had the household settled down, it seemed, when I heard faint pattering on the passageway outside the bedroom, the door opened quietly, and Caroline slipped in. She slid into bed beside me, hissing at me to shove over, and wriggled into my waiting arms.

"M'm," she whispered derisively, "you are pleased to see me! Just as well I didn't wait any longer."

Not dignifying this reference to my embarrassing state with a reply, I quelled her with a kiss, and reached round to slip off her knickers, only to discover that she had already dispensed with them.

Before things had a chance to get much further, however, there was a most alarming development. The door of Cousin James's bedroom, just down the corridor, opened, and we listened, transfixed, as he clumped heavily down the passage towards my door. We lay motionless, waiting to see if he was heading for the lavatory, but to my horror he stopped at my door, and knocked softly. In an instant, I had rolled Caroline over to the far side of the bed, and shoved her down under the blankets. Then I called, softly and sleepily, "Yes?"

Cousin James opened the door, and stuck in his head. I thanked God that electric light had not been introduced into the house in Nyala.

He fuddled around at the door for a moment.

"Very sorry to disturb you, dear boy, but would you by any chance have brought any aspirin? I foolishly forgot, and I don't want to disturb Andy and Louise."

As it happened, I had, along with the condoms, by way of being ready for all emergencies, so I was able to be helpful.

"Yes, actually, I think I do."

I hastily pulled on my pyjama bottoms, climbed out of bed, and felt my way to my washbag on the table. Feeling inside, I put my hand on a bottle of Bayers, and brought them over to him.

"Excellent. Most grateful. I'll just take two, if I may, and leave you the bottle. Must have been Andy's rotgut. Something is bothering me, anyhow."

I wished him goodnight, and he pottered away.

After that, our lovemaking took on a special quality of adventuresomeness. Caroline dug her nails into my rump as I came to a climax, and ordered me to be quiet. If anything, it made it more extreme. I seemed to dissolve all over her.

We prised ourselves apart, and lay quietly for a while, side by side.

"Are you sure your Cousin James is all right?" said Caroline. "He didn't look all that well to me earlier in the evening."

"Oh? Do you think so?" I said, annoyed not to have noticed. "He looks perfectly all right to me. He does like his food, though, and his drink, and it doesn't always agree with him. He's always taking pills of some sort or other, in any case. He has a great medicine chest at home."

"Well, maybe I'm just imagining it. I don't know him well enough to know how he should look." She rolled back into my arms, and we began to explore each other again.

Caroline slipped away to her room some time later, before we could fall asleep and be disgraced in the morning. I dozed off promptly, being by now too exhausted to worry about James or anything else.

Sunday morning was amusing. There was no church to go to, since the Stanfords did not, apparently, attend the native church in the village, although they had been instrumental in the building of it. After a leisurely breakfast, however, an expedition was organised by Louise to go down and watch the *genna*.

The beginning of the game awaited our arrival, as the Brig had the honour of throwing in the ball. This he did with great authority, retreating then with as much speed as was consistent with dignity to a dais that had been erected for us at the side of the pitch, where we now took our places along with the village headman, a stately old fellow in an ornamental *shamma*, and his wife. I could easily see why the Brig wanted to get out of the way.

Pandemonium broke out as soon as the ball, which was an odd-shaped, home-made-looking object, soared through the air. The two sides went at each other with sticks, hands and feet, without much regard to where the ball happened to be. The ultimate object, as with most games, was to get the ball into the opposing goal, but there seemed to be a lot more going on than that. As Louise explained it, this was really a battle of the generations, ritually re-enacted every Christmas, and the aim of the older generation was to keep its end up so as to maintain some respect from the kids for the coming year. The game might go on till sundown, with a feast and a siesta in the middle, so we excused ourselves after about an hour, and processed back to the house for lunch.

James wanted to get back reasonably early, as he had Willy Buhagiar and the Minister coming round for something of a working dinner (they were putting the finishing touches to a new Civil Code), so, after an excellent lunch and a short siesta, we set out in the late afternoon on the journey back. Caroline and I did not have much more chance to talk – or to do anything else – and, as she was now grounded for the immediate future, we couldn't work out when we would see each other again. She promised to try to wangle a few days with the Wigginses the week after next, maybe with the promise that I would chaperone her on all excursions. And she giggled conspiratorially.

The older Stanfords, intent on a final gossip with Cousin James, gave us the chance for a few moments of plotting, but then I was swept into the back seat of the Mercedes, and off we went, as the sun began once again to verge towards the rim of the distant blue mountains to the west. As we drove past the village, the game was still in progress, though the participants were beginning to resemble tired bluebottles, and their ranks had thinned out somewhat.

"A pleasant enough girl, young Caroline," said James, leaning back over the seat towards me, "but I gather from Louise that she's proving a bit of a handful for her. She may have to go home after Christmas."

"Ah," I said, non-committally.

"How did you find her?"

"Well, I suppose she is a bit bored out there, after all. It's a lovely place, of course, but not much in it for a girl like Caroline, really. I expect she probably will go home after Christmas," I added, lightly, but with a weight on my heart.

She probably should indeed, I thought, if things are not to come to some sort of crisis, but if she does, she will take a part of me with her, blast her. If James was trying to pump me, then, he got nowhere, and gave up. I assumed that he had guessed nothing about last night, but I couldn't be quite sure. We subsided into soporific silence as the sun went down, suddenly as always, and as we crested Entotto, the city was a constellation of lights below us, interspersed with dark patches corresponding to the ravines, down which the hyenas were already, no doubt, beginning to move, in their nightly search for carrion and garbage.

Wolde dropped me at the gate of the compound, since I had only a light bag, and I promised James to come to dinner the following Saturday, though I was unhappily conscious that there were a number of parties already scheduled for that evening, and I hadn't heard from Yohannis yet. The pace of life seemed to be steadily increasing in the run-up to Christmas.

CHAPTER TWENTY

Christmas and New Year came and went, in a wild round of parties and bachelor carousals. Christmas itself I spent with Cousin James, and a small party, including Willy Buhagiar and the Hardimans. The expatriate community, it seemed to me, celebrated these festivals with all the more determination because the locals follow the Coptic calendar, at odds with the Western one both in terms of years and annual celebrations. This was especially evident on New Year's Day, when we were on our own, which gave an odd feeling of relativity as we rang in 1962 in the midst of a community which considered itself still in the middle of 1955.

One rather traditional Christmas treat, however, was our triumphant production of *The Pirates of Penzance,* performed in the gymnasium of The English School. I served adequately, if without distinction, as a pirate. Ewan Hardiman was most impressive as the Pirate King, and Mimi Boghossian gave an affecting performance as Ruth.

For New Year, after a few preliminary parties, I ended up in the Bella Napoli, with Simon, Maurice, Knut and a few others. Next morning I didn't remember much about the latter end of that evening, except that I ended up for the night in Berhane's bed, being quite incapable of leaving it once I had got into it.

Not long after we'd celebrated the arrival of 1962, I went on the long-promised safari up north with the Lonsdale's for a week. This was a marvellous introduction to the wonders of the northern Ethiopian landscape, but also not without some reminder of its dangers. Cousin James had made his contribution by arranging an introduction for us with a protegé of his who was currently Governor of Gojjam, with whom, in consequence, we had an invitation to lunch when we got to Gondar. This was a certain *Dejazmatch* Abebe Kassa, a crony of the

Emperor's, who had been high up in the Department of Justice for a while, but who had become rather too outspoken in dealing with one of the old Rasses on the Supreme Court. In consequence, he had been shipped out to the provinces – where, James declared, he was doing very good work, and would probably have to be shifted again, before he become too popular. I looked forward to meeting him. It certainly added a dimension to the trip.

I had longed to wangle it that Caroline could join us, but lacked the courage to raise the matter either with the elder Stanfords or with Alan and Ruth. In any case, with their daughter Judy along, there would have been really no room in the Landrover, and little opportunity for improper goings-on after dark. So it was a celibate safari, so far as I was concerned.

But it did not lack its excitements. After a longish drive across the rather austere highlands of Gojjam – a sparsely inhabited and almost treeless plateau, the skyline punctuated by impressive flat-topped mountains known as *ambas* — our first day brought us to the valley of the Blue Nile. In the early evening sun, an immense green valley opened up before us, partly shrouded in coils of iridescent mist. Alan decided to make camp at a promising spot under some acacias about half way down the gorge, with spectacular views to the north and west. We climbed out and breathed the clear air, a mild evening breeze on our faces. The sun began to slip down the horizon. Under Alan's expert direction, I helped to raise the tent in which he and I would sleep – the ladies would retire to the Landrover, for safety – and then to build a fire from bits of acacia and thorn-bush found lying about. Ruth put together an excellent dinner.

After Ruth and Judy retired to the jeep, Alan and I sat on round the fire, helping it on with gnarled bits of stick from time to time, swigging beers from the bottle, and gossiping about the past term and the recent round of festivities. The sounds of the African night surrounded us. Alan, I noted, had brought along both a revolver and a high-powered rifle, and he had the latter beside him as we talked.

I asked him, jokingly, if he thought we would need to use it. He looked down at it, and patted it reflectively.

"You never know," he said. "But you need to be ready to if you have to. It might be a hyena who gets too close, or a mad dog – or it might be a *shifta*."

"A *shifta*?"

"Yes, you'll find bandits – *shiftas* – out in the countryside from time to time. I mean, there's not a great deal of policing out here, let's face it. And some of the local police aren't much better than *shiftas* themselves. And then your ordinary tribesmen might always be ready to try something on – not above a little thievery and even murder, if occasion offers."

I glanced around instinctively. I didn't like the sound of this at all. Alan seemed remarkably casual about it.

"But, I mean, what chance would we have, if we ran into some trouble, even with the gun and the revolver?"

Alan laughed. "Oh well, if we ran into a big gang, not much perhaps, but we certainly could deal with one or two – and there's always the element of surprise."

I looked at him for a moment, and then relaxed.

"You're having me on," I said. "Putting the wind up the greenhorn!"

He laughed again.

"No, no, I swear to you, there are bad guys out there. But, I admit, you're not that likely to run into them. If I thought so, I wouldn't bring the girls out with me. But I do like to be able to defend myself.'

And he stroked the rifle lovingly.

Just then a hyena whooped, quite close to us. I jumped, and looked around. Sure enough, out of the darkness, eyes gleamed, and more than one set of them.

Alan jumped up, grabbed a medium-sized branch from the fire, and ran in the direction of the eyes, waving it. Then he hurled it into the darkness, with a shout. There was a scampering, and, after a little while, a fainter whoop. He came back and flopped down again, looking satisfied.

"That's all you need with those buggers," he said. "Show them who's boss. They won't bother us again."

I was impressed.

"You've plainly become something of an old Africa hand," I remarked, with mild irony, though mixed with respect.

Alan stretched and scratched himself.

"Well, I wouldn't go so far as to say that. I certainly wouldn't want to claim that I *know* this country, or anything like it. I don't think any *ferenj* can ever really do that. But you do get something of a feel for the place after a while, especially if you do a bit of travelling. I would try never to underestimate it, though. Africa is rather like the sea – it can present itself all calm and beautiful for a lot of the time, but then it can turn nasty very quickly. You never really know what's going to happen next out there. And if things go wrong, you could just vanish without leaving much trace."

I looked out into the darkness beyond the fire. One could just make out, still, a faint line on the horizon between earth and sky, and above, the heavens were full of stars. As I looked up, a shooting star sped across the heavens, and then another. An overpowering sense suffused me of immensity and strangeness.

"Well," said Alan, matter-of-factly, "Better turn in, I suppose. We have a long day in front of us tomorrow if we want to get to Gondar. And we need to take some time at the Tis-Esat Falls. That's a sight not to be missed, I can tell you."

In fact we passed a comfortable and undisturbed night, though I had to get up in the middle of it to relieve myself of some the beer we had consumed. I stood out, rather apprehensively, and peed into the darkness at the other side of the fire, but nothing moved in the vast expanse around, and I crept back thankfully to the shelter of my sleeping-bag.

An early start next morning brought us, first, to the bridge over the Nile, a graceful, single-arched structure, where we paused briefly to look down into the waters of the great river, at this stage still of modest dimensions; and then for a while across a fertile plain, dotted with grazing herds of cattle, eucalyptus trees, and the occasional great kosso tree, with its striking red blossoms. After this there began a steep climb up to the high plateau again at Debra Markos, where we refuelled and had a coffee, and then a slow descent towards Lake Tana, its islands adorned with ancient monasteries.

Somewhat before coming to Lake Tana itself, we turned aside into the bush, along a very rough road, heading for the great falls of Tis-Esat. After a drive of half an hour or so, we came to a clearing, and parked. Then Alan led us forward into the bush, toting, I noticed, the rifle, and with the revolver in his belt. After perhaps a quarter of an hour's slog along a very minimal path, we began to hear a great roaring, which gradually filled the air. Then suddenly we crested a rise, and there it was before us – one of the great waterfalls of the world, a river almost half a mile wide pouring, in a white wall of water, down a drop of at least a couple of hundred feet. From our distance, it seemed almost static, a rumpled curtain of purest white, an aura of spray hanging over it. For some time we just stood there in silence. It was awe-inspiring. Finally, young Judy breathed "Wow!" Her mother put an arm around her shoulder, and smiled down at her. Then Alan spoke, matter-of-factly.

"So there it is, then. *Tis Esat*, 'smoke of the water', is what they call it. Should be one of the wonders of the world, but I don't think it figures on the list."

I shook my head.

"It's actually the only great waterfall I've ever seen," I said. "But I'd say it would be hard to beat."

"Yep," said Alan, "Hard to beat is right."

Our travels next took us around the shore of Lake Tana, another impressive sight, but on a quieter scale, and we then began the climb up to the mediaeval capital of Gondar.

On the way up, though, an incident occurred that brought my conversation with Alan of the previous night into sharp focus. I was sitting with young Judy in the back of the Landrover, the luggage piled behind us, and Alan's trusty rifle slung on straps behind my head. We rounded a bend in the road, and found ourselves confronted by a small group of what seemed to be policemen. At least they were wearing khaki uniforms of some sort. They were all armed with rather antiquated-looking rifles, and they looked pretty villainous. One of them stepped out into the road and waved us down.

"I don't much like the look of this," Alan muttered, glancing back at me. "Luke, would you just unhitch the rifle quickly, and keep it on your knees. Don't let him see you, but have it there. Otherwise, all remain calm."

He slowed down, and stopped beside the figure in khaki, but kept the motor running. Fortunately Alan knew a bit more Amharic than I did, since this fellow did not speak English. He asked for Alan's driving licence and papers. Alan reached into the front pocket of the jeep (where I knew he also kept his revolver), and produced these. The fellow studied them, with the infuriating slowness that native functionaries can often employ when they are really looking for a bribe. We waited patiently. I fingered the stock of the rifle, my hands sweating. I really did not know at all what to expect.

The 'policeman' handed the papers back through the window, and all seemed to be well. But then he stuck his head into the Landrover, looking around with an unpleasant, wolfish grin. His yellowish, bloodshot eyes roved over Ruth and Judy. I pressed the rifle against the back of the seat, hoping he would peer no further. Then he uttered some staccato phrases. What he apparently said to Alan was that the women should step out. That decided it for Alan.

"*Shiftas!*" he roared. "The bastard wants the girls. Let's get out of here!"

He gunned the motor, and the Landrover leapt forward. The 'policeman' jumped back, and unslung his rifle, as did the others behind him. I suddenly felt myself filled with rage instead of terror. The beasts wanted the girls, and then they would presumably have murdered us. I pointed the rifle out the back window and fired. I managed to catch the ringleader in the shoulder, as he was preparing to fire at us, and he swung round with a roar, clutching himself. This fortunately frightened the others, who threw themselves on the ground. By the time they had pulled themselves together, we were a hundred yards down the road. I fired once more for good measure, over their heads, and then we were out of range, round another bend.

Both Ruth and Judy by this time were in hysterics. I was suddenly prostrated by what I had done, but Alan was delighted.

"Great stuff, Luke," he shouted. "You winged the bastard! Probably saved our bacon. That's what I mean. You can never tell what's round the next corner in this bloody country. But I think we're safe from here on" – this, presumably, to reassure the ladies – "We're coming back to relative civilisation."

"Christ!" I gasped weakly, "I wouldn't want to have to do that again. Do you think those were *shiftas* or policemen?"

Alan shrugged. "Like I say, hard to distinguish in this part of the country. But I don't think they can cause much trouble for us, in any case. We might mention them tomorrow, though, to your friend the Governor, when we see him, just to set the record straight."

We did not in fact have any further unpleasantness on our way to

Gondar, and late in the afternoon checked in to the compound of some very pleasant Anglican missionaries, John and Liz Benson, who were friends of Alan and Ruth's. They were most interested in our story, and solicitous for the ladies, and soon had us settled on their verandah with a nice cup of tea – a thoroughly British solution to any emergency, and most welcome.

When we had recovered, and before dinner, they took us on a tour of the old town. Gondar was something of a revelation, after Addis. For one thing, it is a coherent city, almost in the manner of Florence. Its great builder, with the help of Portuguese craftsmen, was a certain King Fasilidas, in the mid-seventeenth century, and his palace in red brick, and a series of fine churches, showing an extraordinary mixture of western and eastern influences, stood gleaming in the evening sun. As we approached the Cathedral, a procession of priests, in elaborate robes, preceded by the usual cluster of boy deacons, began a procession across the courtyard, to the accompaniment of raucous and discordant singing. We watched, fascinated, as they processed round. Our hosts tried to explain, in lowered tones, what it was all about, but it rather passed over our heads.

Our lunch with the governor was both enjoyable and informative. We drove up to his residence, where he welcomed us warmly, on the head of our connexion with Sir James, for whom he plainly had great affection and respect. Over a glass of wine on his verandah, we told him who we were and what we were doing, and he told us something of what he was trying to do, in the way of improvements in health and education, and the encouragement of local industry. He made various suggestions as to what we should see – primarily the ancient capital of Axum, a little way to the north. We assured him that we had that very much in mind, and also Lalibela on the way back. Only the island monasteries of Lake Tana we did not feel that we had time for, though he offered us an official escort, if we wanted to go out.

After an excellent and lengthy lunch of a rather sophisticated wat, with mangoes to follow, we rose to take our leave, and just then Alan felt that he should mention our brush with the *shiftas*. He described what had happened, and that I had winged one of them.

"I hope they weren't police after all," he ended apologetically, "but they were really behaving like bandits, and we didn't feel we could take any chances."

The Governor frowned, plainly much concerned.

"No, no," he assured Alan. "You did quite right. I am only distressed that this occurred in my territory. I will look into it immediately." And he made Alan describe once more, as accurately as he could, with the aid of a detailed map on the wall of his study, where the incident had taken place. We then left him, with repeated thanks on our part, and apologies on his.

"I really liked your friend the Governor," said Alan, as we drove away. "I'd just be afraid that he's a bit too honest and progressive for his own good. He may not last."

"I was thinking much the same thing," I said. "Cousin James did say that he's really half in exile here as it is. If he makes too many waves here, he'll be moved on further – and further down."

We went back to our friends' compound for a siesta, and then a modest supper and an evening round the fire, hearing stories of the outback of Ethiopia, until it was time for bed. John Benson had a pleasantly relaxed attitude, I must say, to the task of spreading the truths of Protestant Christianity in this part of the world. I have always disliked the idea of proselytism, but it didn't seem to me as if the Bensons were doing much harm to anyone. They ran a little school, and a clinic, and I doubted that they thumped the Bible too much. Certainly they had a great respect for the local forms of religion – though properly a bit skeptical about the role of the boy deacons.

We got off fairly early next morning, in order to have enough time to explore the ruins of Axum, so that we could get to a hotel in Makalle well before nightfall. The girls were still too nervous to contemplate any more camping, to Alan's annoyance, but my secret satisfaction. I liked the idea of life under canvass in theory, but in practice I found a little of it went a long way.

Axum was quite fascinating, but also rather baffling. It was a great city in its day – in the first few centuries AD – but it would seem to have been abandoned some time in the late middle ages, and now the main thing to be seen was a series of great stelae, some still standing, rather drunkenly, others lying prone at various angles, over a large open plain.

Little boys came up to us shyly, offering coins. I bought some, for a few dollars, having beaten them down ruthlessly, and found later I had in my possession a selection of classical Axumite coins, presumably of some considerable value. The site was guarded only by one elderly and somnolent *zabanya*, whom we placated with the gift of another few dollars. Despite my ignorance as to the details of what we were looking at, the ruins of Axum brought home to me forcibly what an ancient civilisation one was confronted with in this extraordinary country.

From Axum we cut across country to the seedy hospitality of a little Italian hotel in the dusty and undistinguished town of Makalle, the capital of the province of Tigre. Here, I reflected, I was in the home town of Berhane, and I thought I could see why she left it – apart from any personal reasons she might have had.

We drove out of Makalle and along the remains of a good Italian road. Apart from the continuous wonder of the mountain scenery – the road wound up and down through the spectacular Semien Mountains – just one other wonder was in store for us, and that was the rock churches of Lalibela.

We reached the ancient town in the early afternoon of the following day, after a bumpy drive up from the main road. There were fully eleven of these phenomena, remarkably varied in style, and not all easy to get into. We climbed down into the greatest of them, Medhanie Alem and St Mary's, and admired the extraordinary elaboration of their architecture. Again, I could feel the weight of centuries of ancient civilisation all around me – a further glimmering of what the country was about.

We made it to Dessie that night, and from there it was a relatively easy drive back to Addis on Saturday. By the end of the few days' journey, I felt that I had become quite close to Alan and Ruth. They were a straightforward, uncomplicated pair – despite Alan's complications of the previous year – and I found I liked their attitude to life. They were not about to 'go native' or anything like that, and they were fully aware of the flaws in Ethiopian society, but they were basically positive towards the country, as so many others were not, and prepared to enjoy it for what it could offer, while being sympathetic to its faults – though drawing the line at *shiftas* or rogue policemen!

Upon my return to Addis, I had to gear up to face the new term. Fortunately, I was able to spend a very quiet, studious day on the Sunday.

Simon, as it happened, was sufficiently shagged out from whatever he had been up to the night before as to constitute no danger. He just came over for a beer, listened to my story of the adventure, and complained about his head. Even the account of my heroism with the *shiftas* didn't get him going, beyond a few grunts and a dig at Alan.

"He probably totally misunderstood what the bugger was saying. I bet he was just trying to scrounge a cigarette."

I laughed at him.

"No," I protested. "No way! That character had his eye on the girls all right."

"Oh well," he groaned, "Have it your own way. A genuine heroic adventure!"

And he tottered off to his lair.

CHAPTER TWENTY-ONE

Hardly had the new term started, however, when I received some of the most disturbing news of my life.

One January morning, shortly before eight o'clock. I was still in bed with my morning tea, when there was an urgent knock on the door. TM went to answer it, and admitted a very bothered-looking Graham.

"Luke, old man," he called, "may I come in? I'm afraid it's rather urgent."

"Absolutely," I said, putting down the tea on the bedside table, and straightening up. Graham found himself a chair, and lowered himself on to it deliberately. I did not like the look of this.

He looked me in the eye, and came straight to the point.

"Luke, I'm really very sorry, but I'm afraid that your cousin James has been taken seriously ill during the night, and is now in intensive care in the Ras Desta Hospital. I have to tell you straight that doesn't look as if he'll make it. He is still conscious, though, I'm glad to say, and he's been asking for you urgently. If you'll get yourself up, I'll be glad to take you to him right now."

I looked at him, appalled.

"But, but ... " I stammered. "What ... I mean, what happened?"

"Heart attack, I'm afraid. Pretty bad, by all accounts. Lucky it wasn't immediately fatal. But I gather there's no time to lose. I spoke to his doctor, who's a very good man. Remedios, chap from Goa."

I was already out of the bed, grabbing clothes off the chair.

Graham got up.

"I'll just wait outside," he said, and went back into the living room. I continued to talk at him through the open door.

"I really had no idea he was that ill," I called out.

"Well, no," said Graham. "I knew he'd had a bit of trouble a year or so back, but he seemed very well recently, certainly since your arrival. It's a great shock."

I didn't bother with shaving, and I was into my clothes in a few minutes. We hurried out to the Landrover.

"That's the bugger with heart troubles," said Graham as we drove out of the compound. "You often don't get much warning. He's a big man, though, your cousin James," (this rather tactfully – Cousin James was really pretty stout), "and he does like his food."

"That's certainly true," I agreed, thinking sadly of the many fine meals I had enjoyed under his roof.

There was fortunately not much traffic at that time of the morning, and we made good progress to the hospital, which was on the other side of town, out on the Lekempti road, not too far from where James lived. Even so, it took over half an hour.

We presented ourselves at the front desk. The nurse on duty went to find Dr Remedios, who appeared without delay, gave us a brief account of the situation as he saw it, which was very bad, and then ushered us to a fine, airy room on the ground floor, at the rear of the hospital. Willy Buhagiar was sitting on a chair in the corner of the room, looking tired and haggard. He got to his feet, and embraced me. Then he said, with what seemed a rather special solemnity, "Your cousin James wants to speak with you, my dear Luke. We will leave you alone." And he ushered Graham and Dr Remedios out of the room.

I wondered what this was all about. Why did Willy, of all people, feel it necessary to withdraw? I walked over to the bed, and looked cautiously at James. His eyes were closed, and he was breathing heavily. He looked oddly aged and shrunken in his pajamas.

I hesitated to disturb him, but I felt that in the circumstances I must. I jogged him gently by the shoulder. He opened his eyes and looked up at me, and to my great relief gave a welcoming smile.

"Ah dear boy," he said weakly. "You've come. Splendid, splendid. I'm sorry to have given you such a shock, but there it is. One knows not the day nor the hour. And there is something rather important that I wanted to say to you. Pull up a chair, there, and sit." And he waved a hand weakly.

I pulled up the nearest chair, and sat, looking at him intently.

"Now," he said, "you must listen to me very carefully." He paused, breathing heavily, and looked at me. "My dear Luke, I am sure that this will come as a great shock to you, but I have to tell you that I am not merely your godfather. I fear the truth is that I am your father.'

The room swam before my eyes. I was quite unable to comprehend this.

"But ..." I stammered, "what? How do you mean?"

He reached out his hand, and I instinctively took it.

"Oh," he said, smiling faintly, "I mean it in the real sense, I'm afraid. I don't want to go into the whole story now. Your mother can tell you that some time, if she wants to. But there's no question of it in my mind, though I think – I hope – your father never knew. He wasn't too good at arithmetic, fortunately, despite being an engineer."

He paused, and closed his eyes briefly. Then he continued: "I always loved your mother, you know, and I think she loved me, but I was such a fool, unfortunately, when it came to things like proposing, that your father just got in there first. Swept her off her feet. He was fine-looking man, of course, your father. Pity you had to take after me."

And he smiled. Then, with an effort, he continued.

"It was a difficult time for your mother, you must realise. Your father was away a lot. She was lonely, and I used to come round to dinner pretty regularly to keep her company. That's how it happened, really. I don't want to go into the details. I'm sorry to have spring it on you like this, but I don't think I have much time."

I tried to say something, fighting the lump in my throat. Confused thoughts were shooting through my head like lightning-bolts.

"Gosh, Cousin James," I stammered, "I don't mind, really I don't. In fact, I'm only glad, if anything, to find I have a real father. I don't want to condemn either of you ... But why on earth didn't you ever get together and marry, in all those years since? It would have been so much better."

Tears came into his eyes, and he shook his head.

"I know, dear boy, it might have been so much better for you. Perhaps I should have, but I simply could never bring myself to the point. It somehow didn't seem right, you know, to step into your father's shoes, after what I'd done to him."

This I could not comprehend. The thought of two lives left to moulder in frustration as theirs were was almost too much for me to contemplate.

"But that's terrible. I'm sure that Mother would have loved to marry you. I can remember asking her often, when I was small, 'Why don't you marry Cousin James?' and she would shake her head and smile sadly, 'But darling, he's never asked me. Gentlemen have to ask.' You really should have, you know."

He gripped my hand, and smiled again weakly.

"Well, I'm afraid it's all rather too late now. But do tell her, if you would, that I've always loved her, and that I very much wish that I had married her. My only consolation now is that I have had this little time with you. I hope you have enjoyed yourself these last few months."

Again, I had to choke back tears.

"Yes, of course I have, absolutely. It's been wonderful. And I've loved all our time together. You've been so very good."

"No better than I ought to have been. I am your father, after all." And he smiled again.

"Yes, of course," I said, seeing a chance to cheer him up. "And now what am I to call you? Would you like to be Father, or Dad?"

He actually managed a laugh.

"Whatever you like, dear boy, whatever you like."

"Okay, then – Dad."

The word sounded bizarre, but at the same time I found it deeply satisfying to say it.

He lay back on the pillows, and closed his eyes briefly. Then he roused himself again.

"Of course, you must realise that you are my heir. There will be some complications in tidying up my affairs, here and back in England, and also in Switzerland" – and he looked at me conspiratorially – "but Willy will be able to help you. He's an executor. You should be quite comfortable, and you can look after your mother. See that she has everything she wants. And don't waste it. Go back after this jaunt and do something useful. Go to the Bar, perhaps. I should say you'd be good at that."

He sank back, exhausted. Once again, I was thrown into confusion by this new aspect of the situation.

"But you mustn't be talking this way," I said. "You're not going to die. You've come through this. You're going to be all right."

He shook his head.

"No, no," he said quietly, "this is it, I'm afraid. I've done myself too much damage. I know it. But I'm not complaining. I've had a pretty good innings. And now I've set myself straight with you. This is quite enough for me."

He closed his eyes again, and seemed to want to rest. I had noticed him wincing once or twice while he was speaking, in apparent pain. I waited for a while beside the bed, and then tiptoed to the door to find Willy and Graham.

They were standing talking to Dr Remedios when I came out, and all three turned towards me. I must have looked fairly stunned, because they all started forward anxiously.

"How is he?" asked Graham, anxiously.

"Oh," I said vaguely, "pretty weak, I'm afraid. He seems to want to rest now."

"I had better go in to him," said Dr Remedios, concerned. "You must excuse me. I need to give him an injection." He beckoned to a nurse who was hovering some way down the passage, and she followed him into the room. The door closed.

"Well," said Graham. "I'd better be getting back. You take the rest of the day off, Luke. I'll see to your classes. You can look after him, Dr Buhagiar?"

"Yes, fine," said Willy. "You can leave him with me."

"Thanks for everything," I said. "I'll get back as soon as I can."

Graham patted me on the back.

"Don't you worry about that," he said. "Take your time."

And he disappeared down the corridor.

I turned to Willy, uncertain what to say. He sensed this, and moved to reassure me.

"It's all right, old chap. I know what it was he wanted to tell you. I hope it's not too much of a shock."

I looked at him.

"A shock! I should say it's a shock. And you knew, Willy? How long have you known? How many other people know?"

Willy smiled.

"I have known the secret only since last summer, in fact. Not long before you arrived he told me, one Sunday morning during our walk on Entotto. He obviously wanted to get it off his chest. But don't worry.

I don't believe he told anyone else. Believe me, Luke, it meant a very great deal to him to have you out here. I think he would have told you the truth sooner or later, at least before you went away again, but he found it very difficult. He was a great man, your cousin – I mean, your father – in many ways, but some things, some human things, he found difficult. Like the matter of your mother. He worried about her all the time, but he could never tell her what he felt."

"Oh, I think she knew," I said. "They had a funny sort of relationship, really. I can understand it all now. But, my God, it's a shock!"

Suddenly I felt the whole situation catching up with me. A wave of faintness swept over me. I groped for a chair, and Willy helped me into one. Then I experienced an awful desire to weep. I bent forward with my face in my hands. Here too Willy was most understanding. He patted me on the shoulder.

"Go ahead, old chap. Don't mind me. It's the best thing, believe me."

And so, for a good five minutes, I just sat there sobbing, while he gripped my shoulder intermittently. He was right. By the time Dr Remedios re-emerged I felt much better, and was calm again.

Dr Remedios shook his head ominously.

"I have given him something to make him sleep. But I am afraid that it is just a matter of hours. I feel that someone should be with him."

"That's all right, Doctor," said Willy. "We will stay."

And he guided me into the room.

We sat, I myself by the side of the bed, Willy in a corner of the room, for what seemed an eternity, but was in fact three or four hours. We did not speak. James slept, and Willy seemed to snooze. He must have been up most of the night, I reflected. This is all as bad for him as for me. Worse, really, as an old and close friend.

I tried to focus on my own situation, but found it difficult to take it in. I did not look forward to breaking all this to my mother, but it would be easier, after all, by letter than in person. My distant dream of a father had suddenly been given flesh, in the most dramatic and unsettling way. But as I thought about it, stealing glances at the sleeping form in the bed, I experienced a deep feeling of satisfaction. In a way, various loose strands of my life had now come together. Odd features of it found an explanation. As things had always stood, I was lacking a father, but had instead a remote, but most affectionate and generous godfather, who, from various parts of the world, had overseen, and largely paid for, my upbringing. Now that was all explained. I had in fact a father, who was doing no more than his duty, really, to the greatest extent that he could bring himself to do.

The greatest loser, as I thought about it, had been Mother. All that affection and companionship that she had a right to expect had been very largely withheld – doled out, very circumspectly, in tiny portions. I thought over those visits to Bellevue with a sudden access of annoyance. What fatal lack of resolution had prevented him from bringing matters to a head? Perhaps, I reflected miserably, the very difficulty he would have had in admitting that he was, after all, my father, if this had not happened to him.

At around midday, probably at the instance of Dr Remedios, a boy came in with two brass trays containing coffee and a sort of sticky cake. We sipped and ate in silence. Willy looked over in my direction, and raised his eyebrows in greeting, but said nothing. The silence was broken only by the distant sounds of the hospital, birdsong from the gardens outside the window, and the heavy, irregular breathing of the patient. I longed for something to read, to relieve my mind from its present burden. I could not think this thing through any further.

The heat of the day began to make itself felt through the open windows. At last, shortly after two in the afternoon, James stirred, gave a sort of rattling groan, and seemed to relax. Willy sprang to his feet, and came over to the bed. I watched him anxiously as he bent over my father. He listened for signs of life, and then passed his hands gently over James's eyes.

He straightened up, and looked at me solemnly.

"He's gone, Luke," he said. "I'm very sorry."

I found myself weeping again, quietly, effortlessly. I felt extremely sorry for myself. In the space of little more than six hours, I had gained, and lost, a father. I had no idea what to do next.

In the event, I did not have to worry. Willy moved with great efficiency, first to notify Dr Remedios and the hospital authorities, then to gather me up and drive me back to James's villa, where we had first to console a weeping Wolde, and then make a series of phone calls, and, last but not least, a telegram, drafted by me, to my mother. I kept it short – just "VERY SORRY TO SAY JAMES DIED THIS AFTERNOON STOP AM WRITING WITH DETAILS".

I decided that the task of writing a proper letter to my mother would have to wait. After James's death, I spent the day with Willy in the villa as he took charge of all the arrangements. James was to spend that night in the hospital morgue, where he could be fitted out with a coffin, and then brought home the next morning to lie in state, and we would have to receive visitors. Willy informed the Palace, and a little while later learned, to his mild surprise, that the Emperor himself wished to pay his respects in person, at exactly twelve noon. That would involve considerable protocol, but I looked forward to it greatly, as being probably my only chance to meet the Little Man. After some debate, I decided to spend the night at home, and to return in the morning. Willy left me back to the compound. Fortunately, no one was about, and I was able to flop into bed without having to explain myself to anyone.

In the morning, however, I had to face Graham and Isabel, and then the rest of my colleagues. Graham and Isabel both came over after breakfast to see if I was there, and expressed their sympathy. Isabel gave me an emotional hug. My position was really most peculiar. As far as the outside world was concerned, I had lost a cousin, and a godfather, not a father. This was certainly sad, but not a major tragedy, and I had to be careful to appear moderate in my grief. Simon clapped me on the back a shade perfunctorily, I thought, but then had to remind myself of how it would have seemed to him. As far as he knew, I had lost a source of good dinners, and useful influence, and not much more than that. The others shook me by the hand and made suitably sympathetic noises. It was a remarkably lonely feeling, knowing that I had lost a father but could tell nobody. One is always alone with one's grief, I suppose, but when others cannot even appreciate what one is grieving about, that makes the loneliness a good deal sharper.

Graham asked about the arrangements, and I told him as much as I knew. I believed that the funeral was fixed for the following morning, after a day of lying in state, so to speak. I explained that the Emperor was due at noon, and that I should be there, but assured him that I could teach my classes up to break, if I could be excused the rest. To my relief, Graham made no difficulty. I taught my two classes rather dully, and then slipped away hastily at eleven, to get across town before His Majesty.

I got there at about half past eleven, making good time, threading my way successfully through Addis's chaotic midmorning traffic. Wolde let me in. He was still in a tearful state, and clasped my hands in his, almost as if he knew the truth. I responded, and then looked around for Willy Buhagiar. There were quite a number of people in the house already, sitting around and sipping coffee or drinks. Willy came out of the dining-room, looking pretty anxious, and swept me away into the study to drill me in etiquette before His Majesty arrived.

"I'm sorry, Willy," I explained, "but as far as Graham Wiggins and the rest of my colleagues are concerned, I haven't lost a father, but merely a benevolent cousin, so I can't claim too much consideration. I had to take at least my first two classes."

"Of course, of course," he said. "We must try to remember that. We must not let the cat out of the bag. But you are going to have to concern yourself with your position in the next few weeks, so I will be expecting some of your time for that."

"Oh absolutely," I assured him. "And I really am enormously grateful to you for all this. "

So Willy recovered his equilibrium, and turned to instructing me how to receive the Emperor. Approach him slowly, bow, and wait to be spoken to, then bow again and take one's leave. Above all, one must not turn one's back on him, but walk slowly backwards out of his presence. I tried to take all this in, while wondering also about the rest of the guests.

Then Willy led me out to do my public duty. First we went to pay our respects to James himself, who was laid out in a coffin in his bedroom. The blinds were drawn, and there was only a dim light, but I could see him lying peacefully on his back, hands folded over his stomach, looking somewhat shrunken, but otherwise as if asleep. I reached out cautiously and touched his hands. They were cold, but dry and rough, and somehow reassuring. I looked at him for a while, and turned away.

After that, Willy took me round to meet everyone, being careful to introduce me simply as Sir James's cousin, who was teaching at the moment in the Stanford School. The names flowed past me meaninglessly, until suddenly we came upon Nuri and Mimi Boghossian, and I was on familiar ground. They both embraced me, Mimi with particular warmth.

"You poor boy," she sighed. "He was such a good man, a great man. It is a tragedy for us all, but especially for you."

Again, it was almost as if she knew the truth. I responded, I hoped, suitably. Mr Boghossian gripped me by the arm, and assured me of his willingness to help in any way he could. I thanked him warmly. No doubt I would have much need of him, I thought, in the coming weeks. We discussed the manner of James's death for a while. All I knew was what I had learned from Willy, that he had felt unwell after dinner, had gone to the bathroom, and had collapsed. Fortunately, Wolde heard him fall, had hurried in to see what was the matter, and had then had the presence of mind to phone Willy, who phoned an ambulance, and hurried over himself. The attack had been bad, but not fatal, and fortunately the ambulance crew had some skill, so they managed to give him a shot, and get him still alive to the hospital, where he survived the night. Nuri and Mimi nodded and clucked sympathetically.

We went on then to greet James's friend, the Minister of Justice, whom I had not met again since that evening shortly after my arrival, and Ato Kebede Degachew, both of whom seemed genuinely shattered by the event. I listened to much praise of James's qualities. Finally, we came upon the Hardimans, who had just arrived, in great distress. Ewan clasped me by the hand very firmly, while Susan gave me a long hug.

Conversation, however, was suddenly interrupted by a commotion at the front door. Everyone drew back, and fell silent.

"It's the Little Man," whispered Ewan. "I hope you know what to do."

I nodded. A number of imperial guards filed into the hallway, and then the Emperor himself appeared, accompanied by one of his daughters, Princess Tenagne Worq, whom I recognised from photographs. He was really a tiny figure, but he radiated such authority that one hardly noticed that. He proceeded first into the bedroom, where he gazed down at James for a short time, and then extended his hand, and laid it briefly on James's forehead. Then he turned, and Willy led me forward to be introduced. He explained briefly to the Emperor, in French, who I was. Haile Selassie turned his piercing gaze on me. I froze, but he extended his hand, and I came forward and took it respectfully.

"Je suis désolé," he murmured softly, "vraiment désolé. Il était un trés grand homme, votre cousin, et un vrai ami d'Ethiopie."

I was too overcome to say anything in return, but fortunately that did not seem to be necessary. I got away with bowing deeply. The Emperor gently withdrew his hand. I backed cautiously out of the bedroom and into the hall, where I rejoined the Hardimans. After a few short words with Willy Buhagiar, the Emperor glided out past us and was gone, followed by the Princess and his various aides-de-camp. The Princess smiled at me sympathetically.

After the Emperor's departure, the crowd of well-wishers began to disperse, and within half an hour just a small group of us was left: the Hardimans, the Boghossians, Ato Kebede, and Wendy Thesiger, who seemed to have come over separately from the Hardimans, and whom I hadn't seen earlier. This little company gathered with Willy and myself in the dining-room, and were served by a grieving Wolde with an excellent cold lunch.

The talk, naturally enough, was mainly of James. He had been a man who had loved good company, and would put together an interesting dinner party or picnic lunch almost every week of the year, as far as I could see, and of course he dined out almost as often. His acquaintanceship spanned expatriate businessmen and teachers, embassy personnel, eminent figures in Ethiopian society, and resident foreigners of various kinds, mainly Armenians and Greeks. There was a wide variety of people in whose lives his passing would leave a gap, and I met a good many of them that day.

Nuri Boghossian and Willy were still swapping stories about him a couple of hours later, when there was a further commotion at the front door, and the delegation from Nyala Farm arrived. Louise and the Brig were ushered in, followed by Graham and Isabel – and Caroline. My heart missed a beat. I had not seen her in many weeks. I sprang up and hurried to greet them. Louise was in tears as she pressed me to her.

"You poor boy," she sobbed. "This is such a shock." Again, even more strongly, I had the curious feeling of being sympathised with as a bereaved son. I felt sure that Louise suspected something. The Brig simply shook hands in a manly fashion. "Frightful business, frightful business," he muttered gruffly. "We'll miss him very much, very much indeed." Isabel also gave me a hug.

Then I came to Caroline. She was plainly embarrassed by the whole situation. She came up to me diffidently, and gave me a kiss on the cheek, during which she managed to whisper, "Can we talk?" I nodded, and whispered back, "In a while." Then I had to turn back to the old people, to assist once again in Willy's narrative of how it had all happened. Wolde wanted to get them all lunch, but they would take nothing but coffee for the ladies, and whisky and sodas for the Brig and Graham. The Boghossians and Ato Kebede excused themselves, and the rest of us decided to go out and sit on the verandah.

The conversation followed very much the lines that it had for the previous few hours. I listened to ever more reminiscences of the man that I was now proud, privately, to call my father, and I felt profoundly peculiar doing so. The Brig had, perhaps instinctively, chosen what had been James's favourite chair on the verandah, and my mind strayed back to many evenings over the last few months when I had sat, filled by that time of the evening with rather too much wine and brandy, listening to James and Willy, and usually a few subsidiary characters, discussing the state of the world, and of Ethiopia in particular. It made me miserable to think that that would never be the case again.

I could see Caroline fidgeting in her rather uncomfortable chair, and, after a decent interval, took the chance to slip out of mine, and come over and ask her if she would like to see the house. She jumped at this offer, and I managed to excuse us without causing too much disruption. The older generation were in any case embarked on lines of thought to which we were largely extraneous.

In fact, we headed rather for Wolde's back yard, and stood together, in the late afternoon sun, amid the vegetables and the hens.

"Well," I began, rather fatuously, "how have you been?"

"Never mind about me," she said, impatiently. "How about you?"

"Oh, I'm okay. I'm just in a bit a daze, that's all."

Caroline looked at me shrewdly. "It's sort of weird, isn't it?" she said. "I mean, you're just his cousin, and you're being put into the position, almost, of being the son and heir, having to receive all the guests and so on. Doesn't that feel strange?"

I paused. I had a sudden impulse to tell this girl everything, but I held myself back. That would be reckless. Certainly, this was not the time or place.

"Well yes, it does, rather," I replied noncommittally. "But I'm the only relative on the scene, after all, so I suppose it all just sort of devolves on me." I moved to change the subject. "By the way, are you going to have to go back to Nyala this evening, or do you think you might be able to stay the weekend down here?"

"I could try," she said. "God knows I've served my time down on the farm. And I'm having to go home the middle of next week. Did you know that?"

I was stunned. I had known, of course, that she might have had to go before Christmas, but when Christmas came and went, and Caroline was reported to be still around, I began to assume that she was here for at least most of the year – maybe till Easter. Now I was faced with a sudden crisis.

"No, I certainly did not," I said plaintively. "I haven't seen or heard too much of you at all since Christmas, after all. What's come up?"

She kicked disconsolately at one of Wolde's cabbages.

"Oh, I don't know. A combination of things. Being confined to Nyala really was becoming like a prison sentence. And then my parents were agitating that I come back and do something useful, like spending a while on the continent and brushing up my French or German. And anyhow, even if I did get down to Addis now and again, where is that getting us, really? I mean, there has to be more to life than the occasional surreptitious fuck."

I laughed, in spite of myself. "Nothing much surreptitious about you when you get going," I said.

"Oh hell," she said. "You know what I mean. What's the point of it? This is not going anywhere."

"But I thought that you made quite a point of not wanting it to go anywhere?"

"Well, I've been thinking," she said. "I've had a lot of time to think, after all. I've decided I want to get on with my life. I feel like a fly in amber out there. I mean, this just isn't anywhere, except maybe for a nutcase like you, who decides to take an interest in Ethiopia. My view on Ethiopia is, who needs it? I certainly don't."

Again, this forced from me a laugh, miserable though it made me feel. Then, amidst a flurry of thought too undigested to communicate, it suddenly occurred to me that, owing to the sad event of yesterday, I was now, to some extent as yet unknown, an heir to an inheritance, a person of independent means. I could even, stretching a point, make proposals of marriage. I struck down the thought as grossly premature and reckless, but it hung there in the air between us.

"Look," I said, "just see if you can't persuade Aunt Louise to let you stay down with Graham and Isabel for the weekend – say to keep me company! I can promise to chaperone you, and you can keep me from brooding. How about that?"

Now it was her turn to laugh.

"God, you're a rogue, you know. If they only knew! But okay, I'll try. I've only got six days more, after all."

"Okay," I said. "Maybe we'd better go in. I'm meant to be showing you the house, after all."

We wandered in, and though the dining room and the study, avoiding James's bedroom, and then upstairs to the room I thought of as 'my' bedroom.

Caroline sat down on the bed, and tested it speculatively.

"H'm," she said. "That's nice and comfy."

"Yes, it is," I agreed. "A bit of a tight squeeze for two, though."

"I wasn't thinking about that at all," she said. "God, you have a dirty mind. And your cousin lying dead downstairs!"

I was silenced. We went downstairs and back onto the verandah, where the Nyala delegation was just thinking about getting back. Everyone got up as we reappeared, and I was commiserated with and hugged again. Caroline looked at me meaningfully, and I hoped that she would get her point across with Aunt Louise.

That great lady, meanwhile, was urging me to come up to Nyala Farm as soon as I could.

"Sadly, Caroline is leaving us next week, as I imagine she's told you, but we'll find something to interest you, I'm sure."

"Thank you," I said. "I would love to come up. I'll just wait, though, until things are settled here." But I knew that it would seem empty without Caroline. I had to hope that she might be allowed to remain in Addis for the weekend.

Graham urged me to take my time. He would tell Tekla-Mariam what had happened, and that I mightn't be home tonight. He would also cancel my classes for the following day. I thanked him. In fact, I had no idea what I would be doing, except that I must be at the funeral the next morning at ten.

Willy and I saw everybody out, and waved goodbye to them as they drove out of the compound. Then we returned to the verandah, which seemed the least oppressive place to be. When we were back in our chairs, Willy spoke.

"Well, dear boy – if I may borrow a phrase of your *father's*" – he emphasised the word – "you have some decisions to make. I wouldn't bother you with this sort of thing now, except that some matters need to be decided pretty promptly. James's death is a great tragedy – not least for me – I've lost an old and valued friend – but it leaves you in an interesting position, as his heir. I have no idea how much there is, but I'm fairly sure he salted away a good deal."

He looked around the comfortable old home.

"Among other things, you inherit this house, for instance. Most *ferenji* are not allowed to own houses in this country, and indeed don't really want to, but James had the privilege of owning his, and now it is effectively yours, along with everything in it. Now that is all very well, but it means that we have to consider how you are going to manage it. For one thing, there is poor old Wolde to be considered. He has been with your father for over ten years, and he will be quite bereft. You can see the state he's in, and he's not generally a demonstrative fellow. In the long run, you can let this place, or sell it, but in the short term it really has to be lived in, or things, I'm afraid, are going to disappear."

"Gosh," I said feebly. "I really hadn't thought about that."

"There's no reason why you should have. But I'm afraid that you must now. First of all, if you can stay tonight, I really think it would be better. I can stay too, and keep you company. We can have more of a talk later."

"Okay," I said, looking at my watch. It was a little after five. "I'll ask Wolde to serve dinner for half past eight, which will give us both time to get an overnight bag."

I drove across the city in a thoughtful mood. I was trying to settle in my mind to whom, if anyone, I would tell my news. Was there any need for secrecy at all? I had instinctively felt my new-found parentage at first to be a dark secret, to be kept from the general public at all costs, but it was beginning to appear to me in a different light. There was certainly nothing disgraceful about my situation that I could see. In fact, I felt thoroughly enriched by the revelation, and anyone who was going to hold it against me was not the sort of person I wanted to have anything to do with anyhow. But yet something about the bizarreness of it held me back.

I decided I would not rush to let people know. There were just a few I would let in on the secret; initially perhaps only Simon and Caroline – both sources I could expect a certain amount of slagging from, but I could put up with that. I sort of hoped I could get away with seeing no one until after the funeral.

When I returned, Willy had arrived back in the house before me, and called me out onto the verandah, where Wolde brought me one of his stiff gin and tonics. We sat a while in silence, where the three of us had often sat in the last few months, and where Willy and James had sat together countless times over the last many years. Then Willy spoke, rather briskly.

"Well now, Luke, what do you think you'll do with yourself, eh?"

I found it hard to focus on the question.

"Do with myself? How do you mean? I'll have to finish out the year with the school, of course. Then I'll see. I mean, I'd had the idea of travelling a bit in the summer, round East Africa ..." I trailed off.

"That's not really what I meant," said Willy. "Of course you should honour your contract with the school, at least for this school year. And no reason, I think, why you shouldn't stay another year, if you find you like it. I wouldn't make it any longer than that, though. You have to return to real life sooner or later, and the later you leave it, the harder it will be. No. I'm thinking of the longer term. You know, James's money is going to mean that you'll always be comfortable – at least if you invest it prudently, and I can put you in touch with some good people in that connexion, if you like. But you do need to think of a career." He looked over at me, suddenly hesitant. "I'm sorry to be going on at you like this, but I sort of feel *in loco parentis* to some extent, now that your father is no longer with us."

"No, no," I said, "I really appreciate you taking this trouble about me. I will give it serious thought. Actually, I think I might try the Bar. It's an occupation that's more open than most to Protestants, even English-educated ones. I know a few solicitors, which will be a help. And it will certainly help to have something of an independent income in that case."

Willy nodded approvingly.

"I think that would be an excellent choice. It's a good life. Intellectually satisfying. I think it would suit you."

At this point Wolde appeared and summoned us to dinner, exactly as if James had still been there. It was touching to see how he was trying to keep up the routine. We all tried to put out of our minds the corpse lying in state in the bedroom.

The rest of the evening was interesting. Willy was in the mood for reminiscence, and I got to know a lot more about him, and about James, before the night was out. Only now did I learn, for instance, that Willy had in fact been married, and even had a son, a little older than me, back in London – a merchant banker in the City. His wife still lived in London also. What had gone wrong I did not learn. It seemed strange that someone as amiable and unruffled as Willy should have failed in his marriage, but there it was. I reflected once again how much greater a blow all this was for him than for me. The regular dinners, the Sunday walks on Entotto, the periodic picnics – all out the window. No doubt he had other friends, but none like James.

The lights of Addis twinkled below us through the eucalyptus. A cooling night breeze ruffled the leaves of the bougainvillea. From the neighbouring ravine came the periodic whoop of a hyena. It was getting on towards midnight when Wolde came to say goodnight, and we decided to pack it in. The following day would be a busy one.

In fact, Friday turned out to be rather less strenuous than Thursday, mainly because all arrangements had been made by Willy and others, and were taken out of my hands. James was removed in good time by the pleasant and efficient Greek undertakers, and we followed him to the English Church, where Padre Matthews conducted a simple and moving service, with an excellent sermon, in the presence of all those who had called on Thursday – except, mercifully, the Emperor himself. I performed a reading, and so did the Brig. Willy, as a Roman Catholic, held modestly back.

One unexpected mourner – who, however, slipped in quite unobtrusively, and away very promptly, after just a quick embrace and a promise to get in touch – was Yohannis, who had somehow heard the news. He murmured that he would have come the day before, but he didn't want to run into his uncle. I was touched that he had made the effort.

We buried James in a corner of the English churchyard in Addis Ababa, gathering round the open grave in the bright sunshine, and scattering, each of us, a little handful of earth on the coffin.

CHAPTER TWENTY-TWO

In the aftermath of the funeral, after more refreshments and friends' reminiscences, the older generation had gone back to Nyala, leaving earnest messages for me to visit them as soon as possible. Caroline, however, had been allowed to stay the weekend with Graham and Isabel. We made contingency plans for the night ahead and, hopefully, another 'walk' on Entotto on Saturday or Sunday.

When I got back to my bungalow I found myself with a well-earned hour or so alone, before presenting myself for dinner at the Wiggins', so I took the opportunity to sit down at James's desk and write an overdue letter to my mother:

Dear Mother,

This is to confirm the sad news which you will already have received by telegram, of the sudden death of Cousin James. I hadn't even known he was ill, but he had in fact been taking pills for angina for some time, as well as lots of other pills for everything else, as I have subsequently found out. It did not induce him to change his lifestyle, though. He continued to enjoy himself right up to the end. Even the last dinner party I had with him was on the usual gargantuan scale.

The most momentous and disturbing news, though, I realise, is not news to you, but I want to tell you that I know it. I was able to talk with him for a short while in hospital before he died, and there was obviously something he very much wanted to get off his chest, even though he was barely able to speak.

The first thing I want to say about this is that I am not angry or reproachful. It is not my business to judge what pressures you were under all those years ago. I am only sorry that neither of you, in all the years since, could bring yourselves to pop the question to the other. I know you used always to say to me 'gentlemen have to ask', but you should have known James well enough to realise that he was hopeless about things like that. I know he loved you, and I'm only miserable now to think what you missed out on.

But there's no point now in going on about that. I am at least happy to have gained a father, even if I lost him at the same moment, and to have spent a few very happy months with him before I knew who he really was.

I paused to reflect, trying to think of a way to end my letter, but my mind was filled with buzzing confusion. I decided to simply sign off, and then walked down to post the letter in the Piazza.

That evening, it was just a family gathering in the headmaster's bungalow. We were all rather subdued, I mainly because I was exhausted, everyone else because they thought it was fitting that they should be. After a final nightcap of koniak, I bowed out a little after eleven, to the accompaniment of renewed expressions of sympathy, and congratulations on the success of the funeral. I caught Caroline's eye as I left, and she nodded imperceptibly, in a way I found encouraging.

I left the front door on the latch, and dragged myself to bed. Then I lay in the darkness, listening to the noises of the night, and trying to keep awake. The *abujadid* ceiling flapped gently as the night breezes found their way through gaps in the roof. Hyenas whooped in the ravine. Frogs kept up a constant chorus. Despite their best efforts, though, I dozed off, and the next thing I knew, a teasing voice was telling me to push over in the bed.

"M'm," I mumbled, trying to gather my thoughts, and shifting over to allow Caroline to slip in beside me.

"I don't know why I bother, honestly," she teased. "Couldn't even keep awake for half an hour or so, could he, despite his great enthusiasm! I don't suppose you'll be much good for anything now, will you?"

But in fact the pressure of her naked thighs against mine produced quite a satisfactory reaction in a very short time. I began by nibbling an ear, and then slipped down to get to work on her breasts. I ran my tongue over first one, then the other.

She wriggled and giggled.

"Ow, that tickles. You are a pervert!"

But she made no serious effort to resist. Instead, she cupped her breasts in her hands, and looked down at them speculatively.

"What do you think of them, actually?" she said.

I raised my head, and looked at them. They were small, neat, and round, with inviting nipples.

"I think ye have a grand pair there entoirely," I said judiciously, in my best stage Irish accent.

"Do you really think so?" she said pensively. "I think they're rather small."

"I suppose they're quite small," I said, with unwitting tactlessness, "but I like them small."

"Well, you might, but a lot of men like big breasts."

"Yes, I believe that they're very popular with truck drivers and navvies, in particular. Sailors, too."

"Now don't be snobbish."

"This is a ridiculous conversation," I said, and returned to my explorations, going down by easy stages further and further, to the accompaniment of little squeaks of protest at each level, until I reached the centre of things.

After things had taken their course, we lay for a while side by side, sticky and exhausted. Conversation turned, inevitably, to recent events.

"So," said Caroline, stroking my hair with slightly mocking affection, "poor old Luke! You really have had a traumatic few days, haven't you? It must have taken a lot out of you – though you wouldn't think it just now! But what I don't quite understand" – and here she looked at me cannily – "is why everything seemed to centre so much on you. I mean, I know Sir James was your godfather and all that, and you were on the spot, but didn't he have any nearer relations? And friends like Mr Buhagiar? How close to him were you really?"

I paused a moment, and then came to a decision. It sounded as if she suspected something anyhow. I wondered if there had been any talk out at Nyala. Aunt Louise was a pretty shrewd old bird, after all. I rolled over on my side and faced her.

"Caroline, can you keep a secret?"

She rolled over in turn to face me, grinning, her eyes bright.

"Well, I suppose I can, if I have to," she conceded grudgingly. "So there's a bit more to this than meets the eye, is there?"

I sighed, and ploughed ahead.

"Yes, there is, in fact. But swear not to tell anyone – though really it's nothing very disgraceful, after all. It's just that I'd prefer it not to be known all over town."

"Okay, I swear. So what's going on, then?"

"Just this. I had a chance to talk to James before he died, on Wednesday morning, and he told me an extraordinary thing." I paused. "He told me that he was actually my father."

Her eyes widened.

"Wow," she said, "that is a juicy secret, all right! It's fantastic, in fact. How on earth would that have happened, though? Did you have any clue at all that he might have been?"

"Not really, no, but there's no great mystery, I'm afraid, as to how it might have happened. You see, James was out in Malaya with my parents. He knew Mother before my father appeared on the scene – being a relative, you see. In fact, he introduced them. James was always in love with Mother, and she obviously liked him a lot too, but he just wasn't very good at getting to the point, and my father was, so he lost out. But then, after they got married, my father had to be away a lot, up-country, and James was still around, and Mother was lonely – so, I suppose, one thing led to another. I don't exactly know. But anyhow, here I am. I don't know what to believe, really. I'll wait to hear what my mother has to say, if anything. But I must say I rather like the idea, on the whole."

Caroline was plainly delighted with this story.

"Wow," she said, derisively, "this really is romantic stuff. It's a great story! And you mean to say that all these years you had no idea that your Cousin James was any more than a godfather?"

"Yes, strange as it seems, I really didn't have any inkling. Now that I look back, I can think of various incidents, when he would come and visit us, which I can put a new complexion on, but Mother and he kept the secret very well."

"And now at last it can be told! The cat is out of the bag!"

"Remember," I said, firmly, "you promised! No spreading this around. Willy Buhagiar knows, but no one else, so far as I know. I'll probably tell Simon, sooner or later, but I want to tell him, okay?"

"Okay, I know. Mum's the word. But this is exciting, isn't it? You do look quite a lot like him, actually, come to think of it." She studied me. "And are you the heir, then? You should come in for quite a bit."

I rather shrank from this line of speculation, but it was probably true. There must, after all, be a fair bit there. It was a comfortable feeling.

"Yes, I suppose I might. I really have no idea yet." Then I smiled, reflectively. "But I might turn out to be worth knowing, after all."

It was Caroline's turn to smile.

"Yes, you might be, mightn't you? Pity, though, that I'm not inclined to settle down just yet."

I looked at her speculatively, and reached forward to kiss her where a strand of damp hair had strayed down over her forehead.

"Well, nor am I, frankly. But let's stay in touch."

She looked at me levelly.

"Yes, let's." Then she bounced up. "But I think I'd better be going. I need some sleep, and I'm not going to get much here."

"Will I see you in the morning?"

"Oh yes, probably, but *late* morning. I'm going shopping with Isabel, and then I think we're taking the kids for a swim up at the Embassy."

"And I'll be pretty busy, come to think of it. I must try and catch Simon, and then I'll have to go back to James's place to reassure his man Wolde. How about a bit of a walk on Entotto after Sunday lunch?"

She smiled wickedly.

"Well, maybe. We'll see. But no more Ethiopian antiquities, okay?"

"Okay."

Once again, the sight of her naked back disappearing into the bathroom, and the sounds of her tidying-up, sent further shivers of lust through me, but I had to be content with what I'd had – which had been pretty good, after all. She pulled on her clothes, kissed me goodnight, and slipped out.

The next morning, after a good breakfast of Tekla-Mariam's 'scramble egg', I went out in search of the elusive Simon. There was no particular reason, I reflected, why he should have come to either James's lying-in-state or to the funeral, but I had missed him there nonetheless.

I knocked, a trifle tentatively, on the door of his bungalow. There was initially not much sign of life, but then I heard a muffled thumping and cursing from the recesses.

"Simon?" I called. "Are you up? It's Luke."

The muttering got louder, and the door opened, to reveal a very bleary Blakeney.

"Well, if it isn't La Touche! You're up bright and early, I must say. Bereavement seems to agree with you."

I gulped. This Blakeney was plainly not in a good mood. But then I reflected, as far as he knew, all this fuss was being made simply over a cousin. Why should I have got away with disappearing for a couple of days of class, and without so much as a word to him, really?

So I was not disposed to take offence.

"I'm sorry. You look as if you had a hard night."

Simon rubbed his head, and then scratched his chest.

"Mm," he said. "I rather think I did. I don't remember the end of it too well, to be perfectly frank."

"Well, do you want to come over for coffee in a while, when you've got yourself together?" I decided that I would let him in on the secret. After all, if I didn't, he would go on being aggrieved at the fuss that was being made, and the changes in my lifestyle that were now likely to ensue. "I have something particular I want to tell you."

This intrigued him, as I intended it to, and he promised gruffly to come over when he was ready.

"Maybe I'll just take some breakfast from you. Any of Tekla-Mariam's flapjacks around, I wonder? That'd do me fine."

"Should be."

Tekla-Mariam was by now justly famous among my friends and students for his flapjacks – which he had only revealed to me when the Thursday coffee mornings were well under way. After his first production of them, they were brought back again and again by popular demand.

Something over half an hour later, then, Simon was slumped in my armchair, cup of coffee in one hand and a flapjack in the other, eyeing me balefully, and demanding to be let in on whatever sensational news I had for him.

So I looked him in the eye, and spelled out for him, as fully as I could, the whole story, just as I had told it to Caroline the previous night. Then I sat back and waited for his reaction. To my relief, Simon took it with due seriousness – no mockery, no disbelief. I must have struck the right note.

"Well, of all the bloody fantastic tales!"

He leaned back in the chair and shook his head, releasing his breath with a low whistle. "Jesus, Luke, did you have any *inkling* of this before he told you, or was it a complete bolt from the blue?"

"No," I said, "it was a complete surprise when he sprang it on me. But then again, when I had a chance to think about it, it began to give a new significance to so many details of my life that had always been small mysteries, that it began to fit right into place. And now I find I'm quite at home with the idea. I have just found and lost a father. And in spite of everything, I feel sort of satisfied – as well as very sad, of course, because, father or no father, he was great fun to be around."

"You know," said Simon, reflectively, "it's funny. For most of my teenage years I used to have this persistent fantasy that my dad wasn't really my dad – that my mother had had this passionate and hopeless affair with some artist or poet who had disappeared or died, and I was the result of that, and she'd married my dad on the rebound. Total rubbish, of course. All the evidence points to the fact that he was her only love. But he seemed such a boring old fart that I really wished he wasn't responsible for me. Rather the opposite of your situation, isn't it?"

"That's sort of sad," I said. "Was he really that boring? How do you feel about him now?"

Simon looked at the ceiling.

"Oh, we get on well enough now, I suppose – at a distance." He hesitated. "I shouldn't be too hard on him. He's decent enough, really, and honest, in his way, despite how he treated my mum. He's always looked after us. He manages a chain of cinemas and dance-halls, and he does that pretty well, so far as I know. The main problem, when I was growing up, was that he was the ultimate square. Not an ounce of hipness in his whole body. Funny, I suppose, for a man who ran dance-halls, but there it is. He managed to have no real interest in or understanding of the music that was being played in those dance-halls – and we had most of the main rock-and-roll stars at one time or another. You know, Bill Haley, Jerry Lee Lewis, Tommy Steele, Lonnie Donegan. We even had your hero Little Richard once. He was great. I got to meet him. Crazy guy. But he wasn't interested in any of them. Just a job to him."

I found this fascinating. It was the first I had heard from Simon of anything to do with his family, and it explained a certain amount. But he changed the subject abruptly, back to the matter at hand.

"But what are you going to do about all this? Where does it leave you exactly?"

I spread out my hands helplessly.

"I honestly don't know yet. It's just too early to say. I have a lot of meetings with lawyers and stuff to go through. I may have to look after his house for a while, until we can get it sold. He actually owned it, apparently – a special dispensation from the Emperor."

"Hey, so you should be coming in to quite a bit when all this is sorted out?"

"Yes, I very well may. Indications are that James had quite a lot stashed away in various parts of the world. But cheer up. Simon, old man. I won't forget my old friends."

"No, indeed you won't. You bloody well won't be let. I hope we can expect a few good parties up at the house at least, before you sell up."

"Oh, I think we can count on that. I'll have to respect the feelings of my father's faithful servant, though. He comes with the house, and he's accustomed to a certain standard of civilised behaviour."

So equilibrium was restored between Simon and myself. And yet things were not going to be quite the same, I reflected. I was going to have to maintain two households, for a while at least, and attend to whatever would follow from that. And my position in Addis expatriate society would inevitably be altered. The prospect was exciting, but it was not going to be easy.

After some shopping down at Florides' grocery, and a beer on the verandah of the Ras, Jack Hirschhorn joined us after a little while, and tried to nail me down for the gig that night at the Paradiso. I agreed provisionally, but I was restless, wondering if I should get over to James's villa and make contact with Willy. For Caroline, I was going to have to wait till Sunday, probably, and even that wasn't certain. We were in Simon's Citroen, so I had to persuade him to drive me back with the groceries, which he did begrudgingly. He would have liked nothing better than to occupy his vantage-point on the Ras verandah until well into the afternoon, to see who or what turned up.

By the time I got back to James's, Wolde was very pleased to see me.

"Mr Willy here earlier. He want that you phone him."

Willy Buhagiar was not far from the phone when I rang. He would have been just finishing his siesta.

"Ah good. Excellent. You are at James's? I will come right over."

I mooned about the house until he arrived, exploring the books in James's study, surveying the ornaments in the living room, and finally moving to the verandah, where Wolde brought me coffee. It all felt extremely odd. I was suddenly lord of all this, and with a changed identity to boot. I longed to hear back from my mother, to see how she would take things. I hoped I had struck the right note. I sipped my coffee thoughtfully, gazing out over the city, listening to Wolde pottering in the back yard – feeding the hens, from the sound of it.

When Willy arrived, Wolde ushered him out onto the verandah, where I rose to welcome him. He had not been idle on my behalf, as it turned out. He had set up an appointment with Nuri Boghossian for Monday morning, when, with the help of a young Armenian lawyer who was a protegé of Nuri's, and in whom Willy had every confidence, I would have some important papers to sign.

"You are going to be a rather rich young man," he said austerely. "I hope you will not let this go to your head. You will need to think carefully about your future. That is what your father would have wished."

"Oh absolutely. I'm thinking as hard as I can. It's all a bit confusing at the moment, though."

Willy began to repeat his little lecture of Thursday afternoon, and I was thoroughly disinclined to argue. Privately I felt that I should stay in Addis until I had sorted out the confusion in my head, but there was no sense in telling Willy that. I must also go back as soon as possible and talk to Mother. She deserved no less. Even that, though, would have to wait until at least the Easter holidays. Willy was inclined to bring me out to dinner, but I excused myself with an imaginary engagement, intending to go down to the Paradiso. I'd had about enough of sympathy and inquisitiveness.

Just as I was getting ready to leave, the trumpet case already in my

313

hand, there was a knock at the door. It was Caroline. Her face fell when she saw the trumpet.

"Oh-oh, you're going out."

"Yes," I said. "I have a gig tonight at the Paradiso. I promised Jack this morning."

"Well, you're going to miss a gripping game of scrabble. I wish I could go with you, but I don't think I'd get away with it."

"How about tomorrow, then? Do you think we can take an afternoon walk?"

Again her face fell.

"No such luck, I'm afraid. Graham and Isabel are going to drive me up to Nyala after church. This is it, I'm afraid."

I was devastated.

"Oh God, Caroline, this is awful. I would never have signed on for tonight if I had thought that. I can get back before midnight, though."

She smiled sadly and shook her head.

"No," she said, with a little sigh. "I think we might just as well call it a day. I don't like emotional goodbyes, anyhow. We'll meet again, maybe in a year or so, and then we can see how we feel. This romance mightn't travel, you know. Things seem different at six thousand feet. That's what everyone says."

I looked at her in desolation. She seemed almost to be making a joke of this. I wondered, not for the first time, whether I had not simply been a diversion for her, to be discarded with the rest of Ethiopia when the time came to leave. In that case, Simon was right. I was well out of this, after all.

"Well," I said bleakly, "maybe you're right. If it has to end, it might as well end now. I'll see you tomorrow morning, in any case. Will you leave me an address, or do you want me to write?"

Now it was Caroline's turn to look a little desolate.

"Oh Luke, of course I want you to write. I'm sorry. I was only trying to be brave, and it's coming out as if I didn't care. Of course I'll miss you. You're actually the most interesting person I've met in a long time, I think, even if you do have some soppy ideas. I do want us to meet again, and I hope you'll still like me then. That's what I meant."

And her eyes filled up with tears. I took her in my arms, and kissed first her eyes, licking up a little salt, and then her mouth. Then she slithered out of my embrace, passed a hand over her face, and grinned bravely.

"Okay, I'd better go back and face the family. This was just what I was hoping to avoid, but it seems I can't after all. See you in church!"

And so she slipped away, leaving me both pleased and upset. So she did care for me, then, a little more than she wanted to admit. But perhaps that made it all rather worse. It had been good fun while it had lasted, and we had been operating on the basis of no attachments and no claims. It might have been better to leave it that way. But I could not forget her now.

So I went off pensively to the Paradiso, and played a rather soulful trumpet, to the extent that Jack commented on it jokingly over a beer afterwards. When I told him that Caroline was leaving, he was impressed.

"Shit, man, if you can put that sort of feeling into your horn when you want to, you have quite a future in this business."

I shook my head. "That's good of you to say so, Jack. It's fun doing this, but I really wouldn't fancy it on a serious level."

"Me neither," he grinned. "I'm going to head back after this to Yale Law School, and get stinking rich as a corporation lawyer. Maybe in my dad's law firm, maybe not. How about you? You got any plans?"

"Yes," I said. "I was thinking about law as well, actually. I was going to try and become what we call a barrister."

"Oh yeah," he nodded. "I know about that. It's a weird, old-fashioned system. But I guess it works."

"Yes, it seems to, well enough."

The conversation turned from this, more or less inevitably, to the death of James, which he had heard about. My relationship to James intrigued him.

"So, looks like you may have fallen on your feet there," said Jack. "I have an old granduncle like that back in Connecticut. Owns a bank. But unfortunately he has quite a passel of other nieces and nephews, so I wouldn't reckon on too much from that quarter. It sure is good not to have to worry about money, though."

"Yes, I suppose so," I said cautiously. "It hasn't quite sunk in yet. "

Sunday was rather unsatisfactory, as I was afraid it would be. We went to church, chatted to Padre Matthews, who was particularly concerned about my well-being, and then I said goodbye to Caroline with a chaste peck on the cheek. She slipped me a piece of paper with her address on it, and made me promise to write. Then the Landrover headed off for Nyala. She stuck a hand out of the window and waved. I would not see her again, as they were going to drive straight to the airport on Wednesday.

Willy had invited me for a walk on Entotto, and I felt I couldn't refuse. This was one of the things, I reflected, that he would most miss, as I would miss the Sunday lunches. We stayed off the subject of my future. Willy instead talked of Ethiopian history, about which he knew a good deal, and in particular the founding of Addis Ababa by Menelik, which was quite a story. From that he got on to patterns of property holding around the city inherited from that time, and in that connection mention was inevitably made of one of the largest property owners, Ras Tessema.

"I noticed," said Willy, "that Yohannis attended the funeral. That was thoughtful of him."

"Yes," I agreed. "I was glad to see him there. I hadn't seen him for a while."

"Well," said Willy, with a somewhat disapproving air. "I'm sure he's not a bad sort. Just don't get involved in any of his schemes. "

"I can't really see why he would want to involve me in anything," I said, defensively.

"But Luke, even association with him can be dangerous, as some have found out to their cost already."

"But that would presumably apply to Ethiopians," I said.

"Yes, mostly. But a few eastern European diplomats have been asked to leave in a hurry as well."

"Ah well," I said, "that's another matter entirely. Those fellows are always conspiring." And as I spoke I thought of my pupil Safar Abdolov, who certainly didn't seem to be, but probably was. He was to be found at Yohannis' parties, at any rate.

We went back to what Willy wrily described as a James memorial lunch, prepared lovingly by Wolde, and then parted for the siesta. Willy had made an appointment for me to visit Nuri Boghossian at the bank to sign papers on Monday afternoon after class, at four o'clock, and I promised Wolde that I would return for dinner after that. How I was going to manage my double life for the future, though, I could not yet see.

Back at my own bungalow, Simon was in the mood for at least a short visit to the Bella Napoli, though he had been out boozing with Maurice the previous night, and wasn't in great shape.

"Pity you didn't take in the Paradiso on your pub-crawl," I remarked. "We were really cookin' last night. I have Jack's word for it."

"I thought of it," said Simon, "but you know Maurice. It's a major struggle to get him anywhere near 'zat accursed Hirschhorn'."

I laughed. "He really is an appalling old chauvinist. Jack's a very decent chap. I would say he's a particularly civilised sort of American, actually."

"Well, the French invented chauvinism, of course. He has a soft spot for you, though, has Maurice. It must be the French name. 'And your friend La Touche, 'ow is 'e?' He might almost have come round, if he was sure you were playing."

"Ah well. I wasn't in great form. I was brooding about Caroline. You know she's going home on Wednesday?"

Simon looked over at me cannily. "No, I hadn't heard. But believe me, ye daft bugger, it's all for the best."

"Yes," I said grimly, "I'm well aware of your views on that subject."

"Well, I'm right. Take my advice, stick to Berhane. No complications there, as long as you remember to use a rubber."

We continued in silence for some time.

Our visit to Anna's was somewhat marred by the presence in the bar, once again, of Colonel Tamrat and a number of associates in uniform. He saw us before we could dodge out to the terrace, and rose to greet us, removing his dark glasses as a gesture of friendship. He waved us over to his table, and introduced us to the rest of the company, two army men and a policeman. They all shook hands solemnly.

"Mr La Touche is a good friend of His Highness, Lij Yohannis," explained the colonel. "We have met at his house."

His colleagues exchanged looks.

"I wouldn't claim that we were good friends," I said cautiously. "We were at college together in Oxford, that's all."

"Oh, I think you are too modest," replied the colonel. "The prince has a very high regard for you. I am sure he would think of you as a good friend."

"Well," I said, "I am much flattered. I have a high regard for him also, but we don't really see that much of each other."

Colonel Tamrat smiled.

"Would you care to join us for a drink, you and your friend – Mr Blakeney, do I recall correctly?"

Simon intervened hastily.

"That's very kind, Colonel, but we really wouldn't want to disturb you. We're set up with some friends out on the terrace, in fact."

The Colonel seemed slightly put out by this refusal, but accepted it without further pressing.

"Well, perhaps another time," he said. "It is very nice to meet you again, Mr La Touche, even briefly. And Mr Blakeney also. I have no doubt we will have another occasion for a chat."

So we shook hands all round again, and hurried out onto the verandah.

"Damn and blast!" said Simon. "What the fuck are we going to do now? No way do I want to spend the evening with that bunch of spooks."

"Nor me," I said. "I'm glad you got us out of that. I suggest we just take a table down on the terrace, and see if the girls will join us."

Simon nodded, poked his head back into the bar, and caught Anna's eye. He pointed down towards the terrace, and she nodded comfortably at us, her chins rippling. We took a table under the spreading vine, and in a short while Frewet came out to see to us.

"Just two beers, darling," said Simon, patting her on the behind, "and then maybe we could go out the back, if you're free."

Frewet giggled, and then looked concerned.

"Yes, I come," she said, "but Berhane she is busy tonight. I have other nice friend for Ato Luke, though, if he want." And she looked at me tentatively.

The idea of Berhane being 'busy' sent a pang through me, but I was not going to sit out on the terrace on my own, so I accepted Frewet's offer. In the event, she produced another roundish little girl like herself, giggly and cheerful, Teru by name, who was quite pleased to do various things that I had not dared to ask Berhane for, so I did not feel too bereft. It gnawed at me, though, later, that Berhane might have been commandeered by some friend of Colonel Tamrat, or even the Colonel himself. I disliked being reminded of the realities of her life.

We left soon after our session, glancing cautiously at the door of the bar as we passed, and drove back to the compound rather depressed.

"What I can't understand," said Simon, "is where that fucker fits in in your friend Yohannis' entourage. I'll bet my bottom dollar he's no friend of his."

"It's a mystery to me too. I'm quite sure the Colonel is an agent of the government." For some reason I still could not bring myself to mention the disquieting detail about the visit to TM when I was down with Yohannis at his shooting lodge, but it was very much in my mind. "I can only imagine that the Little Man has assigned Col. Tamrat to keep an eye on Yohannis, and Yohannis can't get rid of him."

"Yeah," said Simon, "I suppose that's possible. He certainly scares the hell out of me. He just seems to represent the dark side of this regime – and it does have a dark side, believe you me, even if we don't see much of it."

"Well," I said reassuringly, "we're not involved in any skullduggery, anyhow, whatever about Yohannis and some of his other pals, so I don't see that we should have to worry about him."

Simon grunted, and we dropped the subject.

On Monday afternoon, I headed downtown to my meeting with Nuri Boghossian, which was to take place in his office at the bank. When I got there, I was met by Nuri himself, Willy, and a youngish man who was introduced as Mr Sarkissian, who was a lawyer and a cousin of Mr Boghossian. As it turned out, he was both very pleasant and good at his job. Willy was in attendance, as an executor (Nuri Boghossian being the other) to hear the will read, and contribute advice.

First of course, it was necessary to have coffee and *loukoumi*, and to discuss general issues. Once again the company sang the praises of my father, then we got down to business. James had named me in his will as his son, which was important from the point of view of inheritance taxes. As regards its contents, while my expectations had been heightened by previous hints from Willy, the reality was still overwhelming when it unfolded before me.

James had made a number of bequests – a thousand to his old school, a thousand to the British Red Cross, and so on, and a nice little legacy for Wolde, which would leave him very comfortable. The balance accruing to me seemed to be in the region of £100,000, even after taxes and legal fees had been subtracted. This left me in a situation I had never contemplated before – of not having to worry about money for the foreseeable future (except, I suppose, as to how it should be invested).

I slumped back in my chair, spread out my hands, and declared myself speechless, to the amusement of all.

"Don't worry, my dear Luke," said Nuri Boghossian cheerfully, "you will get used to it, I assure you."

"Well," I said weakly, "I suppose so. I'd certainly be grateful to you and Dr Buhagiar for advice about what to do with it."

"Of course, of course," he said. "We can discuss all that presently. But for the moment I wouldn't worry too much about it. All you need to do now is to sign on the dotted line."

So I signed with a willing hand various papers which Mr Sarkissian put in front of me. He tried conscientiously to explain the contents of them, but I was not taking very much in. The process did not take long. Then Nuri Boghossian clapped his hands, and a boy brought in champagne and little savoury pastries. We drank to the memory of Sir James, and to my future success in life, and I in turn thanked all three for their help and support.

Willy and I then excused ourselves, and went back to the bungalow for dinner. Willy took time before the meal to communicate to Wolde what he would be coming into, and the poor man in consequence was awash with both sorrow and gratitude. As we ate, I ventured to raise a thought that had occurred to me.

"Willy, I wonder if you would think it proper if I gave a series of dinner parties in the house over the next few weeks. I know that we really should be in mourning, but somehow it doesn't seem all that unsuitable. For one thing, I'd like to be able to repay all the hospitality I've been receiving over the last six months. It would also be a way of carrying on my father's tradition of dinner parties – and it would give poor old Wolde something to do."

To my relief, Willy thought this an excellent idea, and we began to plan some ideal combinations for dinner. Of course we must have the Hardimans, and the Boghossians, and the Stanfords (when they were in town), and Graham and Isabel. I privately noted that I would contrive also a rather wilder party, involving Yohannis and my bachelor friends, but I declined to mention that to Willy. If he were to get to hear of it, I preferred that it should be after the event. One thing that it did occur to me, though, was to ask him whether Abebe Retha, the Minister of Justice, would be likely to come to dinner, if asked. I had found him a most interesting man on my brief meeting with him.

"Oh yes," said Willy, "I'm sure he would come. He was really quite close to your father. But who would you think of having with him?"

"Well, you for a start, if you would come. And then perhaps the Hardimans. Perhaps you could think of someone else?"

Willy proposed a Swiss jurist of his acquaintance who was working in the Department of Justice, and we planned that dinner tentatively for two weeks time. Willy gave me an address for the Minister, and a number to ring for the Swiss, and I promised to get to work.

The next evening, Tuesday, I was in the middle of correcting homework when the phone rang. It was Caroline. I had been thinking of her, of course, and sort of hoping for a letter, but I had really not expected a phone call. Even now, glad as I was to hear her voice, it was a rather unsatisfying experience. The conversation was strained and awkward. The phone was in the sitting-room of Nyala, and the old folks did not approve of frivolous or lengthy phone calls. The Brig regarded the phone as an instrument to be reserved for emergencies.

"I just wanted to phone to say goodbye," said Caroline, brightly but neutrally. "We're going directly to the airport tomorrow. I have a flight just after midday."

"Ah," I said, "It's good to hear you. I was just thinking about you, actually. Are you alone there?"

"Well no, in fact."

"Um. I was afraid of that. Well, what can I say, except that you're taking a piece of me with you, in spite of your best efforts to discourage me."

Caroline giggled, despite the danger of having to explain to Aunt Louise what the joke was.

"And what piece would that be, I wonder?"

"Don't be vulgar," I said. 'What will your Aunt Louise think?"

"Oops. Well, be sure and write, and keep me up with the news – if Simon gets arrested, that sort of thing."

"Don't worry, I will. But I want to hear from you too, mind."

"Okay. I'm not great at letters, but I'll try." A short pause. "Well, cheerio, then. And thanks for everything – showing me round and so on. It was fun. "

"Oh Caroline," I sighed. "Damn it. Look after yourself. You haven't seen the last of me, you know."

"I hope not," she said, in a small voice – and then more brightly, "Byee."

And that was it. I sat in my armchair for quite some time after that, quite unable to turn back to the small pile of essays in front of me, going over in my mind and body a succession of delightful, but now bitter-sweet, occasions.

CHAPTER TWENTY-THREE

On Wednesday a letter arrived from Mother – pretty promptly, really, considering the realities of the postal service. Girma presented it to me at the beginning of break. I looked at the travel-worn envelope with its Irish stamp with deep apprehension, as I hurried across the compound to read it with a cup of Tekla-Mariam's coffee. I wished now that I had taken the opportunity to order her onto a plane to come out and attend the funeral, whatever the cost, but I knew in my heart that she would not have come. For one thing, it would have blown her cover, so to speak. Why would she have come half way across the world to the funeral of a second cousin? People would certainly have asked questions, and she could not have borne that. So there was nothing to be done.

I took a preliminary sip of coffee, and prised open the envelope. In fact, I need not have worried about her reaction. It was calm and serene, grieved though she was at the loss of James. It was plain, however, that she was vastly relieved that I had found out the truth without her having to tell me, and that I had not been angered or shocked.

It is so good, my darling Luke, that it has all come out, but especially that you were able to spend that time with your father, after all these years. I know it was a great joy for him. He wrote to me of it, in his funny, indirect way. Oh, he was such an annoying man, really! I suppose we were both foolishly inhibited, if the truth be told. I don't know, but I think perhaps we were still punishing ourselves for what we did so long ago – though it did produce you, my darling.

She went on to urge me to come home now as soon as I decently could, and do something constructive with my life, as my father would have wished. I leaned back in the armchair, my eyes filling with tears. I felt suddenly extremely lonely and miserable at leaving her to bear this sorrow alone. It was time this little romp was brought to a conclusion, I thought grimly. It was time to be going home.

Meanwhile, though, life had to go on for the moment. I spent a pleasant dinner one evening the following week at the McHugh's, who offered their sincere condolences over the loss of my cousin, as well as some solace from a much welcome bottle of Jameson's.

"We didn't want to intrude on the funeral," explained Mr McHugh, But you were very much in our thoughts.

"It must have been a great shock to you," added his wife.

"Yes, I agreed cautiously. Cousin James has been very good to me since I came here, and I will miss him a lot." I gave them an account of James's death and of the funeral, as well as of the Emperor's visit to the house.

"I hope," I said, "that I'll have a chance to return your hospitality before too long. I find that I've actually inherited my cousin's villa, along with the rest of his estate, so I'll be able to give some proper dinner parties. That'll be some consolation for missing the excellent ones he used to give. I hope that you and Mrs McHugh will be able to come to one of them."

Frank McHugh was most interested.

"Well, of course we'd be delighted. But that must have been quite a surprise to you, surely? Did he have no nearer relatives?"

I tried to cover my tracks as best I could.

"Strangely enough, no. He had some other cousins, of course, but I was his godson. It was indeed quite a surprise, though, certainly."

All this came up again over dinner, to the great interest of both Mrs McHugh and Fiona. By the time I rose to leave, after an excellent dinner and some after-dinner brandy, I was being treated very much as one of the family.

"Well now, Luke," said Mrs. McHugh at the door, "remember that you're always welcome. We'll be glad to give you a feed any time you're at a loose end. Nothing special, now, just a family meal."

I thanked her warmly, and waved goodbye as I got into my car and headed off into the night.

The subject of meals and invitations began to occupy me on a somewhat different level over the following week, as I began to consider my first dinner party, to which I wanted to ask James's friend the Minister of Justice. This turned out not to be too difficult, once I plucked up the courage to phone the number that Willy had given me. This, to my surprise (and, I think, to his) connected me to Abebe Retha directly. I stammered a bit, in confusion, but introduced myself, and said that Dr Buhagiar and I were planning a memorial dinner for Sir James, and we wondered if he could possibly attend. Ato Abebe turned out to be a man of great informality and directness, confirming the brief impression I'd had of him.

"That would be delightful," he said, warmly. "Such a nice idea. I would be very glad to come, if we can fix on a date."

In fact, my suggestion of Saturday, February 17, turned out to be possible for him, and my first dinner-party was launched. After that, it was no trouble to enlist the Hardimans and the Boghossians, and report back to Willy. I was beginning to feel rather important.

In addition, a different sort of plan began to form in my mind. Apart from the series of respectable dinner parties that I was planning with Willy in the villa, I thought I would throw one rather wilder one, featuring Yohannis and some of his pals; my group of bachelors, Simon, Maurice, and so on; Jack Hirschhorn and the rest of the jazz group (we might even do a gig); along with my Russians, Wendy Thesiger and some other embassy people. It was a much less concrete plan, but it served as a kind of distraction, and made me feel as though I were deciding something.

Elsewhere on the social scene, I was being entertained quite regularly either to dinner or to drinks during the week by either the Lonsdales or my nearer neighbours, the Barnes. I had come to enjoy the circulation of gossip about the students, their parents, and the expatriate community in general, as well as the endless rumours as to what was going on in the country as a whole. This was a topic on which the Ethiopian Herald offered only a very superficial and anodyne perspective.

The wife of the headmaster of Medhanie Alem School, for example, got very drunk at a New Year's Eve party, and ran off with one of the Ethiopian teachers and the headmaster went after them with a shotgun, which he fortunately didn't use – the whole thing was settled amicably, but not without the knowledge of the whole British community.

The father of one of our junior Ethiopian students, who was a minister of something-or-other, had suddenly fallen from grace, and been shipped off to be ambassador to Liberia – or so it was rumoured. The boy had been withdrawn in a hurry.

The British military attaché had gone duck-shooting again with the Soviet military attaché, and it was wondered if the Russians were about to make a break for it. That sort of thing.

On a day to day basis, however, life on The English School compound resumed its even tenor, as far as I was concerned. My senior class was becoming more serious, as many of them were having to think about the Overseas GCE in the summer.

One Friday afternoon, when I was on duty during break, however, the attention of the compound was rivetted on the arrival of a large black Mercedes with official number-plates, out of which stepped a courier, with what turned out to be a message for me. With a little quiver of anxiety and excitement, I recognised the familiar monogram.

Yohannis, at his most imperious, was summoning me once again to a weekend at his shooting lodge, not at any remote time in the future, but that very evening. "I thought this time we might try some duck-shooting," he wrote. "I've got together a few other chaps you might like to meet. I realise that this is rather short notice, and you may have other things lined up, but I do hope you can join us."

The arrogant bastard, I thought, with grim amusement. I hear nothing from him for a month or so (though he did come to the funeral, I admit), and then he just thinks he can summon me at a moment's notice. I might very well have been tied up, but as it happened I wasn't – other than the usual possibilities, all of which were disposable, with varying degrees of inconvenience.

So I put in a call to His Highness just at the end of break. The personal secretary with whom I had spoken often before this time put me straight through to Yohannis.

"Ah, Luke old man, good! You caught me as I was just going out. My man delivered the message all right? Any chance that you can join us?"

"Actually," I said. "I think I can, without causing too much bad feeling. I'll have a few apologies to make, but it should be okay. "

"Good. Come in time for a drink or two before dinner. Do you need a lift, or are you all right for transport?"

"The old car should get me there, I think, thanks. I'll take it easy."

"Well, try to get down before dark. It'll be better. I'll let the guards know to expect you. Just give them your name clearly and they won't shoot!" He chuckled ghoulishly. "It'll be great to see you. I'm really sorry for the short notice. These things just come up on the spur of the moment, you know. Suddenly found that I was free, so I organised a little party. We'll mix business and pleasure. I have some surprises I think you'll like."

"Great," I said, not without some unspoken apprehension. "I'll be looking forward to them."

As I put down the phone, it occurred to me to wonder what the business could be with which we were to mix the pleasure. I was not quite sure that I much liked the sound of it, or the surprises either. Whatever Yohannis' business was, I would prefer that he leave me out of it.

I decided that I would excuse myself as early as would be decent on Sunday morning, in order to be back in time for Sunday lunch at the villa with Willy. I had begun to feel responsible, by that stage, for Wolde and the maintenance of the household. As for Simon and our usual Friday night activities, I caught him just before lunch, confessed what I was up to, and received a mixture of derision and fatherly advice. Jack did not need me this weekend, so there was only a couple of cocktail parties to duck out of, and that was no great problem.

I briefed TM, put a few things in a bag, and headed out of town in mid-afternoon, on the road south to Bishoftu, hoping that the old car would provide no surprises.

CHAPTER TWENTY-FOUR

I took it easy, giving a wide berth to donkeys, old ladies with bundles, priests with umbrellas, and small children with herds of goats. The afternoon was hot, and around five o'clock I stopped at an Italian bar and *tej-bet* in Bishoftu to take on a chilled Melotti beer. I took a seat outside under an awning, and watched the world go by for a while, wondering what I was letting myself in for now.

While Yohannis hadn't asked me out that often – I commended myself quietly for not getting myself, so far, too sucked in to his wild and dangerous world, while not snubbing or avoiding him totally as advocated so consistently by my elders and betters. I had to admit that the more I saw of him, the more he fascinated me. He obviously had serious purposes, and no doubt excellent ones, but he seemed determined to live the life of a playboy as well. As he maintains – fathering the sentiment implausibly on none other than Trotsky – there is no reason that, just because one is a Socialist, one shouldn't enjoy oneself.

But where would it all end? From what I'd heard of the Emperor and his style of leadership, it seemed most improbable that he would ever welcome the guidance and assistance of anyone, let alone his frivolous nephew. Far more likely, I thought, that at some point not far in the future, the great paw of the Lion of Judah will descend on this whole scenario, and young Prince Yohannis will be dispatched to the ends of the earth, perhaps even farther than Liberia. And what would happen to his various friends and associates would be another matter again! That, I must say, was bothering me somewhat. I didn't want to be there when the shit hit the fan.

I finished up the beer, and returned to my car. As I opened the driver's door, I glanced back up the main street. Amid the general late-afternoon torpor, my eye fell on an official-looking car about fifty yards away on the opposite side of the street, with two men in dark glasses seated in it. The driver had his arm protruding from the open window, a cigarette between his fingers. I felt a flicker of concern as I saw them pull out after me when I drove off.

The car followed me, at a steady distance of a hundred yards or so, all the way south as far as the turn into Yohannis' estate. Then it swung round and headed back in the direction of Bishoftu. If there was anything calculated to reinforce my uneasiness in having accepted this invitation, that was it. My heart was pounding as I presented myself at the gates of the hunting lodge. However, I preserved my equilibrium sufficiently to give my name loud and slow to the heavily-armed guard who came forward to inspect me, and I was waved through without hesitation.

The party was plainly already well under way by the time I drove up, the old Fiat Millecento standing out rather embarrassingly against a background of Mercedes, Jaguars, and Maseratis. There were in all five other cars drawn up in front of the lodge when I arrived. Plainly quite a house party.

Yohannis and a number of others were reclining on the verandah overlooking the lake, and he sprang up and waved me round to the front door, where he met me, grinning, when I got there with my bag.

"Well, you made it. Jolly good! No problems, I hope?"

I saw no point in mentioning my escort from Bishoftu, so I assured him that I'd had none. Just a pleasant drive down.

"That's great. Come along in, then. I have some surprises for you. But first let's show you to your room." He waved to a servant to take my bag, and accompanied me to the pleasant, airy room that I'd had before. Then I followed him back out to the verandah. On the way, Yohannis turned to me with an ironic smile:

"I hope you won't be embarrassed, old chap, but I actually think you're the only *person of colour* in this particular party. They're all very broad-minded, though."

I laughed. "I'm sure they are. I'll do my best to keep my end up."

There were four or five others draped over chairs on the verandah, and they all lurched to their feet to greet me. They were indeed all

329

Ethiopian, and among them I recognised, to my surprise, my fellow jazz-man, our bass-player, Haile-Mariam Gabre-Hiwot. Then I recalled that of course he was well known to Yohannis.

"Hailu!" I said, delighted. "Good to see you."

Hailu grinned and shook hands. Then Yohannis introduced each of the others, all of whom had been at his previous party, but whose names I could not remember. I resolved to make a serious effort to remember them now, but their names slipped past me this first time. Prince Alex Desta, however, was not amongst them.

Yohannis found a chair for me, and waved me into it.

"Well now, what can we get you?"

"Well," I said, looking around, "what are you all having?"

"Oh, various things, Scotch, gin and tonic – anything you like. And of course a joint to go with it."

I chose a gin and tonic, and a servant departed to get it. Meanwhile, Yohannis rolled a joint, lit it, and passed it to me. I took a deep draw on it, and waited for some results.

With the help of the G&T, which arrived promptly, they were not long in coming. A pleasant fog of relaxation rolled over me. We talked of this and that. I had never really had much chat with Hailu during our sessions together, but now I found myself communing with him casually and easily, mainly on trends in modern jazz, about which he knew a surprising amount, but also about the ins and outs of running a night club, about which he also knew a good deal. Gradually, however, it dawned on me that there were sounds of laughter and splashing coming from the swimming pool round the corner, indicating that not everyone was on the verandah. I gestured to Yohannis interrogatively with my glass.

"Oh yes," he said, "the girls are still having a swim, and one or two of the chaps are with them."

"Girls?" I said. I rose, slightly unsteadily, and walked to the end of the verandah, which provided a view of the pool. An unexpected sight met my eyes. In and around the pool were a bevy of quite outstandingly beautiful girls, all quite naked, as were two young men who were still swimming around them.

"Ah," I said, shaking my head. "Girls! I see what you mean." And I tottered back to my chair.

The evening from then on took a course for which nothing in my previous existence had prepared me. I had heard about orgies, read about them in accounts by disapproving moralists like Suetonius of the decadent society of imperial Rome, but I had never been involved in anything remotely resembling one. Whatever nervousness or embarrassment I would normally have felt, however, was largely dissolved by the effects of alcohol and marijuana.

After some time longer on the verandah, during which the two remaining male members of the party arrived and helped themselves to drinks and joints, dinner was announced. We followed Yohannis down to the poolside, where a series of tables were now laid out, one for each guest, in the Ethiopian manner – or rather, one for each pair, since now each of us was joined by one of the girls, who had in the meantime dressed themselves in loose and flowing garments.

My girl introduced herself as Weinyshet. Her English in fact was quite good, and she seemed comfortably at home in surroundings of this sort, though she was plainly not an aristocrat, but hired for the occasion. The food was a very special *wat*, a melange of various exotic wildfowl, with little eggs, like quail's eggs, mixed in. We shared the *injera*. She tore off a strip first, and I followed her, and dipped in, hoping that the stew would not be so hot as to make me disgrace myself.

In fact, to my great relief, it produced only a slight shock, and I was able to appreciate the various subtle flavours of which it was composed. I praised it to Yohannis, and he responded by naming the components – mainly varieties of wild duck. Weinyshet was most interested to learn where I had come from, and how I knew His Highness. It occurred to me that she was very much the equivalent of what I imagined a Japanese geisha to be, or an ancient Greek courtesan – beautiful, cultivated, and practised in the ways of pleasure.

Flagons of Yohannis' special *tej* were produced, and by the time we had reached the fruit I was feeling curiously disconnected from my surroundings. I began to watch the scene as if it were taking place in a theatre. Fragments of conversation floated past me. Hailu was talking of Miles Davis, and how it seemed to him he was getting already a bit old-fashioned (this a subtle dig at my enthusiasm for him). Had I heard of a new man called Ornette Coleman? He had a trumpeter called Don Cherry. I should listen to him. He seemed remarkably well-informed. I wondered how he knew all this, but I really had not the energy at the moment to do much more than nod.

Then, after the main course was cleared away, one of the young men on the other side of the pool, with a sudden swift gesture, pulled his girl onto his lap, pushing up her dress to reveal her upper leg, and began to kiss her passionately. One or two others, taking their cue from him, began to make the same moves. Despite my befuddled state, I was panic-stricken, mainly by the idea that I might be expected to do the same. Then Yohannis called over to me cheerfully, perhaps sensing that all this might be a bit much for me.

"Luke, old man, you may like to take Weinyshet to your room, perhaps, if you're all through." He reached into his pocket for a little box. "Would you like to try a little coke, perhaps? It very much enhances the sensations."

"No, honestly, Yohannis," I gasped, lurching to my feet, "I think I'll pass on that. The pot and your *tej* is really quite enough for me. But I think I might just take Weinyshet to bed – that is, if she doesn't mind?" And I turned to her, tentatively.

She smiled.

"No, no. I do not mind at all. That would be good. His Highness will excuse us?"

Yohannis raised a princely hand, and Weinyshet supported me tactfully away from the pool-side, and back into the house.

I was able to steer us in the direction of my room, and after that I do not remember anything very clearly until the next morning, except that it was all delightful. The marijuana induced a feeling of detachment, but also of effortlessness. We certainly made love more than once, as I can recall various different positions. Weinyshet was superb, and unfailingly cheerful. I woke up in the morning with my hand caressing her breast, and feeling curiously light-headed, rather than hung over.

This was just as well, because Yohannis appeared a short time later, urging me up to go duck-shooting. His energy seemed boundless. I struggled out of bed, groaning, to Weinyshet's amusement, and to his.

"I hope this time you have brought sensible clothes," he said austerely.

I had in fact brought some khaki shorts and a dark shirt, which I thought would do, and, after a quick shower, which I badly needed, I pulled them on hastily. In about fifteen minutes or so I presented myself on the verandah for breakfast. Coffee and rolls and fruit were laid out, and I helped myself. I looked out at the lake. It was still early morning, just after six. The lake was calm, the sun just catching the tops of the trees which surrounded it. A group of flamingoes was already puddling, some way along the shore, but otherwise all was quiet. I sipped my coffee, and allowed the peace of my surroundings to flow over me – before we got out there and began to shatter it with gunshots.

After a little while, Hailu joined me, looking a little groggy.

"Ah," I said, pleased. "You're going to join the expedition."

"Oh, yes," he groaned. "Yohannis bullied me into it. He has always bullied me, all my life."

I laughed.

"Yes," I said, "I can imagine. He's beginning to bully me a bit. He does make life interesting, though, one must admit."

"Where is the bastard, anyhow?" said Hailu.

"I think he's had his breakfast. He's probably getting stuff ready. I'm sure he'll descend on us in a moment. You'd better get through that fast." Hailu had chosen half a mango with his coffee.

I was right. A few minutes later Yohannis swept in, dressed overall in the most impressive camouflage kit, all greens and browns. He inspected us sternly, but allowed us to pass.

"All right, you'll do. Let's get going. We have a bit of a way to go, and we don't have that much time. The duck are half way round the lake.'

We rose and followed him.

"No one else coming on this expedition?" I said.

"No – I wouldn't even ask them. They're lazy bums when it comes to exercise. They prefer the night life."

We started off down the same lakeside trail that we had followed when we had gone after the pig, preceded by a group of servants carrying the guns, and baskets, presumably for refreshments.

"That was quite a scene last night," I ventured.

Yohannis laughed, a trifle awkwardly, I felt. "Yes, sorry about that, I'm afraid our dinner habits are somewhat crude."

"Well," I said, judiciously, "they'd have been quite in accord with the best practice in either ancient Greece or Rome, in fact, but I suppose I found it all a bit unfamiliar. It was great, though," I added encouragingly, "and thanks for introducing me to Weinyshet. She's a lovely girl."

"Yes," said Yohannis, "she is, isn't she? They all are. We pick them carefully. They're well educated, skilled in all the arts of love, and medically sound."

I was intrigued.

"But who are they? Where do you find them?"

Yohannis laughed, and so did Hailu.

"Oh, they're mainly chosen from the families of our tenants. If they're good-looking, and they want to do this sort of thing, they get free education and a living allowance, and then after a few years, when they've saved up a bit of money for a dowry, they find themselves a nice husband, and settle down. It's not a bad deal, really."

"No," I said, "I suppose it isn't. Meanwhile, anyhow, they seem to be enjoying themselves."

"Oh yes," said Hailu, "they have a pretty good time."

The trek to the ducks took us about half as far again as we had gone for the pig. As we passed to the shore side of the meadow where we had shot the pigs the last time, I thought I heard some contented grunting in the undergrowth some way to our right, but made no comment. As we approached our destination, we fell silent and began to move cautiously. The servants handed over the guns, and melted into the undergrowth.

Yohannis took charge, motioning us forward cautiously until we reached an elaborately camouflaged hide, giving a good view of the lake. Into this we crawled, single file, watching carefully where we put our feet, to avoid the cracking of a twig. The hide gave a good view over the lake. There were some reeds near the shore, but they didn't seriously obstruct the view. Some way out, floating on the still water, we could see quite a considerable flock of duck, many – the males – sporting brilliant plumage. From time to time, one or another would dive, red feet and white tufts poking up into the air. It was a peaceful, domestic scene.

Once again, as with the pig, I felt a pang of guilt at being about to destroy their peace, but there was nothing for it. We each had our shotgun, both barrels loaded, and we would have to fire together, since there would only be one chance. After studying the scene for a short while, Yohannis took charge, raising his gun to his shoulder, and giving us the order to fire on the count of three.

I looked along my sights, trying to remember my minimal skills from rabbit shooting in Wicklow, and picked out a fine drake to the left of the flock. I aimed slightly below him, allowing for the gun to jerk upwards. We all fired more or less together, first one barrel, then the other. I fired my first shot, and then immediately again, blindly into the middle of the flock. There was a second's delay, and then total confusion. The whole flock rose with a terrific quacking. A cloud of feathers hung in the air, and, as the scene cleared, four corpses were revealed floating on the water. The boys rushed forward to do the work of hunting dogs, and catch the ducks before they sank. It looked as if Hailu and I had bagged one each, and Yohannis, as befitted a prince, two. At any rate, honour was served. We emerged from our shelter, and watched the boys bring in our booty. The rest of the duck were by now specks on the horizon.

"That was good shooting," said Yohannis, commending us. "I think we deserve a drink."

We settled down under a large tree a little way in from the shore. The boys brought the ducks for our inspection – three males, beautifully plumaged, and a more modest brown female. I patted one of the wet feathered bodies, with guilty satisfaction. They were undoubtedly fine fat birds. The exhilaration of bagging one – as I was fairly sure I had – outweighed any hesitation I had felt earlier.

To celebrate, Yohannis had arranged some reasonably cool champagne – an Eritrean Asti Spumante, accompanied by a selection of tasty samosas and other nibbles. We sat under our tree and sipped and munched, watching the sun edge itself above the lakeside foliage, and chatting about hunting.

When we had finished our champagne, it was still only about half past eight. Yohannis, after checking the time, now pointed towards a wooded island quite far out in the middle of the lake.

"Now," he said, "I have a little surprise for you, if you would be interested. You see that island out there? On it there is a very old monastery, and if you would like, we could take a boat out and visit it. There are still quite a few monks attached to it, and they have some very fine manuscripts and other things. It is part of my land, and I give them some support, so we will be welcome."

"Well," I said, "I don't know about Hailu, but I'd be fascinated, if you think we have time."

Hailu supported this, though mainly, I felt, to please Yohannis. Yohannis sprang up and went over to the boys to make arrangements. He directed all the rest to set off back to the lodge with the baggage, guns and ducks, and then, with one remaining boy, led us off a little further round the lake shore, to where a little boat-house rose from among the reeds.

Inside, there was a neat launch with an outboard motor, which could be let down into the water by unwinding a winch. We climbed in, the boy attached the motor and topped up the petrol tank, and, with Yohannis at the tiller, we began to chug gently across the smooth surface of the lake. Some way down shore, a cloud of flamingoes rose in alarm at this intrusion. I looked ahead at the island, which was becoming more visible. There did not seem to be much to it.

"It looks pretty small," I shouted across to Yohannis. "How do the monks live?"

"Oh," he said, pointing with his free hand over to the far side of the lake, "they own lands on the mainland. They let the local *Guragis* farm them, and then they go across when they need to and collect supplies. And they can grow a bit on the island as well. You must remember," he added, smiling, "the Church traditionally owns one third of the land of Ethiopia, the nobles one third, and the last third belongs to the Emperor. That isn't quite the way it is any more, but the Church still owns quite a lot."

I laughed.

"Your little spread is part of the Emperor's third, I suppose?" I said. Yohannis nodded, grinning.

"You could say that. But I think that all that has to change, a lot more than it has so far. Of course, I will look after my monks, but I really do not think that they should own so much land."

He paused, and then continued;

"This is a very old monastery, though – like the ones on Lake Tana, but of course much smaller. You see, all the monasteries on the mainland were destroyed by a fellow called Ahmad Granye – nasty fellow, a Somali! When he invaded us in about 1530, but he didn't manage to attack lake monasteries, so ones like this would go back much further than that – perhaps twelfth, thirteenth centuries, I'm not really sure – but old."

I nodded. Conversation was difficult above the noise of the engine, so I contented myself now with watching the island loom up.

As we came round the side of it, an old church appeared amongst the eucalyptus, surrounded by huts. There was a small jetty, with a motor boat already moored at it, and a number of fishing boats drawn up on the shore. Inland I could now see some cultivated land.

As we came in to dock, we were seen by a monk, who first peered at us, and then, seeming to recognise Yohannis, hurried off to summon his superiors. As we climbed onto the jetty, an elderly monk, leaning on a sort of crozier, plainly the abbot, came bustling out of one of the larger huts, followed by some others, and headed down to greet us. As in the case of the little monastery I had come upon on Entotto, there was also, I noticed, a crowd of boy deacons. Scrawny black hens scratched about in the dust between the huts, and a number of curly-tailed Ethiopian dogs contemplated us without interest from shaded vantage-points. Either they did not take their role as watch-dogs very seriously, or they knew not to bark at royalty.

Yohannis advanced with proprietorial authority, and the abbot hastened to kiss his hand, followed by all the other monks. I was amused to observe the relations between church and state, at least in this little corner of the kingdom. We were also greeted warmly, and ushered up to the abbot's quarters for refreshments. Our boy stayed behind with the boat. Yohannis engaged the abbot in animated conversation, presumably enquiring into the affairs of the monastery, and appeared to receive satisfactory replies.

Coffee and little honey cakes were served. When we had taken our fill, Yohannis turned to me and said he was going to ask if we could view their chief manuscript, and perhaps some relics. He put this to the abbot, and as a consequence we were led out of the hut, across a clearing, and into the church.

It certainly seemed ancient enough. Inside it was dark and smoky, cluttered with hangings and ornaments, the walls covered in frescoes. We were led round behind the altar to what seemed like a little sacristy, and there a cupboard in the wall was unlocked, and a number of objects, wrapped in linen cloths, were reverently taken out.

First we were invited to do obeisance to some relics. Yohannis explained them to me in a whisper. The first was a finger of St. Tekla Haymanot, a very great mediaeval monk, one of the founders of Ethiopian monasticism. Fortunately this pickled finger was largely encased in gold, so, following the examples of Yohannis and Hailu, I kissed that, cautiously. Then a garment was unwrapped which Yohannis explained to me, maintaining a very straight face, as being the actual girdle worn by the Virgin Mary. This I found easier to kiss, despite my Protestant reservations about Mariolatry.

These were then reverently packed away, and what was for me the real treasure was produced, from a jewel-encrusted case, a splendid illuminated manuscript of the Gospel of Mark. On a superficial view, it was rather like one of the best old Irish manuscripts, such as the Book of Kells, though perhaps not as elaborately ornamented. Wide-eyed apostles, supplicants, sinners, even animals, not to mention Christ himself, looked out at us from every page. Yohannis, showing off, spelled out some of the *Ge'ez* for me, translating it into one familiar passage or another. I felt enormously privileged to have seen such an object.

After about half an hour we took our leave, accompanied to the boat by the abbot and most of his flock, bowing and scraping to His Highness, who received their homage with dignity. As we chugged out into the lake, and round the island, I turned to Yohannis.

"That was a marvellous experience, Yohannis. I really appreciated seeing that manuscript."

He grinned. "You were actually very privileged," he said. "It is not everyone who gets to see that – or indeed to kiss the girdle of Maryam."

I sat back, and gave way to my thoughts. Once again here, as long ago on the banks of the Awash, when I first arrived, I had the sensation of the utter strangeness of this extraordinary country, and at the same time of the ordinariness within the strangeness. For the monks, this was no doubt a notable occasion, since they had been visited by their prince, but still they were within their normal environment, and would now return to their everyday tasks. Nothing was strange to them. Nor was it, really, for Yohannis, nor even for Hailu. All this is in the eye of the beholder – that is to say, me. I trailed my finger in the water of the lake. It was quite warm. It was now after eleven, and the sun was beginning to make itself felt.

"Any crocodiles hereabouts?" I shouted across to Yohannis.

He shook his head. "No, not up this high. You'll get them in the Omo, but not in these lakes. But if you're thinking of taking a swim, I'd stick to the pool. There are water-snakes, and it's not very clean."

That had not in fact occurred to me, but now that he mentioned it, I began to look forward to a session in and around the pool. We pulled into the boat-house, saw to the stowing of the boat and the engine, and set off back along the trail. The journey back seemed shorter than the one out, as is often the case, and we got back to the lodge a little before noon. The others were by now up, as were the girls, and they were already draped around the pool, having breakfasted and swum.

"Okay," said Yohannis, "time for a swim and a drink before lunch."

I went in and changed, and in a little while joined the party at the pool. The water was still pleasantly cool, and I flopped up and down a few lengths lazily, before rolling over on my back and staring up at the trees and sky. The sun was still only partly over the pool, but what there was of it felt dangerous. After a few minutes I pulled myself out, and went over with my towel to a place that was being kept for me in the shade by Weinyshet.

"Well," she said teasingly, "you have had a nice morning?"

"Oh yes," I said, "quite energetic, and very interesting." And I gave her a description of our visit to the monastery.

'Ah yes," she said. "I know about that monastery, but I have never been there. It is very old. Debre Maryam, it is called. It is dedicated to the Virgin, Maryam, you know. But the funny thing is, they will not allow any women to visit it. That does not make sense to me."

I laughed.

"Yes," I said, "that does seem illogical, certainly. It explains something, though. We were shown the girdle of the Virgin, and allowed to kiss it."

It was Weinyshet's turn to laugh.

"The girdle of the Virgin? Really, they are very silly old men. And of course, you know, even if they will not have women over there, many times the monks come over to the mainland, and then they sleep with women. But really," – and here she lowered her voice – "really, most of them prefer boys. You know what I mean?"

"Yes," I nodded, reflectively, "I did see quite a few boy deacons."

"Well," she said, "they use them, you see, and then when they grow up, they become monks, and so it goes on. Is that the same in your country?"

"Well, you do get clergymen arrested from time to time, in and around public lavatories, for picking up young men, but no, I wouldn't say it's quite the same."

"Oh," said Weinyshet, disdainfully, "priests are the same in all the world, I think. I do not like priests very much."

We dropped the subject, and I snoozed for a while, until a servant appeared with gins and tonics, ordered thoughtfully by Yohannis.

Talk round the pool was relaxed and mainly in Amharic. The young bloods seemed fairly lethargic, after their exertions of the previous night. Lunch, when it came, did not consist of the ducks, but of another roast suckling-pig, which was, once again, delicious.

Lunch was followed by a siesta, which I spent alone, since the guests of the current party, including the girls, now took their leave, and drove off in a convoy of Mercedes and Maseratis, leaving just myself and Yohannis to welcome the next party, which he promised would be more serious and interesting for me.

I slept for a while, and when I roused myself the air seemed a little cooler, and the shadows outside were lengthening. I looked at my watch. To my surprise, I saw that it was almost six o'clock. From the verandah I seemed to hear the sound of voices, so I got myself up, and went to investigate.

On the verandah there was a little group already gathered. They all turned towards me as I appeared. One of them, I was much astonished to see, was my English pupil, the Director of the Soviet Information Service, Safar Abdolov. I knew, of course, that he was an acquaintance of Yohannis', having met him at one of his parties, but I still did not expect to see him here, in this dissolute and sylvan setting. The other two I did not know, but Yohannis, waving me forward, introduced them. One was a pleasant-looking fair-haired middle-aged man, who turned out to be the First Secretary of the Czechoslovak Embassy, a Mr Peter Skrabanek; the other was a young Ethiopian army officer with an intelligent, serious expression, horn-rimmed glasses and a little pencil moustache, who was introduced as Major Samuel Assefa.

"Samuel," said Yohannis, by way of explanation, "spent a couple of years at Sandhurst, you know, Luke. That is where I first met him, in England – just a little while before I met you."

Safar Abdolov broke in cheerfully, explaining to Mr Skrabanek, "Mr La Touche is my instructor in English, you know – and a very good one too! We meet once a week, and I think that I am making great improvements."

"Yes indeed, Safar Akimovich," I said gallantly, "You certainly are."

Mr Skrabanek seemed slightly confused at all these interlaced relationships. A fixed smile had taken possession of his face, as he looked from one of us to the other. Yohannis moved to provide me with a drink. As it happened, Safar Abdolov had contributed some special bottles of vodka, from Soviet Embassy stock, and, not to be outdone, Mr Skrabanek had brought down a case of genuine Pilsener beer, so what was on offer at the moment was beer with vodka chasers. I settled for that, with some misgivings. We were drinking the vodka in the Russian manner, neat, from little glasses which Yohannis had dredged up from somewhere, and at regular intervals Safar would propose a toast – to World Peace, to Progress, to Ethiopian-Soviet Friendship, even to Irish-Soviet Friendship – after each of which we had to lower our vodka at one gulp. Too much of this could make conversation difficult.

Yohannis, however, was keeping his end up admirably. As the sun went down, and the moon rose over the lake, he engaged Safar and Mr Skrabanek on a series of topics which concerned him: nationalisation of the means of production, worker control of industry, the theory of surplus value, and the question of whether a transition from feudalism to socialism was possible without passing through the stage of capitalism. Safar Abdolov, though his English idiom sometimes failed him, was never at a loss for a response, while Mr Skrabanek tended rather to throw in supporting remarks, glancing deferentially at his more voluble colleague.

I listened with one ear, while paying attention mainly to Major Samuel. He interested me by speaking very frankly about what he saw as the dangers facing the country, and the role which he felt the army would have to play in them.

"Our problem," he told me with great emphasis, "is simply whether we will have progressed far enough before His Majesty passes on, to prevent the country sliding back into darkness. And of course, as you know, he is not young. You see, the only other element in the state which can possibly keep things going, apart from the Emperor himself, is the armed forces. And even there, many of the senior ranks still have very old-fashioned attitudes. Really, we are in a race against time."

I nodded, fascinated. This was talk I had not expected to hear. Major Samuel must have been quite sure that he was among friends.

I asked him where he was from. Did he come from Addis?

"No," he said, "I am not from Addis. I was brought up in the North, in Gondar. Have you been there?"

I told him that I had visited it briefly, on my trip north with the Lonsdales after Christmas, and had found it fascinating, especially the palaces.

"Ah yes," said Major Samuel, "they are very fine. But where I am based now is also very fine. That is Harar. Have you been to visit there?"

"No, I haven't. I'd like to," I said.

"It's an old Arab-style town," he told me, "down in the south-east, with many fine buildings. I'm attached to a large army base there."

Soon, servants came in with the traditional Ethiopian individual wicker tables on which our *wat* and *injera* would be served. It was plain that Yohannis was once again going for something traditional. In fact, we were served with a deliciously aromatic lamb *wat*, washed down, as before, by flagons of Yohannis's special *tej*. Safar was moved to propose toasts with the *tej* also, but at least we were not compelled to down a flagon each time. The conversation became progressively wilder and more disconnected.

Safar, who was in fact, as I had discovered, quite well read, in a rather selective way, asked me my opinion of Sean O'Casey as a playwright. I had seen his early plays, of course, and enjoyed them greatly, but only once had I seen one of his later ones, Purple Dust, and had found it rather dismal, so I told him that.

"Aha!" he said, triumphantly, "That you say because he has become communist, is it not?"

"No, Safar," I said firmly, "it is not. He is quite welcome to be a communist if he wants to be, but I'm afraid it just causes him to write lousy plays. I think it's really more that he has lost touch with his roots by living abroad. I mean, Brecht's a communist, and no one holds that against him, as long as he can write a good play."

Then in return I began to tease Safar about Yevgeni Yevtushenko, who was much in the news at the time as a dissident poet.

"What do you think about Yevtushenko? He reads very well in translation, at least."

Safar shook his head sorrowfully.

"Ah yes, Yevtushenko. Of course he is excellent poet – but ideologically he is not sound."

"And that's important?"

"Yes, of course it is important. A poet must be intellectual leader. He must assist in building better society."

"Oh? And you don't feel he's doing that?"

Safar raised his hands in a despairing gesture.

"He speak too much of negative things. It is not good. One must be positive." He moved to change the subject. "And let us now be positive. I want to propose a toast..."

And so it went on. Even Mr Skrabanek became rather jolly, and was prevailed upon to sing a sad Czech song. Then Yohannis pulled a fast one on me. He left the verandah for a moment, and came back carrying a black box which looked very like a trumpet case. That indeed it proved to be.

"Look what I managed to find!" he announced with a grin, opening it, and brandishing a gleaming trumpet. "Now I can invite Mr Luke La Touche, Addis Ababa's greatest jazz trumpeter, to play us a few tunes."

I was appalled. "Yohannis, what are you doing to me? I'm in no condition to play a trumpet. I'm totally plastered!"

"Nonsense!" he said gaily. "You'll find you play even better. Come on, don't be modest. Play us a tune!"

I was trapped. I accepted the horn from Yohannis, and fingered it tentatively, fitting in the mouthpiece. It was in good shape. I tried a middle C. It came out smoothly. I thought for a moment, searching for a tune that would be simple, and sound well as a solo, and then picked on an old favourite, 'Summertime'. I closed my eyes, and caressed the tune langourously. The notes rang out into the darkness, disturbing water birds round the lake.

I tried no Milesian elaborations, no frills – simply laid out the main tune. The audience listened in appreciative silence, and then called for more. Again, I paused a while to think, and then belted out the St. Louis Blues. Having regard for my audience, I thought it best to keep things pretty basic. That went down well too. Even Mr Skrabanek seemed to know the tune. After that, however, my head began to swim. Even some powerful Ethiopian coffee after dinner had neither sobered me nor helped to keep me awake.

"Yohannis," I said feebly, "I think you are going to have to excuse me. This has been quite a long day. I have just got to go to bed."

Fortunately, Yohannis made no great difficulty about this, apart from trying to press a final brandy on me as a nightcap, which I declined. I handed him back the trumpet.

"That's a very fine horn," I said. "Where did you find it?"

"Ah," he smiled, putting it back in its case. "I have my sources. I'm glad you liked it."

I shook hands with each of my three fellow guests in turn, and accepted their congratulations. Yohannis accompanied me out into the hall, and clapped me on the back as I staggered off to bed.

Next morning we shared a leisurely and lateish breakfast on the verandah with Yohannis, who had already had a swim in the pool, and was looking quite unaffected by the events of the weekend. Only he and Major Samuel had risen yet, though it was after nine.

"Well," said Yohannis, "the others really had quite a lot to drink by the end of the evening, and I don't think they are very used to that."

"Russians are usually pretty good at knocking back the vodka," I remarked, critically.

"Yes, but there was also the *tej*. I don't think they took that seriously enough, frankly. However," continued Yohannis, after a pause, during which he cut a slice out of a mango, "I had a most interesting discussion with them earlier. Skrabanek doesn't look like much at first, but he is actually very sound theoretically."

"Ah," I said, not wishing to sound too committed to the direction which the conversation was taking.

"And Safar, of course, has an answer for everything."

"So you clarified various issues?" I said, with mild irony. The contradictions between two sides of Yohannis' life, as revealed in the course of this weekend, filled me with amused astonishment.

"Oh yes," said Yohannis, with entire seriousness. "I am much clearer now, for one thing, on the possibilities, as well as the difficulties, of moving directly from feudalism to socialism."

I decided that I had better get going. Major Samuel had been listening in respectful silence, but now he rose and urged me to look him up if I ever decided to visit Harar, and gave me his card. I promised faithfully to do that. It sounded like a place well worth seeing, and I had found Major Samuel both interesting and congenial. Yohannis came with me to the car, followed by one servant carrying my bag, and another my duck, wrapped in plastic, all ready for Tekla-Mariam to deal with.

"A pity we did not have more time to chat, but we had some good fun, did we not?"

"Absolutely," I said. "It was great." To tell the truth, though, I was not sorry to have avoided too much heavy chat with Yohannis on the future of his country. He gave me a vigorous embrace before I climbed into the car.

"It was great having you down here, Luke old man. I really appreciated it. We must do it again."

I nodded feebly. Well, I thought to myself, not all of it, and not too often.

CHAPTER TWENTY-FIVE

I made good time on the road back to Addis, without anyone obvious on my tail, and reached James's bungalow comfortably early for lunch, leaving myself a little time to change and settle in before Willy arrived. I suspected that, from force of habit, he was probably taking himself for a lonely walk on Entotto. Wolde was very pleased to see me, and brought me a fairly stiff gin and tonic on the verandah, where I sat contemplating the city below me, and thinking on the curious and varied events of the weekend.

I was increasingly having to admit to myself that all those well-meaning folk, from James himself on down, who warned me against associating with Yohannis, were probably quite right. The problem was, though, that in addition to not wanting to cause offence, I liked him. I liked him a lot. Also, he was undeniably interesting. He made things happen. I went over in my mind the duck-shoot, and the trip to the monastery. I thought fondly also of Weinyshet, and wondered if I would ever see her again. I made a resolve, though, to back off, so far as I could.

A commotion at the door indicated that Willy had arrived. He bustled out onto the verandah, followed by Wolde. I rose to greet him.

"Mr Willy, you like gin and tonic too?" asked Wolde, hovering.

"No, Wolde, I'll take a beer, I think, if you have one cold."

And Willy subsided into one of the cane chairs, fanning himself with his hat.

"You were up on Entotto?" I said.

"Yes," he said, a little sadly, "it's a habit of long standing. It's not quite the same, of course, without your ... your father." He paused. "What have you been doing with yourself? I gave you a call earlier, just to see if you'd like to join me."

346

"Oh, I'm sorry," I said – and then, not willing to reveal the awful truth, "I was away for the weekend with a friend, down by Lake Langano. We were camping."

"Ah? That must have been pleasant."

"Yes, it was."

"You must try to use the house more, though, at the weekends, if you can, just for the moment. It would be a great consolation to Wolde. He was devoted to your father, you know, and he misses him a lot."

"Yes, I know," I said with a twinge of repentance, "I really must. We'll be able to have this series of dinner parties, though, for the next few weeks. That should keep him happy."

After a pleasant lunch, during which Willy gave me the gossip of the courts, most of it thoroughly amusing, he then parted for the siesta. I decided to rest in what I regarded as my room, just to keep Wolde company, and only at around five o'clock did I head back to the compound.

Although I was rather hoping to slip in unnoticed and get some preparation done for Monday's classes, Simon must have been watching out for me. Shortly after I had settled down in my armchair, having handed over the duck to Tekla-Mariam, there was a knock on the door, and he stuck his head in.

'Where the hell have you been?" he said, indignantly.

"Oh?" I said. "I'm sorry. Didn't I say? I was down at Yohannis' hunting lodge again. I thought I told you that."

"Not that I remember," he grumbled. "I think that at the very least you owe me a generous measure of that whiskey of yours."

I grinned and headed for the sideboard to fulfil the order. I had been able to keep up the supply of Jameson's, in fact, through the courtesy of Frank McHugh, who ordered bottles through the UN, and presented me with one from time to time.

"So!" said Simon, cheered up considerably by the generous measure I'd poured for us both. "Where to tonight, then?"

I hesitated. I had really had quite enough today, but I was conscious of having neglected Simon somewhat of late, and I couldn't be quite sure I hadn't told him I was going off for the weekend. I tried a compromise.

"I really don't want to go too far. I'm pretty bushed, and I have a bit to prepare for tomorrow. Could we just go down to Arat Kilo and have a drink there? I know quite a nice little *tej-bet* I've dropped in on a few times. Then, if you like, you can come back and join me for duck. I shot it yesterday morning, and I'll get TM to cook it up."

Simon guffawed.

"Well fuck and stroll about! You uppity bastard! Shot a duck when out with 'is 'Ighness, eh? And now my manservant will prepare it. Okay, great! I could do with a bit of duck. I just hope it isn't too tough, though. Maybe he'd better cut it up small."

So I went into the kitchen and told TM that Mr Simon would be there for dinner and we agreed on a duck wat, which seemed on the whole the safest option.

We headed down the road in his car, and established ourselves at a table beside the window where a smiling plump girl, wrapped in a *shamma*, brought us two Melotti beers. A little cluster of other girls, gathered against the inner wall, giggled and eyed us speculatively, but Simon decided he was not really in the mood this evening, and I certainly wasn't, so we decided to leave them for another time. We addressed our beers, and I looked out the window.

There was little action round the square at this time of the evening. A few cars, millecentos mainly, nosed round the central roundabout in one direction or the other, bringing passengers in or out of town. Across from us, the buildings of the university looked quite deserted, as one might expect on a Sunday evening.

"Well, how was your friend the prince? As full of fun as ever, I suppose."

I reckoned I owed Simon an account of the weekend, so we called for another pair of beers, and I gave him an extended and dramatised narrative, pointing up the contrast between the two evenings. Simon chortled at the goings-on of the Friday evening, and snorted sceptically at those of the Saturday.

"He's getting into deep water there, I'd say, is your prince. I mean, you can't just invite chaps like that down for the weekend, and not end up compromised. And I'll bet that's been noted. From what I hear, the Old Man is no slouch when it comes to security. He can't afford not to be. I'd be pretty sure that his boys know all about that little get-together. And of course you shouldn't have been anywhere near it!"

"Oh, I know, I know," I said, miserably. "But how could I know what he was cooking up? Once I was there, I was stuck. There was no way out. I don't think I'll accept any more invitations like that from Yohannis, though, unless I can get a look at the guest-list first."

And then, just to inflame Simon the more, I told him about my encounter in Bishoftu, and how I was tailed right to the entrance to the lodge.

"Oh Jesus," groaned Simon. "I tell you, you are in trouble. You had better just stay very quiet until further notice. I don't know if I should even be seen talking to you."

He looked at his watch. The sun had sunk behind the eucalyptus that fringed the west of the square.

"I think we should get back and have a look at this duck of yours. I'm starving. I just hope Tekla-Mariam hasn't made a complete balls of it."

In fact, he had not. Within about twenty minutes of our return, we had a very respectable duck *wat* on the table, which Simon enjoyed to the full, plunging his *injera* into it copiously, and wolfing it down. He had produced a bottle of Eritrean chianti from his cellars, so we ended up in a less than ideal state to address ourselves to preparation for Monday's classes when I finally ushered him out the door.

Next morning, when I returned to my bungalow at break for coffee, I found a letter from Caroline. I looked at it intently while Tekla-Mariam poured my coffee, savouring the anticipation of opening it, but nervous, too, at what it might contain.

In fact, though, it was a rather satisfying document, sent from an address near Banbury, in Oxfordshire.

> *"Darling Luke,*
> *I'm sorry for not writing earlier, but things have been rather hectic. It really is weird to be back here. I thought it would be great to get back to civilisation, but strangely enough I'm feeling just a little homesick for dear old Nyala – and even a bit for you, you bastard. It's hard to settle in, and there isn't really much to do. I think I might go down to London and see if I can get a job, and take in a bit of intellectual life. I don't want to get involved with you-know-who again, and that might happen if*

I was just hanging around. How about you? Do you miss me at all? Or have you taken up with that little girl in your Latin class? I suppose you're having to get used to being a man of property now. How are you managing? Do write and give me the news. And give regards to Simon. I hope he's staying out of trouble!
Lots of love, Caroline.

So there it was. I read it over again. Not much to it, really. But then she didn't seem to be having a very interesting time. And she sounded as if she might be missing me a little. I decided to write soon, but not quite yet, and put the letter in the top drawer of the desk.

The rest of the week passed pretty quickly, as the weeks were beginning to do once again, after the upheavals of mid-January. A certain routine was setting in. I tended to go shopping, buy a paper or a book at Giannopoulos', meet Simon and others at the Ras Bar, drop in for a drink, perhaps, before or after dinner with the Lonsdales or the Barnes'.

At school, we had begun to prepare for Sports Day, which was to occur just before the Easter holidays, on the last Saturday of term.

The school was divided into three 'houses', Green, Yellow and Red, based patriotically on the colours of the Ethiopian flag. I had to take my part in training my 'house', Green, in various sports which I really knew very little about – soccer, basket-ball, and track and field. Alan filled me in on the rules of basket-ball, and I had become, on Wednesday afternoons, quite a committed sports coach, roaring at people from the sidelines, and blowing my whistle. To balance this rude physical activity, I organised a chess tournament, in which I managed to involve about a dozen people, from almost as many nationalities, but including at least two very proficient candidates, one Yugoslav, one Indian. All this activity, then, kept me busy.

The session with my Russian pupils the following the weekend at Langano was amusing, as Safar was full of my trumpet-playing down at the lodge, and was only with difficulty persuaded that I could not play for them now without disturbing the whole compound. Indeed, in general I was having to do my practising either with a mute instrument, or by driving up into the hills and playing to the birds and goats, which

I did from time to time – though there one never quite knew when a countryman might not appear round a corner on his mule. At any rate, on this occasion we had a rather laborious discussion as to whether jazz was a progressive or a decadent art-form, Safar advancing the latter thesis, I the former, and the rest of the group maintaining a certain caution, tending to glance at Safar for guidance.

On the Saturday of that week, I gave a little experimental dinner party, just for Graham and Isabel, with Willy in attendance, and that was pleasant and nostalgic, but not otherwise worthy of note. We were officially still in mourning after all, and not exactly inclined to be boisterous, and I was feeling my way into my new role as host. Wolde served an excellent meal, however, and was obviously pleased at the re-establishment of traditional norms. I stayed the night over in the villa, and accompanied Willy on a walk on Entotto the next morning, after church.

I had to duck out of performing at the Paradiso that night, but had done my duty on Friday, dragging along a rather unwilling Simon, who would have preferred Anna's. I was conscious, indeed, of not having seen Berhane for a couple of weeks now. Simon said she had been asking for me rather plaintively last weekend. We agreed to try to drop in on the following Wednesday evening, after sports practice, if we could get away.

In the event, we did manage to go out to the Bella Napoli, Simon doing the driving, for an early evening pasta under the vine trellis, followed by some leisurely love-making out the back. Berhane was indeed pleased to see me, though a little reproachful.

"I think you find other girl you like better, perhaps."

"Oh no, Berhane," I protested, as if stung by the suggestion, "you are definitely the only girl for me. It's just that I have been very busy, really, these last weeks. Much work in school."

She seemed to accept that, and giggled and wriggled happily as we made love. As she lay in my arms afterwards, though, she revealed something else that had been bothering her.

"You know, last week, last Saturday, you were not here, and there come this policeman, he want to make love with me. I do not like him, but nothing I can do. Then he ask me questions about you."

351

I froze. This was appalling.

"Good God," I said. "What was his name, Berhane? It wasn't that Colonel Tamrat, was it? Nasty looking fellow with a little moustache."

I pointed to my upper lip. She nodded.

"Tamrat. Yes, Tamrat. That is him. He is often here, but he has never chosen me before."

I was enraged at the idea of Berhane having to submit to the filthy embraces of Colonel Tamrat, but also seriously disturbed.

"Damn it. What was he asking?"

Berhane looked worried.

"Oh, he ask if you talk about politics at all, if you mention any Ethiopian friends you have. I say no, never. We just make love. That is all."

"Good. Good girl." My mind was going round in circles.

"But he say to me, you are dangerous person. Are you dangerous person?"

"No, that's absurd. He's crazy." I paused, wondering if I was going beyond the limits of discretion. But then I reflected, after all, that it was better for her to know the situation. "It is just... I think that it is because I am a friend of Lij Yohannis Tessema. You have heard of him?"

She shook her head, rather to my relief.

"Fine. Well, there's no reason that you should have, I suppose. He is a nephew of the Emperor. His father is a brother of Empress Menen." Her eyes widened in alarm. "There is nothing to worry about, though. He and I were at university together in England for a while. That is why I know him. I think that Colonel Tamrat has been set to watch Lij Yohannis, to protect him. I actually met him in His Highness's house, at a party. But if he bothers you again, you tell him that I have no interest in politics here at all. Okay?"

"Okay," said Berhane, looking rather subdued. "I tell him that."

This piece of news, though, bothered me in all sorts of ways. I told Simon about it on the way home. This time he was not inclined to guffaw, or to tease me. Instead, he looked grim.

"You know, La Touche, this is getting somewhat beyond a joke. I would suggest the next time you see that fucker at Anna's, or anywhere else, you just go right up and confront him. Tell him if he has any questions, to put them directly to you, and you'll be glad to answer them, but not to go scaring the living daylights out of innocent girls like Berhane."

"Yes," I said, firmly. "Good idea. I'll do that. That is just what I will do."

That opportunity, however, did not arise. On Friday we had a rather lively party over at Maurice's pad, more or less equally divided between francophones and anglophones, with a great deal of wine consumed. And on Saturday, still slightly hung over, I presided at the second of my dinner parties — my first serious one – featuring James's friend, Minister Abebe Retha, Willy, and the Boghossians. The Minister proved in the event to be delightfully informal, and most likeable, as was his charming but quiet wife. The knowledge I had accumulated of Ethiopian history pleased him very much, as also the modest amount of Amharic I had learned, and he made great efforts to teach me more, across the dinner table. He drew Nuri out also, getting him to tell stories of his family, how his grandfather as an orphaned child had been given sanctuary in Addis by the Emperor Menelik, and how his father had built up his business. I learned a good deal that evening.

As he was leaving, Dejazmatch Abebe pressed his hand on mine, and urged me to let him know if I had any difficulty with anything connected with settling the estate, or indeed anything else. I thanked him, and hoped it would not be necessary to bother him.

"Ah well," he said, with a smile, "of course you have the best of advice here already. I am sure that you will not need me. But if ever you do, do not hesitate to call."

And he was gone, ushering his wife out in front of him.

The Boghossians excused themselves shortly afterwards with Mimi reminding me about the next playreading as she left. Willy and I were left alone sipping a final brandy on the verandah.

"Well," said Willy, with a smile, "I must say I think that passed off splendidly. I was not really sure, you know, how well Nuri would get on with Abebe. Of course Nuri is the soul of diplomacy, but his relations with the Ethiopian aristocracy have not always been very comfortable. Abebe is a very good fellow, though, and the atmosphere that you created was very positive."

"I would have thought," I countered, "that it was rather the ghost of James that was responsible for the atmosphere – and yourself, of course."

"No, no," insisted Willy, "you handled yourself very well. You will find the Minister a useful friend, though I naturally hope you will never need him." He drained his glass. "And now I think we may head for our beds. We have earned them."

Willy went home up the hill to his bungalow, and I headed up to my bedroom under the eaves, for which I was developing a great affection. My own bungalow was fine, but there was a certain quiet luxury about my bedroom in my Father's house that appealed to me greatly. Wolde was still pottering about in the kitchen, and I wished him goodnight, and thanked him for an excellent dinner.

"Good night, *getoich*," he said, happily. Wolde liked a good dinner party, especially one with government ministers involved. "You go to church in the morning?"

"Yes, Wolde, I think I will."

Somehow, church had become more important in this environment. It was a purely cultural event so far as I was concerned, but I liked old Padre Matthews, and I valued the bit of colonial conviviality afterwards. It was curious how, when based in James's bungalow for the weekend, I found myself slipping into his role.

"Good," said Wolde, "I bring you tea, nine o'clock."

Routines, routines. And now another thoroughly pleasant routine was added to all the others. I was beginning to feel like an old Ethiopia hand.

CHAPTER TWENTY-SIX

The year drew on into the Ethiopian Lenten period, which that year overlapped with Ramadan, so that about half my pupils were pretty dopey most of the time. The so-called Little Rains were also in progress, so many of the afternoons were pretty wet. I couldn't begrudge them the rain, but it all conspired to make life just a bit gloomy.

It was cheering to head for Nyala at the weekends; it was becoming one of my favourite places. The routines out there appealed to me: afternoon tea, then a bath or a walk, then the nine o'clock news on the BBC, with the hurricane lamps hissing and swaying gently above us, and then dinner and bridge and brandy and eventually, bed.

One Sunday morning, Isabel took me for a tour of the village, to show me what sort of things her parents had been doing over the last ten years or so. Everywhere she was greeted with great affection, since she had more or less grown up on the farm, and she chatted familiarly, in fluent Amharic, with young and old, male and female. She would then fill me in on who this or that person was, often with amusing details. We looked into the school, and to the community health clinic, and to the co-operative dairy, all developed by the Stanfords. Finally, we went to pay our respects to the headman of the village, a stately grizzled old boy sporting a large flywhisk, whom I had met briefly before Christmas, when he was presiding at the game of *genna*.

"The Ethiopians are a lovely people, really," she remarked to me as we strolled back up to the house to lunch, "but if Daddy wasn't there to keep an eye on things, none of this would survive. They only keep it going to please him. I'm convinced of that. I don't know whether there will ever be change. Not in my lifetime, I don't think. But I like things the way they are, after all. I just look around, and I think, who needs progress?"

"Yes," I nodded. "After all, what have we got to offer? The Cold War? The arms race? Either rampant capitalism, which will make paupers out of most of them, or a grim Communist regime, which will make paupers out of all of them. That's what I came out here to get away from, after all. I wouldn't wish it on anyone."

"Oh well," said Isabel, not wishing to seem to criticise her father's efforts, "I don't think we've contributed very much to their ruin here, I must say. And above all, it's all been done only after consultation with the elders, and endless debate, so at least it's the community that has chosen it, to some extent. It hasn't just been imposed on them from above, as it so often is."

"Yes," I agreed hastily, "it does seem like a very happy community. Your parents have obviously done a great job here."

And indeed they had. Nyala Farm was a sort of paradise, at least to the casual observer like myself. The only question was, I thought, how long the outside world would let it alone.

We had a copious leisurely lunch, during which the Brig was in a reminiscent mood, particularly about James. Louise also reported that they had received a nice letter from Caroline, saying how much she missed them, so I revealed that I had got one as well, saying the same sort of thing.

Louise looked at me shrewdly. "You know, Luke, I think that Caroline was rather taken with you, if the truth be told. But it's probably just as well that she went back, after all."

"Yes," I said, mildly, "I'm sure you're right."

After lunch, we all retired for a siesta and then, after a (comparatively) quick cup of tea, we set off in the Landrover for the ride back to town. Despite my Aunt's words, as we drove along the bumpy road, I found that my mind was on Caroline – the smell of her hair and skin, the feel of her body against mine.

Coming up to the Easter Holidays, I had an unexpected adventure when, after a number of postponements, I accepted an invitation from Manolis Hadjidakis to visit his father's plantation down in Metahara. He also invited also a number of the other seniors, with the plan of hunting some wild pig or oribi, so it was quite an occasion. I felt curiously honoured, while also somewhat out of place.

We went down on the train on a Friday the afternoon. The drive to the station was a tight squeeze, since I had offered to drive everyone there in the Fiat! I left it there for the weekend, hoping the Somalis wouldn't set their eyes on it for spare parts. It was my first journey on an Ethiopian train, and it was quite an experience. Pretty slow, for a start. The train stopped at a series of little stations, at each of which there was more or less the same degree of confusion – much shouting and waving of hands, as people and bundles were piled on and off. Hucksters bustled up and down selling fruit, bottles of beer and soft drinks, and various dangerous-looking concoctions. I stuck to bananas and beer, bargained for ferociously by Manolis on my behalf.

It was pretty crowded and malodorous, even in first class, so it was a great relief when, after about three hours, we stopped, very briefly, at the little station that served the plantation. Manolis had warned us to have our bags ready, and to jump out as soon as we were stopped, but I still managed to jump only as the train was starting to move out again, and rolled over and over down a grassy bank, clutching my bag, much to the amusement of everyone, particularly Manolis.

"Ah sir, truly, that was a great jump! Where you learn to do that? You did not tell me you were in the army."

Metahara was a hundred miles or so down on the way to the coast at Djibouti, so once again, as at the Awash, or even at Yohannis' hunting lodge, the air was warmer than at Addis, even as the sun was going down.

There was a Landrover waiting for us, driven by the foreman, Mr Lefteris, a stately old Greek with silvery handlebar moustaches.

"Eh, Manoli," he greeted Manolis with a bear-hug and a punch on the arm, "Ti kaneis? And who are your friends? You are all very welcome."

Manolis introduced us. I was put in a place of honour in the front seat, with Manolis sandwiched between me and Mr Lefteris, over the gears, and the others in the back. We bumped away up a dusty trail into the gathering dark.

It took us almost half an hour to reach the main complex of buildings which housed the personnel of the plantation. We drove into a spacious yard, one side of which constituted the rear of the owner's bungalow. I was shown to a room of my own, while the boys had to bed down together in a sort of dormitory.

I settled myself in, and made my way cautiously into the front of the house, where I found Manolis' father waiting for me in a large, spacious sitting-room, the walls of which were hung with native rugs, and adorned with shields, spears and a number of useful-looking rifles. Mr Hadjidakis was a tall, impressive Greek gentleman, with piercing blue eyes, and a fine, greying moustache. He greeted me, offered me a choice of beer or ouzo – of which I chose the latter, to his pleasure – and ushered me out onto the verandah, from which there seemed to be a fine view of rolling savannah, though the darkness obscured any detail. The African night embraced us gently, crickets and frogs providing a soothing background chorus.

"The boys will be along in a little while," said Mr Hadjidakis, "but I wanted to say to you right now, before Manolis comes, how much I am grateful to you for your kindness to him. He speaks of it often."

I gulped, all too conscious of the nature of the kindnesses I had been conferring upon Manolis, but it seemed as if he had not been too specific, after all, in describing them to his father.

"Oh," I said, airily, "I must say I enjoy our conversations. I'm glad that he does too. He's an intelligent fellow, Manolis, I must say. He has an enquiring mind."

"Yes," said his father, "I think that that is true. That is why I wish to give him a good education. But he finds it hard to be away from home, boarding in this school. That is why it is a great pleasure for him to be able to come and talk to you."

We went on to talk about why I had come to Ethiopia, and then Mr Hadjidakis told me why he had come.

"It was after the war. I was really sickened, I must tell you, with what was happening in my country. You see, we had fought, many of us, to get rid of the Germans, and also to get rid of the king. He was a German too, after all. And you know, some of us were Communists, and some were socialists, like me. But we were all Greeks. We all wanted the best for our country. But then the Americans and the British, they come in, they put the king back. And they start a civil war, a very bad civil war. So I say to myself, this is no good, I get out. I take my son Manolis – he was just a little kid – and I get out. I know there are Greeks in this country, so I try here. And here it is not bad. One can make a living. Old Lefteris here, for example, he have been here since the thirties.

All through the Italian times he stay. He keep his head down, do his job, help the Ethiopians when he can, and he survive. Now he is my foreman. Very good man."

I was fascinated at this account. I found it strange that he had not mentioned a wife, such as he must surely have had, but I didn't like to ask. I had no real knowledge of what had happened immediately after the war in Greece, except that I believed that it had been saved for democracy from Stalin's clutches. But the truth, as usual, seemed to be somewhat more complicated. I felt confirmed in my decision to retreat from the Cold War.

The boys made their appearance, and we went in to dinner. I was amused to be in the company of a number of my toughest customers, all pretty difficult to keep in order in the classroom, but now transformed into serious and disciplined hunters: Manolis himself, his fellow-Greeks Basil Kremastiotis and Theodoros Katsargyris, who were 'town' Greeks, and thus slightly out of their usual stamping-grounds here, and Vartan Malkhassian, a large and villainous-looking Armenian, who, however, when the chips were down, revealed a heart of gold. A good company to go tiger-hunting with, as James used to like to say about people he approved of.

The next day we were scheduled to climb a neighbouring volcano, Mt. Fantale, officially dormant, and bag any game we came across, which would probably be kudu or oryx. That night, if we still had any energy left, we could go after pig on the plantation itself, where we might catch them raiding the sugar-cane.

We were up at dawn, and after a quick breakfast piled into Mr Lefteris' Landrover, which took us to the foot of the mountain, a journey of about half an hour along a dirt track. We all carried satchels with picnic lunches and water, but we also had a local boy as guide, who carried more supplies. Only Manolis and Vartan carried guns. At the foot of the mountain the trail petered out, and Mr Lefteris deposited us, promising to come back at around five o'clock that evening.

The climb was at first quite easy. Manolis engaged me in conversation as we trudged along.

"Well, sir, how you like our part of the country?"

"I think it's just great, Manoli. I love it. I haven't got out in the countryside very often, and I miss it. I live in the country back home in Ireland, so I'm used to having it around me."

"Ah, sir, I think Ireland must be very beautiful."

"Well, it is, yes, in its way. The part where I live, Wicklow, is particularly so. But it is not as beautiful as here. And it does rain a lot."

Manolis spat contemptuously.

"This place is not beautiful, sir. How you can say that? It is uncivilised. It is full of savages. Look at it! It is a mess."

I laughed.

"Now, Manoli, you're being unreasonable, and you know it."

He grinned broadly, but would not give in.

"No, no, sir, I tell you, these people are really savages."

We had by this time reached a small plateau, which ended the easy part of the ascent. In the middle distance, under some acacia trees, a small herd of oryx were shading themselves. Beyond them to the right, and back behind us, stretched an endless vista of apparently empty country. Manolis waved an arm at it. "Down there, sir, there are Carayou. You have heard of Carayou?"

I shook my head.

"Ah, the Carayou, if they catch you – excuse me for saying it, sir, but we must be frank – they will cut off your orchides – what is that? Balls, I think you say – and hang them round their necks, as a trophy. That is savages! That is why I carry a gun always when I leave the plantation." He patted the rifle slung over his shoulder.

I gulped. I had not heard of the Carayou, and I was not quite sure that I believed in them, but I had heard stories of the habits of the Danakil, further down in the lowlands towards Djibouti, so one couldn't be sure.

"Are there likely to be any of them around here?" I asked, tentatively.

"No no, they will usually be down in the plain. But one must always be careful."

We stopped for a drink and a snack before attempting the serious climb, and then started up the ascent to the crater. I found the going tougher than I cared to admit, not having taken that much exercise since I had come out here, apart from rather gentle hikes with James and Willy on Entotto. Otherwise, I reflected shamefacedly, my most strenuous exertions had taken place in bed. Manolis noted that I was dropping behind, and fell back to encourage me.

"Ah, sir, I think that perhaps you have been drinking too much beer with Mr Blakeney."

I attempted indignation, but laughter got the better of me.

"What do you know about my beer-drinking with Mr Blakeney?" I expostulated.

"Aha," said Manolis, craftily, "such things cannot be hidden, you know, sir. But this will be very good for you. You will see."

I hoped he was right, but for quite some time it seemed more probable that I would perish there on the mountain, to become a trophy for a Carayou. The slope seemed to get steeper and steeper. The ground under foot became little more than cinders and volcanic ash. We found a rudimentary path, whether of beast or man one couldn't tell, which wound gradually round the mountain towards the summit. It was now past noon, and the sun was becoming very hot. Conversation declined to a trickle. Theodoros and the others got further and further in front, the native boy padding along behind them.

Suddenly, however, after about two hours of this, we rounded a bend, and found ourselves within a hundred yards or so of the top. This provoked me to a final burst of energy, and I floundered up after Manolis to join the others at the rim of the crater.

The view that met my eyes was awesome. The crater itself was more than two miles across, largely blackened lava, with columns of steam rising at various points, but with some rudimentary scrub also beginning to assert itself, indicating at least that it was not currently too active. Beyond the crater, however, and behind us, stretched a vast panorama of Africa. To my left I could see the plain of the Awash, and the river itself, marked out by a slash of green. Directly behind us lay the beginning of the Danakil depression, extending off to the horizon. I picked my way down from the rim, found a large boulder, and slumped down in the shade of it to take in all this in comfort. The others gathered around me, and supplies were opened up. Now that the hard part of the climb was over, more serious refreshments were produced, including beer, hard-boiled eggs, and lightly-spiced legs of chicken. I looked out over the endless plains below.

"Now, Manoli," I said, "you surely have to admit that this is impressive." But Manolis was not inclined to concede anything. He shook his head.

"No, sir, all I see out there is wilderness. Apart from our plantation, which we cannot see, it is wasted space, with just some savages wandering around in it." He paused, and then added, with passion, "I really have to get out of this country, you know, sir. I think perhaps, when I am finished with this school, I will go to Australia. I have an uncle there. Here, I tell you, you are stuck."

The others started arguing with him, and a general discussion began, which I merely listened to with interest. Vartan, the large Armenian, spoke up most strongly in defence of the country. Ethiopia had plainly been good to his family, as it had to many of his compatriots, despite a degree of prejudice. But Manolis remained unrepentant, emphasizing his points with a brandished chicken-leg. Apart from anything else, as I had occasion to know, he was a man who liked an argument.

We spent a half an hour or so at this, polishing off a few beers each in the process, and then packed up the remains of the lunch, and headed back down the mountain. In many ways, going down is more dangerous than going up. My knees now began to get very shaky, and I had a number of close brushes with a sprained ankle, but managed to reach the lower plateau with no harm done. Now a debate ensued as to whether we should try to shoot a buck.

The buck themselves, whether they had sensed some danger or were just retreating from the heat, had all withdrawn from sight, but Manolis and Vartan decided, since we still had something over an hour to wait for Mr Lefteris and the Landrover, to go in search of them. The rest of us settled down in the shade of some acacias to have a snooze.

Having downed a couple of beers earlier, I had no trouble with this. I awoke, about half an hour later, to the sound of two shots, in quick succession. We all sat up and listened.

"Sounds like they may have got something, sir," ventured Basil. "Maybe we should go see if they need some help?"

That sounded a good idea, so we headed off in the direction of the shots, over the rim of the plateau to the east. As we reached the rim, and got a first view down into the valley beneath, we saw Manolis and Vartan some way below us, struggling with a medium-sized kudu, which they were dragging between them, their guns slung over their shoulders. They were moving as fast as they could, and seemed unduly agitated, frequently looking over their shoulders at something.

We started down the slope towards them. When they saw us, they waved frantically, and made signs that we should be quiet. I was suddenly anxious. Could there be a lion about, or a leopard? When we got up to them, we had our answer.

"Quick!" hissed Manolis. "Carayou – a bit way behind us, in the valley. But I think they hear the shots. They will come to search. Help us with this."

Each of the boys grabbed hold of a leg of the beast, and started to drag vigorously. To be of some help, I took hold of the head by a horn, and hurried along beside them. It was a fine animal, I couldn't help observing.

Manolis pointed at clump of bushes at the edge of the plateau, round a little way from where we were, and we headed for that as fast as we could. A few minutes later we had hidden the buck and ourselves in the bushes, and were peering out the way we had come, alert for any sound. Manolis and Vartan reloaded their rifles. Basil and Theodoros took out long knives from the leather scabbards at their sides, and tested them against their thumbs. Silence settled over the scene, except for some scattered birdsong. My leg became uncomfortable, and I shifted cautiously, snapping a twig.

"Shh!" said Manolis fiercely, and then continued in a whisper, turning towards me. "I am sorry, sir, but this is important."

I nodded. Five minutes later I could see what he meant. Over the crest of the rise there appeared four murderous-looking individuals, dressed only in loin-cloths and skins draped over their shoulders, but with ornaments of wire round their necks and rings in their ears. Each carried a spear, but fortunately no guns. They stood and looked around, seeming to sniff the wind. Then they moved cautiously forward across the plateau, heading for the acacias where we had been resting. They did not think to investigate our thicket.

"Damn it," whispered Vartan, "they will see our packs. We will have to deal with them. I hope that we can frighten them. I do not want to shoot. Come on!"

We let them get some distance from us, and then stepped out into the open behind them, Manolis and Vartan in front, guns at the ready. Manolis called to the Carayou harshly in Amharic.

They jumped round, startled. Manolis continued to shout at them.

He was not wasting time with courtesies. He was plainly telling them to fuck off out of there and mind their own business.

The Carayou hesitated, fingering their spears, weighing us up. Then Manolis aimed his rifle just a fraction in front of their feet, and fired. A spurt of dust rose up just in front of the group. The Carayou jumped, and backed away a few feet. Manolis hastily reloaded, and shouted at them again.

The Carayou muttered amongst themselves. We waited. I was conscious, suddenly, of being positively lightheaded with terror. If they charged us, what would we do? We could shoot two of them, but the other two might be onto us before the boys could reload. Then it would be knives against spears. And I was unarmed and useless. I felt humiliated.

After some muttering among themselves, though, the Carayou decided that discretion was the better part of valour. We had the jump on them, after all. They plainly weighed up the odds, and decided to back off. They made their way at an angle to us back across the plateau, giving off a stream of rather plaintive abuse at Manolis, until they disappeared over the rim. We waited for a short while, and then Manolis told the three of us to lay hold of the kudu and pull it down to our agreed rendezvous, while Vartan and he brought up the rear, guns at the ready.

We collected our packs, and moved off down the slope, half-dragging, half-carrying the kudu. As we reached the clearing from which we had started, we heard with great relief the sound of the Landrover in the distance, and within five minutes Mr Lefteris appeared on the scene. The boys gathered round him, telling him the story excitedly in Greek. They were now quite recovered from the previous tension, laughing at the memory of it. Mr Lefteris rubbed his chin, and looked speculatively up at the mountain, whence no sign of life was now visible.

"Come on," he said in English, out of courtesy, presumably, to me, "you get that deer on the roof, and we get out of here. I don't like this situation. Those Carayou, they come back with their friends. I no think they were so near here this time of year, or I no let you climb."

The boys heaved the kudu up on the roof, and tied it down securely with ropes. Its head drooped sadly over the windscreen, its mild eyes staring at nothing. Once again, I was given the seat of honour in the front, with Manolis in the middle over the gears.

"Manoli, old man," I said admiringly, as we got bumpily underway, "that was pretty impressive back there. You're a useful fellow to have around in a tight spot."

He grinned in mild embarrassment.

"Oh, that was nothing, really, sir. But you have to show them that you are serious. I am sorry, by the way, that I speak rudely to you back there, but it is important to be very quiet. These savages, they hear very good."

"Oh no," I said, laughing, "you were quite right. I think I'll remember that, though, when we get back to class, the next time I can't get you to be quiet. Pretend like I'm a Carayou, or a wild pig."

At this they all laughed. We travelled back to the plantation in a state of exaltation, with Mr Lefteris shaking his head sceptically.

The rest of the weekend was somewhat less eventful, though nonetheless very pleasant. The kudu was taken charge of by the kitchen staff, and made into a rather stringy, but tasty, stew for dinner, after which the boys went off to play cards while I stayed a while on the verandah with Mr Hadjidakis, sipping five-star Metaxa, and he told me stories of his adventures in the Ethiopian countryside.

We continued the conversation the following morning, when, after a leisurely breakfast, Mr Hadjidakis took me for a walk round the plantation, and told me more about the Greek civil war. He had been quite an activist, it seemed, fighting with the socialist militia, rather than the communists. One evening, he told me, he came back to his village to find that it had been bombed, and a lot of the women and children killed, including his wife and baby daughter. This had sickened him utterly. It was then that he decided to get out, with his remaining child, Manolis, and head for Ethiopia, where he had a cousin. Some time later his brother emigrated to Australia. If things got bad in Ethiopia, that was where he would head. He wished never to return to Greece.

It was a sad story, and greatly heightened my sympathy for Manolis, as well as for his father. I had wondered about his wife, whom he had not mentioned the previous evening. Now I knew. We'd had our civil war in Ireland, and that was nasty enough while it lasted, especially in its latter stages, but it had been nothing like this. It was strange to me, really, how calmly he related the story, as we stood gazing at an experimental field of pineapples that he was quite proud of.

Later, we caught the afternoon train to Addis from the little station, and reached the city towards dusk. There was less conversation on the way back. I studied my Amharic grammar, which I had brought with me in my backpack. The boys played cards. But I returned enriched in various ways, as it seemed to me. New dimensions had been opened up on various of my students. It was borne in upon me how superficial, after all, is the view one gets of someone in a classroom situation. I was not at all sure how well I had come out of the adventure myself – though a new level of friendliness certainly developed with the lads as a consequence – but I certainly gained an increased respect for them, and particularly for Manolis.

CHAPTER TWENTY-SEVEN

The winter term trundled uneventfully towards its close, and Simon and I, looking towards the Easter holidays, were making plans for an expedition to Harar. My curiosity had been aroused, I must say, by my conversation at the hunting lodge, on that notable occasion, with Major Samuel, and I had no difficulty in interesting Simon in the idea. We would not attempt to drive – that would be offering too many hostages to fortune – but take the train to Dire Dawa, and then go up to Harar by bus or taxi. I undertook to get in touch with the Major.

In the meantime, to bring some cheer to the drudgery of the Little Rains, I held a dinner party in James's for the McHughs, to which I decided to ask Safar Abdolov and his wife, in return for their hospitality. I found, to my relief and pleasure, that, as with previous social occasions with the Soviets and despite the Cold War, the Irish and Russians got on very well. Safar insisted on downing little shots of Jameson's along with wine between courses and became very cheerful indeed. He and Frank sang a number of songs after dinner, and exchanged Kerryman and Chuckchi jokes.

Then, two weeks later, I contrived to have my bachelor party in James's, having checked that Yohannis was available. Wolde was a bit bewildered by the whole project, but he went along with it, and I managed to keep the full enormity of what I was planning from Willy Buhagiar. Yohannis brought a consignment of his best pot, and his best *tej*. At my request, he brought along Prince Alex Desta, and a few of his other friends, including ladies. Maurice came, and also Knut. I even asked Marco, since many of his most faithful customers would be present. He was very pleased to come, and settled himself on the verandah with Maurice, swopping increasingly improbable stories about their respective adventures. Simon even suggested that we ask along Frewet and Berhane, but I regretfully drew the line at that. It occurred to me that Wolde might somehow get wind of who they were, and be outraged. As it was, he bore up manfully, and supervised an excellent buffet dinner, though it all must have been rather a shock for him. Jack and the rest of the band came, and we set ourselves up in the living room to play a few tunes.

Towards the end of the evening, when I was already fairly far gone, there occurred a little incident that left me a bit uneasy. Yohannis came to find me, took my arm, and led me out into the garden at the back, among Wolde's vegetables. The hens, in their little house, shifted on their perches and uttered muffled clucks, perhaps fearing a hyena. Yohannis seemed a trifle conspiratorial, and I was both intrigued and apprehensive. It emerged, though, that all he wanted was to ask about my planned visit to Harar. I told him that Simon and I were going to go down after Easter.

"Right," said Yohannis. "And you'll be visiting my friend Samuel, I think."

"That's right," I said. "He has very kindly asked us to dinner."

"Good! Well then, would you mind delivering a little letter to him from me?"

I paused. This sounded a little odd.

"Yes," I said, somewhat cautiously, "I'll be glad to, Yohannis. But what's wrong with using the post?"

"Ah!" he said. "The thing about this packet is that it is important that Samuel gets it, and that no one else does. One just can't trust the mails in this country, I'm afraid. And since you will be seeing him anyway ... "

I nodded, not much liking the sound of this, but not wanting to be churlish.

"Okay, no problem. Do you have it with you?"

"No, but I will have it sent round to you nearer the time. Okay?"

"Okay."

He patted me on the back.

"Thanks, Luke, old man. I am very grateful. And now let us just have one last joint – one for the road, as you say."

And he turned to go in. I followed him, conscious now, despite my fuddled state, of a distinct feeling of apprehension.

Simon and I took off for Harar as soon as possible after Easter, to give ourselves the best part of a week before term began for what we hoped would be a naughty as well as interesting few days.

The promised letter for Major Samuel turned out to be rather bulky – plainly not just a letter of introduction, which in any case I didn't need. I looked on it with some suspicion, but I felt there was really nothing to be done but deliver it as promised. I swore to myself, though, that this was positively the last time I would allow myself to get involved in any scheme of Yohannis's, however trivial.

Major Samuel himself had also written, very courteously, inviting us to dinner at his home on the Wednesday after we arrived.

We had a reasonably pleasant train journey down to Dire Dawa – first class was not too crowded – and then, after some haggling, contracted with a taxi at the station to take us up into the hills to Harar. It was a spectacular drive up, with the vast expanse of the Ogaden stretching out below us to the left. Harar itself, too, was all that we had been led to expect. The old town was an impressive sight, still surrounded by its mediaeval walls. We got there towards evening, and our driver took us to the hotel that Major Samuel had selected for us, which was on a narrow, picturesque old street near the Market, run (as usual) by an Italian. The cost was very moderate – no doubt the intervention of the Major inhibited any tendency to undue inflation. We were shown to a spacious double room, with a bath down the corridor, unpacked our things, had a wash, and went out to explore.

Harar was unlike any other city I had previously visited. It dated from the sixteenth or seventeenth century and featured predominantly Arab architecture, with some admixture of French colonial (like our hotel). It was throbbing with life; the marketplace in particular a hive of activity. There was lots of interesting silverwork and baskets and ancient weaponry, muskets, swords and spears. We accepted invitations to look at many things, but resisted buying on our first visit. There were beggars and urchins about, but they were not too bothersome. No lack of tell-tale red lights above doors, so we would not be short of entertainment, if we dared. The girls, we noted, seemed particularly beautiful, as they stood outside their doors in the evening light.

In a street off the Market, we came upon a sign directing us to Rimbaud's house, and went and paid our respects to that – a rather splendid, if delapidated old palazzo, more or less contemporaneous with our hotel, where the poet had held court in the 1880's, when dabbling in the import-export business.

As the sun was going down, we wandered through a gate, outside the walls, and joined a small crowd gathered to gawk at something, we knew not what. What was attracting them was in fact something rather entertaining. At a short distance from the crowd there sat an old man on a large stone, clutching a bag of bones, and around him was gathered a group of hyenas, to whom he was rationing out the bones. The hyenas would dart forward in turn, accept a bone, and slink off with it into the jumbled mass of ruins and undergrowth that edged this part of the city. I had never had such a good look at a hyena before. Usually they were just a shape loping across the road in front of one's headlights, or a ghoulish whooping in a nearby ravine. Here they were in plain view. They were remarkably ugly, awkward brutes, but no doubt excellently adapted to their role in life. Their shifty eyes scanned the crowd malevolently, and their great forequarters and jaws reminded one of what formidable scavengers they were. We learned later from the Major that the Hyena Man was a well-known figure, a half-mad eccentric who did little else but feed the hyenas. He was now something of a tourist attraction, and he had an old basket for contributions, into which we dropped a fifty-cent piece each.

After tiring of this spectacle, we turned back into the city and found a little Indian restaurant in a corner of the Market, where we had quite a hot chicken curry, washed down by beer. Then we decided to seek out a *tej-bet*, to see if we could find some congenial girls. Simon was particularly keen to try out the girls of Harar, of whom he had heard great praise. We saw what seemed a jolly little bar not far from our hotel, pushed through a variegated bead curtain, stepped inside, and found a table by the window. I looked around. There were native rugs on the floor and walls, giving the otherwise rather basic room a pleasantly exotic tone. A portrait of His Majesty looked down sternly on us from above the bar. At the other end of the room, a group of rather attractive girls eyed us speculatively, and giggled. Europeans were rare enough in town to be of special interest.

An older lady, not unlike Anna in dimensions, but Ethiopian, came over from behind the bar to take our orders.

Simon was in an expansive mood.

"'Ullo, love," he said. "I'll 'ave a beer – Melotti beer? How about you, Luke?"

I opted for a koniak.

"And my friend here will 'ave a cognac. Okay?"

Fortunately, she spoke some English. She smiled broadly.

"Okay, fine, I bring. You boys here for holiday? You like some fun, yes?"

"Oh yes, love," said Simon emphatically. "Fun is what we're here for."

"That's very good. We have nice girls here. You take a look?"

"Yes," said Simon, nodding appreciatively, "so I see. We'll 'ave a little drink first, though, and then we'll see how we feel, okay?"

"Okay. You boys make yourselves comfortable."

Our hostess went off to get the drinks, and Simon leaned back in his chair with a contented sigh.

"Well, what d'ye think, Luke, old chap? I reckon I like this town. It's got character. Knocks poor old Addis into a cocked hat in that respect."

"Absolutely," I agreed. "The difference is, it's a real city. I can see how Rimbaud could feel at home here."

The drinks came, and Simon turned to serious consideration of the girls.

"I reckon I'll take that tall one on the right," he said. "She has a lovely bum."

I picked a little round, cheerful-looking girl in the middle of the group, and we communicated our choices to Madame. She went over and brought the girls, giggling, back to our table. She took five dollars off each of us, plus a dollar each for the drinks, and gave the girls each a key.

"Five dollars is charge," she said, "but you like, you can give more. Okay?"

I found myself in a curious frame of mind, realising that while I'd had a number of casual, once-off sexual encounters over the previous few months, I had never considered sex consciously as a commodity. In Anna's, with Berhane, it should have been like that, but I had, perhaps foolishly, established a relationship with Berhane that made it into something more than a mere transaction. Here, however, there was no

371

question of that, and I found it pleasantly liberating. Since my girl spoke no English at all, and my Amharic was still pretty limited, there was not much chance of intellectual interchange. We communicated mainly by signs. There is love, in its various forms and degrees, and there is sex, and this was sex.

She slipped off her *shamma*, and then her frilly knickers, and climbed onto the bed, and I followed. Then she surprised me by rolling over, and presenting me her buttocks. I thought of rolling her back, but then decided to try this new position, since she had offered it. It worked surprisingly well, and proved most exciting, though not quite so convenient afterwards. There was a mirror at the head of the bed, and just as I was coming, I looked up and found myself framed in this. The ridiculous thought passed through my mind, for some reason: 'If Mother could see me now!' and I suddenly began to giggle. She looked up, and began to giggle too, and we ended our session in helpless, happy laughter. She slipped out of me, demurely tidied me up, and then herself, and dressed again. I pressed another five dollars into her hand. She kissed my hand in gratitude, and slipped out of the room.

"How was that, then?" said Simon, as we strolled back to the hotel.

I was still in a mildly pensive mood, meditating on the nature of the sexual transaction. In a way, that was what Caroline was aiming at – a mutually enjoyable encounter, without any emotional baggage attached. Caroline missed this ideal by a mile, as far as I was concerned, but this was much more like it. I hoped that it was mutual – at least my girl liked her five dollars, whatever about the rest of it. I hoped, also, that I was not oppressing or exploiting her. She was already in this position, after all, for whatever reasons of her own (perhaps just trying to raise a dowry?) and she seemed pretty cheerful about it. That was something I liked about the girls here – no sense of sleaze or corruption. No guilt, no furtiveness, no pimps. I had never dared to try a prostitute in Europe, where my impression of the scene involved all of that, and it did not attract me.

All this, however, I felt, was a little too philosophical for Simon in his present mood, so I kept it to myself.

"Oh, that was great," I said. "She was a nice little thing – very obliging. How about you?"

"Ahhh!" Simon smacked his lips reflectively. "She was a bit of all right. Great figure. Great legs. Very obliging, too!"

He didn't elaborate, and I didn't ask him to. We had another drink in the lounge of the hotel, and then went up to bed.

As we were lying in the dark, however, listening to the muted noises of the street, Simon spoke. His mood had changed to something more serious.

"La Touche, you bugger, are you awake?"

I grunted.

"You know," he continued, "I almost don't like to mention this, because it seems sort of paranoid, but I had a very strange vision back in that *tej-bet*. I came out a little before you back into the bar, and just as I came in, I saw a fellow slipping out through the bead curtain onto the street. It looked as if he'd just been having a word with Madame, and damn me if he didn't look like one of your chum Tamrat's friends. He had all the look of a spook – the smooth suit, the dark glasses. I wonder what the fucker was up to?"

A shiver went down my spine. I had not mentioned to Simon the number of previous disquieting incidents I had experienced, and I was not inclined to now, but I had a nasty feeling that he was not fantasising. And in fact, now that I came to think of it, Madame had been somewhat restrained in bidding us goodnight, as we left. What could be going on, though? Did Tamrat and his cohorts really have nothing better to do but to follow me around the country simply because I was a friend of Yohannis'? It was infuriating, as well as unsettling.

"That is certainly weird," I said, cautiously. "I wish I'd got a look at him myself. I hope you are imagining it, but I suppose it's possible that we're being kept under surveillance. This is a police state, after all, when all's said and done. There's probably no sense in worrying about it, though. We're not doing anything wrong, after all. Fucking is not illegal in this country, God knows! And Harar's not out of bounds, or anything."

"No," said Simon, "not as far as I know. The only thing that occurred to me that might interest him, if he knew about it, would be our visit to your friend the Major. They mightn't like us fraternising with the army. What do you think?"

That thought had in fact occurred to me, and it bothered me, but I was really not prepared to give in to it.

"Well," I said, grudgingly, "I suppose that's true, but I can't see how we can decently get out of it now. And anyhow, God damn it, if they have some objection to that, let them just say so, instead of snooping around in the shadows. Otherwise, I feel free to accept invitations to dinner from members of the armed forces. I'm certainly not conspiring to overthrow the goddamned state, so I don't have anything to hide."

As I said that, I thought of the packet, but I firmly put it to the back of my mind. I was not going to mention it to Simon, for fear of causing a row. The packet and its possible contents were not my business, anyhow. If Samuel was up to something with Yohannis, then that was his lookout, not mine.

"Oh well," said Simon, "the hell with it. We're here to have a good time. Let's just do that." And he rolled over and went to sleep.

I stayed awake rather longer, staring at the ceiling, but finally I too rolled over, and the exertions of the day mercifully caught up with me.

CHAPTER TWENTY-EIGHT

Next day we poked around the town again during the morning, and then decided to take a local bus to the neighbouring town of Jigjiga, which had been recommended by our host in the hotel, a cheerful Italian called Signor Salvatori. Simon engaged him in conversation after breakfast, and asked him for recommendations. It seemed as if we had seen most of what Harar had to offer, so he suggested perhaps we would like to take a drive to this other place – not as interesting as Harar, but the countryside would be worth seeing, in particular a succession of curious standing or balancing stones that had been left by some geological upheaval or other, which we should look out for.

Signor Salvatori proposed a taxi, but we decided that a local bus would be more fun. There was one every hour, and the ride would take about two hours. We were due at Major Samuel's around seven, so we had lots of time, since the bus left from the Market at eleven o'clock. It was in fact a rather bumpy and smelly ride – lots of old ladies with baskets of groceries, chickens, and even a goat – but we were not willing to admit that Signor Salvatori had been right about the taxi. We felt that we were communing with the people, and were determined to make the best of it.

Our immediate conditions may have been trying, but the scenery was extraordinary. We travelled over a high, rather barren plain, up from which there protruded, at intervals, these strange rock-formations, either standing stones, or, even more remarkable, stones balanced on stones. It was hard to imagine how they could ever have got into such positions. As we were admiring some of these, about half an hour out on the road, a voice broke in on us from across the aisle. We looked over at a smiling, fresh-faced young Ethiopian, in military fatigues, who seemed determined to engage us in conversation.

"Hallo!" he said, "How are you? You are interested in our stones?"

"Yes," I said. "They're certainly remarkable. Do you know how they got like that?"

He laughed.

"The people here, they say they are put there by the *zar* – you know, by devils. But me, I do not believe that. I think it is just nature. Maybe a big flood some time – something like that."

He introduced himself as Tesfaye, and explained that he was an officer cadet in the military camp at Harar. He was going back to his family for a few days for his brother's wedding. We introduced ourselves, and told him that we were teachers in Addis Ababa, having a short holiday in Harar. Tesfaye, it seemed, had just graduated from the Haile Selassie I High School in Harar, from which many students were recruited directly into the army. Since he lived in Jigjiga, he had to be a boarder, but he had been given a scholarship. He was obviously a bright lad, and his English was pretty good. We decided that we liked him, and chatted to him fairly continuously across the aisle for the rest of the journey, he being pleased to practise his English, and we being by now rather bored with the scenery.

We reached Jigjiga, and stepped down from the bus into the midday heat and dust of the market-place. It looked a rather nondescript town, not by any means the equal of Harar, and we were rather wondering what we would do with ourselves for the next few hours, when Tesfaye solved our problem by insisting that we come to visit his home. We protested that we didn't wish to intrude on the wedding preparations, but our new friend was most insistent that it would be an honour. Simon and I looked at each other, and decided that really we might as well be doing that as anything else, so we accepted the invitation with thanks.

"We won't stay very long, though, Tesfaye, if you don't mind, because we need to get back to Harar in time to go out to dinner."

"Ah!" he said, interested. "You have friend in Harar?"

"Yes. In fact, it is someone that you might even know of. You don't by chance know anything of a Major Samuel Assefa, in the Military Academy?"

Tesfaye's face lit up.

"Major Samuel? Oh yes, certainly I do! Major Samuel is my commanding officer. He instructs us in strategy. That is very remarkable. How do you know him?"

At this point I began to wonder if I had not already said too much. Certainly I did not want to reveal how I had met the major.

"Oh," I said, vaguely. "We met at a party in Addis Ababa, and he very kindly said that, if I ever visited Harar, I must come and call on him. So now we are doing that."

This satisfied Tesfaye, and he was plainly most impressed. It was quite a short walk to his parents' house, which was a spacious bungalow inside a large wooden fence. Already by this time the compound was filling up with wedding preparations. I knew an Ethiopian wedding to be a major affair, which might very well go on for three days, so I was hesitant about imposing on his unfortunate parents, but in fact we were received very hospitably, ushered into an impressive, rug-strewn living-room, and made to sit in seats of honour, while various tasty snacks, together with *tej* and coffee, were served to us. The parents spoke no English, so Tesfaye interpreted, while his younger siblings looked on wide-eyed. The bridegroom, we gathered, was busy elsewhere. Tesfaye explained who we were, and who we were going to visit for dinner, and this was received with great astonishment. We had to explain what country we were from, and to identify Ireland (England was no trouble) Tesfaye had to go and get a school atlas of the world, and everyone studied that in wonder, shaking their heads and muttering.

Then an old patriarch, whom Tesfaye introduced as his grandfather, began a series of searching questions. Were we married? No, we assured him, we were not. He shook his head, and pursed his lips. Then he pursued his interrogation. How many cattle did we have at home? How many goats? Simon failed on both counts. I was able to lay claim to ten cows (stretching the truth somewhat – they really belonged to one of the neighbouring farmers), but no goats. This seemed satisfactory. The old gentleman nodded appreciatively, but advised me to get some goats. Then he seemed to lose interest in us, and younger persons took up the questioning. One of Tesfaye's younger brothers, half-astonished at his own boldness, asked us if we knew Elvis Presley.

Simon laughed. "No, Tesfaye, tell him I've not met Presley. But I 'ave met Little Richard, and he's even better. The real thing. Presley's just a poof."

But no one had heard of Little Richard.

We excused ourselves after about an hour, though we were urged to stay, as we thought that if we were caught up in the wedding proper we would never get out. Tesfaye accompanied us a little way back down the road, but then, with many apologies, went back to the festivities, so we had a little time to stroll round the town before getting back on a mid-afternoon bus.

"That was actually pretty jolly," commented Simon. "Pity we couldn't stay for the wedding, in fact. It would have been quite an experience."

I agreed. The encounter had transformed what could have been a rather dull excursion into something special. The dusty town took on a more pleasing aspect through a mild mist of *tej*.

The drive back was less crowded, but rather less pleasant. Nobody interesting accosted us, though my attention was caught, some way into the journey, by a rather grim-looking individual near the back of the bus who seemed to be keeping an eye on us. At least, on a number of occasions that I turned round, I found him gazing in our direction. He didn't seem to be in any sort of uniform, however, so I wasn't sure what significance to attach to him.

"Simon," I said, "just take a look back there at that fellow in the suit near the back. He wouldn't be anything like the character you saw last night, I suppose?"

Simon glanced back casually, and scowled.

"Fuck it," he muttered. "I can't be sure, but it could be."

"Oh well," I said, "the hell with him. If they want to put a tail on us, that's their privilege. Our conscience is clear." But I had to admit to myself that my own conscience was not entirely clear.

We got back around five-thirty, leaving just time for a shower and change before heading off for our dinner. We found a taxi without difficulty in the market, and spelled out where we wanted to go. Signor Salvatori had told us it would be no more than a fifteen-minute drive.

Major Samuel lived in a fine modern bungalow in a suburb of the city adjacent to the army base, plainly set aside for the military. The neat lawns and tree-shaded streets gave it a distinctly European look. The Major himself welcomed us at the front door, and ushered us into the living-room to meet his wife and one other couple, a Swedish officer, Col. Lindstrom, and his wife. After we had been introduced, I unobtrusively presented him with Yohannis' packet. He looked at it a moment, thanked me, and then stored it away in an inside pocket.

It was a pleasant evening. Nothing controversial or revolutionary was touched upon. Instead, the Swedish couple and ourselves exchanged impressions of the country. They had travelled more extensively than either of us, having been in Ethiopia for nearly five years, as Col. Lindstrom was seconded from the Swedish army on a five-year contract. Samuel explained certain geographical features on which we expressed confusion, and his knowledge of his country's history and geography was most impressive. I scored a success with my description of the climb up Mt. Fantale with the boys, and our confrontation with the Carayou.

"Aha!" said Samuel. "I must tell you that you were quite lucky there, in fact. There have been many examples of fatal encounters of travellers with the Carayou."

"I had never heard of them," I said. "I had heard tales of the Danakil, though."

"Ah well," Samuel explained, "these people are a branch of the Danakil, and they have much the same habits, I'm sorry to say. We have to be careful in making expeditions too far out of here. They do not like Amharas at all!"

Samuel's wife had not been in England with him – he had married after he came back – but her English was good too, and she had quite a lot to say for herself. She had gone to university, which was still quite unusual for girls, and now taught school in the town.

They served a very pleasant Western-style meal of roast lamb, with an apple pie to follow. Samuel had developed quite a liking for English food when he was in Sandhurst, and liked to keep up the tradition.

After dinner, I asked about his student Tesfaye. At first he had to think, since we had never learned his second name, but when I mentioned Jigjiga he recognised who he was, and praised him as a bright lad.

"That is a good thing that is happening," he remarked, in what was really the most controversial utterance of the evening, "boys like Tesfaye, who could otherwise not afford to continue their education, are picked out of the secondary schools and given scholarships if they will go into the army. Of course, that is a fine thing for us in a way, but it means that a lot of very intelligent people are concentrated in the army, and that could bring trouble in the future – especially if they don't find enough for them to do." He cast a glance at Colonel Lindstrom and smiled. "Intelligence is not necessarily the best basis for building a well-disciplined and obedient army, I think you will agree, Anders."

Colonel Lindstrom laughed.

"I am afraid that you are right, Samuel. Somebody has to have intelligence in an army, of course, but ideally not too many."

We did not stay late, as the army men had to be up early. Major Samuel drove us back to the hotel, since a taxi would have been hard to find at that hour. I did, however, notice another car, parked further down the street, which started up when we left, and followed us back into town.

CHAPTER TWENTY-NINE

I awoke in the middle of the night, in a state of confusion. The lights were on in the room, and it seemed to be full of policemen, all heavily armed. Simon and I were hustled out of bed, and made to stand facing the wall, with our hands above our heads. An older man, who appeared to be in charge, told us roughly, in rather broken English, to get dressed quickly, and to give no trouble. I thought I recognised him as the unpleasant-looking fellow at the back of the bus coming back from Jigjiga, but I couldn't be sure. Other members of the squad took charge of our bags, and began to look through them.

I found myself beginning to tremble uncontrollably as I tried to button my shirt, pull on my trousers, and tie my shoes. I tried not to look at Simon. Neither of us said anything. We were both operating in a kind of daze.

Then it occurred to me that by acquiescing in this intrusion in silence we would seem to be admitting some sort of guilt, and this steadied me. I stood up.

"Wait a minute!" I said, "What is going on here? Who are you? What are you doing in our room?" I turned towards the officer in charge, trying to summon up all the indignation I felt was called for. "I demand an explanation!"

Even as I uttered this rather stereotyped protest, there was a dead weight in the pit of my stomach. With blinding clarity it came to me – it was that damned packet. I should never have touched it. Just to confirm my suspicions, the officer in charge reached into the inside pocket of his jacket, and took out the accursed object. Then he advanced towards me, eyeing me with venom. He thrust his face close to mine, and when he spoke, it was in tones of concentrated rage.

"So! You wish to know what we are doing here, Mr La Touche? You demand an explanation?" He shook the packet in front of my nose. "This is the explanation. You know what this is? You have seen it before?"

Then he suddenly struck me across the face with the back of his hand. It was a stinging blow. I reeled back across the bed, clutching my jaw. It was a long time since I had experienced physical violence, and it sent me into shock. I lay prostrate on the bed, trying to gather my thoughts. I tried to think of other things that innocent victims should be calling for, but they all sounded absurd. Ask to see a warrant? Demand to be allowed to consult my solicitor? Make a phone call? All these requests seemed grossly inappropriate to a hotel room in the depths of Africa, in the middle of the night. Simon, I noticed, was saying nothing, and I found that particularly ominous in a man known for his belligerence. Doubtless he was blaming me for all this, and I had to concede that he would be largely justified in that.

A hand seized me roughly by the arm, and dragged me up off the bed.

"Come on," snapped the officer in charge, "Get moving."

Simon and I had our hands handcuffed behind our backs. Then we were hustled out of the room, and down the stairs of the hotel. As we were being pushed through the hall, I caught a glimpse of the horrified gaze of our previously jovial host, Signor Salvatori, standing in an old-fashioned nightgown at the entrance to his personal quarters. I felt an absurd impulse to apologise, but I was frog-marched through the front door before I could do anything about it.

Outside, we were bundled into the back of a van, with a number of armed police to guard us, and driven away at speed. Simon and I sat side by side on a bench at one side of the van, our guards facing us on the other, machine-guns at the ready. Only now did Simon exhibit some reaction.

"You fucking idiot!" he hissed into my ear. "Now what have you got us into? You and your royal chum!"

One of the guards opposite made a gesture with his gun, and told us to shut up. It was just as well. I had no answer to make.

We lurched uncomfortably along a bumpy road for about twenty minutes, seeming to drive out of the town into the countryside, and turned abruptly off the road, into a military aerodrome. Before we even got out of the van we could hear the engines of a plane warming up. Then the doors were flung open, and we were pushed out onto the runway. My jaw was still sore, and I had no way of rubbing it. I saw the officer in charge, who had just got out of the front of the van, and had come round to give orders to the soldiers and some crewmen. I called to him in what I hoped was a suitably respectful tone.

"Excuse me, officer, but may we know where we are being taken?"

He turned and walked towards me. I thought he was going to hit me again, but he contented himself with words this time.

"No, Mr La Touche, you may not know where you are being taken. You may not know anything. I do not want to hear any more from you, do you understand?"

I nodded, thoroughly cowed. Nothing like this had ever happened to me before, and I had not the least idea how to behave. With hands handcuffed behind my back I felt especially vulnerable. There was obviously nothing to be gained by provoking this man. Simon had grasped that better than I.

We were bundled onto a small plane, crudely furnished with benches running the length of the interior. At least now our hands were untied, or we would have been falling helplessly all over the place. Without much delay, the door was closed and we rumbled off into the night sky. We were able to see out through the portholes, though there was very little to see, except a bright crescent moon, which appeared and disappeared according to the direction our course took. Below us, the ground was dark.

After about half an hour the lights of a large city began to appear, which I felt had to be Addis. This seemed better, at least, than being spirited off to Gamu Gofa or some other remote corner of the Empire, as I had feared for a while. The plane's wing dipped, and we came in to land.

I began to realise how, in an appalling situation such as this, a fatalistic acquiescence sets in. One begins to fall into a kind of stereotype: 'the prisoner'. I no longer wished to protest or struggle against the indignities being imposed on me. I simply wanted to know what I had to do next, and to do it. I had become an automaton in the hands of my captors. My state of mind was not helped by the fact that I recognised that I was guilty of something, if only of monstrous stupidity. And I had sucked poor old Simon into it as well. At least, I resolved, if I can ever get to someone who is prepared to listen, I will insist that Simon had nothing to do with anything, and must be released immediately.

As for myself, I was resolved to indulge in no heroics. I would tell them anything they wanted to know. I felt no obligation to Yohannis whatever. In fact, I was furious with him. He had cynically used me as a pawn in whatever crazy game he was playing, and had now dumped me in the shit. I felt no sympathy for the fact that he had probably got himself, and the unfortunate Major Samuel, who was plainly a decent man, into far worse trouble, through an extraordinary degree of naiveté on his part.

How could he have been oblivious to the fact that his every move was being watched, and that sending me with a letter was really no different than sending it through the post! I resolved again that if Col. Tamrat, or anyone else, wanted information, I would not stint them. I would sing like a canary. I tried to console myself that if they just intended to shoot us, they could have done that before now. No need to bring us back to Addis for that, surely.

The plane came in for a very bumpy landing, and we found ourselves deposited on the runway. Our handcuffs were replaced, and once again we were bundled into a police van. Neither of us attempted to say anything on the short journey into town. This van had windows, so we were able to get some idea of where we were going. We ended up in a large compound on the south of the city, which I presumed was some kind of police headquarters. The van drove in through the gates, and came to a stop in the middle of a courtyard. Again, we were bundled out. As we stood together on the concrete, fearing that we might be separated after this, I contrived to whisper to Simon.

"Look, as soon as I get to see anyone, I will insist that you had absolutely nothing to do with anything, and must be released. Okay?"

To my relief, Simon glanced at me and smiled, though somewhat ruefully.

"Thanks," he whispered back. "Good luck with that. I'll be saying the same, you can rely on it."

A guard stepped forward and silenced us roughly. Then we were marched off into the adjacent building. As I feared, we were in fact separated. I was taken to one cell and Simon to another somewhere down the same corridor.

It was still dark outside. My watch told me that it was a little before five o'clock. Our gaolers, having no doubt checked through our belongings, returned us our bags, so we had at least wash-things, and a change of clothes. We had not even had to hand over the contents of our pockets, so I still had my wallet, and even a penknife. Doubtless, I felt, they would get round to this in good time, but for the moment I was left alone, to brood on my situation and wait for the next move.

The bed was hard, and the pillow unpleasantly clammy. There was a single, rank-smelling blanket, which I was rather unwilling to pull over me, but the early morning air was rather chill, so I took a chance on it. I lay on my back, and tried to think calmly. I presumed that in the morning there would be an interrogation of some sort. Perhaps I would get to see Colonel Tamrat himself. I rather hoped so, much though I disliked him, since he would at least be a familiar face.

Surely any reasonable person would see that my role in anything that was going on was insignificant, indeed non-existent. It only required the application of reason. As I thought of this, I began to feel a little better. I began to go over all the signs and warnings I'd had over the previous months. I was inclined to curse my stupidity and obstinacy, but then I reflected, as I had often before, that really I'd had little choice, unless I was prepared to tell Yohannis unequivocally to his face that I wanted to have no more to do with him. And that I had simply not been willing to do. I could have refused to take that packet, though. As I thought the whole thing over, I seemed to be the victim of an ineluctable chain of events.

I must have slept for a while in these unpromising surroundings, because I was nudged awake in the light of day by a rather casual, non-threatening young policeman, who beckoned to me to follow him. Good, I thought. Now we can sort all this out. I pulled myself up off the bed, rubbed the sleep out of my eyes, pulled on my shoes, and followed him down the passage. However, all that awaited me was a very uncommunicative sergeant, or whatever he was, who (quite superfluously, it seemed to me) demanded my name, wrote it in a ledger, in Amharic transliteration, and then demanded that I take off my watch and turn out my pockets. Fortunately, the previous night, on arrival, I had taken out of my wallet a number of personal documents, and transferred them to an inner pocket of my coat, since now my wallet, watch, pen, penknife and house and car keys were impounded, and put into a bag.

I tried to get some information out of the sergeant, but got nowhere.

"Excuse me," I said, slowly and clearly. "Can you help me? I wish to speak to someone in authority. I wish to make a phone call."

He looked at me with a blank expression, and waved a hand.

"No, no," he said. "After, after."

I was then led I was led down the corridor to wash and go to the lavatory (a vile hole in the ground), then back to my cell. I hoped to catch some glimpse of Simon in the course of this, but no luck. The young policeman returned with a breakfast, in the form of a sort of chapati and sweet tea, which was not too bad. After that, however, I was faced with a complete blank.

Very little happened for the whole of that day, and it was a very long day. It was probably the most unpleasant day of my life so far, I reflected, although nothing very dreadful actually happened to me, it was simply the fact that nothing did happen, along with the anticipation of what might be in store for me. The crushing effect of sensory deprivation should not be underestimated. I had nothing to read, obviously, or even to look at, except the walls and door of the cell.

My only distraction was a letter that I had been carrying in my wallet for a month or so now, my mother's reply to my news of James's death. I pulled it out now from my inside pocket, and read through it once again, with difficulty, by the light of the miserable bulb hanging above me.

The reading of it again, in the circumstances in which I now found myself, suddenly made me feel very sorry for myself indeed. A lump came to my throat, and tears filled my eyes. I sat on my malodorous bed, staring at the opposite wall. Just as my life had taken a significant turn for the better, and just as my mother needed me most, I now, through my own stupidity, found myself in a situation that I might never get out of alive. As it seemed to me now, it would be fatally easy for these people just to take Simon and me out to the back yard and shoot us, and then dump our bodies in some remote part of the country. They could choose a ravine where no one would ever find us except some passing wild beast. There might be enquiries from the British Embassy and others, there might even by a formal protest, but what the hell?

They could deny everything, if need be. As I thought it over, I began to feel very vulnerable.

I lay back on the bed and stared miserably at the ceiling. I listened to the various distant noises, trying to make some sense of them. A cell door clanged, somewhere down the corridor; somewhere outside the window some heavy machinery was being manipulated, perhaps a tractor or a crane. From my immediate vicinity, though, I could make out nothing.

Taking my cue from the letter, I tried to visualise various aspects of Bellevue. I imagined myself turning off the main Dublin-Wicklow road, up the winding, narrow side-road leading to the estate. Then through the front gates, neat little gate lodge on the left, perhaps with Mrs O'Toole's washing hanging out in the garden beside it. Then slowly up the avenue, trying to avoid the worst of the potholes – I deliberately took my time about this, trying to visualise the various trees and shrubs, the cattle in the front field – and pull up on the gravel in front of the house. I actually managed to conjure up for myself the smell of wet leaves, of mown grass, of horse manure, of wood smoke.

In through the front door, dining room on the right, with La Touche ancestors looking down from the walls onto to the long mahogany table; christening cups on the mantelpiece; sideboard with silver, badly in need of polishing; tallboy, topped by its two cut glass decanters. Across then to the drawingroom, with its great mirror above the marble mantlepiece, sofa and armchairs, two glass-fronted cabinets full of books, bay windows looking out on the walled garden – beautiful in its way, but eternally in need of weeding and mowing. Sometimes my mother would conspire to allow a donkey or a goat to get into it, in the hope that they would keep down the grass. They spent most of their time and energy, in fact, polishing off the few remaining shrubs, or any vegetables that appeared above the surface, and then shitting all over the place.

I continued through to the back of the house, past a dark cubbyhole full of coats, boots, golf clubs and croquet mallets, into the kitchen, centre of my mother's world (Granny would probably still be up in her bedroom – only fairly late in the day would she appear, if at all). I imagined my mother at the kitchen table, cigarette in the corner of her mouth, cup of tea or instant coffee in front of her, in her ratty old cardigan, reading a letter from me that would have just been delivered.

All this helped to pass the time, but it also made me feel worse. I had never felt such nostalgic affection for the cold, draughty, dilapidated pile of rubble that I called home. I felt now that, if by some happy chance I ever got back to it, I would devote all my resources to repairing it and making it liveable. My new-found wealth made this a realistic proposition. All I had to do was somehow to extricate myself from my present situation.

Many hours later – it was hard to tell exactly how many without my watch – a different guard appeared with a bowl of chicken *wat* and some *injera*, and a bottle of water, which I hoped was reasonably clean. I ate the food eagerly, though the wat was fiery, and drank the water, though with misgivings. I tried to ask the guard when someone would see me, but he seemed not to understand English.

After this lunch, feeling now rather uncomfortable, I decided to try and take some exercise. Reckoning on seventeen hundred and sixty paces as covering one mile, I set out to cover that distance, pacing up and down my cell. It was only five paces long in each direction, so covering a mile was a tedious business, but it did serve to pass the time. I came to the conclusion that Col. Tamrat, or whoever was now in charge of the case, was deliberately trying to wear us down by this delay. It was in fact not at all a bad tactic, no doubt employed by police forces everywhere – simply leave the suspect to wait and brood, until he or she will be so pleased to see anyone that they will be quite ready to talk. In my case, I reflected, they didn't really have to bother. I was quite ready to talk already. But perhaps they didn't realise that.

I walked a full two miles, and then lay down again on my bed, and managed to doze for a while. I was woken in what I assumed was the early evening by the same guard, and escorted out to the lavatory, which I was glad of. Then again a tedious wait, and I was served with another meal of *wat* – a vegetarian, bean *wat* this time – and some more water.

I was just on the point of devising some other mind-game for myself when I heard a loud commotion from the other end of the corridor. There was the sound of scuffling, the banging of a door, and over all that the clear sound of Simon's voice raised in anger. He seemed to have completely lost control of himself. A cold fear gripped my stomach as

I heard him roaring that he was a British subject, that he was totally innocent of everything, and that he demanded to be allowed to call his embassy. He was plainly putting up quite a struggle. I heard the thud of footsteps as reinforcements came to control him.

"My God," I said to myself, "the fool – they'll destroy him!" I shouted through the cell door, telling him for God's sake to shut up and be patient, but no one heard me. The scuffling and the shouting receded down the corridor, and emerged out into the yard. Simon was plainly being led, kicking and roaring, away to some other part of the compound. I wondered whether this was premeditated, or did they simply not know what to do with him? Why was he not just shoved back into his cell? I began to have the most ominous premonitions.

Then suddenly shots rang out in the middle distance – one, two, and a third – followed by a dreadful silence. I stood frozen to the spot. Surely they could not have just taken Simon out and shot him? But that was very much what it had sounded like. In that case, they would be coming for me very shortly. I felt totally weak. I realised that, though I had toyed with the idea that they might execute us, I had not really taken the possibility seriously. Despite our rough handling, I had tacitly assumed that the worst that awaited us was a few days in jail, a sharp interrogation and reprimand, and perhaps summary expulsion from the country. Now I was confronted with a far more terrifying prospect.

I lurched back towards the bed, fell down on my knees, and, in my confused mental state, tried to pray. As it seemed to me then, it would probably be my only chance to do that. I found that I could not think of any prayers. Instead, all sorts of things passed through my mind. I would never see my home again. My mother's life would be shattered. I would never see Caroline again. There were so many things I had wanted to do, I realised now – write, travel, perhaps do a higher degree. Suddenly, my life, which had seemed hitherto to have very little direction, appeared a promising, purposeful enterprise, rudely cut off before its prime. I buried my head in the rancid pillow and wept bitterly.

But ten minutes, twenty minutes later, the silence continued unbroken. No one came to drag me away. No one came at all, for many hours. Then a sleepy guard, different from the one before, came to take me out once again for a wash and a visit to the lavatory. He also seemed to speak no English, and refused to be spoken to, so I was left no wiser, and racked with anxiety and remorse.

That night I lay awake till near dawn, in a state of the utmost misery. It seemed to me plain that, whatever their ultimate plans for me, they had simply taken Simon out and shot him. Had that been their plan all along, or had he provoked them? Either way, there was no avoiding the conclusion that it was all my fault. Whatever about myself, he was a totally innocent bystander in this scenario, who had actually warned me repeatedly against involving myself in Yohannis' crazy schemes; now I had become the cause of his death. Even if I got out of there myself, how could I face the rest of the world after that? How could I face myself?

I did in fact get to sleep for a while, and awoke to try and come to terms with another day. I found that my anger against my captors was rising steadily. If I had come face to face with Col. Tamrat at that moment, I would have torn strips off him. After all, I was not entirely without friends or influence in this state, and I intended to make the fullest use of this if given the chance. But that was the question gnawing at me – would I be given any such chance?

Once again, a wash and breakfast was provided by a stubbornly taciturn guard, and I settled down miserably to wait. This time, however, this time I did not have to wait very long. I had just decided to do my exercise routine again, when the door of my cell was thrown open. Two armed policemen appeared, and I was ordered to go with them. I still did not know whether I was going to my death or not, but I decided not to provoke them by carrying on as Simon had done. Instead, I walked out and down the passage, with one leading me and the other going behind.

We marched out of the building and across the compound to a rather pleasant, single-story structure which seemed to house the administration. I was marched up the front steps, and down a corridor into a large, bright room. At a desk in the room, with his back to the window, sat my old friend Colonel Tamrat. Good, I thought to myself grimly. Just the man I wanted to see.

The colonel rose from his chair, and greeted me blandly, waving me to a chair in front of him. The guards saluted, and withdrew. The Colonel resumed his seat.

"Well now, Mr La Touche!" he said, with a faint, thin-lipped smile. "What is all this about?"

I looked at him. "That is very much the question that I would like to ask you, Colonel," I said.

"Oh?" he said, rather more brusquely now. "Surely, Mr La Touche, you know why you are here?"

I paused.

"Well, I suppose it has something to do with the letter I brought to Major Samuel."

"It has indeed very much to do with that."

"Well," I said, "let me make it absolutely clear straight away, Colonel, that I am quite prepared to tell you anything that I can in connection with that. But first of all," and I straightened myself in my chair, "I want to know what you have done with my friend Mr Blakeney. Whatever about myself, he is absolutely innocent in this matter. He knew nothing of any letter. He must be released immediately."

Colonel Tamrat's face darkened, and he slammed a hand down on the desk in front of him.

"Mr La Touche, I will ask the questions here. You are not here to ask questions, but to answer them. You need not concern yourself with Mr Blakeney. He has been taken care of. We are here to talk about you, and what we are to do with you."

A cold shudder went through me, but at the same time a rising sense of anger. I decided to respond calmly, though, to give him less excuse for violence. As long as I could keep talking, I felt, I had some hope. The Colonel, I had to admit, interested me, much though I disliked him. His English, like that of Yohannis, was virtually perfect, though he spoke it with something of an American accent, indicating, no doubt, a period of study in that part of the world, no doubt with the CIA.

"I have said that I am perfectly ready to answer all questions that I can," I said coolly, "but I must ask first to be allowed to make contact with a legal representative. I wish to make a phone call."

Col. Tamrat leaned back in his chair, and gave an incredulous laugh.

"Mr La Touche, you do not seem to understand your situation. You are not going to be making any phone calls."

"You may not be aware of this, Colonel," I said, firmly, "but in civilised countries any person arrested is permitted to contact a legal representative. Even a mass murderer is permitted to do that."

He paused, apparently intrigued by the proposition.

"Well, well," he said, with heavy irony, "and to whom would you wish to make your phone call?"

I thought for a moment. A number of possibilities suggested themselves. Ewan Hardiman for one, at the Embassy. Or Willy. Or perhaps Nuri Boghossian. But then a better idea struck me. Why not go for the top?

"I would like to speak to the Minister of Justice, Dejazmatch Abebe Retha." Again, this provoked the Colonel to a sarcastic snort of laughter.

"You want to speak to the Minister! I do not think that the Minister will want to speak to you. Why would the Minister concern himself with you?"

I looked him in the eye, and spoke with all the authority I could muster.

"The Minister, as you should be well aware, was a good friend of my cousin, Sir James Mallory, and he knows me perfectly well. In fact, I entertained him to dinner two weeks ago, and he urged me particularly on that occasion to let him know if he could ever be of help to me. So I would like to make contact with him now."

The colonel's yellowish eyes narrowed, and he seemed to hesitate. I got the feeling that I had scored a hit here, and I decided to try and press my advantage. First, however, he blustered.

"This matter is no concern of the Minister's."

"Oh?" I said. "Is he not your boss, then? I rather thought he was."

Again, there was a pause. The colonel seemed to be turning things over in his mind.

"The Minister is a busy man," he blustered. "He cannot be bothered with matters like this."

"Well, I suggest you try him," I said. "I think you will find that you are wrong, Colonel. I can give you his personal phone number, if you like. Or at least I could if you would give me back my diary."

Again, I had the sense of scoring a hit. He looked at me with venom, but at the same time a flicker of anxiety crossed his face.

"Well," he said, "we will see about that in a little while. Meanwhile, you have some questions to answer."

I decided not to press the matter further, and to cooperate with him for a while.

"As I have said, Colonel, I will be glad to do so, if I can. I have no desire at all to be mixed up in any schemes which Lij Yohannis may be engaged on, and I certainly do not appreciate being used by him in the way that I seem to have been, As far as I was concerned, I was bringing a letter of introduction from him to Major Samuel. If that is not what it was, then I would be most annoyed to hear it, but I have no knowledge of that."

Colonel Tamrat leaned forward in his chair menacingly.

"So, you thought that you were bringing a letter of introduction, did you? Do you expect me to believe that? For what did you need a letter of introduction? Did you not know Major Samuel perfectly well? Had you not met him with Lij Yohannis at his hunting lodge?"

I had to admit to myself that he had scored a point there. This was shaping up in my mind like a sort of deadly chess game. If I had managed to capture the colonel's bishop, then he had just clawed back a pawn. My mind was racing, but I managed to remain calm.

"That is true," I said, "but I certainly did not know him very well. It did not seem strange that Lij Yohannis should give me a letter of introduction to him. Whatever else he may have wanted to say to him was not my concern at all."

I was conscious of being less than candid here, but I felt it to be important not to concede anything.

"But did you not wonder, perhaps, why His Highness could not pick up a phone and call Major Samuel? Why would he need to write a letter?"

I shrugged my shoulders.

"Colonel, I have no idea. I tell you, it did not concern me. It just seemed a reasonably natural thing for him to do, since I had told him that I was going to visit Harar."

The colonel grunted, and seemed to concede the point. He changed the subject.

"Well now, I wish to hear more about this party at His Highness's hunting lodge. There were some interesting guests there, were there not?"

"Well, there were actually two quite different parties, of course. The group on Friday were quite separate from that on Saturday."

"All right. And who were the guests on Friday?"

"I really didn't ever learn their names, I'm afraid," I said. "I am not very good with names unless I can attach something to them, and I did not have very much conversation with that group."

"Well," said the colonel, shrewdly, "you did at least know one of them, did you not?"

Then I remembered. "Yes, of course, I'm sorry. I did know Haile-Mariam Gabre-Hiwot. We play jazz together – as you know, I'm sure, since you seem to know everything. But I can assure you that our conversation did not touch on politics or revolution. It was not that kind of party at all."

The colonel leered. "No, I believe it was not, I have had some report of it. However, the party on Saturday was of a different sort, no?"

"Yes," I said.

"And who was there?"

"Now, Colonel, I think you know very well who was there."

"Well, I would like to hear you tell me."

"All right," I said, with a sigh. "There was Mr Safar Abdolov – who is also a pupil of mine, as again you doubtless know – and a Mr Peter Skrabanek, of the Czech Embassy. And of course Major Samuel Assefa."

"Good. And what did you all talk about?"

"Well," I said. "Major Samuel and I talked mainly about the beauties of Ethiopia, and its history, on which he is quite an authority. As far as I could gather, Lij Yohannis and the other two talked mainly about economics. It sounded rather boring. And then I talked a bit with Mr Abdolov about literature."

"Ah? About literature?"

"Yes. About Sean O'Casey and Yevgeni Yevtushenko, as I recall."

Again the colonel grunted.

"Colonel," I continued. "If what you want to know is whether anyone within my hearing was plotting violent revolution, then the answer is simply no. His Highness was certainly interested in Marxist theory on various subjects, but it was all very theoretical."

The Colonel leaned back in his chair, and surveyed me. He was plainly trying to make up his mind about something. Then he leaned forward towards me, pressing his fingertips together.

"Tell me, Mr La Touche, what is your opinion of Lij Yohannis? Do you admire him? Do you like him?"

I thought for a moment.

"Colonel, if you had asked me that just a couple of days ago, I would have replied without hesitation, yes, I both like and admire him. Right at this moment, however, I must say that I am angry with him, for having got me into this mess. But let me tell you my opinion of his Highness and what he is up to, if you are interested. I think that in fact Lij Yohannis is one of the best assets this country has got, and it is a great pity that his talents, and his patriotism, are not put to better use. So far as I can see, he only wants what is best for his country and for the Emperor. He just has a strong sense of what the dangers of progress are, and he wants to try and avoid them."

The colonel shifted impatiently in his chair. It was plain that this encomium was not going down very well.

"Ah!" he said sarcastically, "so that is your view? I thought that you told me that you were not interested in the politics of this country? Now I see that you are quite interested."

"No," I said firmly, "I did not claim not to have any interest. I could hardly fail to be interested. What I do assert is that I realise that it is not my business to interfere in your internal affairs, and I would not dream of doing that. Lij Yohannis is an old friend of mine from Oxford, and of course I am interested in what he is doing. But I must insist that I have no desire to be involved with it."

"And yet," said the colonel, with a nasty gleam on his eye, "you are involved, you see. Why were you carrying this letter?"

I sighed, and spread out my hands.

"Surely we've been through that. It was simply a courtesy to His Highness."

"Ah? A courtesy, you say. But I thought you said that you felt it was just a letter of introduction?"

My heart sank a little. We did not seem to be getting anywhere.

"Colonel," I said doggedly, "I have explained to you that I did not regard it as any business of mine what it was. As far as I was concerned, it was a letter of introduction." I paused. " I don't suppose you would care to tell me what in fact the wretched letter was about, just for the record?"

"You have really no idea?"

"Absolutely not."

"Well, perhaps in that case it is best to leave it that way."

I shrugged my shoulders.

"That is certainly fine with me. And now," I continued, "I really would appreciate it if you would either let me call the Minister, or call him yourself."

The colonel's face darkened. His fingers drummed on the table. But if he contemplated some violent response, he plainly thought the better of it.

"You are not here to give me orders," he snapped, though a trifle defensively, I thought. "I am giving the orders."

"I am not trying to give you orders, Colonel, I assure you," I said pacifically. "I am just making a request."

He pressed a buzzer on his desk, and the two guards reappeared. He had plainly had enough of me, at least for the moment. Colonel Tamrat addressed no further word to me as I was escorted from his presence.

I very much hoped that I had got my message across, but there was no way of telling. At least I had impressed on him, I hoped, that I was not without friends – that I was not just a piece of rubbish that could be thrown into a ravine without questions being asked. What bothered me now most was what they had done with Simon. Had they felt, perhaps, that he was easily expendable? There seemed no point, however, on pressing that question again now.

Back in my cell, I was left for the rest of the afternoon to brood further on my fate. I took my mile walk, and then lay down on my bed. I fell to thinking about my future. I resolved, if I ever got out of this, to change my attitude to life. It seemed to me that, in striking a pose of aimlessness and futility, I was giving in to gross self-indulgence. The last eight months or so began to seem somehow pivotal. A good many strands of my life had straightened themselves out, and come together. I now conceded that, apart from my present desperate situation, I had very little to complain about after all.

Certainly, being a public-school educated Protestant in contemporary Ireland was something that could be made an excuse for alienation, if one wanted to feel alienated, but I knew in my heart that after all, for all its faults, Ireland was an easy-going, hospitable sort of place, in which anyone who was prepared to muck in was granted a role in society. There was actually a pretty good network of people in the various professions, particularly the law, who would give me a helping hand if I presented myself to them, and there were various opportunities to make a good living, if I was prepared to take them. I felt suddenly as if I had grown up a couple of years in the previous few days alone, never mind the previous eight months. Such a pity, then, if I was just going to be taken out the back and riddled with bullets. Such a waste.

In fact, however, my interview with Colonel Tamrat must have been a success. Towards evening, I heard footsteps once again down the passage. This time it was the bad-tempered officer who had arrested me in the first place, accompanied by two guards with machine-guns. I stood up and looked him in the eye, ready to meet whatever fate awaited me. But the officer was now in a rather sunnier mood, to my great relief.

"Well, Mr La Touche, you are a very lucky man, I think. I am here to tell you that you are to be released. However, you have violated in the most serious way the terms under which you were admitted to this country, and consequently you are ordered to leave here within one week."

I looked at him, uncertain how to respond. A wave of relief flooded over me, but at the same time I felt indignant that I was still being judged guilty of something. However, this hardly seemed the time or place to enter into dispute on that issue. Above all, I wanted to get out of there. I felt as though I had been confined in that cell for weeks.

"Thank you, officer," I said in what I hoped was a neutral tone.

I gathered up my few possessions, and followed him down to the corridor. A policeman at a desk returned to me my wallet, watch, diary and other objects, and I was escorted out to a waiting car. A half-hour's drive across the darkened city, and I was deposited at the gate of The English School. I shook hands with the officer, whose name I never learned, and then walked the last few yards to the freedom of my bungalow.

CHAPTER THIRTY

My first concern, after I had dumped my things, was about Simon. He had never been far from my thoughts since the awful events of the previous night, but now I felt I must break the news to Graham without delay. Since we were still in the holidays, no one, I supposed, would necessarily have begun to worry about us, so I was gloomily prepared to have to unveil the grim news, and set in train whatever diplomatic processes were open to us. As I was making my way over to the Wiggins's bungalow, however, I looked across, rather wistfully, at Simon's, and noticed, to my surprise, that the lights were on.

Nothing was visible clearly through the window, since the curtains were across, so I knocked. There was a shuffling around inside, the door opened, and, to my enormous relief, it was Simon himself who stood in front of me. He had a black eye, and a bandage round his head, but otherwise he didn't look too bad at all. I have rarely been so pleased to see anything in my life. I would have embraced him, if he hadn't looked at me so malevolently.

"Well, look who's here!" he said. "It's La Touche, Ethiopia's most wanted man! I really thought we'd seen the last of you."

"My God, Simon," I gasped, "I really did think I'd seen the last of you. I was absolutely sure I heard you being dragged out and shot last night. What in the hell happened to you? How did you get out?"

"No thanks to you, La Touche, I can tell you. Come on in, you miserable fucker." And he led the way back into his sitting-room, where he slumped down in an armchair. I lowered myself into the other one.

"You want a beer?"

I shook my head.

"Okay. I can't drink myself at the moment, worse luck. Ol' Ratna gave me some painkillers. No, well, there was a little misunderstanding there, I admit. The silly buggers had actually come to release me, but they couldn't speak any English, and I was in a flaming bad mood by that time, and I really thought they were planning to take me out and shoot me. So I started to give them a hard time."

"Yes," I interjected. "I heard you doing that, all right. I was just up the passage."

"Well, they dragged me out into the yard and round a corner, but I was putting up such a struggle that one of them started firing into the air. Another one hit me on the head with a rifle butt, and that's all I remember until I found myself in a hospital ward, having my head bound up. By then, there was a fellow who could speak English, and he told me they were letting me go. Pity they couldn't have said that in the first place. Then they brought me back here. By the way, have you seen Graham yet?"

"No. I was just heading over to him, to give the sad news about you, when I saw your light on."

Simon laughed grimly.

"Ha! Well, I gave him the sad news about you, and the poor sod has been phoning up all over the place, trying to get something organised. You'd better go over and put him out of his misery. How did you get out, by the way? At least I was totally innocent. You were guilty as hell."

I sighed.

"I suppose I talked my way out. I had a rather sticky interview with our old friend Colonel Tamrat, but I survived it. So I'm free all right, but on the other hand I've been given a week to leave the country, which is pretty miserable, and damned unfair. I'm going to see what I can do to appeal that. All I'm guilty of, really, is crass stupidity, and I think they know that. Otherwise I assume I wouldn't be here at all. But as you say, I'd better go and break the news to poor old Graham. Christ, am I glad to see you, though! I really thought you were finished in there."

So with that I went back across the compound to the headmaster's bungalow, to face the headmaster's wrath. Graham, however, when he had recovered from the initial shock of seeing me safe and sound, was very nice about it all. He in particular could very well have been aggrieved, as I was considerably complicating his life, and that as a result of disregarding his repeated warnings and advice. But his dominant reaction seemed to be overwhelming relief that Simon and I were safe.

I was given a warm welcome – a protracted hug from Isabel, and a stiff gin and tonic. I had to tell the whole story again, from my perspective, ending with a description of my interrogation, and the ultimate sentence of expulsion. I assured him that I would try and have this reversed, but Graham's mind was turning already to setting up substitute teaching.

"I really am extremely sorry about this," I said. "I was well warned about Yohannis and his goings-on by all and sundry, not least yourselves, and I still pressed ahead. But I was sort of caught in a bind, really."

"Don't worry about it, old chap. It really wasn't your fault. As you said yourself on occasion, you didn't want to be rude to him, and it's hard to see at what point you could have stopped. It wasn't very smart to take that letter for him, I will admit. But there again, what do you say when he asks you directly?"

He really was being most magnanimous, and I appreciated it.

"It's very good of you to take it this way," I said. "As it seems to me now, I was just a disaster waiting to happen, one way or another. I'm only sorry that I involved other people in it. At least Simon is safe. But I wish I knew what was going to happen to poor Major Samuel, for example."

"Nothing good, I'm afraid. They're pretty rough with their own people. And it does look as if he was involved in something, after all. Presumably some sort of coup attempt."

"Yes," I said, "I'm afraid he possibly was, though I can't really believe that it was anything violent– he's a very fine fellow. And then what about the ringleader of all this himself? I'd really hate to see Yohannis destroyed, angry though I am with him at the moment."

"Oh," said Graham dismissively, "I imagine his uncle will just shunt him off somewhere out of harm's way – probably some minor diplomatic job. I don't know if they've got an embassy in Paraguay, but that'd be about right. Blood is thicker than water, after all. I wouldn't waste any sympathy on him. It's the others that he has involved in this that I would worry about. As for you, we'll have to see if we can get the authorities to reverse their decision, but I'm afraid I wouldn't count on it. They don't like *ferenji* to get involved in their internal affairs – except of course as a total apologist for the regime, like Richard Pankhurst or someone. So I'll have to start thinking about replacing you."

"I'm really sick about that aspect of the situation," I said. "At least, though, I can start them off next week, and help to break in whoever we can find – that is, if I can't get a reprieve."

Isabel was for making me stay to dinner, but I excused myself by saying that I had trespassed on them long enough. I went back to my bungalow to call Willy Buhagiar, who was about to set out to dinner. He had heard nothing of my adventures, since Graham had not thought to call him yet, and he was predictably appalled. I agreed to come over to his place in the morning around ten o'clock and discuss the situation in detail. Meanwhile, I had to possess myself in patience.

I tried to call Ewan and Susan Hardiman, but their houseboy informed me that they were away for the weekend. Then I thought of Simon again. I presumed that he was not fit for going out on the town. I certainly wasn't in the mood for any night-life myself, though it might have taken my mind off my problems. In the event, I gave him a call, to see if he'd like a drink or a bit of dinner. Tekla-Mariam had appeared, just in case I had returned (fortunately for his peace of mind, he knew nothing of my adventures either), and was preparing me a chicken pilaf.

Simon reminded me with some asperity that he was on pain-killers, and so off drink for a day or so, to his great annoyance. He was already having his dinner, but he agreed to come over for a coffee afterwards. I was glad of that, as I wasn't really sure if he had forgiven me or not for our nightmarish adventure. Anyhow, I needed company. Dinner with the Wigginses would have been too much, but a bit of a post-mortem with Simon would be welcome.

We sat for quite a time over our coffees, to which we added some whiskey – in Simon's case, in defiance of Dr Ratna's instructions. After playing it over a few times, the whole experience began to seem like a bit of a romp, but I could not get out of my head how I had felt at various times over the previous two days, and I still had to face the problem that this Ethiopian adventure was in danger of coming to an abrupt end. Simon tried to console me about this, if in a rather ham-fisted sort of way.

"Look on the bright side, you bollocks, for Chrissake. You're out of this crazy scene, and you can get on with the rest of your life. The die is cast! You don't even have to think about whether maybe you should stay one or two more years, or whether that might lead to your being trapped here forever. Look at me. I probably am stuck. I certainly don't know what the hell else I'm going to do, except that I don't relish going back to the good old UK. I might head for Australia or Canada eventually, not that I know exactly what I'd do there. I'll probably stick on here until I'm thrown out too – or have to run for my life, more likely, when the political shit hits the fan. Because that will happen sooner or later, whether with the help of your great pal the Prince or some other."

I thought about that for a moment, and found it both consoling and saddening.

"You wouldn't go back to England, then?"

Simon shook his head mournfully. "Naw. I reckon I'm spoiled already. I don't think I'd ever get Africa out of my blood. I'd just be restless, and then I'd be boring everyone rigid about how great it all was in Addis in the old days. Probably end up taking to drink." He gazed out of the window at the darkened compound. "No, count your blessings, Luke, old fruit. You're just as well out of all this."

I got up and poured another shot of Jameson's into our cooling coffee.

"Well," I said hesitantly, "maybe you're right. I was really getting to like this bloody place, though. Over this last half-year or so I've been actually getting myself together, you know, getting a new perspective on life."

Simon snorted. "Illusions, La Touche, illusions! All that was happening is that you were beginning to slip into the Addis way of life. That's the danger."

I took a slurp of the now rather alcoholic coffee, and shook my head.

"No, I really feel better able to face the outside world now, I think – that is, if I have to! Damn. I'll miss Berhane, though, and evenings at Anna's. I'll even miss old Jack and the jazz at the Paradiso. And tennis parties and film nights at the embassy. And play readings at Mimi Boghossian's. And safaris up country. And weekends at Nyala. Oh Christ. And I was really looking forward to going down to Kenya over the summer, if you'd have come with me. Shit!"

What I didn't like to say, as it would have grossly embarrassed him, is that I would miss Simon as much as anything. But perhaps he understood. I hoped he did. At any rate, he gestured with his cup.

"But this is just what I mean. You were getting sucked into the life here. I'd say you're getting out not a moment too soon."

"Well," I said, grimly. "I'm not gone yet. I have a few shots still in my locker, I think."

CHAPTER THIRTY-ONE

Simon began to develop a bit of a headache, in consequence of disobeying orders, so we broke it up not long afterwards, and I crawled into bed, not waking again till TM came in with the tea next morning.

At around ten, I drove across town to meet with Willy, and see what ideas he might have. It occurred to me as I drove that I had never been to Willy's place, though I knew where it was, and I was rather curious to see it. He had a small villa on the same road as James, about a quarter of a mile further out of town on the road to Gojjam.

Willy himself came to the door to let me in. He was in a rather grave mood. He led me into his study, which was a fine mess, the desk and floor strewn with law-books and papers. He must have forbidden his servant to touch it.

"Now, you'll have coffee, won't you? I'll tell Sahle."

He bustled out to the kitchen, gave some instructions in Amharic, and returned. He sat down behind his desk, waved me into the only other habitable chair, and contemplated me.

"Well, Luke," he said, "you have been a very foolish young man – and a rather lucky one, I think. I hear you pulled rank on a secret policeman."

I looked at him in astonishment.

"How did you know that?" I said. "I haven't told you the story yet."

"Ah!" said Willy, craftily, tapping a finger on the side of his nose. "I have my informants." He paused. "To be perfectly frank, I was having dinner with the Minister last night – or rather, he was there – and before I could approach him on the subject, he came up to me, and took me aside."

"Gosh!" I said. "So Colonel Tamrat did phone him after all?"

Willy nodded.

"What you weren't considering, though, when you engaged in your bit of name-dropping, is how far you might be compromising Abebe Retha himself."

"Oh?" I said, anxiously. "No, I'm afraid I wasn't thinking of that. I was just trying to save my skin."

"Well, you did that all right. But you see, you have to realise that Abebe's position is not really all that secure. As you know, he's quite a critic of the Emperor himself, and creatures like your Colonel Tamrat have a good deal of power to make trouble if they want to, even for him. You see, Tamrat is Secret Police. He's actually under the Minister of the Interior, who is a pretty nasty piece of work; not under Abebe – though he would have to defer to his views. However, don't worry too much. Abebe wasn't really annoyed – he had offered to be of help if you ever needed him. He did that in my hearing, after all. But he had to be pretty polite to your colonel, I can tell you. He managed to convince him that there was really no harm in you – but he had to agree to send you packing within a week."

I spread my hands in bafflement.

"But if I'm agreed to be harmless – and God knows I am harmless – why in hell do I have to be deported?"

"No, sadly, the Secret Police mind does not see things that way. The thing is that you have been involved in subversion, even unwittingly, and you have been in contact with people you should not have been in contact with. Moreover, I think, you seem to have got the better of the Secret Police, and you are being punished for that. They don't want you around on the expatriate cocktail circuit boasting about your adventures. They want you out. Whether or not you choose to tell your story in the rest of the world does not concern them so much."

Willy's servant brought in the coffee, and some *loukoumi*. As I stirred sugar into my coffee, I thought about the situation from this angle. It really seemed, as Willy laid it out, that the game was up.

"But look on the bright side," he continued (everyone seemed to be telling me this, I reflected). "You have had a most interesting few months, you found your father, you have acquired a considerable inheritance, and now it is high time that you went home and got on with your life. The man I'm most sorry for, I must say, is your unfortunate headmaster. He has a devil of a problem on his hands as to how to finish out the year."

"Yes, I agree. That's what really embarrasses me at the moment. But I had a talk with him last night, and he was really very decent about it. I can help a bit next week, if he can just come up with someone to hold the fort for the next few months."

"Oh well," said Willy, "we could have had a double 'disappearance' on our hands – or a 'shot-attempting-to-escape' scenario. Such things have certainly happened. I think you have been pretty lucky, really, though it did help to have influential friends! But anyhow, tell me the whole story from the beginning. I am most curious to hear it."

So I had to give Willy pretty much a blow-by-blow account of our adventure, glossing over such details as our visit to the *tej-bet*, but giving due weight to everything else. He shook his head and chuckled at intervals, but most of the time he listened pretty solemnly.

"Well," he said finally. "I don't think we'll be seeing any more of your friend Lij Yohannis for quite some time."

"He'll be all right, though, I hope?" I said anxiously.

"Oh, he'll survive," said Willy, with bitter irony. "And he'll be back in due course, when the Little Man has decided he can be trusted to do a useful job without stirring things up. No, it's the unfortunate Major Samuel that I would worry about. I'm afraid he's a dead duck, when they've extracted all the information they can out of him. Very sad – it sounds to me as though he was a very fine officer. Just the sort of fellow the country needs, really. But there it is."

"I suppose it is the army that will take over after the Emperor dies?" I said. "That's what everyone seems to think, anyhow."

"Oh, they do, do they?" said Willy. "Well, I expect that 'everyone' is probably right. But it all depends on what sort of army man takes over. They have some pretty nasty specimens in there, as well as fine fellows like your Major Samuel. It's more likely that the Colonel Tamrats of this world will take over. They're likely to be better organised, and more ruthless. And then I'm afraid we'll all have to get out as fast as we can."

It saddened me to think that this ramshackle playground for expatriates, with all its faults, could, and probably would, come to an abrupt, and possibly bloody, end, but it did serve to reconcile me a little more to the fact that I was going to have to leave it. I turned to broach that subject, on which I was conscious that I would need a lot of help from Willy.

"Well," I said tentatively, " I suppose I'd better start thinking of sorting out my affairs. I hate to give you this trouble, Willy, but on certain matters I don't know who else I can turn to – except Nuri Boghossian, of course."

"Don't worry. I'll be glad to help sort things out, and so will Nuri, I'm sure. We'll have to sell the villa, of course, and I can have your things shipped back easily enough. It's not entirely easy to send money out of the country in any quantity, but Nuri has various devices he can use – mainly by dealing with people who have foreign bank accounts. Being the President of the Supreme Court, I don't enquire too closely. And then I can put you in touch with James's Swiss bankers. I think you can just have his account switched to your name, but you may have to fly into Zürich in person to set things up. That could be quite enjoyable, though. Bring your mother along. She deserves a break. I would keep on that account, actually, if I were you. You never know when it might come in useful." And he smiled.

Something now occurred to me.

"Willy," I said, "a couple of things I wanted to say. First of all, would you please have a look round James's – my father's – things, and choose whatever you would like by way of mementoes. I would really like you to have a few things to remember him by."

Willy's eyes suddenly filled with tears. He looked away, down at the papers with which his desk was strewn.

"It is very kind of you to think of that, my dear boy. Of course, I would not wish to take anything of value, but certainly I would be very grateful for some things which would bring him to mind. His walking-stick, for instance. That sort of thing."

"Oh please, Willy, anything you like. I mean that. The other thing is that I must provide properly for Wolde, and for Tekla-Mariam. I thought I would give Tekla-Mariam my car, and pay for some driving lessons for him, and then give him a few hundred dollars over and above, but Wolde I think should have some kind of pension, if we can arrange that."

And so we spent the rest of the morning planning. Willy made a phone call to Nuri Boghossian at home, and he arranged to have a conference of the three of us on Monday afternoon, after school. Nuri was greatly shocked to learn that I had to leave, and the reasons for it, which Willy sketched for him briefly, but he was most anxious to be of help.

I was gradually coming to terms with the reality that my adventure in Addis was substantially at an end, and even that this might not necessarily be a bad thing. It was now mainly a question of tidying up loose ends, and making quite sure that I got into no further trouble.

On Saturday night I performed what was going to be my last gig at the Paradiso, and over beers afterwards I had to tell my story again. My American colleagues were wide-eyed with alarm, since an essential part of their Peace Corps training was never to get mixed up in local politics in any way, shape or form. Young Hailu, it seemed, had been questioned, but released – partly, I imagined, because of his father's wide influence, but partly also because he had not been implicated in the subversive aspect of our weekend at the hunting lodge. He was in a pretty chastened mood, though.

"Jeez, Luke," said Jack, "you were really playing with fire there. If that happened to any of us we'd be shipped out on the next plane – no kidding."

"And probably quite right too," I said ruefully. "It's become quite obvious to me now that this regime is not to be fooled around with. But I was just stuck, in a peculiar way. Yohannis was a friend of mine, and I couldn't just snub him and break off all contact with him. And anyhow, to tell the truth, he was good fun to be around, the bastard."

And so I parted from my jazz group, with many expressions of regret and mutual esteem.

On Sunday, I went to my final Addis Ababa church service, with its strange congregation of expatriates and exiles. The Padre gave his usual sermon and after I took leave of acquaintances there, Willy and I went for our now customary walk on Entotto. Wolde served a copious lunch at James's house, which I very much enjoyed, of course, but could not help reflecting, sadly, that it was for the last time.

Following a siesta back in my bungalow, I woke up refreshed and read for the evening Simon had proposed: a visit to *La Bella Napoli*. This I felt I had to do, though I did not look forward to having to say goodbye to Berhane.

When we arrived, however, a grim surprise was waiting for me. Berhane was no longer there. We checked in with the Signora, who was in her usual place behind the bar, but we found her in a reproachful mood.

"Ah, Signor La Touche," she said, wagging a fat finger at me, "I think that Signor Blakeney here is the bad boy, and you are a good boy, but now it seems as if you are very dangerous man. I don't know if I should have you around my place."

I was astonished at this.

"But Signora Anna," I protested, "what makes you say that?"

She shook her ample jowls at me.

"You mix yourself up in politics, that is what. I no know what you have been up to, but I know that the police they come and take away Berhane, and they say it is because of you."

A cold hand of fear gripped me. Simon looked at me in horror. I put a hand on the counter to steady myself.

"They did what? Why on earth would they have taken away Berhane? She would know nothing about anything. Did they say?"

"They think maybe you talk to her about things. I say no, they no talk politics, they just fuck, but is no good. They take her."

My sense of panic was displaced by fury. If I could have come face to face with Colonel Tamrat at this moment, I would have gone for him with everything I had – and thus doubtless sealed my fate. Instead, Simon ordered dinner for us both under the vine trellis, and guided me out of the bar. I was speechless and shaking. I sank down in a chair and stared at him.

"My God," I finally managed to say, "we are certainly seeing the other side of this country in the last few days. I'm really not so sorry to be getting out after all. But I wish I could do something about Berhane. The poor girl is an utterly innocent victim of all this. I feel so fucking helpless!"

Simon shook his head.

"Yes, I agree, it's disgusting. But I don't honestly see what you can do about it, without getting yourself right back in the shit."

Just then, Frewet appeared, bringing out tableware, glasses, and a jug of wine. She had been crying, and she looked over at me with reproach in her eyes, sending a pang of guilt through me. As she put the things on the table. Simon caught her gently by the waist, and pulled her to him.

"Now, love," he said soothingly, "don't you cry, there's a good girl. I'm quite sure Berhane's all right. They'll let her back soon. They just want to ask her some questions, that's all. And it isn't Mr La Touche's fault, you know. He didn't want to involve her in anything. Did you, Luke?"

She looked at Simon doubtfully, and then at me.

"No, no, Frewet," I assured her, "they can't do anything to Berhane. She knows nothing about anything. It is all a mistake."

Frewet's large eyes filled up with tears. She turned and rested her head on Simon's shoulder, and began to weep bitterly. I felt very miserable. Simon put an arm round her, and patted her.

And then a thought occurred to me. The one person who could perhaps help Berhane was Signora Anna herself. She at least was on reasonable terms with Tamrat and his cronies, since they came to drink here. I would offer her a significant amount of money – say, a hundred dollars – to put in a word with them, and perhaps that would help. In my distracted state, at least, it seemed worth trying.

Frewet pulled herself together, and went off to get the rest of the dinner. I put the proposition to Simon. To my relief he didn't rubbish the idea, but nodded thoughtfully.

"Yeah, it might just help," he said. "Anna does have some clout with these bastards. And I'm sure she wants Berhane back, so she'd be on your side for a start. And, as you say, the poor girl's absolutely innocent. In fact, they may well have just taken her for questioning – who knows?"

I reached in my wallet. I still had quite a bit of money left over from the holiday, which our captors, to their credit, had not appropriated. I picked out a hundred-dollar bill. We went in to consult Anna at the bar. She looked up as we came in.

"You boys want something?"

We went over to her, and leaned on the bar.

"Anna," said Simon confidentially, "Signor Luke wants to ask you a great favour."

"Aha," she said, her eyes gleaming. "Great favour, eh?"

"Yes, Anna," I said. "I am having to leave the country in this next week. I have been told that I must leave. And I want to try and do something to help Berhane before I go."

"Hey, Signor Luke," she interrupted. "What you do that is so wrong? That is what I want to know. You seem such a nice young man. Not like this Blakeney here. Why they not throw him out?"

"I *am* a nice young man, Anna," I protested. "The problem was that I had a friend, I knew him from university in England, Lij Yohannis Tessema – you have heard of him?"

Anna nodded and rolled her eyes.

"Yes, well, I don't want to go into details, but he got me into trouble – and almost he got Signor Simon into trouble as well. As a result your friend Colonel Tamrat wants me out of the country, and now he has taken away Berhane because she was a friend of mine. But she knows absolutely nothing. It was a horrible thing for him to do."

"Oh, that Tamrat," she scowled. "He no friend of mine. He is pig."

"But he does drink here, doesn't he?" I persisted.

"Oh yes, he drink here, with his friends. And of course I am polite to him, because he is dangerous. But I no like him one bit."

"Well, all I was going to suggest was that you might put in a word with him for Berhane, next time he comes? And I was wondering if perhaps this hundred dollars would be any help if you had to bribe him, perhaps? Or more? I could raise a bit more next week, I think."

I held out the notes. Anna raised her hand.

"No, I tell you, I speak to him anyway, when I see him. I no need your money. But I am worried for Berhane. These are very bad men, very bad. You lucky you escape from them."

"Oh, Signor Luke has important friends, Anna," said Simon ironically. "He is friends with the Minister of Justice. That was a help."

Signora Anna opened her eyes wide, and smiled.

"Well," I said, "maybe my friends did me some good, but not that much good. I am really sorry to be leaving. I will miss coming out here, and I will miss Berhane. But perhaps you would keep the hundred dollars, and give them to her when she comes back. It would just be a sign of how sorry I am for all this."

Anna took the money, and concealed it in her ample bosom. Then she patted my cheek with a fat hand.

"Signor Luke, you are good boy. I am sure that Berhane will come back, and she will be sorry not to see you any more, but she will be happy with this." She patted the concealed money. "And now, here is your dinner coming."

Indeed, Frewet was just bringing out what would be my final *pollo alla diavola*. We returned to our table under the trellis.

After dinner, Simon wanted to go out the back with Frewet, and I was resigning myself to a lonely brandy under the vines, but then Frewet had an idea. She hurried back into the restaurant.

"What's she up to, I wonder," I said.

"I dunno," said Simon, "but she seems to have some plans for you. I wonder if that involves some disloyalty to Berhane."

"I hope not," I said. "I don't feel like being disloyal to Berhane in the present circumstances."

"Oh, I wouldn't think of it like that," said Simon, grinning. "These girls don't think that way, really. I think she probably knows what you did in there."

I shrugged, not really knowing what to think. I did feel sort of disloyal, but I appreciated Simon's point, and it occurred to me that it might be along time before I would get a girl into bed after my return to the eminently respectable environment of County Wicklow.

In the event, Frewet re-appeared with Teru, whom I had made love with once before when Berhane was busy. Simon and Frewet then went off, leaving us alone. Teru smiled at me, and beckoned. I felt really rather peculiar about this, but rose and followed her. As Simon said, these girls looked at things rather differently from us.

In fact it was a peculiar, bitter-sweet love-making. When we got to our room, she sat me down on the bed and said, hesitantly:

"You are good man. You are good to Berhane. Berhane is my friend. I do this for no money, as a friend."

I looked at her in astonishment, tears coming to my eyes.

"But Teru," I protested. "There is no need for you to do this. I want to give you money. You deserve it."

When she saw the tears in my eyes, Teru also began to cry.

"No, no, I no want money this time. This for Berhane."

I took her in my arms and kissed her eyelids gently, and hugged her. Then we undressed and made love, rather gently, and very weepily. It was all most peculiar. Afterwards, I tried again to press ten dollars into her hand, but she refused firmly, and slipped out of the room. I was left sitting on the bed, staring into space, with a lump in my throat.

"That was most bizarre," I said to Simon as we drove back. "Teru wouldn't take any money. She was doing this in honour of Berhane, in some way. I was really touched."

"Yes, well," said Simon, "the word got around about your little gift. Anna must have let Frewet in on it, and she would have told Teru. I just hope poor Berhane gets back to enjoy it." Then a thought occurred to him, and he cackled. "*The Berhane Memorial Fuck*! God, La Touche, you do fall on your feet, you know."

"Well," I said, "I imagine that's my last one for quite some time. Not much chance of that sort of thing in dear old Ireland – or certainly not in the circles in which I move." As I said that, I thought of Caroline, but I didn't care to mention that to Simon. I wasn't sure that that relationship would travel too well. We would have to see.

"Well, you'll just have to stir up some action, won't you?" said Simon, laughing. "Or just fly over to gay Paree for the odd weekend?"

I shook my head.

"I've a nasty feeling it wouldn't be the same thing at all. It's a pretty sleazy scene in Europe, so far as I can see. I don't think I'd enjoy it after this."

The beginning of term brought its own pressures. Graham decided that we should say nothing about my imminent departure, and I launched my classes into their various tasks as if nothing had happened. Meanwhile, Graham had been active, calling around. To my great relief he quickly found a temporary substitute, in the person of none other than Susan Hardiman. The Hardimans had got back on Sunday night, and Graham had called Ewan on the Monday morning, to ask his advice. In the event, it turned out that Susan had a degree from Somerville in English, and she declared herself quite prepared to help out, if I would give her proper instructions. I phoned during break, and arranged to come up that very evening for dinner and a briefing session.

My meeting with Nuri Boghossian and Willy in the late afternoon was most satisfactory. After some preliminary tut-tutting from Nuri, he undertook to make all the necessary financial arrangements. We would advertise the villa, and he would arrange a pension for Wolde. He also phoned up Ethiopian Airlines on my behalf, and booked a flight to London for the Thursday morning. I left him much encouraged. More loose ends were being tidied up. Leaving was not so difficult after all. I began to focus more clearly on my departure.

The evening with Ewan and Susan was very pleasant, though I

had to withstand some criticism of my recklessness and naiveté. Ewan was quite impressed by my escape from Col. Tamrat, though he did feel that I would be wise to get out of the country while I could, since I was unlikely to be forgiven for that.

"We have our eyes on a number of figures in the army and the police," he said, "and he is one of them. It's our feeling that there is a multiplicity of factions forming in those areas, some which one might call 'progressive', others frankly reactionary, who are anticipating the death or incapacity of the Emperor, and waiting to take over. Tamrat and his cronies have just neutralised – with some help from you – a progressive group in the army with whom your friend Yohannis was in contact. Of course they've disposed of him as well, for the moment – and I'm sure they're feeling very pleased with themselves. But I doubt that that is going to be the end of the story."

This was the longest discourse I'd yet heard from Ewan on the political situation. He continued with some gravity.

"This sort of activity – in-fighting between rival groups – is going to intensify in the coming few years, and it's going to be a bit of a battleground between ourselves and the Russians. You have just had the dubious privilege of being a very small part of it. I wouldn't give much for the future of Asfa Wossen, or indeed any of the royal family. They're a pretty futile lot, except perhaps young Alex Desta, but I doubt that even he will stand much of a chance. So much for the Lion of Judah and all his progeny. But now I'd better leave you to work things out with Susan." And he retired to his study to work at some papers.

I was able to put into Susan's hands all that she would need to take over from me. Unfortunately, she would have to step in already on Thursday, but she did not seem too overawed by the prospect. I told her that she could have the senior class to coffee in my bungalow on the Thursday, if she liked, and that might help to break the ice, and she liked that idea.

On Tuesday, I had a serious talk with Tekla-Mariam. He was horrified at the news, but I reassured him that I would look after him. I would see that his pay was continued to the end of the school year. I would bequeath him my old banger; and I would pay for driving lessons for him, in case he would like to become a driver. Poor TM wept, and knelt and kissed my hands, to my great embarrassment, but I think he was pleased in contemplating his future.

Another problem was the Latin class. Graham had actually persuaded Padre Matthews to come up and do the Latin at least till the end of the year, so that was taken care of, but I felt I had to break it to the class, especially since young Tewodros would have had a pretty shrewd idea of what had happened, in view of the disgrace of his big brother. I did not really expect that he would be there, but plainly his father had decided on business as usual. He was rather subdued, however, and made no comment when I announced that I had to leave.

At the end of class, Fiona hung back, and with tears in her eyes, begged that I might come round that evening and say goodbye, and tell her parents exactly what had happened. She was sure that they would want to see me. I hesitated. Various people, particularly the Lonsdales and the Barneses, were wanting to give me a farewell party, and I also wanted to say goodbye to the gang down at the Ras Bar. But I agreed to phone her parents and check with them. We could have a farewell party on the compound on the Wednesday, I calculated, and I could go down to the Ras that evening before dinner.

In fact, the McHughs insisted that I come down and dine with them, so I agreed to be there at around half-past seven. Frank McHugh was most disturbed to hear my news, and I promised to give him a full account when we met. Then Simon came round, and we decided to go down in convoy to the Piazza, since I would have to leave separately.

Everything suddenly became a last time round, and clothed in a mist of nostalgia. A last drive down to the Piazza, a last visit to Giannopoulos' Bookstore, where I picked up a last *Manchester Guardian Weekly*, and a last beer on the verandah of the Ras. Maurice was there, and Knut, and Jack Hirschhorn. Marco turned up, looking, as so often, as if he had come straight from under a lorry. Even Dr Ratna appeared, enquiring after Simon's injuries, the traces of which were beginning to fade.

They all had to hear the story, and offered their commiserations and encouragement. I began to feel like a minor hero. The curious feeling impressed itself upon me that, in a way, all these people were trapped here, and rather envied me my enforced escape. As for me, I envied them their oddly carefree, almost timeless existence. I felt as if I was being dragged kicking and screaming from the land of the Lotus-Eaters.

At about a quarter past seven, I rose to go. I had to embrace everyone there except Simon, whom I was going to see again, and promise not to forget them. I told Marco what I was going to do with the car, and he agreed to go on looking after it, if TM would call on him. Maurice promised to advise me on Parisian prostitutes, if I applied to him at a later stage.

The evening at the McHughs passed off well enough. Over dinner, of course, I recounted my tale, and accepted more reproof, commiseration, and advice. Frank had had a Polish colleague who'd had a similar adventure the previous year. He had become too friendly with a young Ethiopian official in his ministry who was too advanced in his thinking. The Pole was arrested, and then sent packing very promptly, and the young Ethiopian just disappeared.

"Yes," I said, sadly. "I'm afraid that Mr Abdolov and Mr Skrabanek will be leaving shortly, if they haven't left already. And as for poor Major Samuel, I dread to think."

"Oh, you just have to learn here," Frank said solemnly. "There are boundaries, and you don't go beyond them."

I excused myself soon after dinner, on the plea of packing and so on. I promised to keep in touch with them, and to get together whenever they got back to Ireland. Fiona I would see the following day in class, but her parents both embraced me in farewell. I realised that I would miss them a lot. Frank and Maura McHugh were the first Irish people of a quite different background to my own that I had ever really got to know. They had accepted me with open-minded hospitality as a fellow-Irishman, and I deeply appreciated that. And, I reflected, I'd had to come out here, to the ends of the earth, to make their acquaintance. I certainly would never have met them, in the normal course of things, back in Ireland.

CHAPTER THIRTY-TWO

My final full day in Addis was something of a blur. I taught my classes as calmly as I could, but somehow the rumour had swept through the school that I was going, and in some mysterious way, my senior class had managed to have a whip-round, and bought me a delightful little gift. It was an ashtray made out of three Maria Theresa thalers, with a ten-cent piece to rest the cigarette on. Tewodros and Manolis presented it to me at the end of class, amid much applause, and a little speech.

"Sir," said Manolis, in his august tones, "we wanted you to know that we appreciate all that you have done for us. We have had a lot of fun during the year, and we are sorry if we ever made life difficult for you by making disturbances."

I was actually so affected that I doubted if I could reply without making a fool of myself. I raised a deprecatory hand and tried to defuse the situation by making a little joke.

"It it particularly thoughtful of you all," I remarked, "to give me this beautiful gift of an ashtray, since you know I don't smoke!"

Tewodros was equal to that.

"Ah sir," he said solemnly, "we are trying to educate you into better habits. It will be good for you to take up smoking. It will make you calmer. You will be grateful for this."

There were loud cheers, and a round of applause. I felt greatly consoled. We had all ended as friends, and I thought that I might have done them some good, which is the best that one can hope for as a teacher.

My afternoon was spent in doing a sort of inventory of the villa with Willy, and in consoling Wolde. The poor man had lost two masters in almost as many months, and was feeling thoroughly bereft, but Willy was able to explain to him that he was amply provided for in James's will, and that did seem to cheer him up a little. There were so many strange and lovely things up and down the house, particularly in the living room and study, that I was quite unable to take them in, though I had looked at many of them individually before this. Willy I prevailed upon to choose, not just the walking stick, but a number of trinkets from around the world which he had long admired. The rest would be packed up in the next week or so, and shipped.

I went back then to face a farewell party at the Wigginses. All this was much more, I felt, than I deserved. Despite my manifest foolishness, and the inconvenience I was causing to all and sundry, I was being given something of a hero's send-off. Ewan and Susan came down, as did Wendy Thesiger. A number of people came also from the university. Various good-humoured speeches were made, as we all got boozier and boozier. When it came my turn to reply, I almost broke down again. It seemed to me at this moment that the previous eight months had been a turning-point in my life, and I tried to communicate that without embarrassing everyone beyond measure. I had enjoyed hospitality and companionship here beyond anything I had ever expected, and I was only sorry that it all had had to end this way. If I ever had a chance to get back, I pledged, I would not fail to do so.

Back safe in my bed, much later, I lay and stared at the darkened ceiling, listening, for the last time, to the *abujadid* rustling to the night breezes, and the hyenas whooping in the ravine. My mind turned back to my best and worst times of the previous eight months. Two images pushed themselves to the fore; first, the ecstasy of my first love-making with Caroline, on that trip to the lower farm in Nyala – so long ago, it seemed now; and secondly, the utter despair I had felt in that prison cell only the week before, when I heard those three shots, and Simon's voice fall silent. Many other memories, the vast majority pleasant, floated up the surface of my consciousness, but those two stood out.

The next morning, it was again quite affecting to see my things all laid out in the front room. My bags were packed and all was ready for departure. The plane left at noon, a very civilised time. With an hour or so's stop in Athens, it was timed to get in to London early the following morning. Another short hop, and I would be in Dublin, back into another world, the 'real' world, where the serious business of life was waiting for me.

Willy had insisted that he would do the honours and drive me to the airport. His Mercedes arrived punctually at half past ten. A small crowd of my colleagues gathered to see me off, led by Graham and Isabel. Simon stepped forward, punched me on the arm, and pressed a small packet into my hand as a farewell present. Opening it later in the plane, I found it was a packet of Durex, with a derisive note, reminding me that these would be difficult to find in Ireland, but then I probably wouldn't have much need of them.

I waved goodbye, and we drove out of the leafy compound. As we made our way along the airport road, the colours of the now familiar landscape seemed richer than ever, and the modern hulk of the airport dull and forbidding in contrast. Willy saw me through the customs, and embraced me emotionally in parting.

"Good luck, my boy," he said. "I feel now almost as if you were my own son. We have been through quite a lot together. You have my address. Let me know how you get on."

I had to choke back tears. All I could say was:

"I will certainly, Willy. Thanks again for everything."

We shook hands, and on such a banal note the whole adventure ended. I turned to go through the gate, swinging back for a last wave.

Addis Ababa from the air is, truly, a memorable sight. I looked down at a scene which was now familiar to me, and which I knew would never entirely fade from my memory. The plane swung out first over the open country to the south, and then veered round to fly directly over the chaotic jumble of the city, over the eucalyptus-covered heights of Entotto, and so north, towards the blue mountains of Gojjam, and then into mile after mile of nothingness.

ABOUT THE AUTHOR

John Dillon is Regius Professor of Greek (Emeritus) in Trinity College Dublin, having returned there in 1980 from a period in the University of California, Berkeley, where he was a member of the Classics Department from 1969 onwards. Prior to that, after graduating from Oxford in 1961, he spent some years in Ethiopia, teaching English in Addis Ababa. His chief area of interest is the philosophy of Plato and the tradition deriving from him, on which he has written and edited a number of books, but he has always had an interest in more popular forms of writing as well, together with a weakness for practical politics, which he does his best to resist. This is his only novel (so far).

451
Editions

www.451Editions.com